Trans

For Rachel Kranz, my first editor, and a woman who taught me a lot about writing, poker, and friendship. You'll be missed by many.

Transient

Part One

Chapter 1

I remember when I saw my first murder.

I say *first* as though I've seen a lot of them. The truth is I've only had two happen right in front of me. The first was two years ago and I don't talk about that one. I remember it—I'll always remember it—but I don't talk about it.

The second was about an hour ago.

I take a drink from my beer bottle, the liquid warm and somewhat flat as it slips over my tongue and down my throat. It leaves an acidic and bitter feeling in my stomach as it sits there. I know *bitter* is a taste, or possibly an emotional reaction and not actually a physical feeling, but I can't think of a better word to describe the daggers in my stomach as the beer churns in my gut. I haven't eaten today and that's probably part of the reason the tepid beer isn't sitting well with me.

Lyrics from *Paul Revere*, the old Beastie Boys song, spring unbidden into my mind:

One lonely Beastie I be,
All by myself without nobody.
The sun is beating down on my baseball hat,
The air is gettin' hot, the beer is getting flat.

There's a line later in the song about a sheriff's posse being on his tail. That line is even more apropos to my current situation.

I need to figure out what to do about the murder I just saw.

There are options of course. There are always options. Mine are more limited than yours would be though.

 If you witnessed a murder—saw it happen right in front of your eyes—what would you do?

I'm guessing some of you are tough guys and you're thinking you would have done something to stop it. You would have played the hero; you'd have jumped at the killer and wrestled the gun away from him and then held him until the police arrived.

I snort at that thought, some of the beer coming back up my esophagus, burning my throat as it tends to do. This is the worst part about drinking warm beer. It doesn't want to stay where it belongs, always bubbling around down there, threatening to rise back up. I read somewhere once that Germans drink their beer warm on purpose. They don't have a history of good decision-making skills though, do they?

It's rare that I actually have a good, cold beer, so you'd think I'd be used to the warm stuff. I suppose there are some things a civilized person was just never meant to get used to.

If you haven't guessed by now, I'm no hero. I didn't even consider trying to stop the murder I just witnessed. My life may not seem like much to you, but it's the only one I've got and I'd rather prefer to keep it.

Be a good witness. That's what the cops always tell civilians when the civilians ask what they should do when they see a crime happening. *Be a good witness. Don't get involved.*

Those of you who aren't heroes—like me—are probably thinking that if you witnessed a murder you would be a good witness, just like the police recommend. You would watch the murder happen, and then take note of the killer's appearance: his clothing, height, weight, complexion, hair color and style, any facial hair, any noticeable scars or visible tattoos. You'd take note of the gun, filing away whether it was an automatic or a revolver, stainless or blued. Perhaps you'd even notice the make and model of the gun (stainless Beretta 92FS in this case). You'd take note of anything unusual, like the thing he'd been carrying in his left hand, something he grabbed from the car after he fired the fatal shot. I couldn't see what it was as it was blocked by his body, but it was small and white in color, and if you'd seen that, you would add that to your mental report.

Once you'd filed all that information away in your memory, you'd then pay attention to the killer's escape method. If he left the scene in a car, such as he did in this case, you'd note the make, model, color, any distinguishing characteristics such as body damage or custom equipment, and, if you could safely get close enough, you'd take note of the license plate number, memorizing it or typing it into your phone so you didn't forget. And of course, you would note the direction of travel after he left the scene.

Then you would call the police, giving the critical information to the dispatcher so he or she could relay it to the responding police officers. When they arrived on the scene, you would give a detailed statement of what you had witnessed. With your superior powers of observation, there would be an excellent chance of the killer getting caught.

I'm a superb witness and I did everything listed above...with one exception.

I didn't call the police.

A cockroach scurries out from some crevice in the wall behind me, scooting past my leg and stopping at the edge of the shade, instinctively, or perhaps learnedly avoiding the hot sun. Its antennae quiver and I lift my heel to crush it before thinking better of it and gently lowering my foot. The insect pauses a second further, blissfully unaware of its brush with death, before it turns and runs off, following a crack in the sidewalk.

I take another swig of the beer, grimacing again at the lukewarm liquid before tossing the nearly empty bottle at my feet. It would be better for my image if I finished it, but I just can't bring myself to do it. Besides, I don't think anybody's watching me. It's getting hot and the sun's rays are beginning to encroach on my little protected area. I move my legs to the right a foot or so, twisting my body to keep everything in the shade, and burrowing deeper into my sitting area.

I don't know the exact time, but based on the sun's position, I would guess it's somewhere around 8 o'clock in the morning. That would mean the murder I witnessed happened around 7 o'clock. I glance over at the car where the homicidal violence took place. I can still see the blood droplets, now more like rivulets as they start to run on the interior driver's side window. Even blood droplets are subject to the laws of gravity, stretching and extending as they make their distinct tracks down the glass. The victim is a man with

8

black hair, but I can't tell you much more than that. His head is all I can make out, just a spot of dark hair that's resting in the middle of the canvas of red gore. I did watch for a while for any movement after the shooting happened, thinking the guy could still be alive. That is the kind of wistful naïveté that has no place in my life, and its resurfacing from my past life annoys me.

I need to do something, but I don't know what. It's not like I have a predetermined plan in place for what to do in case I witness a murder.

While I decide what to do, I should probably tell you a little something about myself. First, my name is David Sands and I'm 37 years old. That's not my actual name, nor is it my actual age, but you'll have to forgive me as I'm not willing to give out the real information at this time. The point is, that this is the information printed on my driver's license, which is a fake. Actually, more accurately, it's a real driver's license, it just belongs to someone else. Someone named David Sands presumably.

Finding the David Sands license was just good luck. I think. The name fits me as well as any I might have chosen for myself. Sands: shifting sands, blowing sands, wandering sands, subject to the forces of wind and earth, traveling grains nearly unnoticeable, irrelevant and anonymous. Me in a nutshell. I chuckle as I usually do when I think of the term *me in a nutshell*. It always conjures images of Mike Myers doing the *me in a nutshell* skit in Austin Powers. Hilarious.

I don't know who the actual David Sands is, or even if he's still alive as those things don't matter to me. In fact, the driver's license I hold with that name is expired, and I'm sure the real David Sands, if he is indeed still alive, has replaced the one he lost, the one I'm currently using. I'm actually quite a bit older than 37, truth be told, but I do look enough like the image of David Sands on the license so that the few times I've had to show the identification to someone in authority, none have questioned its authenticity.

It certainly helps that I'm careful to maintain a shield of invisibility. Not the magical kind like you might find in a Dungeons and Dragons game or a Harry Potter novel, but rather the societal kind, which is actually a much stronger spell than the magic kind.

You'd be amazed at how many people look right through me as if I'm not there. When they do look at me and actually notice me, more often than not they quickly avert their eyes, as if they might catch whatever disease I must have simply by looking at me.

I don't have an actual physical disease (at least not that I know of), but I do have a social disease; I'm a vagrant. A homeless person, a bum, an itinerant, a drifter, a wanderer, a transient. The last couple aren't technically accurate as I don't actually move around much, other than maybe in an area about one-mile square. But you get the idea anyway. These are the words that I've heard whispered as people pass near me, those brave enough to pierce the veil of my societal invisibility. Usually one of those words is preceded by the f-word, as in, "Hey, don't get too close to that fucking bum over there."

Those words bothered and angered me in the beginning, but they don't anymore. I've developed my own type of shield, an auditory deflection shield, if you will. I *hear* the words but I don't *register* the words.

My invisibility shield was working full force today when the blond guy with the Ray-Ban sunglasses killed the man in the car. I saw the blond guy glance around, his careful, halting, nervous manner catching my attention as surely as if he was glowing or had two heads. His gaze passed right over me, even though I wasn't even attempting to hide. I suppose I was probably in the shadows somewhat, and my clothing is quite drab—appropriate for street living, as well as for unintentional invisibility cloaking.

I don't know if it's a good thing he didn't see me or not. If he had, perhaps he wouldn't have followed through with the homicide. Or perhaps he would have still murdered the man in the car and then

11

proceeded to murder the witness, aka Yours Truly. That would have definitely ruined my day, as I imagined it had ruined the day of the poor mope in the Olds Cutlass, whose blood was currently drying in what was certainly becoming a scorcher of a car.

I still don't know what I'm planning to do, but I decide it would probably be a good idea to move myself to a different location at the very least. Up to this point, nobody has noticed the dead man in the car, probably due to the fact that it's Sunday morning and there just aren't that many people wandering around yet. It's only a matter of time before somebody finds him though.

Once someone sees the dead guy, they'll surely call the police who will arrive in force and then proceed to canvass the area. Canvass is a cop word that means search, and my invisibility shield isn't good enough to protect me from that kind of scrutiny, nor is my false ID good enough to stand up to a suspicious cop's thorough examination.

The police have a habit of being thorough when investigating a murder, as I'm well aware. Even when they're not as thorough as they should be, they're certainly not going to fail to take a close look at a vagrant found in proximity to the scene of said murder. It's time to put some distance between myself and the immediate search area.

I stand up, stretching my tired muscles as my eyes do their searching thing, a relic from my past that's served me well in my present. I'm always on the lookout, maintaining a vigilant awareness that would certainly mark me as an outsider should any of my brethren notice it. Of course, the lack of vigilant awareness in my compadres makes notice of my own unlikely.

I gather my blankets and stuff them into my large backpack. Once an expensive gem from REI, it's now a faded and worn carryall, shoulder straps ragged and broken, tied together in a knot to keep them intact. I could probably find a shopping cart to push around, but that would limit my mobility.

I stuff my last two warm beers in the pocket of my olive-green jacket and sling the pack onto my shoulders. It's hot already, too hot for the jacket I'm wearing, but I don't take it off. Warmth is a commodity on the street, and the true vagrant doesn't shed a commodity without careful consideration. There's room in the pack for the jacket and it'll be joining the blankets soon enough, but for now, while the heat is still bearable, the jacket stays on.

I make one last inspection of the area and then head south, away from the car that's currently becoming a dead guy's personal oven and away from the immediate vicinity of the impending police scrutiny. I don't see anybody else until I reach Fremont Street where people are already beginning to stir.

This isn't the part of Fremont Street that's famous for its kaleidoscopic canopy of lights and music where tourists gather every night to get drunk and gamble in the casinos. I'll make my way to that part of Fremont later, most likely after dark, when the police are more interested in keeping the inebriated tourists from killing themselves through stupid antics than they are in hassling the vagrants.

The part of Fremont where I'm currently standing is several blocks away from the touristy part. It actually used to be a haven for people like me, a place where you never had to worry about being contacted by the police. Lately it's been changing though, and I can recognize that the free-wheeling days of the homeless in this part of the town will soon be coming to an end.

For now, though, it's safe for me. There are people walking around, lazily going about their business, blissfully unaware that someone was murdered just two blocks away, the victim's body heating rapidly in his enclosed car.

The memory of the murder comes unbidden to my mind. The flash from the car, the loud pop that startled me from my resting spot.

The killer emerging from the car, glancing around carefully, his gaze traveling right over me as I lay frozen in place.

I shake my head, push the image down, and move on.

I make my way to the doorway of a building that's long been abandoned. The doorway is set well back in the entrance, creating a hallway that makes a right turn as it leaves the street, a terrible design for a store that would need to rely on walk-by traffic, as it makes the entrance all but invisible to the passersby. Probably why the shop went out of business in the first place. Or perhaps it was because it was a shop selling antique furniture in a section of town where even a couch placed on the curb was likely to be gone within the hour. Nobody around here has the money to buy antique furniture, and the people who do have the money for such a frivolous expenditure sure aren't going to be looking to spend it down here in what passes as Las Vegas' version of Skid Row.

Although the doorway design is terrible from a business perspective, it's perfect from a vagrant perspective. The right turn means the alcove is away from the flow of pedestrians and out of the direct rays of the hot desert sun.

I fully expect it to be occupied when I arrive, but I'm pleasantly surprised to find it empty. I remember that it's Sunday morning, and I suppose that even the vagrants are getting a late start to the day.

Being the first to arrive, the code of the homeless means that I get to decide who's allowed to join me in this cozy alcove and who won't be allowed. Of course, strength is also a big part of that code. The animal kingdom version of diplomacy that requires concessions toward those much stronger than you is alive and well on the street.

I drop my pack and take off my jacket, carefully removing the two bottles of beer so they don't break. Then, spreading the jacket onto the concrete, I settle in, using the pack as a back rest and twisting the top off one beer, taking a big chug. My gut does the stirring thing as the beer settles in it, a sharp pang reminding me that my system needs some calories that don't come from the mouth of a bottle.

I ignore the jabs from my belly and think about the murder I just witnessed.

Despite my current living conditions and lack of contribution to society, I consider myself a good citizen. I'm sure you're laughing at that statement right now and I don't blame you. The deplorable way I've chosen to exist for the last two years leads to a negative judgement, though I assure you, I have my reasons, my excuses, and either way, your opinion doesn't bother me.

Anyway, despite what you may think of me, I know I'm a good citizen and because of that, I can't ignore what I just witnessed.

I consider making an anonymous call to the police with the information I have, but this is tougher than it may sound. If you doubt that, think about this: when was the last time you saw a payphone?

Even living on the street as I do, I can't think of a single payphone that exists in my life circle. Without a payphone, how do I make the anonymous call? If I approached you on the street, would you lend me your cellphone to make a call? If you owned a business and I walked in asking to use the phone, would you let me?

Even if you're one of those rare types that says yes (and I don't believe you, by the way), there's still a big problem with either of those options. Contacting the police and telling them what I know, what I witnessed, would cause the owner of said phone to watch me in near disbelief, that amazement causing him to register the details of my appearance. You better believe the police will be following up on a phone call like I would need to make, and getting my description from the owner of the phone would lead them to discovering me eventually. Once they contacted me about a case such as this, they would take a pretty thorough look into my background, and that would be that for *moi*.

So, the anonymous call to the cops seems to be out of the question. Perhaps I could mail a letter. Or write down my observations and just drop it off at the police department. These are potential options, though I would need to make sure I didn't leave any fingerprints on the letter or on the envelope. Or DNA. I don't know if you're aware, but it's pretty tough to not leave your DNA lying around these days. If I do take this route and I drop a letter off at the police department, I need to make sure I don't get caught on their surveillance cameras. It's not like I have a wide variety of clothing or disguises I can wear to mask my appearance, and I'm not willing to take any risks to myself in order to report my observations.

I take another drink of the beer while I mull over the situation. I'm pretty sure I know what my only logical option is, but I'm trying my best to talk myself out of it.

While I'm thinking, a shadow appears in the doorway and grows larger as it morphs into a man. Allen Iverson peers through the doorway and peers at me, concern grooved into his face as he waits for his eyes to adjust.

He finally recognizes me and steps fully inside the alcove.

"Sandman. How you doin' brotha?" he asks.

"I'm alright, Allen." I nod to the empty space next to me. "Come on in."

A smile lights up his face and he shuffles in out of the sun. He plops down next to me and exhales sharply as he leans his head back against the wall.

"You just saved my life, man," he says to me, peering earnestly into my eyes. "They're after me. They're gettin' close, man. Real close. I can feel 'em."

Allen has a strong belief that the government is after him. His entire life is spent running and hiding from mysterious, shadowy figures that he's convinced are trying to kill him. I've asked him before why the government would possibly be after him.

"I've seen stuff, man. Bad stuff, and they know it. They can't have me seein' stuff, can't have nobody seein' stuff like I've seen. They gotta stop me, before I can tell anybody what I seen."

That's all he'll say on the matter. Normally when he's asked any further questions, he gets a wrinkle of concern on his face, glares at his questioner suspiciously, and then wanders off, checking back over his shoulder. He didn't talk to me for weeks after the first time I pressed him on the things he thinks he's seen. I haven't asked him since then.

Allen Iverson isn't his real name, probably. Nobody knows his actual name. He got the moniker from the 76er's jersey with the number 3 on it that he has worn every day that I've known him, nearly two years now. As I'm well aware, monikers on these streets are more common than real names. As you may have guessed, Allen has some serious mental health issues.

Allen leans forward and shrugs out of his jacket, taking the opportunity to peek out from our cubbyhole and glance around at the street before ducking back in. He's a black man, tall and lean, somewhere around 40 years old though he appears to be somewhat older, as most of us living on the street do. He claims that he's a Vietnam veteran, though that is, of course, impossible. Unless he's actually much older than he appears. An implausible scenario here on the streets.

He mumbles to himself, words that I can't understand, then leans back again and studies me. I take a swig of the beer and then hand him the bottle. His dirty facial features light up in a smile and he takes the bottle from me gratefully.

"You da man, Sandman. You da man," he says, staring adoringly for a moment at the bottle.

He takes a long drink and tries to hand it back to me but I wave him off. The beer is for my image, but I need to be careful of actually falling into the pits of alcoholism and drug use that are prevalent in this lifestyle. It's an easy path into oblivion out here, and as I start drinking earlier and earlier each day, I recognize I'm taking steps down that path.

"You see any police activity out there?" I ask him.

He gives me a long stare. "They always out there. Always watching."

"I'm talking about the regular cops—black and white cars, uniforms, blue lights. Anything like that?"

He shakes his head. "Not that I seen. You got somethin' goin'?"

"Nah. You know, just stayin' low," I say to him, keeping my facial features blank. Iverson has moments of clarity, and despite his mental problems, he's often very observant. When he's lucid he remembers conversations we've had from all the way back to when I first met him.

I think about having him tell the police what I witnessed, having him tell the story as if it were his own. But that's a problem just because it's impossible to know when he's going to slip into his more agitated and paranoid states. He's also afraid of the cops— the ones that we can all see, in addition to the ones that he thinks

21

are hiding in plain clothes and following his every move. I doubt he'd be too keen on cooperating with my request and approaching a uniformed officer, even if he could be counted on to relay the information correctly.

I know what I have to do, even though I've been avoiding the obvious solution since I witnessed the murder. As Steinbeck once said though, *"A man's got to do what a man's got to do."*

"I gotta run, my friend," I say to Iverson, standing up and stuffing my last beer into the jacket pocket. I then shove the jacket into the top of the pack, slinging the worn straps over my shoulders. "You're in charge of the spot now, take care of yourself."

"You gonna see Lizzy today?" he asks as I turn to make my way back onto the street. Lizzy is a prostitute who's been working the downtown area here as long as I've been around. She and I are friends, though not in the way you're probably thinking. We've never had any kind of romantic involvement and that's why Iverson is asking me about her. He's in love with Lizzy and I'm about the only person he knows out here on the street who hasn't taken a run at her. It's one of the reasons he likes me so much.

"I doubt it, but if I see her, I'll tell her where to find you."

He gives me a big smile and tips the beer up to his lips, finishing the remainder in one big gulp.

I lean my head out of the doorway and make a quick scan in both directions before setting off westbound on Fremont Street. I need to make my way north eventually, but I want to avoid using the street where the dead guy is. As I walk past that street, I see two police cars, lights flashing, one officer stringing up yellow crime scene tape while another talks to two pedestrians. I would have been one of those interviewees if I hadn't vacated the scene when I did.

Chapter 2

I scoot quickly up two more blocks and then make the right turn,

ambling north. I walk at a slow pace, not wanting to warm up too much in the hot sun and also not wanting to draw any attention to myself. Even though I'm moving at a faster pace than most of the vagrants out here, not performing the "bum shuffle" that really contributes to the invisibility shield, I still get few looks from anybody.

I work my way under the I-515 overpass, near where it meets up with I-15 and I-215, the area known as The Spaghetti Bowl in downtown Las Vegas, and then continue north, paralleling I-15. I need to walk almost a mile and I manage that distance in just less than thirty minutes. A little too fast for a homeless guy I suppose, but I'm anxious to get to my task, now that I've made the hard decision to proceed.

My destination is a truck stop, a *Flying J Travel Plaza* to be exact, and this one in particular. It's the only spot I know of that meets all the conditions for what I need.

It's early on a Sunday and there are only a few trucks topping off at the pumps. This isn't the ideal situation for me. I'd much prefer a busy time of the day and a little bit of chaos, but I don't have much choice. I approach the chain link fence that marks the boundary of the Flying J property, brown plastic privacy strips inserted into the links of the fence giving the place both privacy and trashiness at the same time. The trashiness is amplified by actual trash that has collected in wind-blown piles against the fence. I scuttle along the perimeter, shuffling slowly and occasionally bending down to study a piece of the trash that litters the ground. I'm not the slightest bit interested in the garbage, but again, it's all done for appearance's sake. All done to aid my cloak of invisibility.

Eyeing the truckers filling their tanks, I figure the time is right to make my move. The time for discretion has passed, and I step around the end of the fence and pick up my pace, making a beeline for the rear entrance to the store. This is the overnight truckers' entrance and it leads directly to the showers.

Nobody notices me, or at least nobody cares if they do notice me, and I cautiously pull open the door, peering inside for any employees before slipping in. I'm in a hallway, the storefront and merchandise at the end of the white-tiled corridor, the truckers' lounge through an open doorway to my right. The lounge is empty, the television tuned to CNN blaring some report about the presidential primaries. I have no idea who's running for election and I couldn't care less. I only care that the lounge is vacant, the comfortable recliners meant to cater to the long-haul truckers seeming forlorn in their emptiness.

On my left is a door with a plastic sign that declares the room to be "Showers." Under that is a hand-printed sign that says, *Drivers: Please check in at the counter prior to using showers.* I'm not a driver so I don't have any issue ignoring that request. I push my way through the door and walk confidently into the shower room.

The reason I needed this particular truck stop is in front of me. There is a row of coin-operated lockers with a wooden bench in front of them. Beyond that are the showers, five in total with doors instead of shower curtains. That's all helpful, but the real important part is the coin-operating mechanisms set into the wall by each shower door.

Most truck stops that I've seen these days are controlled by the counter clerks. It's rare that they're coin operated like this one. I would never be allowed in to take a shower if I'd had to check in with the clerk, and the shower is the reason for my visit today.

Digging into the backpack, I remove a plastic bag that's full of quarters. There's a dollar bill changer mounted on the wall, but I've seen it broken in the past, a sign on it advising the drivers to get change from the front counter clerk. That won't work for me obviously, so I always keep the bag of quarters handy.

Digging even further into the backpack, I remove another bag. This one is a black plastic garbage bag and I have to dig almost all the way to the bottom of the pack to remove it. I set it carefully aside. There are a few more items in the backpack, my most valuable items, and I'll need some of them later. For now, I cover them back up with my other belongings.

The change machine seems to be working today, so I dig a crumpled five-dollar bill from my pocket and smooth it out the best I can, rubbing it back and forth on the side of the dollar changer. I glance warily toward the door, dreading the thought that somebody might come in, report me, and have me kicked out. Or worse, call the police and have me arrested for trespassing. That would be an unmitigated disaster.

The coin machine accepts my dilapidated bill on the third try, spitting out a handful of quarters which I quickly add to the plastic bag containing my previous collection. Grabbing two of the quarters, I feed them into the coin slot on the lockers, open a locker and quickly stuff the backpack inside, slamming it closed and removing the key with its lanyard from the slot on the front of the locker door. I gather the black plastic garbage bag and step over to shower number one, opening the door and hanging the garbage bag from a hook, along with the locker key.

Moving quickly now, I step over to the coin slot and start feeding quarters into the machine. Two dollars gets you six minutes in the shower and I'm going to need more than that. I feed a total of four dollars into the machine, the shower turning on automatically when I reach the eighth quarter, steam appearing by the time I've entered the sixteenth. I step into the shower fully clothed and close the door behind me.

I'm safe now; there's nobody who will come into the shower stall itself, and my presence is hidden from plain view thanks to the lockers that house my backpack.

Stepping into the spray, I adjust the temperature to the hottest level I can stand, letting it run over my filthy hair and long beard, over my t-shirt, jeans, broken-down tennis shoes. The water feels amazing and I allow myself the luxury of just standing in the torrid stream for a minute, eyes closed, basking in the long-missed bliss of a hot shower.

I can spare only a minute of the extravagance though, before I force myself to get to work. On the wall of the shower is a triad of cleansers housed in a plastic dispenser. Liquid soap, shampoo, and conditioner.

I start with the shampoo, filling my palm with it and massaging it into the hair on top of my head. The hair is in knots, so oil-filled that it tries to shed water without actually getting wet. It takes some time, but I feel it loosening as I wash, the oil and the shampoo running down my dirty clothes, taking the accumulation of dirt and grime with it. I stare down and see that I'm standing in brown water, a sight that makes me smile despite what I'm sure is pure disgust from you as you picture it.

Letting the hot water wash the suds from my hair, I fill my palm again from the shampoo dispenser, moving to my beard. I repeat the process, using my fingers to comb through the beard, removing months of accumulated dirt and food debris.

My clothing is now soaked and I use the soap from the dispenser, rubbing it into my clothes and letting the water stream wash it out. I remove the t-shirt, throwing it into a corner of the shower, then my jeans, shoes and socks, and eventually my underwear, rubbing soap into each item before tossing it aside.

I'm running out of time so I quickly scrub down my body, spending extra time on my armpits and my undercarriage, enjoying the feeling and the luxury of cleanliness after so much time on the street. It's been three months since I've last taken this risk and the twelve minutes pass much too quickly.

The shower shuts off suddenly but I continue to stand in the steam-filled room, enjoying the humid warmth as I squeeze the water out of my hair, using the droplets to make sure all the suds are off my body. I grab my articles of clothing and wring them out, snapping them in the air to shake off the last of the water. Opening the shower door, I hang each item on a hook next to the shower. If anybody should come in now, it would certainly seem strange, the wet clothing hanging next to the shower, but I doubt it would be strange enough to report to anybody in charge.

Now I unwrap the garbage bag and open it, pulling out a towel and using it to rub myself down, enjoying the feel of the clean cloth against my head and my skin. Wrapping it around my waist, I step out of the shower, bringing the bag and locker key with me and rubbernecking around to make sure I haven't missed anything.

I step over to the mirror on the wall and take a moment to examine myself. I've lost weight since I last observed my reflection, and it's not good. I'm pale and emaciated. I decide I need to take better care of myself, try to eat better, stop drinking beer for breakfast. Living on the street is tough, but I don't need to fall into the mental decline that so many of my friends have succumbed to. I need to be more cognizant, more self-aware than I've been.

I had a mission at one time, a reason for my being, for my existence on the street. I've allowed myself to fall into a type of depression, a self-loathing that is already degrading into the self-fulfilling prophecy of the street vagrant. Staring into my own eyes, I'm aware of this, yet strangely I feel powerless to stop it. I feel a strong sense of apathy, and consciously I know I need to fight it. I remind myself of what it was that led me to this point in my life and why I'm out here. It's a good reminder and one I need to keep giving myself.

Reaching back into the garbage bag, I empty it of the remaining items. Fresh clothes: a Henley t-shirt, cotton pants, underwear and socks, sandals with straps. Everything is in earth tones, browns and greens. All part of the image I'm now creating. There are hair ties as well, and I use them first, one to tie my hair into a ponytail, and two more to do the same with my woolly beard.

Hipster. That's the look I'm going for and I think I've achieved it. I now resemble a granola-eating, tree-hugging, environmentalist-liberal, searching the country for the greater meaning of life. Believe it or not, I prefer the homeless persona to this one. Unfortunately, what I witnessed this morning, along with my social responsibility and need for anonymity, rules out maintaining the image I've cultivated for so long now. As much as I abhor the persona I'm now emulating, it's a necessary evil.

Gathering up my pack from the locker, I stuff the wet clothes into the garbage bag along with the towel, and put the bundle into the pack. I'll get the clothes hung up later and the hot, dry, Vegas air will suck the water out of them as quickly as an industrial clothes dryer.

Slinging the pack over my shoulders, I exit the showers and turn left toward the store. It doesn't matter now if anybody sees me. I've shed the image that causes such fear and loathing in business owners and now personify the image that causes only disdain. An improvement? Maybe.

I walk to the drink coolers and stare for just a minute at the beer section. My mouth begins to water as I stare at the cold bottles of beer. The desire to grab one and drink it down is both powerful and frightening at the same time. The intellectual part of me recognizes these physical pangs for what they are—the early stages of alcoholism. I muster all the willpower I can and instead of the beer, I grab a large Gatorade from the cooler and take it up to the counter. I tell the clerk I'll also take two burritos from the hot food case. My mouth waters at the thought of the food and my stomach gives a little flip. This is an extravagance that I can just barely afford, but I know I'm going to need my energy for the day ahead. The distraction of the hot food helps to diminish the desire for alcohol, my body realizing it needs the sustenance of the fat and protein-filled burritos more than the empty calories of the beer.

The clerk stuffs the two burritos into a paper sleeve and rings me up. I watch him carefully as he does so, watching for any sense that he's not bought into my image, any suspicion that would mean I'd forgotten something. I see nothing as he gives me the total. $4.12. I dig another crumpled five-dollar bill from my pocket, along with a dime. I motion toward the small bin on the counter that holds a handful of pennies, and the clerk nods and takes two from the bin, dumping the bill and coins into the register and handing me a dollar back. Luckily for me, saving the two pennies works for both my normal image and the new one.

Nodding my thanks, I make my way back to the truckers' lounge, ravenously stuffing one of the burritos into my mouth. My four-dollar expenditure will buy me some time back here, hopefully enough time to accomplish what I need to get done before the clerk starts to wonder which truck I'm driving.

Settling into one of the comfortable lounge chairs, I open my backpack and begin removing items, setting them on the ground and digging all the way to the bottom of the pack. I carefully push aside the thick envelope near the bottom, leaving it securely in the pack. Emergencies only. I have to remind myself of that whenever I see it.

At the bottom of the pack is a hard-plastic case which I leave there. There's a chance I'll need that later, though part of me hopes I won't. On top of that case is a padded neoprene sleeve and that's what I pull out. I open the zippered top of the neoprene and remove the item inside. My laptop computer, stored safely inside the pack since the last time I used it, more than six months ago.

The power cord is coiled up inside too and I remove that, plugging in to the outlet beside the chair and powering up the laptop. The Wi-Fi here is free for the truckers' use and the password is posted on the door. I connect to that and then immediately launch a program I have installed called "IPAnon." This is an IP hider and it's a good one that I paid quite a bit of money for two years ago. It takes my IP address and bounces it around to different servers across the world, switching every five minutes and making it seem as if I'm anywhere but where I actually am, sitting in a truck stop in Las Vegas. If anybody decides to track me during my online session, it will appear that I'm in Switzerland, then five minutes later, Australia, then five minutes after that, New York City or some other random spot. I have no doubt that a top-notch computer specialist could get around this IP jumper and find my actual location, but the company that makes the program claims even the NSA would have a hard time with that. I don't think the people searching for me care enough to be using resources of that caliber.

Once the program is active, I launch a web browser and do a Google search for my current IP, just as a precautionary check. It shows my location as Sao Paulo, Brazil. Perfect.

Next, I launch an instant messaging program that sends anonymous text messages to any phone number. Entering the ten-digit number from memory, I type in my greeting, *How you doing, partner?* and then I sit back and wait.

The reply comes back just two minutes later. *You ok?*

Leaning forward, I type the response he'll be expecting to see, the one that confirms it's me and tells him that I am indeed okay. *Code 4.* I hit send and then, *Florida weather sure is nice, my tan has never been better.*

I don't think he'll believe for a second that I'm in Florida, but I always tell him that's where I am. I don't want him getting in trouble and if he's reporting this conversation, as he should be, he'll be able to truthfully tell them that as far as he knows I'm hiding out in Florida. I don't *think* he's reporting these chats, but I never want to put him in a position where he has to lie for me.

He sends back a smiley face, then, *A sends love and best wishes. Nothing new on this front, still searching.*

"A" stands for his wife, Alexa. And the rest...well, basically it means that I still need to continue in my present ways.

I need a favor, if you can. 28, 29 on NV 549TPE, I type to him, hitting send and leaning back, waiting. "28, 29" means a registration check and owner criminal history on the Nevada license plate 549TPE. That's the plate number that I memorized this morning, the plate on the vehicle the murderer was driving.

If you haven't already guessed, the person I'm typing to is a police officer. He also happens to be my best friend. He also happens to be my former partner, which you might have guessed from my initial message to him. Which means that I used to be a police officer, which I have no doubt you've now come to realize.

If he's still my best friend, he'll send me back the information I'm requesting, though I certainly won't blame him if he chooses not to send it to me, just like I wouldn't blame him if he chose to report this conversation. I'm putting him in a tough spot and I know it. Again, you're getting a view at all of my secrets here, so I'm sure you've figured out that I just happen to be a fugitive from justice. That means I'm putting my best friend in a spot where I'm asking him to assist a fugitive from justice, in and of itself a felony. I'm asking my best friend, who's a police officer, to commit a felony. Some friend I am, huh?

I know you're judging me and I don't blame you. I'm judging myself too, believe me. I feel terrible about it, but I also feel that I don't have a choice.

I know you're also wondering why I don't just tell my friend what I saw and let him deal with it. Well, that's a big problem and it would put him in a tough spot. My friend is a cop in Henderson, a city to the south and east of Las Vegas. The murder occurred in Las Vegas which means my friend would have to call the Las Vegas cops to pass on the information I gave him. They would wonder where he got it and would want the name and contact information for his source. Obviously at that point, he would have to give me up or lie about it. Neither of those are good options. I'm never going to ask my friend to lie for me, even though I'm asking him to assist me which might be just as bad. I justify it though by telling myself I'm not actually asking for assistance for myself, I'm asking him for information to help me track down a murderer and therefore it's not as bad as it might seem. Is that a poor justification for a felony? I don't know the answer to that and I chew on my lip as I think about it, worrying about the position I'm taking.

The other reason I can't just pass on the info to my friend to pass on to the Las Vegas police is because that would tell him that I witnessed the crime. And that would mean he would know that

I'm in Las Vegas, something I've taken great pains to hide from him and from the rest of the law enforcement community. That's not an option. Not only would that vastly magnify the risk to myself, it would put him in another position where he would feel compelled, both legally and morally, to tell his superiors that he knows where I am. As of now, if he reports these conversations, he can plausibly tell them as far as he knows, I'm in Florida.

Do you see the position I'm in? Does it change your judgement of me and of my actions? If not, I don't blame you.

It's funny, I think, as I wait for a reply, how I would have passed the downtime just two years ago. Facebook, Twitter, email, online news services...I spent hours, wasted hours, on internet searches for things I now couldn't care less about. I can tell you, I don't miss it, not anymore. At first it was difficult to be away from the crutch of social media, but now I don't think I'll ever be back on Facebook, even if my life someday goes back to normal.

His reply is taking some time, and though logically I understand that he may not even be on duty, or may be on a call, just busy, or whatever, I find myself starting to get nervous. Pulling up a web browser again, I do a search for my IP address. It comes back quickly with my location as Vancouver, British Columbia. That's a good sign, but does little to quell my apprehension and my paranoia. I set the laptop on the table next to the lounge chair and move over to the doorway, glancing to the right and left. The left is clear, but to the right I see a clerk staring at me, a milk crate balanced on her hip as she stocks the full- sized cooler with drinks. She gives me a funny look, a frown on her features as I duck back inside the lounge. Cursing at myself for drawing attention, and for my unremitting paranoia, I start back toward my laptop just as it beeps with an incoming message.

Settling back into the chair, I pull up the message.

Comes back to a 2014 Chevy Tahoe / Joseph Panattiere. This is not a good dude. Convictions for bribery, extortion, robbery, suspected in murder, kidnapping, etc. What are you into, partner? You okay?

That message was followed with a screenshot showing a picture of Panattiere's driver's license. It listed his height and weight, along with his address here in Las Vegas and a nice clear picture of a man I recognize as the murderer from this morning. Bingo.

I type back to him: *Thanks. I'm okay, not in trouble. Guy lives there, so he's your problem I guess. Hope you're all well, will be in touch when I can.*

I wait for his reply which comes: *Take care buddy. Always here for you.* It brings a smile to my face and, I'm not ashamed to admit it, a tear to my eye. I sign out of the messaging program and then close the IP hider program and shut down the computer. I got the information I needed, but it came at a cost...a feeling of melancholy, an overwhelming sense of loss and despair. I know I'll feel better a little later, but for the moment, I take a few minutes to wallow in my own self-pity.

Chapter 3

I'm standing in front of Joseph Panattiere's house, or at least the address on the driver's license my ex-partner sent me. I haven't seen any people yet or the car I saw this morning, so I can't say for sure this is his place. I'm waiting and I'm hiding in plain sight while I wait. I've become quite good over the last two years at both of those things.

Luckily for me, Panattiere's house is directly across from a park, and I'm sitting on one of the park benches, sipping my Gatorade while I steal discreet glances at what I hope is his residence.

It took me just over an hour to walk here from the Flying J Travel Plaza. While I walked, I had a lot of time to think. The obvious solution and the easiest path to take, now that I'd altered my appearance significantly, was to borrow a phone at a business somewhere and call the police, making an anonymous report. This was the obvious solution, but it still carried some risk. The police would show up at whatever location the call came from, and they would ask questions. There might be security footage of me, either from the business where I make the call or another business nearby. The clerk or a customer might give them a description of me, almost certainly would in fact, and that could end up being an issue. I think it would be a fairly safe route to take, but there is still some risk there. That's the kind of risk I just can't accept. I'm not going to be caught because of a momentary lapse of judgement.

It was certainly a lot easier for those in dilemmas such as my current one when there were payphones available on every other corner. Making an anonymous call to the cops back then was a near guarantee. There were no cameras, very poor tracking ability, even enhanced 911 which automatically gives the location of the call and holds the line open is a fairly new advancement that certainly didn't exist when payphones were in their prime.

My risk-averse nature has led me to this spot in this park, watching the house of a known criminal and all-around bad guy, and trying

41

to formulate a plan on the fly. If I'm being completely honest, I could probably stand the small amount of risk involved in notifying the cops of what I saw. I could justify taking that limited risk and could possibly find a way to limit it even further. But honestly, I guess I miss the action a little bit.

I'm excited just sitting here, watching the house, being a part of something, even if it is mainly manufactured in my head. Still, for the last two years I've mostly sat around all day on the street, waiting for something to happen. Waiting for the moment that I can safely make my return into society, triumphant though sad. My life has lost nearly all meaning in those two years; my purpose, iron strong when I began this transient journey, has withered away to something that lives at the back of my mind, getting smaller and smaller every day, further suppressed by the all-encompassing pull of alcoholism.

Now, I feel that surge of adrenaline, the *joie de vivre* that comes from having a purpose, a mission. It helps immensely that the mission I've set for myself is righteous, the antagonist evil, and the hero true. Of course, you may feel differently, seeing that you know my carefully guarded secret, or at least part of it. Being a fugitive from justice does dampen the enthusiasm somewhat.

Nevertheless, I feel my heart rate pick up, my eyes widen and my breath quicken slightly as a jolt of adrenaline hits me. A black Chevy Tahoe has just turned onto the street in front of Panattiere's house, and sure enough, it slows and turns into his driveway. The door opens and Joseph Panattiere himself steps out, blonde hair and sunglasses, still wearing the same clothes he was wearing this morning when I watched him murder the guy in the car. This tells me he's extremely cocky and arrogant or extremely stupid.

He pulled the trigger this morning while sitting next to the victim in the victim's car. Blood spatter certainly blew back at him, got onto his clothing, probably a decent amount of it, yet it appears that he didn't even bother to change clothes. Or maybe he owns more than one of the current wardrobe he's so proud of. That adds the possible tag of douchebag to the previous list.

Joseph takes a quick peep around, his gaze passing right over me without slowing down, my own gaze slipping from his direction naturally as his crosses the distance. Much like this morning when he didn't notice me, he's once again overlooked my presence, a mistake he'll live to regret if I have anything to say about it.

My gaze settles back on him as he turns away and walks up to the front door, using a key to let himself in and slamming the door behind him. I glance up at the sun which has begun to dip into its final arc toward the western horizon. Although I have no idea what time it is, I have become phenomenal at determining how much daylight is left, and the sun's position tells me I have a good five or six hours before it gets dark. I don't have much of a plan with regard to Joseph, but the beginning of one is there and I'm going to need to wait until full dark to implement it.

I'm on the west side of town, just a couple of blocks west of I-15 and close to Charleston Avenue. While I have time to kill, there's something I want to do, something I haven't done in too long, and now that I'm in this area, it seems like a good time to get it done.

Slinging the pack onto my shoulders, I slip the Gatorade bottle into a pouch on the side and start walking, taking one last gaze back at Panattiere's house before I turn to the south and lose sight of it.

It takes me about an hour to reach my new destination, a charming house on a corner lot, west and south of Panattiere's house, probably two miles as the crow flies, a little farther as the coyote walks. Or the transient. Or the Gatorade-sipping, bleeding-heart tree hugger. My pace slows significantly as I get close, memories and emotions bubbling to the surface, along with a sense of caution that is quite obviously unnecessary, yet still hard to shake. As I turn the final corner onto west Rosemont Street, I notice my hands shaking slightly, my palms wet, my heartrate elevated beyond what should be expected for the walking exercise I've just done.

The house comes into sight looking lonely and forlorn. A house has a feel when it's unoccupied, an empty feel that's tough to accurately articulate, but that most people can sense. The longer a house sits empty, the more that feeling grows, until it eventually reaches a level where the neighborhood kids, even in their iPad and video game-induced, nearly comatose lack of perception, can feel it. That's when the house gets the tag *haunted* and its path to ruin becomes inevitable.

This house hasn't reached that point of no return yet. It has a despondent and abandoned feel, something the house and I have in common, I suspect. But I doubt it's been elevated to haunted status. Nonetheless, it feels haunted to me, likely my own memories making that seem true.

The shrubs that once surrounded the house in lush greens are now brown. The lawn, once manicured and trimmed nicely, now weed-choked and overgrown, a sickly yellow color. Apparently, the water has been turned off, something that shouldn't surprise me but somehow does.

The house is dark inside of course; empty houses usually are. I think I expected to see at least one light on, maybe a lamp or porch light, but perhaps the power has suffered the same fate as the water.

One immediately obvious change has taken place since my last visit a year ago—the crime scene tape has been removed. I don't know why I expected it to be there still...perhaps in my mind this continues to be an active crime scene. Apparently, Las Vegas Metro doesn't think so. At some point, some detectives decided the tape could come down, and I don't blame them I guess. In their minds, the case has been solved; they have a prime suspect. There's no more evidence to be discovered, no more sleuthing to be done. All that's left for them is to find their suspect and bring him to trial.

My pace has slowed to almost a halt and I realize that I'm staring at the house, definitely drawing attention to myself if anybody happens to be watching. That I absolutely can't have and I force my eyes away from the structure and back to the street in front of me. It was a terrible risk coming here before dark, an unnecessary risk, and I don't even feel better. The sight of the house looking so despairing and disconsolate seems to transfer those emotions right to myself. I lost everything in this house, that night that seems so long ago.

I shuffle past, thinking back to that night which was actually only a little more than two years ago. I believe I mentioned to you already that I've seen a murder before the one this morning. I don't talk about that night two years ago, but I wonder if I should. Who would I talk to about it though? Allen Iverson? One of my other brothers in homelessness with whom I wander the streets? None of those seems appropriate. All of us have our tales of woe and none want to hear about somebody else's. Mine is probably worse than most and undoubtedly nobody wants to hear a tale that makes their own seem less significant.

I focus upwards and say a quick prayer, a prayer to God—if he even exists. That was something I was confident of before that night two years prior, and something I greatly doubt now. I say a prayer to Him that if He exists, my wife and my son are with Him now, protected by Him in death the way that I was unable to protect them in life.

Chapter 4

Back on my bench in the park across from Panattiere's house,

I've managed to shake off most of the melancholy feelings and I'm now focused on the task at hand. The sun has all but disappeared behind the mountains to the west and street lights are beginning to come on. I laid out my wet clothes on the grass when I got back here an hour ago and they're nearly dry already, the sun and the dry desert air doing as good a job as any man-made dryer. I was getting a few funny looks from some of the park-goers so I also had my laptop sitting open on the picnic table in front of me, pretending to work. Even in my current disguise, dressed as a hipster gypsy traveler, I suppose the clothing laid out next to me might make me appear once again like a vagrant. The laptop certainly obliterates that perception though.

Nonetheless, I won't be able to sit here much longer without raising suspicion. I don't think normal people sit in parks in the dark working on their laptops.

I pack up my clothes again, ignoring the slightly damp feel, knowing that a little mold or mildew growing on them won't hurt my image when I need to go back to the transient look. The backpack is going to be a problem for the tasks I've laid out for myself this evening, but I don't have many options. I can't store it anywhere nearby and I don't want to risk stashing it in some bushes or somewhere else, at least not while residents are still out and about, moving around, taking walks, enjoying the evening. Literally everything I own is in that pack, including some valuable items that I need. Or hope I'll need someday.

Grabbing the backpack, I sling it over my shoulders and leave the park, walking away to the north and hitting the cross street which I follow back to a wash. Vegas is full of these washes, designed to carry away flash flood waters that otherwise would come roaring down from the mountains with every rain. The ground around here is like concrete; a million years of sediment has settled into this valley, and the water doesn't soak into the ground very well. The washes are a great way for coyotes to travel from the desert into the neighborhoods hunting for stray cats as a late-night snack. They're also a great way for homeless hipsters to sneak in behind your house.

By the time I'm in the wash and I've worked my way behind Panattiere's house, it's fully dark. A large masonry wall separates the back of his house from the wash and I can see only his roof from my side of the wall as I'm crouched behind it. When I stand up to my full height I should be able to just see over the top of the wall, hopefully into his backyard. It's a nice Sunday evening, temperature cooling off quickly, and I can hear the clatter of dishes

49

from residents eating dinner, windows and doors open to let in the fresh evening air. I ignore the hunger pangs in my stomach, something I've grown accustomed to doing. What is harder to ignore are the feelings of envy toward the residents, enjoying time with their families, happily tucked into their homes.

Despite my desire to not leave my backpack behind, I realize I'm not going to have a choice. It's too bulky and unwieldy for the maneuvering I'm going to have to do tonight. Not for the first time, I wonder what exactly I'm getting myself into. What the hell I'm doing out here playing a one-man game of hide-and-seek, spying on the monster in the house behind the wall.

You're probably wondering just what the hell my plan is. I'd love to lay it out for you, but truth be told, I don't quite know what it is myself. I have a semblance of a plan, the beginnings of something, but mostly I'm playing it by ear, allowing the wind to take me where it will, much like my life over the last two years.

Making the decision that the pack will probably be safe for a short amount of time in this wash, an area where few people probably ever travel and virtually none after dark. I quickly unshoulder it and stash it behind some sage that's clinging stubbornly to the slope. The pack has faded over time to the color of the street, meaning no real sharp colors, and it blends in nicely with the loose rock and sediment of the wash. From a few feet away it appears to be nothing more than a lump of earth or a rock in the dark night.

Satisfied, I move back to the wall and slowly stand on tip-toe, peering over it and into Panattiere's yard. There are lights on in his house, and I can see the rear end of the Tahoe sticking out around the side of the residence. The backyard is small and almost entirely dirt, tufts of weeds and grass sprouting up in random blooms throughout. It's not the kind of backyard where you'd spend any time hanging out, enjoying the evening, and I don't expect to see anybody out there. What I'm actually looking for, and concerned about, is a dog.

I search for any sign one might live here, doghouse, tie-up lines, worn paths in the dirt, piles of dog crap, etc. I don't see anything and I exhale with relief. Next, I peer at the windows of the rear of the house. I can see light streaming through both of the windows and the sliding glass door, but can't see into the house itself. All the blinds are closed and the two windows appear to have some sort of privacy screens over them. I suspect one of the windows is probably a bedroom window and the other should be a kitchen or dining room.

Not seeing anything more, I take one last glance both ways down the wash, place my hands flat on the wall, and boost myself up and over. It takes more effort than I expected, my strength having waned significantly over the last two years. Luckily my weight has also waned, and I'm able to get myself to the top of the wall, lying flat and then lowering myself to the other side, landing softly on my feet and crouching down immediately, listening for any sign my presence was noted.

I don't hear or see anything disturbing and I scoot over to the window, staying low and then pressing myself against the house and peering up toward the corner of the glass, trying to see inside. There is some kind of film over the window, a sort of hazy plastic, possibly designed to block the sunlight from coming in. Of course, it's a north facing window, I realize, so the amount of sun coming in should be pretty minimal. That leads me to think the purpose is more along the lines of not allowing anyone to see in. So, yeah. Suspicious.

I can hear a low murmur coming from inside, voices speaking or perhaps a television; it's tough to tell. If I can't see in, they can't see out either, so I walk quickly over to the sliding glass door. The blinds here are long, vertical, plastic slats, and there are minute gaps on the edges where they don't quite overlap the door. Cupping my hand to the door and leaning up to the glass, I peer inside.

Directly in front of the slider I can see a kitchen table—a folding card table it actually appears—set up in the place you would expect to see a dining room table. It sits under an eighties-style, cheap chandelier. The card table is piled with dishes, plates, cups, ashtrays with cigarette butts, and an honest to God lava lamp, plugged into an outlet in the wall, blobs of red whatever floating up and down in the glass cylinder. I haven't seen one of those since I was a kid and I'm slightly mesmerized by the sight of it.

Finally tearing my gaze away from the floating red orbs, I focus past the table into what appears to be a living room. I can just see the left edge of a large-screen television, some type of action movie playing. Across from the TV I can make out a pair of legs, feet encased in black socks, elevated up on the leg rest of a recliner, hands on the arms of the chair, remote control in the right hand. I can't see the face of the person because of the way the wall to the dining room blocks part of the living room, but it's clearly a man sitting in the chair. I need to see if it's Joseph Panattiere so I can plan my next move.

Hoping that the other side of the glass door will allow a better view of the living room, I decide to make my move and cross the small concrete slab that serves as a back porch. As I take the first step, I realize two things. The first is that there were two sets of dishes on the dining room table set up in front of two plastic

53

chairs. The second is that under the eave on the back of the house, invisible from my earlier position on the other side of the wall due to the overhanging roof, but clearly visible now, is a security camera, pointed right at me. Simultaneously as I realize these two critical pieces of information, I hear the cocking of a pistol and a quiet voice saying, "Move and you die."

Chapter 5

I don't move. I certainly don't want to die, and if this is Joseph

Panattiere behind me, he's already shown a willingness to commit murder. I silently curse myself for my lapse of attention and judgement.

"Really slowly I want you to turn around and keep your hands in plain sight."

I do as he says, turning slowly to my right, hands held out to my side, palms open. When I get turned, I can see my captor's face from the light streaming in from the kitchen. It's Joseph Panattiere and he has the same pistol I saw this morning when he murdered the man in the car, the stainless Beretta 92, hammer pulled back, pointed at me and held with a steady hand.

Panattiere studies me for a second and then pulls a cell phone out of his jeans pocket with his left hand. He glances at the screen and then back up at me, too quickly for me to consider making any kind of move. He's seven feet away from me and I know the time it takes me to cover that distance is much greater than the typical person's reaction time, especially with the hammer cocked back and a finger on the trigger. Not good trigger safety, and it worries me, but I'm in no position to complain at the moment.

He takes another quick glance at his phone and pushes a button, holding it up to his ear, eyes and gun steady on me. My first fear is that he's calling the police. If he holds me and waits for them to show up, they're going to run me and probably arrest me. If my David Sands ID doesn't pass muster, they'll book me into jail and fingerprint me. That will be the end of my life as I know it. I quickly dismiss this as an option though. There's no way a guy like Joseph Panattiere would be calling the police to help him with a trespasser. Particularly when he's holding the same gun he used to commit a murder just twelve hours ago.

I notice he's wearing his sunglasses on the top of his blond crew-cut hair, even though it's been dark for almost an hour. I know from his driver's license that he's 32 years of age. He's also 6 feet 2 inches, weighs 200 pounds, and he's in great shape. A hooked nose marks him as a fighter, and what appears to be a small amount of cauliflower ear on the left side of his head tells me that he's spent some time wrestling as well. I missed the cauliflower ear this morning, too far away to have spotted it.

"Reggie," he says when someone answers on the other end. "Come to the back slider and open it up. Hurry up." He disconnects the line and slips the phone back in his pocket, continuing to stare at me in a cold and calculated manner, not saying a word. This guy has been around the block, and I'd be lying if I said I wasn't nervous and apprehensive.

The blinds on the slider abruptly move and then open partially. A man stands there, Reggie presumably, gawking at me with a curious expression. A gaunt figure, he has a mop of unruly red hair and bags around his eyes, his pale, freckled skin meeting the purplish bloats of sleeplessness, the contrast stark and shocking. He's wearing jeans and a t-shirt that used to be white but is now much closer to gray. Black socks on his feet mark him as the man in the recliner. On his left arm, I see the easily recognizable sign of a heroin user—the track marks of a chronic needle sticker. I recognize his look—not the man himself, but the *look* of the man. He's well on his way to a life right next to me on the street unless he makes some changes, and quickly. Of course, I doubt he'd appreciate the warning if I were to give it. Which I won't. He unlocks and pulls open the door and Joseph motions with the gun toward the opening, his expression stoic and icy. I turn toward the open door and enter the kitchen, moving slowly, hands still held out and open.

"What's this, Joey?" Reggie asks.

"Saw this guy on the camera snooping around outside." He points with the gun to one of the kitchen chairs. "Sit."

I sit, still not saying anything, glancing around the filthy kitchen. Dirty dishes are everywhere, the sink full of them, overflowing onto the counter and stacked in precarious piles. I see a cockroach scurry across the counter, probably on his way to one of the many cornucopias of dried food littering the surfaces. As I sit, I glance at the lava lamp which glows behind me, silently and magically sending the blobs of goo up and down the glass cylinder.

"Who are you?" Joseph asks, the gun still pointed at me.

I focus on him but don't say anything, not sure what I should say. My mind is racing and I can't seem to make myself focus. It seems like I should say something cool, like I should be intimidating right back to him, maybe do some martial arts shit or something and take the gun from him. But I'm pretty worried right now and I can't seem to make my tongue work. Joseph apparently takes my silence as defiance and smiles. Without breaking eye contact, he casually lifts the pistol slightly, pointing the barrel toward the ceiling and then bringing the butt end of the grip down rapidly at my face.

It's too fast for me to react properly and I'm embarrassed to say I barely see it coming. My reflexes have apparently slowed considerably over the last two years, and the pistol grip hits me on the cheekbone. My vision goes dim and the pain receptors in my brain scream out. Unbidden, my hand reaches for the wound and comes away bloody. Now my heart is working overtime and adrenaline courses through my body. This may turn out to be a good thing because it's helping me think.

"Let's try this again," he says, his expression unchanged. "Who are you?"

"My name is David," I say, cowering slightly in the chair. "I'm sorry, I didn't mean to be here. I was just passing by."

"You were passing by? And decided to take a detour into my backyard?" he replies, an expression of disbelief on his face.

"I saw something. A cat. I saw a cat and wanted to pet it." This sounds slightly stupid, even to me, but maybe stupid is the best play in this scenario. Also, I'm presenting a scenario that fits my current image as a tree-hugging animal lover. I hope it sounds more believable considering my appearance. If I hadn't changed into these clothes, washed my hair and tied it up, I would have said I'd been searching for a safe place to sleep for the night.

"You saw a cat?" Joseph regards Reggie, disbelief on his face. "He saw a cat, Reggie. What do you think of that?"

Reggie smiles, crooked and yellowed teeth doing nothing to improve his appearance. "I didn't see no cat," he replies.

"Me neither. Search him," Joseph orders Reggie.

Reggie steps to me and grabs my beard by the ponytail I've tied it in, pulling hard to make me stand up. I stand, still slightly wobbly from the smack to the head, a pounding headache beginning to surface and a slight feeling of nausea stirring in my gut. Reggie roughly pats me down, a poor attempt at a frisk that he must have learned watching cop movies. I doubt he would have found a weapon even if I had one. He shoves me back down in the chair.

"He's clean."

"Look, I'm sorry. I know this sounds dumb. I was walking on the street one block over and saw a cat. I love cats. I tried to call to him and he ran down the wash behind your place here. I was worried he was going to get eaten by a coyote so I chased him. He jumped the fence behind here and I followed. I just wanted to make sure he was okay."

Joseph appears disbelieving and I don't blame him. The story is stupid but it's all I could think of and now I'm stuck with it. Changing it now would be a bad move and might get me killed.

"What do you think we should do with him?" he asks Reggie.

"I think we oughtta kill him!" Reggie growls, trying to appear scary.

"You're a fucking idiot, Reggie," Joey says, still staring at me. "He always wants me to kill everybody. The problem is that once you start killing everybody, the bodies start piling up and the cops start asking too many questions. Don't you agree?" he says to me.

I nod, vigorously. At the moment, I couldn't agree more. "Please don't kill me. I'll never come back. I just wanted to protect the cat. I didn't mean any harm." I hate myself for groveling. As my vision returns fully and the blood stops collecting in my beard, my anger is growing. The immediate situation is still dangerous of course, but I'm already planning my revenge. If I can manage to escape.

Reggie cackles at my whining tone but stops immediately when Joseph says, "Okay, you can go. Get up, get out of here."

Reggie stares at him in disbelief and I start to rise, turning toward the glass slider and taking a step, immediately falling to the floor as the gun strikes me again, in the temple this time. I hear Reggie cackling loudly as my face hits the filthy linoleum floor. I've lain in worse places of course, so the dirty linoleum doesn't bother me, but I'm struggling to stay conscious, my head pounding and my ears ringing. I shake my head slowly, trying to push my hands under me. Joseph kicks me in the ribs with a boot, hard, and I curl up into a ball. He squats down close to me and rubs the barrel of the gun across my face, slowly, poking the front sight of the weapon into the original wound on my cheek, causing more blood to flow. I realize in some abstract way that my DNA is now on the murder weapon from this morning. This presents all kinds of potential future problems for me. Of course, my current problem is much more pressing.

"I don't like you. I don't ever want to see you again. If you see me, even if it's just on the street, you run the other way. Am I clear?" Joseph asks me. He's playing the badass, showing off for Reggie possibly, but he holds all the cards. For now, I nod, my head screaming with the up and down motion.

"Go." He points to the front door this time.

I push myself up, unsteady and dizzy, glancing warily at Reggie who grabs me by the back of my shirt and prods me through the living room toward the front door. He unlocks two deadbolts and pulls open the door, shoving me hard. I stumble but manage to keep my feet.

"And you don't never come back!" I hear Reggie yell from behind me as I walk carefully past the Tahoe. The contrast of the newer model, well-taken-care-of Chevy Tahoe to the state of the house behind me is marked and interesting. Joseph clearly cares more about his public image than his private one.

The door slams behind me and I walk out to the street, turning left and getting out of sight of the house. I cross the street and track backwards to enter the park, finding a dark corner and laying down on the cool grass. My head is pounding and I take a minute to close my eyes and try to relax my brain. The gash on my cheek has stopped bleeding, but I can feel the blood matted in my beard, hardening on the whiskers. My ribs ache and I hope nothing is broken in there. I have no means to go to a hospital, nor could I stand the kind of scrutiny that might bring.

After a few minutes, I remember my backpack and I sit up rapidly. Too rapidly. I feel the blood pound into my skull, causing another wave of sickness. This feels like a concussion and that's a big problem, obviously. My backpack is the priority though; I can't lose that, so I fight down the nausea and get to my feet, holding onto the chain link fence behind me to steady myself.

After another minute, I feel slightly better and start walking, staying in the shadows until I reach the street and then moving as quickly as I can toward the wash. I spend a moment at the entrance to the wash, letting my eyes adjust to the darkness and peering warily down toward the wall behind Joseph and Reggie's house. My eyes seem to adjust fine and focus seems improved. Maybe I don't have a concussion after all, but I do have a splitting headache.

I wait five minutes and then creep cautiously down the alley, avoiding loose rocks and the branches of shrubs. There's a slight breeze developing and that helps mask the minor noises I make with my sandals in the gravel bottom. I get to the shrub where I stored the pack and I'm relieved to find it still there. As I pull it away from the bush, I hear voices from the other side of the wall and see the overspray of light from a flashlight as its beam wanders over the backyard. I set the pack down again and crouch next to the wall, straining to hear.

"I'm tellin' you, there ain't no cat. I think he was a cop, man."

"You're paranoid, Reggie. He wasn't no cop."

"Well I don't know, man. He looked familiar to me anyway. I'm sure I've seen him before. Din't he look familiar to you, man?"

"No."

"Well, I think I oughtta get outta here for a day or two."

"Reggie, you think I give a rat's ass what you do or where you go? Leave. In fact, you can stay gone for all I care. All you do is sit around all day and shoot up and I've had about enough of that."

"Screw you, man. I'm the one who brings all the work in."

"I'm the one who has to *do* all the work, you punkass bitch."

"Yeah but I got the contact for all the work, Joey. Without that, you got nothin'."

The voices fade away and I hear the sliding door move noisily on its track and slam shut, the click of the lock engaging. The conversation was interesting. It's not surprising that they're afraid of the cops, but I wonder what "the work" is. Drug dealing seems the most plausible scenario, particularly with the filmed-over windows and the nice SUV in the driveway. I don't know many successful drug dealers who use their own product though, as Reggie obviously does. And the last thing I heard, Reggie saying he has the contact for all the work, doesn't quite make sense either.

Grabbing the pack, I slide quietly out of the wash and then work my way around the block, catching it again on the other side, a hundred yards or more away from Joey and Reggie's place and across a major street, well out of any search area they may have if they get suspicious again and start searching around. I need a dark and quiet place and I'm worried the park may get some after-dinner traffic, people walking their dogs or just going on a stroll themselves. The park has a sign that says it closes at 10pm and I want to remain clear until after that, which gives me a couple of hours.

Positioning myself halfway down the wash between two streets, with corridors of inky blackness protecting me from the streetlights on each of them, I squat on my haunches, leaning back against the wall and closing my eyes. The backpack is between my legs, my arms wrapped around it as I wait for my headache to subside.

Sometime later, I awake with a start. It's gotten noticeably colder and I shiver slightly. It takes me a minute to realize my headache is mostly gone, and I'm relieved. There's still pain from the cut on my cheek, and I feel up to the side of my head where the second hit occurred. There's a knot there and it's swollen and tender. I get carefully to my feet, feeling the soreness in my ribs and pressing my fingertips against them to check for anything that feels

65

unnatural. They feel normal, though I suspect there may be a crack or two. As long as they're not actually broken, they'll heal fine.

There's nobody in sight other than the occasional car as it passes by on the street on either side of me. I open the backpack and begin pulling items out, setting them to the side as I dig for the bottom of the pack. The item I'm after has been in the bottom of the pack for the last two years, my need of it non-existent until now. What I'm about to do will put myself at great risk, but to be honest, I'm pissed. Wouldn't you be? I know I should be scared and I am a little, but my anger overrides my fear. For the last two years I've had this need for revenge, and recently it's diminished into a dull murmur, far back in my head. I've allowed myself to become complacent, to worry less about what I should be doing and more about what my life has become, a serene acceptance of my circumstances because the concept of my mission is too difficult to consider.

If this event has done one thing decent, it's woken me up, made me realize that I need to reestablish my previous purpose, my intent. I've let myself down and I've let down those I once loved, allowing my despondency to govern my decisions and lack of action.

That ends tonight. You're my witness, and my sincere hope is that you'll hold me responsible from this moment on.

At the bottom of the pack, under the laptop case, is a hard-plastic box, and I pull that out, stuffing the other items back in. This case has seen its last days at the bottom of the pack.

Opening the case, I stare for a minute at the contents, transfixed by the small gleam of light off the cold metal. The gun is a Glock, a nine-millimeter Glock 17 to be exact, one magazine inserted into the grip, another nestled into the foam next to it. Each magazine holds seventeen rounds, and there's a box of fifty silvertip hollow-points sitting next to it.

I open the box and eject the magazine, feeding rounds into it until it's full, then smacking the magazine against my thigh, an old habit to seat the rounds correctly, a motion I make without thinking about it. I insert the magazine into the gun and rack one round into the chamber, trying to do it as quietly as possible to avoid anyone hearing the distinctive sound. Ejecting the magazine again, I fill that last slot with one more round and slam it back home into the grip.

The gun feels great in my hand, the balance perfect and comforting. I hold it up, sighting down the barrel and see the soft glow of three green lights on top of the gun. Tritium night sights, slightly radioactive and still perfectly effective after two years in the dark.

I consider the other magazine and then decide not to carry it. I know I'm out of practice with a gun, but if I need more than eighteen rounds, I'm dead anyway. I grab the leather holster that sits next to the gun and close the lid of the box. There are a couple more items in there, but I'm not going to be using them tonight. They would mark me if I used them, and I still need to avoid that. Of course, the gun will mark me as well, but I'm only taking it as a last resort. I hope I won't have to use it, or at least that I won't have to fire it. In the hands of a righteous person, the power of a gun is like the power of an aircraft carrier or a nuclear weapon. Its power is deadly when used, but the real intent is the *projection* of that power, rather than the actual use of it.

Putting the box back into the pack, I place my jacket and the plastic bag containing my still damp clothing on top of it. The gun will stay with me for a little while, but I hope to be putting it back in the case soon.

I stand up and slide the holster into the waistband of my cotton pants, putting it right in the front where I know I can most easily get to it. I take the time to practice drawing the gun from the holster, adjusting its position and getting the feel right. Try not to judge me. It's been a long time since I've carried a gun and it takes some getting used to.

Finally, I'm satisfied with the feel and the position and I drop my untucked shirt over the grip, concealing the weapon from view. I need to pee and I do so here, the soft splash against the rock nearly inaudible in the breezy night. I finish and then swing the big pack over my shoulders and cautiously exit the wash.

Chapter 6

Judging by the position of the moon, I think it's close to 11pm.

Joey's truck is gone, his house is dark, and I'm standing in the park across the street, watching from the shadows. The moon is a crescent tonight, not giving off too much light despite the lack of any cloud cover, so the shadows on the edge of the park conceal me completely.

There's a fountain near the playground and I've filled my belly, as well as the Gatorade bottle from earlier with water. It's a good thing for a transient to always know where to get clean water, and this is a great source, though a far distance from my usual hangouts.

Dropping the pack, I take out my big, green, Army jacket, the last warm beer still in the pocket. focusing on the beer for a moment, I open the bottle and pour it out. I'm on a new mission, and there's no place for the alcoholic-like plunge my life has recently been taking.

I put on the jacket. Not because of the temperature, it's not quite cold enough for that, but because I need it for the camouflage. Pushing the pack back into the darkest corner of the shadows against the fence, I walk confidently out of the park, across the street, and up to Joey's front door. Knocking loudly and quickly, I step back and slightly to the side, my hand going under my shirt to rest on the grip of the gun. I don't expect anybody to be here—the house is dark and empty feeling, and the Tahoe is gone, but I'm ready in case anybody does come to the door.

Nobody answers and I walk over to the side of the house, inspecting the area carefully to make sure no neighbors are watching. A car drives by, its headlights not quite reaching beyond Joey and Reggie's driveway, but I don't move until it passes out of sight.

The yard is dark, the streetlight nearby defective or possibly shot out or otherwise disabled by Joey or Reggie. Those two are like a fungus, much preferring to live and operate in the dark, like most criminals I've known, and if I'm being completely honest, much like myself in my current lifestyle.

I scan the driveway and calculate what areas might be illuminated by headlights from a car turning in from either direction. Figuring out the best spot to remain hidden, I hunker down, jacket wrapped around my legs, at one with the night.

I wish I had a partner, somebody I could call to help me. A friend, a relative, anybody. But I don't. I'm alone and I'm on my own, and I need to accept that.

One lonely Beastie I be,
All by myself without nobody.

I fall asleep while I'm waiting, but wake up before too long, disturbed by the sound of a car engine slowing to make a turn. I glance up and see the Tahoe as it turns into the driveway and parks. I've got the Glock in my hand and I'm motionless as the headlights are extinguished and the engine shuts off. If it's both of them, this is going to be difficult, but I'm hoping, based on the conversation that I've overheard, that Reggie has indeed decided to leave.

The driver's door opens and I'm happy to see that it's Joseph himself and that he's alone. He slams the car door and hits the lock button on the remote fob, the Tahoe's headlights flashing once. By the time he reaches the door, fumbling for the key on the key ring, I've moved into position and I quickly and quietly walk up behind him, any noise I'm making masked by the sound of the key ring as he unlocks the door.

The Glock doesn't have a hammer, so I can't cock it and get the same effect that he did, but I do press the metal barrel up against his neck while saying, "Move and you die."

Much like me, Joey apparently values his life, and he doesn't move. His hands freeze and I add, "Open the door, nice and slowly, then get your hands up in the air."

He complies. "Now use your foot and push the door open. If you make any sudden movements, I will blow your head off."

I'm disguising my voice of course, I want him to think this is a nothing more than a robbery and I need to get him inside, away from the street and anybody that might come by and see us. Although it would be extremely difficult for anybody to see that I'm holding a gun in the dark, I want to minimize any exposure.

Joey pushes open the door and I tell him to walk in and stay turned away. I stop him when he reaches the middle of the living room

72

and then I shut the door behind me, locking both of the deadbolts while watching him out of the corner of my eye. I leave the lights off and tell him to walk into the kitchen, and sit in the chair, keeping his hands above his head. The glow from the still-illuminated lava lamp casts enough light for him to see and he takes a seat in the chair. Once he's done that, I reach over and turn on the overhead light. He immediately swivels his head toward me and I see an expression of worry and confusion that immediately turns to rage as he recognizes me.

"You motherfu...," he begins, his hands lowering.

I motion with the gun. "Uh-uh. Keep the hands up. I'm probably going to kill you anyway for what you did to me, but it's going to happen a lot quicker if you don't do what I tell you."

He puts his hands back up and stares at me, fuming.

There's no doubt in my mind that he has a gun on him, so I tell him to lie down on the floor. He glares at me and doesn't move fast enough so I take a step toward him, elevating the gun slightly as if to strike him with it. That gets him down on his belly and I tell him to keep his hands and feet spread, as far as the small kitchen will allow.

Putting the barrel of the gun against the back of his head, I stand over him and pat down his back with my left hand. Sure enough, I find the Beretta in a holster similar to mine under his shirt on the right side. I remove it and slip it into the holster on my waist. In another life, I was trained that where you find one gun, you should expect another, so I keep searching, patting his waistband underneath him, then following his pant legs down to his ankles. I'm glad I remember my training because I find a .38 revolver in an ankle holster on his left leg. Removing that, I open the cylinder and empty the shells into the sink, all five of them rattling among the dishes and dropping down into the basin.

I toss the .38 onto the counter and tell him to get up, sitting him back into the chair.

"What do you want?" he asks.

I just smile at him and begin to scan around the kitchen.

"Who the hell are you?" he asks, agitated. I ignore him.

In a drawer next to the refrigerator, I find what I'm searching for, a roll of duct tape. Walking over to him, I give him a love tap on the head with the pistol and tell him to put his hands behind his back, intertwining his fingers. He does that, but I notice his muscles tensing, his body rigid.

"Okay, here's the deal," I say to him. "I'm going to set the gun down and I'm going to tape your hands together. I know you think this is going to be a great time for you to attack me. Your plan is probably to shove your chair back into me with your feet and then jump on me. You will die at the slightest movement. I just want you to know that. You move, you die. I'm going to tie you up, then I'm going to ask you a few questions about something that happened earlier, then I'm going to leave. That's it. You comply you live; you fight you die. Fair enough?"

He pauses for a moment and then nods, stiffly. I don't believe him of course, but I also don't have much choice. I need him tied up and I'm alone here. Holding the gun against his head so he can feel it, I grab his hands and squeeze his fingers together with my left hand, locking them behind his back.

"Now, stick your legs straight out in front of you. Hold them in the air and hold them up, as high as you can. If those legs drop, I pick up the gun and put a bullet in your head. If you think you can move faster than me, go for it. I have no problem killing you right here."

He sticks his legs out in front of him, grunting with the effort it takes for his core muscles to hold them there. This is as disabled as I can make him and I audibly smack the floor with the gun and then wait just a moment before sticking it in the waistband at my back. If he does attack me, the gun won't be on the floor where he thinks it is. If he was going to attack, it should have been just after he heard what he thought was me setting the gun down.

I keep the pressure on his fingers, holding his hands together while I pick up the duct tape and use my teeth to start unrolling it. I then lower it to his wrists and wrap it quickly around them, moving the roll over to the legs of the chair to secure his wrists to the chair itself. Using more than enough tape to hold him, I tell him he can lower his legs back down. I then use the tape to tightly tie his legs to those of the chair.

I'm sweating now, more from tension and nerves than from the exertion, but the dangerous part is over. Joey has been curiously silent during this, and I walk around in front of him to focus on his face. He seems calm, staring at me, his face a mixture that's more curiosity than anger.

"What do you want?" he asks.

I ignore him and walk over to his fridge, opening it and peering inside. There's not much there. A half-gallon of milk with an expiration date that I think has already passed, though I'm not sure of today's exact date, a package of lunch meat and another of processed cheese that seem fine. A two-liter bottle of soda that's half gone, some condiments, and half a roasted chicken.

I grab the lunch meat and the cheese and open them, stacking them up and shoving them in my mouth, keeping my eyes on Joey. I'm hungry and he's not going to need these things anyway. I cautiously smell the milk which seems okay, and drink it straight from the container. I then start picking at the chicken while Joey watches me, a bemused smile on his face.

"I really hope you're enjoying yourself," he says to me. "You have no idea who you're messing with."

I swallow a piece of chicken and wash it down with more milk. "Your name is Joseph Panattiere. You're thirty-two years old and your birthday was March 5th. You're a two-bit thug who thinks he's something special but who's really just a classic piece of shit who doesn't deserve to be breathing."

Joey's face wrinkles in confusion which morphs into fury as I spout this off to him. I continue calmly eating the chicken, watching his face as it reddens.

"Let's talk about this morning," I say to him. "Tell me about the guy you shot."

He stares at me, a cold, calculating expression on his face, his eyes widening. He didn't know what this was before, and he now seems worried.

"Are you with Dominic's crew?" he asks.

I shrug, noncommittally and continue to pick at the chicken.

"Why's he sending you here?" he asks, his voice rising in what seems to be fear. "I did what I was supposed to. I followed orders exactly."

I stare at him, picking chicken from my teeth. I obviously have no idea who Dominic is, and I don't want to say the wrong thing to enlighten him to that. The best I can do is hope he keeps talking.

"Look man," he says finally. "I've worked with you guys for years; I've always done what I was supposed to. I don't know what you think I did wrong, man. I did just what Dominic told me to do!"

He's agitated and repeating himself. I stare at him and raise my eyebrows slightly. Joey is sweating, his face shiny. The moving light from the lava lamp reflects off his skin. I wait, my arms crossed, staring. I'm done here and should be wrapping things up, but I can't help my curiosity. I don't care what he did wrong. I don't care who he killed or why, or who Dominic is. It seems like it was part of a Mafia deal or a drug deal, or something along those lines, and I don't need to get involved in anything about that. My whole goal with this mission was just to be a good citizen, and I've done what I needed to do. It's time to get going.

"Please, man, just tell me what Dominic wants. Tell me what I need to do. I'll do it like I always have."

I walk over to the front door and unlock the deadbolts, using my shirt to wipe them clean of my fingerprints. Joey sees me do this and gets the wrong idea.

"Okay, okay, okay man. I just took something from the car, that's all I did. It wasn't a big deal, man, it wasn't like anybody was going to miss it. Don't do this, man. I'm a good guy to know, I can get things done for you."

I walk behind him and bend down. He cringes and begins straining at his bonds.

"Relax," I tell him. I use my shirt to wipe the surface of the duct tape, hopefully removing all my fingerprints. I can't do anything now about the saliva and my DNA on the end of the tape where I used my teeth to get it started, but it's doubtful the police will be going to that length to try to figure out who did this to Joey.

I step back to the sink and peer under it, moving things aside until I find the bottle I want. Clorox bleach. Great for disinfecting things, killing germs, and obliterating DNA. The cops are unlikely to test the duct tape for my DNA, but they're quite certain to test the gun used to kill the guy in the car this morning. And running a DNA test on the murder weapon will return several hits, my own most prominently from my blood on the front sight.

I take Joey's gun from my waistband and hold it over the sink, pouring bleach over the front sights and then over the bottom of the grip. It would be better and safer if I immersed the gun in bleach, but I don't want to destroy evidence that the cops might need to prove Joey was the murderer. His close proximity to the victim this morning all but guarantees there was blowback of blood from the dead guy onto the barrel of the gun. I want to make sure that part doesn't get destroyed.

I finish and dry the gun on a filthy dish towel, taking the opportunity to wipe it clean of any of my fingerprints. I walk back over to Joey and reach down behind him with the gun. He flinches and I again tell him to relax, pressing the gun into his fingers in several places, and then using my shirt to place it on the table next to him.

I scan around the kitchen, making sure I didn't miss anything that I might have touched. Walking over to the fridge, I wipe the handle. I'll take the food wrappers and milk carton with me and dispose of them elsewhere.

"Where's your cell phone?" I ask, turning back to Joey.

His eyes are bulging and sweat is now heavy on his brow. He's been watching me cleaning my presence away, and he's sure I'm getting ready to whack him.

"My jeans," he croaks out.

I walk back to him and feel his pocket for his cell, pulling it from his right jeans pocket.

"What are you going to do?" he asks me.

I ignore him. The cell phone is locked, but that doesn't matter. I hit the call button which brings up the emergency calling feature. I hit that button and the phone automatically dials 911.

"911, what's your emergency?"

I lower my voice, both in tone and volume. "My name is Reggie. My friend killed a man this morning and tried to kill me just now. I've taped him up and taken his gun." I give the operator the location of the murder this morning and then give her Joey's address and his name. He stares at me silently, confused and uncertain about what's happening. The operator tries to ask my last name and I disconnect the call. I wipe the phone of any prints and then set it on the table next to the gun.

I gather the food items and head for the front door. "See ya' later, Joey," I call over my shoulder.

"Wait! What the hell was this all about?" he yells at me. He can't fathom the good citizen concept, apparently. He's sure this has to be more.

I smile and turn my back to him as his phone starts to vibrate. I stop and glance back at it—it's the 911 operator trying to call back. Ignoring it, I start back toward the front door, my task complete. Suddenly I stop. Something isn't right and I'm not sure what it is.

You know that feeling you get when you're missing something, when something just doesn't feel right? I have it now. I missed something and I don't know what. I glance around, rapidly. Was it something I touched, something I left? I can't find it and I know the police are on their way.

I can't find it and I'm scanning around wildly. Joey stares at me like I'm mentally ill, a stare I've seen often enough to recognize. His phone lights up again, buzzing on the table, and my eyes go to it. The 911 operator trying to call back again. I don't care about that but the buzzing of the phone is distracting. I can't figure out what it is that's making me feel that I'm missing something.

The lava lamp draws my attention again and my gaze drifts toward it. The blobs still float around, doing their mesmerizing dance inside the illuminated water. Suddenly I see it. Behind the lava lamp. I realize at this moment that it's been there the entire time, but the surprising and unexpected sight of the lava lamp had drawn my attention, made me miss seeing the object every time I glanced in that direction. I must have caught it the last time as I was on my way out and my subconscious realized it, finally screaming to my conscious brain that there was something important here.

I jump over to the table and shove the lava lamp out of the way. It tips over and falls to the floor with a huge crash but I ignore it. I have no idea if it broke or not and I don't care. My gaze is captured by the object that was behind the lamp.

It's a figurine, a woman holding a child, made of porcelain and intricately painted. The figurine is about five inches tall and the woman is wearing a necklace and bracelet that sparkle with what appear to be real gems.

I can't breathe, my hands are shaking and my vision is narrowing. I know this figurine. I know it well. I turn it over, my palms sweaty, the figurine slipping in them. Taking a deep breath, I focus on the bottom and my heart nearly flips. There on the base is an inscription carved carefully into the porcelain.

H.C. + T.C. = Forever

I close my eyes and try to steady myself but my mind is racing and I feel dizzy. My brain tries to deny the existence of the statuette in this time and place. How could this be here? How is it possible that I find this figurine in this house?

Trying to calm myself, I turn to Joey. "Where did you get this?" I ask, as smoothly and quietly as I can, though my voice still trembles.

"Whatever, man. Fuck off."

I don't say a word; I give him no warning. I step back and then kick him in the stomach. Hard. He doubles over, all the air gone from his lungs, retching noises coming from his mouth. Nothing else comes out and I wait, trying my best to be patient, knowing time is running out. Peering around the kitchen, I spot a knife rack, empty of knives but containing a pair of scissors. I pull the scissors from the rack and walk back over to him. He's still trying to catch his breath, face red, still bent over in the chair. His arm muscles are corded and he's straining against his bonds. Right now I don't care if he breaks free. I want to hit something and I'd welcome a fight at this moment.

"Where did you get this?" I ask again, holding the figurine up.

He can't talk and he shakes his head. I take the scissors and slam them into his thigh as hard as I can, the blades sinking in several inches.

Joey gives a blood-curdling scream and I let go of the handle, stepping back, waiting to see if he breaks free. He doesn't, but begins to cry, tears streaming down his face.

"Jesus Christ, what the fuck, man?!" he screams at me.

I hold up the figurine. "One more time. WHERE DID YOU GET THIS?" I yell at him.

"I took it from the job this morning, man. From the car. I thought it might be worth something and I would sell it. Look what you did to me, man. I'm going to bleed to death! Jesus Christ, you fucking lunatic!"

He wasn't going to bleed to death; there was no danger of that. The scissors didn't go anywhere near an artery, though I wouldn't have cared if they had. This was the white object I saw in his left hand when he got out of the car after killing the guy this morning. The white object I couldn't identify at the time. I could have told him the figurine was worth about a hundred bucks. Without the inscription. I know this because that's what I paid for it. I bought it for my wife when our son was born. She kept it on the dresser in our bedroom for four years and I haven't seen it for two years...since the night they were both murdered.

"What was the name of the man you killed this morning?" I ask. I realize I can hear sirens in the distance. I'm out of time.

85

"Go fuck yourself, man. The cops are almost here." He smirks at me. I reach forward and twist the scissors 90 degrees in his leg. He screams again, long and loud.

The sirens are closer and I scream at him, "HIS NAME, GODDAMMIT! WHAT WAS HIS NAME? WHO ORDERED HIM KILLED? WHY DID HE HAVE THIS FIGURINE?"

Joey just shakes his head, refusing to answer. I want to hurt him, want to kill him actually, but I can't. I'm out of time. I grab the food packages and stuff them in my pockets, then grab the figurine from the table. The sirens suddenly shut off and I know that means the cops are close, probably turning onto the street here, sirens off to allow them to roll in silently the last few blocks.

I step over to Joey and grab the scissors, pulling them out of his leg and dropping them into my jacket, not worried about the blood that's all over the blades. I can't leave them; my fingerprints are on them, and I don't have time to clean them. He screams again when I pull them out of his leg, but then starts laughing at me.

"This is far from over, asshole," he says to me, teeth gritted, mouth snarling. "Run. Run far and run fast because I'm coming for you. I'm coming for you and I'm coming hard, and you'll be dying slowly and painfully when I catch you."

I turn without a word and stroll to the slider door. I hear a car door shut out front and know the police will surround the house if more than one officer has arrived. If there's only one, he'll wait for backup. I use my shirt to open the back door, not watching for the cops, walking straight back to the wall. If they're there, they're there, and it's all over anyway.

Nobody challenges me and I set the figurine on top of the wall, boost myself over, grab the precious statue and run west through the wash.

Chapter 7

I'm back on the street in my old haunts and in my old clothes. I

don't quite fit in, obviously. My appearance isn't right, and though the average person might not notice, my fellow transients certainly will. I'm still clean and that's a problem. My hair and beard are long, wild and scraggly since I removed them from the ties that held them, but they don't have the matted, filthy appearance they had yesterday, the look that would make me fit in.

After I left Joey's house last night, I ran down the wash as fast as I could move, stopping at each street to check for cops before crossing. After three blocks, I left the wash, moved through neighborhoods until I came to a grocery store, walked in one entrance and right back out the other, trying to confuse any police dog that might be tracking me. I strongly doubted they would deploy one, doubted Joseph Panattiere would talk to the cops, would tell them who injured him. He wasn't the type. I didn't want to take any chances though, so I kept moving after the grocery store, constantly working away from Panattiere's house, changing directions at random until I was lost.

I dropped the scissors in a storm drain and the food cartons in someone's garbage can as I walked. If I was caught, the only evidence against me would be a little bit of Joey's blood on my jacket.

After an hour of wandering around, I began working my way back to Panattiere's, taking the long route, arriving more than three hours after I'd left. The police were gone, his house empty and dark. I crossed over to the park where I'd stashed my backpack and was relieved to find it still there. Removing the gun from my waist,

I unloaded it and returned it to the case, then changed clothes, carefully wrapping the figurine in my hipster clothes and placing it into the pack surrounded by my blankets so it wouldn't break.

My homeless clothes were still damp and they chilled me, but I put my jacket over them and started walking. Before sunrise I was back in the downtown area, lying under the I-515 overpass and trying to get some sleep. My mind was racing, though, and sleep came hard despite my exhaustion.

Where did the man in the car get the figurine? Who was he, why did he keep it in his car, how long had he had it, did he get it from someone else, or is he the one who pilfered it from my house?

So many unanswered questions, and so many bad memories of that night two years ago, the night my life ended, or at least I wished it had ended. The night that put me on the run, the prime suspect in the murder of my wife and son, the only suspect the police had, despite my insistence that someone had been in the house, had broken in and knocked me unconscious.

Can you imagine the feeling of being knocked unconscious, then waking up and finding your wife and son brutally murdered, you left alive for some unknown reason? Can you imagine the police arriving and instead of searching for the killer, focusing their attention on you? A never-ending nightmare, that's what that would be, and that's what I've lived for two years now.

I was a cop at the time in the city of Henderson, though I lived in Las Vegas. Las Vegas Metro had identified me as the prime suspect and was about to arrest me, when I was tipped off and I fled. I ran with all the money I could grab and just a few belongings. When they found I was gone, they froze my bank account, revoked my passport, issued an arrest warrant and sent it to all surrounding states.

I could have fled far, could have tried to get to the east coast and blend in, but I was innocent. I wanted to stay, wanted to work the case myself, find the killer, get my revenge and clear my name. More than anything, I wanted the opportunity to grieve, to mourn the unimaginable loss I'd suffered, yet my grief had been denied by the cloud of suspicion that hung over me.

Finding the David Sands ID had been a godsend because I'd been contacted by the cops four months after I moved to the streets. I'd been sitting in an alley, a sign asking for help and a cup in front of me, doing nothing but mourning, thinking of very little but that devastating night. An ambitious cop approached me and asked for ID. He hadn't questioned the discrepancies that should have been obvious between the picture on the ID and my own face. It was close enough and he just wanted to move on, and I realized that the ID was good enough with my homeless camouflage.

Over the last year, I realize now, I've sunk into a depression that's caused me to forget my goal when I stayed…the goal of finding my family's killer and clearing my name. I've reached a level of acceptance with my situation, and I can hardly believe I've allowed myself to forget, to become so complacent.

It ends here. It ends now.

Sleep continues to elude me and so I sit up and pull out the figurine, unwrapping it from my clothing and running my fingers over it, cherishing it. I vow to never again forget, never again allow my despondency to distract me from finding my family's killers.

Who was the man in the car and why did he have this precious artifact from my past life? Who is Dominic and how does he fit into this? Who killed my family and why? Why was I left alive? These questions and many others race through my mind.

My desire to be a good citizen, to help solve the murder of a man I didn't know, led me to a clue about the murder of my family two years prior. The odds of that are mind-blowing, astronomical, yet it had happened and it has given me new life, a new purpose.

I won't squander this one. That's a promise, and you can hold me to it.

91

The Desert Sun Sentinel

Monday, May 2nd 2017

LV Metro Police make arrest in downtown slaying

Las Vegas Metro Police have made an arrest in the Sunday morning slaying of local businessman Jerry Bastain. Metro spokesperson, Sergeant Denise Titofski, announced that Metro Police, acting on an anonymous tip, arrested Joseph Panattiere at his residence at approximately 11:15pm without incident.

"Panattiere was taken into custody and booked on suspicion of first-degree murder," said Titofski. "He was arrested without incident by police acting on a tip from an anonymous caller."

Titofski went on to say that in Panattiere's possession was a pistol that is currently undergoing ballistics testing by the crime lab.

Panattiere will be arraigned in Superior Court on Thursday morning.

Jerry Bastain was found dead in his car yesterday morning after a passerby observed blood on the inside of the window and an unresponsive male in the car. There were no witnesses to his slaying.

Police say the investigation is ongoing.

Part Two

Chapter 1

"Yo, Sandman! Over here, man!"

I recognize Allen Iverson's voice yelling at me and I glance over. I'm shuffling down the street, moving in that slow, rambling gait that marks me as a man who has nowhere to be and nothing to hurry to, but what I see stops me cold.

Iverson is standing next to a police officer, waving his arms at me; the cop is staring at me, an impatient expression on his face.

My heart falters when I see this. Iverson has always avoided the cops and I thought I'd made it abundantly clear to him that I was trying to avoid them as well.

Apparently not.

"Sandman! Come 'ere man!" he yells again, waving his arm in a big pirouette as if he can pull me over by generating enough wind in that direction.

The cop is frowning now and I'm frozen to my spot. Should I run for it? That seems like a bad idea. The cop *shouldn't* chase me—as far as he knows I've done nothing wrong—but cops are like wolves; they see game running away and they tend to give chase, even if they aren't hungry.

If he chases me, he'll probably catch me. He's not one of those donut-eating, never-leave-the-patrol-car types who love to sit on cold cases all day avoiding real police work. He's a bicycle cop, dressed in a yellow Las Vegas Metro Coolmax shirt, shorts and tennis shoes, obviously in good shape. He also has a bicycle—as you'd expect for a bicycle cop—and I can't outrun a cop on a bike, even if I could outrun one on foot.

Help me out here. What do I do?

Knowing I have no choice, with Allen waving his arms like a buffoon and the cop impatiently waiting for me, I turn toward them, crossing Fremont Street and shuffling slowly, dread building as I approach.

"You gotta tell him about Lizzy, Sandman. You gotta tell him," Iverson says when I get close. He's agitated, his features contorted in an expression of mixed worry and fear.

Since I've known him, Iverson has always had an abjectly suspicious view of the police. He feels there are government agents tracking his every move, following him on the street and planning to snatch him if they find him alone. He spends his life in fear of this, hiding from the fictional shadowy agents as he moves through his constantly changing daily routine. He's also always felt that the uniformed cops are simply agents of the secret police officers who are trying to find him, which is why I'm shocked that he's currently talking to one.

The cop focuses on me now and asks, "Do you know this Lizzy he's talking about?"

Allen knows only one Lizzy to my knowledge, a prostitute who works the streets here in downtown Las Vegas. Allen is in love with Lizzy and is sure that the two of them are meant to be together forever. Lizzy and I are good friends as well, but I actually haven't seen her around in the last day or two, a bit unusual now that I think about it. Of course, I've been pretty busy with my own personal things.

Not having seen Lizzy notwithstanding, I now have to address the fact that a police officer is currently asking me questions, something I try to avoid at all costs and something I now have to deal with thanks to Allen.

"I guess so, maybe," I say to the cop, avoiding eye contact with him while trying to appear confused and unworthy of his attention.

"Okay, well this guy says she's missing. Have you seen her around lately?" He asks me, his exasperated tone conveying his annoyance, something I may be able to take advantage of.

"She's gone man. Somebody took her, she's in trouble!" Allen yells, his own voice rising, his arms doing their waving thing.

"Alright, look, settle down buddy, you hear me?" The cop says to Allen, his right hand moving in a casual way to rest on the butt of his gun, his left coming up to chest level, a move I recognize well as a cautionary defensive stance. "I'm sure she's fine."

The cop glances back at me. "Have you seen her lately?" he asks again.

I scrutinize the sidewalk and shrug. I don't recognize this officer but I have no doubt my picture is still active in the law enforcement wanted books, and I don't want to take any chances that he might recognize me.

"Okay," he says, taking a deep breath and letting it out sharply. "Do either of you know her last name. Or her full first name?"

I continue to gawk at the sidewalk, kicking the curb with my torn and beat up tennis shoe, shrugging again.

"Yeah, I know her name, man, it's Elizabe...," Iverson begins.

"Officer!" I say, loudly interrupting Iverson before he can continue. I don't actually know Lizzy's full name but if Allen shouts it out, the cop might write it down and then might decide to begin an actual report. That report would entail taking down information that would include my name. I need to end this before the cop decides to start asking for ID from us. Even though I have my fake driver's license, I always prefer not to have an encounter with the police get that far.

"Officer, can I talk to you a minute, alone?" I ask, fear and dread evident in my voice as I make this move. I don't know if this is a good decision, drawing even more attention to myself. I could have simply mumbled and acted like an imbecile or faked some mental issues. That probably would have been safer than this move, yet I don't want this cop following up in any way, or trying to do any real police work. I know that most cops hate dealing with both the homeless and the mentally ill, so my plan is to give him a reason why he can ethically walk away, his conscience clean. Which I know is what he wants to do anyway.

He tells Iverson to wait there and takes a few steps backward, me following him. We get out of earshot of Allen who's pacing back and forth, talking to himself in a voice that alternates between a mumble and a yell. He glances suspiciously at the large backpack I'm wearing, and I know I need to end this encounter. Quickly.

"Officer, Allen has some issues. Lizzy isn't even a real person, she's a figment of his imagination," I say to him, still avoiding eye contact, trying to keep my face turned away as much as possible.

"Hmm," he says. "Maybe I should take him to the hospital, try to get him some help."

This isn't what I want at all. Why did this guy have to be Mr. All-American cop actually trying to help? Ninety percent of them would have already left or would have ignored Allen to begin with.

"I'll get him to the free clinic," I tell him quickly. "It's time for his meds anyway; he was supposed to be there this morning and I think he missed it."

The cop nods. "Okay, if you think you can get him there safely, then go ahead."

I mumble my thanks and walk back to Iverson, grabbing his arm and turning him away.

"Come with me," I say. "I'll take you to Lizzy."

He goes with me willingly, something I'm grateful for. I don't glance back to see if the cop's still watching us. Looking back would be suspicious, but it takes all my effort not to do it.

"You know where she is, Sandman?" Allen asks.

"Just keep walking, Allen," I lower my voice, conspiratorially. "They're watching right now."

Allen shuts up quickly and his pace slows, his body seeming to shrink as he leans in toward me.

"They are?" He knows "they" are the secret police who are always searching for him.

I nod. "Come on. Just keep walking."

I get us around the corner and out of sight, off Fremont Street and down an alley where there are two large dumpsters. Walking behind the dumpsters, I finally turn to Allen.

"What the hell are you doing, man? You're talking to the cops now?"

"I was worried about Lizzy, Sandman."

"That's fine, Allen, but you can't involve me with the cops. Ever. Do you understand?"

He nods, looking contrite, and I force myself to relax. It's over now, there was no harm, and there's no need to browbeat him. I'm one of Allen's only friends and I don't want to hurt him by getting too angry at him.

"Okay. Tell me what happened with Lizzy."

"She's gone, man. We was s'posed to meet at her place. She said she was gonna cook breakfast for me but she wasn't there."

His voice rises at the end and he's agitated again, waving his arms and regarding me with a crazed look in his eyes.

This actually concerns me a little bit. Lizzy knows how Allen feels about her. She knows he's in love with her and that he has some mental health issues and she would never knowingly hurt him or worry him in this way. If she said she was going to be somewhere to meet him, she'd be there, come hell or high water.

Lizzy has never told me her last name or if Lizzy is even her real name. We don't ask those kinds of things in this community where everyone is either running from something or hiding from something. Or someone. That doesn't mean we don't talk though. In fact, I've had a lot of deep conversations with Lizzy, usually over a bottle of booze one of us scraped up the money to buy or a cigarette she bummed from some tourist by flashing him her tits.

Lizzy first appeared on the streets down here a little more than a year ago. Somewhat naïve and fresh from whatever hell she'd run from, she's aged significantly after twelve months plying her trade. I would guess she was probably in her late teens when she arrived, though she now appears to be in her late twenties. This life doesn't tend to lead to a Glamour cover appearance, even when you avoid the worst of it.

The worst of it, of course, is drugs, and Lizzy has struggled with that demon since she first arrived. I suspect she originally got started on them to block out the memories or possibly to ease herself into the job she'd chosen. Seeing some of the guys that

Lizzy willingly lays with, it's hard to find fault in her chosen method of mental escape.

The most likely explanation for her disappearance is that she went on some sort of drug bender and she's still sleeping it off. She wouldn't be the first person to blow off a commitment while in a narcotic-induced crash. Of course, it is early evening, the sun beginning to dip behind the Plaza Hotel off to the west, and even if she had gone on a bender last night, she should have surfaced by now.

"Okay, try to stay calm, Allen. I'm going to help you. What time were you supposed to meet her?"

"We was s'posed to meet before noon in front of her building. I asked everybody I could find what time it was, all morning long. I wasn't gonna miss my 'pointment, no way, no how. I was there by eleven, waitin' for her." He takes a deep breath and stares at me, pointedly focused and more alert than normal. "I waited for hours, Sandman. She never showed, man. She wouldn't do that to me, man."

"I know, Allen. I know," I say to him, trying to console him while I think. He's right that she wouldn't no-show him on purpose. "Let's go take a peek at her place, whatta ya' say?" I ask him. His mouth turns up in a big grin and he slaps me on the back with one hand while he wipes away a tear with the other.

"I knew I could count on you, Sandman. I knew you wouldn't let me down!"

I smile at him and we head toward Lizzy's apartment, me leading with my slow shuffle, maintaining my bearing, my cover, my societal invisibility shield at all times.

Chapter 2

As a homeless man, I would never judge the home of another.

That would be awfully presumptuous and petty and you would lose whatever respect you might have for me. Oddly enough though, I don't envy Lizzy her home, and in fact, I wouldn't trade places with her.

I suppose I've become accustomed to the freedom of laying my head wherever I like. And of course, the lack of a rent payment has a lot to do with my feeling. I don't know what Lizzy pays to live here, but whatever it is, it's too much.

Her apartment is in the Gold Dust Condominiums, just to the east of the El Cortez Hotel and Casino. I don't see any gold dust laying around but I sure see a lot of other dust as well as dirt, garbage, syringes, rank and rotted clothing, and an old couch that even I wouldn't sit on. The paint on the building has faded to a salmon color from what used to be a deep burgundy, the stucco having been neglected for well over a decade.

A sign out front, placed high off the ground, advertises that condos are available for lease with weekly or monthly lease options.

There's a rusty metal fence that guards the entrance to the courtyard. Where the gate once hung, only a tall, metal arch remains, stretching from one wall to the other, the opening no longer protected from the likes of Allen Iverson and me. I suppose the owners feel the building can't be further despoiled even by the homeless wandering around unfettered.

Allen and I make our way through the open archway and into the courtyard, Allen yacking at me the entire time, explaining over and over again that he's sure Lizzy wouldn't have stood him up. I can't seem to assure him that I believe him. He's near frantic with worry and I pat him on the back, trying to calm him a bit.

The courtyard is anchored by an empty swimming pool, another old couch laying at the bottom of the cracked and faded concrete of the pool. I suppose that's the Gold Dust Condo safety measure, giving a person falling into the empty pool something soft to land on. The sun beats down on the courtyard, continuing its relentless task of fading the paint of every surface it touches.

Surrounding the courtyard are two levels of condos, doors facing the pool area, a staircase on both the right and left sides leading up to the second-floor rooms. A woman holding a child and talking on an honest-to-God cordless phone, the metal antenna sticking up above her head, glares at us as we enter before turning around and going back into her room, slamming the door behind her. A child of about four years sits on a Big Wheel in the shade, staring at us with a vacant expression, eyes peering out from a dirty face, his only attire a pair of almost-white underwear.

Ignoring the boy, as well as a pang of conscience resulting from both his abysmal living conditions and my own guilt over my son's murder at about the same age, I make my way to the staircase and Lizzy's condo on the second floor, Iverson in tow.

"You waited for her outside the fence?" I ask Iverson as we start up the stairs.

"Yeah man, I waited all morning."

"Did you come up and knock on her door, see if she was home waiting for you?"

"Yeah man, she didn't answer." We reach the top of the staircase and turn left toward her apartment, and I glance back to see a concerned look on Allen's face. "Do you think she might be in there? Maybe she's hurt? Oh man, Sandman, what if she's hurt and I could have helped her? She might be dead in there!"

He's freaking out again and I try to calm him. "Relax, Allen. I'm sure she's okay. Let's see if she's home."

Reaching her apartment door, I knock loudly.

I've been to her place twice previously and I know the apartment is a studio--not big enough for Lizzy to be in the apartment and not hear the knocking. Nevertheless, I wait a minute and then knock again, even louder.

"Oh man, oh man, oh man, there's something wrong, man!" Allen exclaims behind me. He's staring at her door as if willing it to open while he paces back and forth along the walkway.

Reaching down, I grab the knob and twist it. It turns in my hand and the door opens.

"Lizzy?" I call out, not wanting to step inside, reluctant to disturb her sanctuary without an invitation and concerned about the unlocked door.

Iverson has no such qualms. His fear for Lizzy's safety overriding societal conventions, he pushes by me and walks through the door, calling her name. I step in behind him, glancing around the small apartment. It's mostly clean, sparsely furnished, orderly, tidy, and conspicuously empty of Lizzy. Or anybody else. Allen takes a quick peek into the open door of the bathroom and comes back shaking his head.

On the nightstand next to Lizzy's bed is an older alarm clock with big red numerals that show the time as 6:16pm. There's a lamp on the nightstand and a piece of paper folded in quarters. I can see something written on the piece of paper and I step over to it. I'm not sure what I expect to find, but I know I never expected to find what I do. Written in black ink on the folded piece of paper is my name, *David Sands*.

I pick it up, shocked to find my name on it. I glance over at Allen who's watching me expectantly.

"What is it?"

I shrug and unfold the paper with a mixture of curiosity, confusion and fear. The words are written with a pen, in block letters, the handwriting poor but readable.

David,

I took Lizzy to my house. She's not feeling well. She really needs to see you as soon as possible. Hope you come by soon.

Joey P.

My fingers have gone numb and the letter nearly falls from them. I recognize that I'm in shock, my heart thumping, blood pooling in my core as adrenaline courses through my body.

"Sandman?" Allen asks, regarding me with a frown.

I don't answer him. I'm speechless and my head doesn't want to process the meaning of this note. I only know one Joey P. and he should be in jail, awaiting trial for murder. Joseph Panattiere was arrested after I tracked him down, detained him, and called the police, leaving the murder weapon and other evidence for them to find. That was two weeks ago and I haven't had the means nor the inclination to follow his case in the media, my time having been spent following other, more important paths. I never thought I would see that name again and I can't put together how Lizzy could possibly have a connection to him. Or how he could even be out of jail to leave the note.

Not only that, I can't figure out how he could have tracked me down. He didn't know who I was, he'd never seen me prior to the night I captured him, and I was careful to leave no evidence: no fingerprints, no DNA, nothing he could have used to track me down. As I fled, he threatened that he would find me. He also threatened that I would die slow and hard when he did. It seems he's followed through with his first threat.

My head is spinning and I hear Allen asking me what the letter says, but I still can't answer. When I'd cleaned up at Joey's house that night two weeks ago, I'd been thinking of the police, trying not to leave anything that they could have used to find who had left Joseph Panattiere for them to arrest. I can't think of anything I did wrong, yet somehow Panattiere found out who I am and where to find me. It's unfathomable and yet the evidence is right in my hand.

I finally manage to pull myself together and glance at Allen.

"I'll explain what's happening, but we need to leave. Right now."

I stuff the paper in my pocket and head for the door. Allen is protesting but I ignore him, pushing him out the door and pulling it shut behind us. I scan around, a feeling of dread causing my paranoia to rise. If Panattiere was able to leave this letter in Lizzy's apartment, he could be watching us right now. He could have seen us come in, could be coming after me this very second.

I practically run for the stairs, trying to stay calm but failing badly. Allen is trying to keep up, asking me what's happening, but I ignore him. My backpack is slowing me down, bouncing around on my back and I worry about the straps breaking. It's well suited for my normal slow shuffle, but too old for the drumming it's taking as I pound down the stairs, taking them two at a time.

I race for the exit and turn right heading west toward the El Cortez and then turning left to get back to Fremont Street. There are people on Fremont and right now, people equate to safety for me.

Chapter 3

I turn down an alleyway off Fremont and drop down into a spot behind a dumpster. The dumpster is positioned away from a wall just enough for me to peer through the gap behind it and see down the alley back toward Fremont, concealing me from view but still allowing me to see if anybody enters the street. Allen is out of breath, his hands on his knees, his eyes wild as he stares at me. I haven't had time to explain to him what's happening and I feel badly, but I still can't get my thoughts organized. My brain is racing, confusion and paranoia blending together making it difficult to think.

"Sandman," Allen says between breaths. "Lizzy. Where is she, man? She's hurt isn't she? She's been kidnapped, huh?"

Staring at him, I realize just how perceptive he's been. When Lizzy didn't show up for their breakfast date, Allen knew immediately that something bad had happened to her. He'd overcome an almost paralyzing fear of the police to make contact with an officer to try to get help for her. And now, after my wordless and headlong flight from her apartment, he doesn't understand what's wrong but he knows that it's about her and that she's in trouble.

I pat the ground next to me, motioning Allen to have a seat. Taking a glance toward the mouth of the alleyway and finding it empty, I pull the note from my pocket and read it again. I know that once I read it to Allen, there will be a barrage of questions that I can't answer and I need some time to think.

My first thought is whether or not I know another Joey P., another person besides Panattiere, who could have left that letter. Wracking my brain, I can't think of even another Joe that I know, at least not one that would know me under my pseudonym, David Sands. The note can only be from Joseph Panattiere, and he's supposed to be in jail. Apparently this is no longer true.

Thinking back to that night, I realize that I did give him my first name, David. I hadn't thought there was any need to give him a fake name. Hell, David isn't even my real name, giving a *different* fake one seemed unnecessarily complicated at the time.

How could he track me down with nothing more than a first name? And even if he did, how could that have led him to Lizzy? And if it did somehow lead him to Lizzy, how would he know I would find the note—that Lizzy's abduction would even come to my attention?

Allen is rocking back and forth next to me, mumbling and talking to himself, his words inaudible.

"Allen," I say to him, taking hold of his arm. I feel bad that I've been letting him suffer, his confusion and fear at least the equal of mine. "Allen, take a deep breath. Lizzy is going to be okay. I'm going to find her, okay? You and I together are going to find her, and she's going to be just fine."

He regards me, hope mixed with fear on his face. "For reals, Sandman? You ain't lying to me are you?"

109

"Never, Allen. We're going to find her, I promise you."

I hate giving a promise that I have no idea if I can keep, but I'm going to need Allen's help and I'm going to need him focused as much as possible.

"Do you have any money?" I ask him.

He shrugs. "A buck or two."

I lean forward and shrug out of my backpack, taking another second to glance at the mouth of the alleyway which remains mercifully empty. I dig into the pack, down to the bottom where I find the padded envelope.

This is my emergency stash. When I fled for my life two years ago, the police on their way to my house to arrest me on a warrant for murder, I'd grabbed all the money I had at the house and then left, pulling everything I could from my debit card, plus cash advances on all of my credit cards before tossing the entire wallet in the trash and melting into the homeless lifestyle on the street. That money had amounted to just over $5000 at the time, and I'd been extremely careful with it. I'd needed to use it in the beginning as I'd been an obvious outsider. I bought food and water at night and spent the days hiding in remote spots to the north of town. Once my beard started to grow and my clothes and body had begun to stink, my skin darkening with dirt and exposure to the sun, I'd been able to take more risks, coming out during the day and begging for coins on the street. I'd stopped using the emergency stash, living on what I could beg, eating in soup kitchens and finding food where I could. I'd only dug into the emergency stash twice since those early days, once to help a friend who'd run into trouble and once about six months ago when I'd pursued a lead into the murders of my wife and son...a lead that turned out to be nothing but a false trail and had gone nowhere.

My stash is now down to a little less than $3000, and I reach into the envelope, shielding it from Allen who is watching me curiously. I thumb through the money and pull out two $20 bills. I then close the envelope, stuffing it back down to the bottom of the pack and closing the top.

Handing one of the bills to Allen, I watch as his eyes widen in surprise.

"What's this for, Sandman?"

"Listen closely, Allen. I need you to do exactly what I tell you, okay?"

He nods his head, staring at me intently, the bill held tightly in his hand. I realize just how much he's counting on me at this moment, and I feel the weight of that responsibility. It's been a long time since someone has counted on me, and it feels surprisingly good. I don't want to let him down. Even more importantly, it appears that Lizzy may be in trouble and her trouble might be my fault. She's also likely to be counting on me, and there's even more on the line for her if she has indeed been kidnapped.

"I want you to go get some food first. Some food and some beer. Spend as much of that as you want. Make sure you get plenty to eat and drink." I notice him lick his lips, his mouth watering as a dog's might when food is mentioned. It makes me wonder how long it's been since he's eaten anything at all, let alone had a good meal.

"Once you get the food and the beer, take it to the spot, the cove in front of the antique store, you know where I mean?"

He nods.

"When you get there, if anybody else is there, kick them out. Offer them some of your beer or your food if you need to, but make sure you have the spot to yourself and then keep it. Eat the food, drink some beer, and wait for me."

He nods. "But what about Lizzy, man?"

"I'm going to work on that. I need to do a couple of things first and I have to move fast. I need you to wait for me there. I'm going to need your help later and I'll come get you."

"What if the cops find me?" he asks, his voice lowering to a whisper.

"They're not searching for you right now, Allen. They're looking for someone else. You're safe today."

He nods uncertainly. "Okay."

We get up and walk to the end of the alley. I see him on his way, watching carefully for any signs that somebody might be following him or watching me. There are a number of people walking around, businesses open, storefronts where somebody might be concealed. I'm looking for anything unusual, anyone that seems out of place. Nothing draws my attention and I don't get that sixth sense that somebody's watching me. If you've ever been in a quiet and lonely place and felt that sense, you know what I'm talking about. It can be a disquieting feeling and I've learned it's important to trust it. Oftentimes it's nothing more than your subconscious, trying to tell your conscious mind something that it's missed.

Iverson turns into a small restaurant that I know sells cheap Mexican food to go. It's inexpensive but it's also pretty tasty. The owner sometimes leaves the leftovers out in Styrofoam boxes in the alley behind the restaurant for us homeless to feed on at the end of the night. I'm glad to see Allen using the money to support a restaurant with such a compassionate owner.

I turn left and begin walking slowly, headed west toward Panattiere's house. It's hot and the sun beats down on my shoulders, making me realize I haven't brought any water with me. I consider scouting about for an empty bottle in a trash can and finding a place to fill it, but quickly realize that will take more time than I'm willing to expend at the moment. Taking a deep breath, I make a quick stop at a small mom-and-pop store to buy a bottle, parting with some of my precious funds. The woman behind the counter holds her nose as I pay, not bothering with any social nicety at all. I'm sure I actually do smell bad; after all, it's a hot day and I haven't showered in a couple of weeks.

The homeless are easy to hate, easy to fear. You find it easy to hold us in contempt because you know deep down that you're only a short string of bad decisions or bad luck from becoming one of us. You probably deny it, and in fact the root of the contempt is in the desire to justifiably deny it, but I know it's true. I used to be you before a streak of bad luck drove me to what I am today. I don't find fault with the storekeeper's attitude, though I do begrudge her the outward display of that disdain. I collect my change wordlessly, vowing to avoid giving this store any future business.

I continue my walk, sipping the bottle of water and thinking about my next move. I walk slowly, trying to stay cool on this warm evening. I'm wearing only a t-shirt and pants which I've rolled up above the knees, the remainder of my clothing stuffed into the backpack. The slow pace I've set accomplishes more than keeping me cool, it allows me time to think. I don't want to arrive at Panattiere's until dark, probably two hours away, and I also need some time to figure out what's going on.

I made a promise two weeks ago that I wouldn't squander this opportunity, this new evidence that I found when I was leaving Panattiere's house, and I assure you now, I haven't. I've been busy the last two weeks, running down leads and trying to figure out just how my wife's figurine ended up in Panattiere's possession.

He told me that night that he'd taken it from the car of the man he'd killed, a man I later discovered was named Jerry Bastain. It seemed that the logical place for me to start was by looking into Bastain.

I'd gone to the downtown Las Vegas branch of the Clark County library to begin my research. Still clean from my recent shower, they'd given me hardly a glance as I settled in at a computer station and went to work. I'd discovered several articles about Bastain while searching the online archives of the Desert Sun Sentinel.

The oldest article in the archives was from three years earlier announcing Jerry Bastain had won the "Asian Businessperson of the Year" award. There was a picture of him, smiling and holding up his plaque, Las Vegas' mayor standing to his right and a woman identified as his wife, Jackie, on his left. I hadn't expected him to be Asian with the name Jerry Bastain. His wife, I noticed, was not Asian, a white woman, blonde, slender and pretty. She appeared to be in her early forties, about the same age as Jerry. I studied his picture, wishing desperately for some way to ask him how the figurine had come to be in his possession.

On the surface, Bastain seemed to be an upstanding citizen. The article reported that he owned a chain of successful coffee shops, an anomaly today with the near stranglehold that Starbucks has on the industry.

Bastain donated to numerous charity organizations in the Asian community. He sponsored Asian-owned small business startups with interest-free loans and gave full-ride scholarships to a few students each year. Asian students of course. He was a leader of the community and well regarded, even outside of the Asian bubble of influence with which he seemed to surround himself.

The article gave some information about his earlier life. He had immigrated to the United States from China in the mid-eighties as a teenager, taking an Anglo name in an attempt to circumvent anti-Asian sentiment that he claimed was rampant at the time. I didn't recall any such wanton prejudice in the eighties but perhaps as a white man, I'm not a good judge of such things.

There was nothing in the article that gave any indication of what would have led to his murder by Joseph Panattiere three years later.

I'd spent the next few days visiting each of the six coffee shops he owned scattered around the Vegas area. I'd been able to take The Deuce, the big double-decker buses that pass for mass transport here, to stops adjacent to each of the coffee houses. These rides cost me a few precious dollars each, but I felt they were a necessary expenditure.

The coffee shop chain was called *Shanghai Espresso* and as I went to each store, sitting outside and watching the clientele, I began to see why they were so successful. Each shop was frequented almost exclusively by Asians. They filled the shops all day long, eating the pre-packaged Asian food in the display cases, sitting under the umbrellas at the front of the store, sipping Asian teas and coffees. Business was booming and it became clear that Jerry Bastain had created a niche market, one that catered exclusively to the Asian population who came out in droves to support his businesses.

I didn't know if it was just a simple matter of his products being of high quality, a brilliant marketing campaign, or some other more nefarious scheme, but it was clear that his had been a thriving business.

So why was he driving a beat-up Oldsmobile Cutlass on the morning of his murder?

I'd been able to locate Bastain's home address through a simple property search with the county Assessor's website, and I took the bus out there one evening about a week ago. Bastain had lived in a country estate in a gated community, and I waited until an hour after dark before climbing over the wall and finding his house.

He owned a palatial home near the foothills of Red Rock Canyon with an unobstructed, beautiful view of the Las Vegas Strip. The house had felt empty, and I imagined his family had left the home to deal with their grief somewhere else. I'd snuck into the backyard and taken off my shoes, rolling up my pant legs and letting my feet soak in his expansive swimming pool while I enjoyed the view of The Strip and thought about his death, trying to make sense of the figurine I'd found at Panattiere's house, the one he claimed he'd taken from Bastain's car after he killed him.

None of it made sense, and my quiet reflection in the darkness of Bastain's backyard yielded nothing to enlighten me.

Before I left Bastain's house that night, I'd taken the opportunity to peer in the windows of his garage. Inside was a Tesla Model S, plugged into a wall-mounted supercharger. This was a $100,000 plus car. Jerry Bastain might have been the only person in history who had ever left a Tesla in the garage to go meet his appointment with death in an Olds Cutlass.

Stepping out to the street, I'd peered around at the neighboring houses, quiet and still this late at night. I couldn't see Bastain, an award-winning pillar of the community, driving a junker Cutlass into this neighborhood and parking it at his house. It didn't fit.

Perhaps the car might not have belonged to him. So why was he driving it that morning?

The other name Panattiere had mentioned that night a few weeks ago had been Dominic. He'd thought I worked for Dominic and that I'd been sent to his house because of something he'd screwed up. He'd actually implied that Dominic had been the one who ordered Bastain's death.

After I left Bastain's place, I'd spent the next couple of days trying to track down Dominic. With nothing more than a first name to go on, I'd been unable to find anything. I wish I could have accessed the police database. The police keep records of all known associates of criminals, particularly with regard to organized crime or gangs. With that information I could have pulled up Panattiere and likely found out who he associated with. Even if there was no Dominic listed, I could have cross-referenced other criminals to figure it out. I also could have reached out to the LVMPD Gang and Organized Crime Units for help. Unfortunately, those resources were not available to me and I couldn't contact my former partner for help there either. With Panattiere's recent arrest after my earlier questions, had I asked him about associates, he would have realized I was likely in Las Vegas.

I was sure the murder of my wife and son had something to do with my previous job. As a police officer, I had made numerous enemies over a career spanning more than ten years. I'd sent many felons away to prison for sentences ranging from a few years to life. There had been no doubt in my mind that the killer was someone exacting revenge on me for an arrest I'd made.

One of the other things I'd spent some time doing these last couple of weeks was figuring out if I had ever had any contact with Bastain or with anybody named Dominic in my law enforcement capacity. Panattiere clearly had links to organized crime and I tried to remember if I'd wronged any mob figures. There was no connection I could think of, but it had to be there somewhere. My wife had been a geologist and I had been a cop. It was obvious to me that her murder had something to do with my job and not with hers.

The problem was, the figurine had been in Bastain's possession before Panattiere had taken it. I couldn't tie Bastain to anything illegal at all, much less to any arrest I'd made in my career. He'd been the Asian Businessperson of the Year for crying out loud, not a criminal who felt wronged by me. So how had he come to be in possession of my murdered wife's figurine?

I'd been sort of stuck and trying to figure out what else I could do when Allen had called me over to talk to the cop today. Now my priorities have shifted to Lizzy. Somehow my actions have put her in grave danger and it's on me to get her out of it.

The problem right now though, is that I don't know what I'm going to do.

All I can do for now is go to Panattiere's house and see what's there. The only thing I have going for me at the moment is that I don't appear much like the person Panattiere saw just two weeks ago. I was in my hipster disguise then, and that look is long gone. It doesn't take too many days of sweating in the mid-May Vegas heat to get grimy, and I'd had two weeks of it. Vegas is full of dust from the surrounding desert, and that dust sticks to sweat, caking onto the skin and making one seem darker than usual. My hair, which had been cleaned and tied up neatly when he last saw me, is now dirty and matted, stringy and hanging wildly on my head. My beard is grungy as well.

So, it's possible that Panattiere might see me and not recognize me, although I was still holding out hope he might not see me at all, thus the reason behind my plan to arrive at his house after dark.

Chapter 4

I'm sitting in the park across from Panattiere's house. If you'd told me two weeks ago that I'd be back here tonight, I definitely would not have believed you.

The house is dark and the driveway is empty. It's somewhere around 9 o'clock and I've been sitting in the park half an hour. Luckily there was nobody here when I arrived, and only one person has come by since I've been here. That guy was walking a little dog that smelled me and began barking and growling, threatening to out me from my place of concealment behind some bushes. I was worried about that and had prepared to jump the wall behind me and hightail it through the neighborhood, but the guy had been distracted by something on his phone. He jerked the dog's leash impatiently and dragged it off down the street, the dog glancing back and growling until it was out of sight.

Panattiere's house is located in a subdivision that has just two entrances from the main road, one on each side of the

120

neighborhood. Either entrance could be used to access his house by car, with the north entrance being by far the closest. Not wanting to be predictable, particularly since whoever left that note must be planning for me to show up at some point, I didn't come into the sub through either entrance. Instead I jumped over the wall on the east side of the neighborhood, skirting quickly between two houses and approaching the park from the back side, hopping the stone wall that borders the back of the park, a completely different direction than anybody who might be waiting for me should be expecting.

This was a trap, obviously. It had to be. I'd fled from Lizzy's apartment earlier in fear that her place was the trap, but in retrospect, I realized it couldn't have been. Whoever kidnapped her couldn't be sure who would come looking for her, who would find the note. They had to hope that whoever found it delivered it to me. The note had been intentionally vague, designed to make whoever found it think that Lizzy was just sick and being taken care of somewhere. Only I would know the actual meaning and only I would understand who Joey P. was and where his house was. That meant this place had to be the trap...Joey's trap to find me and exact his revenge.

I'm settled in behind the shrubs, watching Panattiere's house through some gaps in the leaves, watching for any sign of activity. The neighborhood has begun to quiet down and I can hear the humming from one of the sodium vapor lights nearby. The street light directly overhead that I'd noticed was out on my previous trip is still out, conveniently casting my hiding place in deep shadow. A cricket sounds off somewhere in the park behind me and I hear a dog start barking a few houses off to my left. A man yells something at the dog and it stops barking, quiet settling again over the neighborhood. I shift and catch a whiff of my own body odor, the smell no longer bothering me after two years having it for my almost constant companion.

Is Lizzy inside? Is she even still alive? He doesn't have any reason to kill her. She's bait to him, nothing more, designed to draw me in, and any fisherman will tell you that live bait is better than dead. At least I hope that's the way Panattiere will look at it. I know he's a killer but I hope he doesn't kill unless he has to.

I still can't understand how he can be out of jail. Bail for a murder charge doesn't usually happen and when it does, it's always a prominent citizen with no criminal record and no risk of flight. Panattiere is anything but a good citizen and he's a known criminal.

A couple walks by, hand in hand, talking softly to each other, expressions of happiness and contentment on their faces. Pangs of envy hit me but I try to quell them. I don't have the luxury to feel sorry for myself and my situation. Besides, I've spent enough time over the last two years wallowing in self-pity.

I wonder if this could be somebody else, not Joey Panattiere. It's obviously somebody who knows him, somebody who knows that I would understand where to go, where he lives. I remember Joey's friend Reggie who was at his house that night two weeks ago. Could Reggie be exacting revenge on Joey's behalf? Could it be somebody else, somebody I haven't met yet?

The wind shifts slightly and I can hear the soft idle of a car somewhere off to my right. The couple on their walk has left my sight and the evening seems calm yet again, the breeze dying down.

Five minutes later, I've still seen nothing from Panattiere's house and the breeze shifts again, bringing the soft noise of the idling car back to my ears. I frown. Why would someone let their car idle for so long?

When you get in your car and start it, how long do you let it idle? Five minutes or more? I doubt it. The only reason you'd leave your car idling would be if you were sitting in it, and on a hot night like this, you'd want to run the air conditioning. It's got to be close to 85 degrees out here right now, and even if the windows were down, sitting in a car would get hot and stuffy. If I was tasked to watch this house and wait for someone to show up, I wouldn't sit in my car. Actually, I would sit right where I am now, but the average person isn't quite as comfortable huddling in the dirt as I am.

Is this the trap?

If I were Joseph, or whoever it is that's waiting for me, I think I would just wait in the house. Why have someone sitting in a car watching? If I'm coming, I have to make the first move, all they have to do is sit in the house and wait.

There's still no movement at the house and so I have only a few options. I can wait here all night and sneak out before dawn if nothing happens. I can try to make an approach to the house, peek in the windows, see if anybody is there. Or I can check out the idling car.

I would be pretty dumb to approach the house without checking out the idling car first, so my options are limited to waiting and watching or checking out the car. My curiosity, as well as my nearly forgotten good tradecraft, isn't going to let me ignore the idling car which means I've narrowed it down to just the one option. Besides, I don't need to approach the house at all. My opponents probably think I'm without resources, and they're mostly correct. But not completely. I do have one ace up my sleeve, and it's about to come into play.

I scan around carefully for any sign of activity and, not seeing anything, I slink cautiously out of my hiding spot in the shrubs, leaving my backpack behind. It should be safe where it is and I don't want to be hampered by it as I move down toward the street.

Hugging the wall and staying in its shadow, I shuffle as far as I can toward the street, stopping behind the trunk of a pine tree and listening. The car engine noise was coming from my right, but I can no longer hear it. I peek around the corner of the wall, my head between the wall and the trunk of the tree. I would feel somewhat foolish with my head sticking out this way if the stakes weren't so high.

The street is empty of cars. I now see that there are *No Parking* signs scattered along the edge of the road, some kind of neighborhood covenant I suppose. I can see a few cars but all are parked in the driveways of the houses. I would have heard the car had it left, so whichever car was idling is still here, but which one is it?

I watch for a while, searching for movement, any sign of life from inside any of the cars. Everything is still. If somebody is sitting in one of the cars, they're not moving. I consider waiting for them to start the car again. My guess is whoever is watching starts the car every once in a while, to run the air conditioning for a bit, then shuts it off to maintain some element of stealth.

If I was in the car watching for someone, I would want to be positioned where I could watch both the target house and the logical approach routes to the house. None of the cars I can see parked in driveways meets those criteria.

I frown, puzzled. The noise of the idling car had definitely been coming from the right, in the direction of the northern entrance to the neighborhood. But that would, in reality, be a terrible place to sit and watch the house. If I had entered the neighborhood from that direction, I would walk up behind anybody watching the house, which would mean they would have to split their observation both to the front and to the rear. The optimal place to be sitting would be to the east of Panattiere's house, to my left.

I realize this and glance to my left at the same time. There's a car parked on the street just a block away and I become aware that I've been in the open ever since I snuck up along the wall. Only the trunk of the pine tree and the deep shadows of the wall itself have obscured me from view of anybody sitting in that car. Have I been spotted?

As I watch the car, frozen in place, I hear the sound of an engine turning over and starting. It comes from the car sitting there and it comes from behind me at the same time. I realize that the earlier engine noise I heard had actually come from the east and not from

125

the west as it seemed. The noise had bounced off the wall to my right, making it seem as if it was coming from that direction. The car is a sedan, a newer model, four-door that's dark in color. I can't tell the exact color or the make, and I can't see inside it to tell if there's anybody sitting in it. Nor do I have a prayer of seeing the license plate.

I can't move now. I'm in the open but I don't think I've been seen yet. If I move, I certainly might be. Being seen right now would completely destroy the plan I've put into place…the plan that should be executing any moment.

I turn my head, moving painfully slowly, to focus back to my right. I'm just in time to see a man turn the corner, walking up the sidewalk toward me. He's moving slowly, shuffling in a manner that I'm quite familiar with. If the man in the car is indeed waiting for somebody to approach the house, his attention should be on the man walking up. The car shuts off and I glance back toward it, seeing motion inside the car for the first time as somebody moves around on the driver's side.

This is about to get interesting at the very least.

A light comes on in the car, a glow I recognize as a cell phone. Whoever's in the car is employing terrible stakeout practices by allowing that glow to be seen.

Despite the bad procedure, the man approaching the house doesn't seem to notice the activity in the car fifty feet in front of him. He stops directly in front of Joey's house, studies it for just a moment, and then shuffles up the driveway toward the front door. He stops to peer in the window and I turn to see the man in the car lift the cellphone up to his head, the glow just briefly illuminating him before it goes out as he puts the phone to his ear. He's making a call and that wipes out any doubt that he's part of the plot.

I'm a little concerned about the man who's now peering in the windows of Joey's house, working his way around to the back where he'll peer in every window there before coming back around to knock on the front door. At least those are the instructions I gave him when I paid him the $20, offering him an additional $40 if he performed the job exactly as I said.

I'd found him at the Charleston onramp to I-15 on my way out here to Joey's place. He'd been sitting there with a sign that read, "Homeless and hungry vet, anything helps. God bless!" He'd introduced himself as Nick and when I'd handed him the $20 bill I'd pulled from my envelope earlier, he'd been grateful but suspicious. When I told him how he could earn $40 more, he'd been intrigued, and when I told him he would be helping someone who was in trouble while he did it, he'd been instantly willing. I hoped now that I wasn't going to get him hurt, that somebody in the house wasn't going to jump out and grab him.

Nick is still at the rear of the house, and I turn back to the man in the car just in time to see him pull the phone away from his ear, the glow still illuminating the interior of the car as he plays with it for a second and then puts it back to his head, making another phone call. I want to know who he's calling, but I have no way of finding out.

I wish I'd taken the time to dig my gun out of my backpack before this went down. I'm worried for Nick. I'd hoped whoever was in the house would simply show themselves and tell him to get lost, allowing me the chance to see who they were, how many they were, and to check out any defensive measures they'd taken. I'm using him as a decoy but I hadn't considered the danger I might be putting him in.

Nick comes around the side of the house, moving slowly and staying in the shadows. He works his way to the porch and I hear the sharp sound of knocking as he follows my instructions exactly. I see him step back and wait. There's no motion from the car and nothing from the house either. Nick waits just a moment and then knocks again, louder. Still nothing. I don't understand why nothing at all is happening. This isn't what I expected.

My head is on a swivel, turning back and forth between the car and the house. I'm starting to wonder if perhaps the watcher in the car has realized Nick isn't the target. Maybe he thinks Nick's appearance is random, perhaps he could see him well enough to know it's not me. Could one of the calls he made have been to someone in the house, telling them not to answer the door? If Lizzy's in the house, is she tied up? Can she yell out?

Suddenly, from my right comes the screech of tires—a car, moving fast. I whip my head that way and see headlights round the corner. Behind the headlights, I can see a paint scheme that I recognize well—a Las Vegas Metro Police car.

As it approaches the house, the spotlight on the passenger side comes on and lights up Nick standing on the porch. The car screeches to a halt and both front doors open. Cops jump out, guns drawn and pointed at Nick who has turned around to face them. One of the cops screams at him, "Police, get your hands in the air, now!"

I'm silently begging Nick to comply, not wanting to see him get hurt. Of all the possible scenarios, the cops showing up was not one I'd considered. I'm relieved to see him put his hands up immediately, his face frozen in fear. Another police car comes around the corner from the opposite direction and a second spotlight centers on Nick, another pair of doors opens and another pair of guns line him up in their sights. This is quite a response by the police, certainly more than you'd expect to see if it was a routine prowler call.

One of the cops shouts orders to Nick, demanding he turn around and drop to his knees. He does as they order and the four cops approach him at gunpoint, one of them shoving him to the ground and handcuffing him.

I glance over at the sedan just in time to see its headlights come on, the driver pulling away from the curb. He drives toward the police cars, passing my position and I stand up, attempting to see his face. He's turned away from me, watching the cops arrest Nick and I'm unable to see him. The police officers don't even glance in his direction as he accelerates down the road, heading toward the north entrance to the subdivision.

I need to stop him. It's become quite obvious to me that Lizzy is not in Panattiere's house and the driver of the sedan is my only link to finding her now.

Turning, I run for the back wall of the park, counting on the cops to be distracted enough by their arrest that they won't notice me in the dark. Reaching the wall, I vault over it, landing on the sidewalk on the other side and twisting my ankle. Two years of inactivity does not an Olympian make.

Wincing with the pain in my ankle, I race down the sidewalk for the gap between houses where I know I can hop another wall and end up on Charleston Avenue. I need to get there before the sedan does. I reach the alley between the houses and run for the wall. Planting my hands on the top, I lift myself up and see the sedan nosing out of the subdivision to my left. I need him to turn right on Charleston to come in my direction. I suddenly realize that I have no idea what I'm going to do. I've got some kind of half-baked notion that I'm going to jump out into the street and stop the car, confront the driver. I don't know what I'm doing. I only know that if the man in the sedan gets away, I have no chance of finding Lizzy.

I jump down to the sidewalk, hurting my ankle again but ignore sharp needles of pain. The sedan pulls out and to my dismay, turns left, accelerating as it heads west on Charleston. I start running, a futile attempt to catch the sedan, my panic at losing Lizzy surging up. Even with two good ankles I wouldn't have had a chance. I slowly come to a stop, watching in frustration as the sedan pulls away, taking my only clue to Lizzy's whereabouts with it.

Chapter 5

The sky over the lofty hills to the east of the Las Vegas valley is just beginning to lighten when I finally reach the cove in front of the antiques store. I wasn't sure whether Allen Iverson would still be waiting for me but he is. He's lying across the entrance to the abandoned store, asleep under his ratty blanket, an empty beer bottle sitting against the wall next to him. I try to come in quietly and not wake him, but he opens his eyes as soon as I round the corner.

"Lizzy?" he asks, sitting up and peering at me. His eyes are clear and I suspect he didn't get much sleep during the night.

I shake my head. "Not yet, buddy. I'm working on it though."

I try to convey assurance in my voice, but in truth, I have no idea how I'm going to find her now. My only lead disappeared with the sedan that turned the wrong way.

After I watched the sedan drive away down Charleston, I returned limping to the park, taking my time and letting my ankle recover. By the time I got back there, the police were gone and the neighborhood was quiet again. I watched the house for a while, waiting to see if the sedan would return, but to no avail.

Going to my backpack, I pulled some more cash from my precious supply, shouldered the pack and left the neighborhood, walking down Charleston until I hit Decatur. There's a gas station there where I'd agreed to meet Nick to pay him the money I owed him. Nick was there waiting for me, happy to see I'd lived up to my end of the bargain. He told me he'd been frightened nearly to death when the cops had arrived. After they handcuffed him, they'd asked for his name. Luckily he had a wallet in his pocket and that wallet contained his ID card. They'd asked what he was doing at the house and, as we'd rehearsed (expecting him to have to tell the story for the kidnappers, not the cops), he told them he had heard this was a place where he could score some weed.

I laughed in spite of my anger, fear, and confusion when he told me that. It had seemed like it would be a good story for him to use if the door was answered by a criminal element, especially if he produced the $20 bill I'd already given him. I was surprised he'd stuck with that story when confronted by the cops, but I was glad he had. No cop would expect someone to use that story as a lie and therefore it had worked well. It's a dumb thing to say to a police officer generally but worked perfectly in this situation as they had bigger fish to fry.

Nick also told me that a total of three police cars had been on the scene while he was detained, the third arriving a few minutes after the other two. There had been only two when I ran off, chasing down the observer in the sedan, and the overwhelming police response confirmed that it was a setup. He said the late-arriving officer had told the others that Nick was not the guy they were searching for. They'd then taken off the cuffs, told him to leave the neighborhood and never come back, something with which he was happy to oblige.

If Joey Panattiere or one of his buddies had kidnapped Lizzy in an attempt to draw me in, why would they then call the police when they'd thought they had me? And when they found out they had the wrong guy, wouldn't they have come back and continued the stakeout?

These were questions Nick couldn't help me with, of course, so I handed him the other two twenties I owed him and started back downtown. The Deuce had quit running at midnight and I had to hike the entire way back. Luckily the night had cooled considerably and the walk was pleasant, giving me time to think about Lizzy and what I was going to do next.

Thankfully, Allen has saved some food for me, and I scarf it down with gusto. Despite my worry, I'm exhausted and I ask Allen to wake me in three hours. I spread out my blanket on the cool concrete and lower myself onto it, my jacket over me. Just before I drift off to sleep, it occurs to me to wonder how Allen is going to know when three hours have passed.

Chapter 6

It's the heat penetrating the shaded cove where I'm resting that finally wakes me up. May mornings in Vegas tend to get hot pretty early, though not as scorching as the mornings in the three upcoming months. Being homeless is pretty miserable most of the time, but in Vegas it's even worse during June, July and August.

Allen is sitting next to me, staring at me, and he sees my eyes open.

"I didn't know when to wake you."

"That's okay," I assure him. "Do you have any water?"

He hands me a jug that he's been able to fill somewhere. Like all of us who live on the Vegas streets, he's managed to find a reliable source of water.

I drink my fill, hydrating my body for the day ahead. My muscles are stiff and sore from lying on the hard concrete with only a blanket for padding, but I'm used to waking up this way. I do my normal stretching exercises to get my blood moving.

"What are we going to do? We need to find Lizzy!"

I try to mask my frustration. I know he's worried but I'm doing everything I can with the limited resources I have at my disposal. I consider calling my ex-partner at the Henderson Police Department and getting him involved. That would alert him to the fact that I'm still in the Vegas area, though, and I've already gone over the reasons that would be bad, both for him and for me. That option will have to be a last resort.

"We're going to go back to Lizzy's apartment and look around some more, see if we can find any other clues," I tell him.

I don't share with him my concern about this trip to Lizzy's. I'll share it with you, though. Joey, or whoever was waiting for me at Joey's house last night, whoever was in that sedan and called the police when they saw Nick, my decoy, approach the house, long hair and matted beard, time and place making them think it was me...whoever they were...by now they know that the police arrested someone else that night and that David Sands is still out there. They can't know whether I got the note, they can't know if I set them up with Nick or if he was just a person in the wrong place at the wrong time. All they can know is that they screwed up and they need to try again. Trying again might mean going back to Lizzy's place to see if the note has been removed; if we go back there, that might mean a confrontation.

I still don't know why Joey would want to call the police on me or how he found me in the first place. And unless the person who found my name knows it's not my real name, and what my real name actually is, why would they think the cops would be remotely interested in me?

Could it have been the way I reacted over the figurine I found at Joey's that night? I had freaked out, shoving those scissors into his leg and screaming at him to tell me where he got it. If he'd told somebody about that, and that person knew about the figurine, maybe they'd put two and two together and figured out that only I would react in such a way to this specific figurine. That was a possibility that I'd have to explore. It could mean that Lizzy's kidnappers were the same people, or associates of the same people, who murdered my wife and son.

I like Lizzy and I like Allen and even if there was no relationship between her disappearance and the murder of my family, I would still want to get involved and do whatever I could to help. With the possible connection, though, I'm even more anxious to put the pieces of the puzzle together.

So, even though going to Lizzy's place *might* mean an encounter with the kidnappers on their terms, I know that going to Joey's place *definitely* means a confrontation on their terms. That confrontation may be coming up either way, but I need to start with the most remote of the two options.

Allen and I pack up our gear and step out into the hot sun. I glance up and estimate the time as somewhere between 11 o'clock and noon. We're getting a late start but at least I'm well rested. This might be a long day.

It's only three blocks to Lizzy's apartment, but we take our time getting there. I'm sort of ashamed to admit it, but I play on Allen's paranoia, telling him that I think there are secret agents of the government looking for us and we need to make sure we aren't being followed. This may not be far from the truth though; I know somebody is searching for me at least, and I need his watchful eyes to help me look for them.

It takes us about thirty minutes to cover the three blocks and we don't see anybody that doesn't seem to belong. I've been walking these streets every day for the last two years, and Allen longer than that, so between the two of us we should notice anybody out of place.

We're standing together now in a doorway of yet another abandoned business across from the Gold Dust Condominiums. This was once a small corner grocery that probably did good business at one time from the residents of the Gold Dust and the other foot traffic in the area, before the slumping economy came knocking on the doors of downtown Las Vegas two decades ago. Interestingly, this area is finally beginning to make a comeback, mostly due to a large influx of money from Tony Hsieh, the CEO of Zappos. Even before I came to live on these streets, Hsieh had been investing heavily in this downtown area, spending hundreds of millions of dollars for renovations. Those dollars have been spent mostly in the few blocks just to the east of the Fremont casinos. This area, just north and east of there, remains a haven for the people of the street, the homeless, the addicts, the criminal element. People like me.

I think it won't be long before wealth begins to work its way this direction though, and I wonder what will happen to the people who live in this area when it does. There was a time in my life when I held great disdain for the people who now surround me, for the choices they made in their lives that got them to a point of despair. I'd always felt that everybody has choices and these people made terrible ones and deserved the conditions under which they're living. My perspective has shifted now that I call some of them my friends and now that I've walked the storied mile in their shoes. Many of them are here because of bad luck. Many are running from something, the circumstances of which were beyond their control. And many of them, an astonishingly high percentage actually, have moderate to severe mental health issues, like my friend Allen here.

Those people, the ones with the mental health problems are the most tragic of all. The ones who got here through drug abuse or because they're just bad people who made a series of bad decisions are one thing. Those who got here because they were unable to get help for something completely out of their control are another thing. If I ever do get out of the situation I'm in, I suspect I'll be spending a lot of time trying to help people like Allen.

Anyway, we're standing together in the doorway peering into the courtyard of the Gold Dust Condominiums, and I don't see anybody out of the ordinary. The tanned, dirty, skinny kid with the mop of blond hair wearing only underwear is back again today riding around on his Big Wheel, ripping between the poles that support the second-floor walkway. He comes perilously close to the edge of the empty swimming pool on a couple of occasions, which causes me to wince each time.

A girl who appears to be about the same age as the boy is watching him race around, a doll clutched tightly in one hand, the other placed on her hip in a manner that conveys disgust and impatience toward the boy and his antics. That pang of nostalgia, sorrow and loss hits me again and I turn away from the children.

"Everything look normal to you?" I ask Allen.

He nods. "I don't see any agents right now," he tells me, his voice a conspiratorial whisper.

"Okay, let's go."

I start across the street, still scanning the area, still anxious, waiting for a trap to spring shut on us. No voice shouts out, there's no screech of tires from an oncoming car, and nobody runs toward us. We make it to the rusted, metal arch over the missing gate and cross under it and into the courtyard of the Gold Dust. The girl turns to inspect us, the hand that's not clutching the doll going up to her mouth, her thumb slipping inside. The boy ignores us and continues to race around on the Big Wheel. All the doors are closed and there are no adults in sight.

Allen and I move quickly now, climbing the stairs and turning to the left toward Lizzy's door. I try the doorknob which is still unlocked and open the door cautiously, pushing it open while we remain standing outside. It swings to its stop revealing the interior of the small apartment.

Everything appears the same as it was when we left it yesterday. I walk quickly inside and check the bathroom, then walk back and motion Allen inside, closing the door behind him and locking the deadbolt.

If anybody was waiting for us, watching for me to arrive back here, they were well hidden and I didn't see them. If that is the case, then I guess the police will be showing up soon, but there's nothing I can do about that now. I'll have to hope and trust that we were vigilant enough to have seen anybody if they'd been there to see.

"What do we do now?" Allen asks.

"Let's look around some more. Be thorough. If you see anything at all that seems like it doesn't belong, anything the bad guys might have dropped, let me know."

Somebody left the note for me yesterday, so somebody was in this room. I would have loved to have the support of a competent forensics team to help me scout for trace evidence that might identify the suspect, but alas, my ability to call for that kind of help is long ended.

Nonetheless, I hope we're able to find some clue, something that will lead us to Lizzy's kidnappers, because I don't know where else to begin to look.

It doesn't take us long to search the small apartment. We find absolutely nothing that looks as if it doesn't belong.

I sit down on the edge of Lizzy's bed to think while Allen paces back and forth in the room.

"What now, Sandman?" he asks, impatiently.

"Hang on, Allen, let me think a minute."

If Lizzy had been kidnapped from the apartment here, there should be some kind of a sign of that. She would have fought, things would be disturbed, chairs knocked over, something. Even if the kidnappers picked things up, there should be some sign of a disturbance and there's nothing at all.

"Allen, we've never talked about this and I don't want to be insensitive to your feelings at all, but I have to ask you this. You know what Lizzy does for a living, right?"

He gets a distasteful expression on his face but nods his head.

"Okay, so I need to know, did she bring clients back here to her room, or did she take them somewhere else?"

"I don't know where she took them," he replies. "Not back here though. This was her place, man, her castle. She didn't never take nobody back here for that stuff."

"Does she have anybody who took care of her? You know, anybody who looks out for her while she's working?"

"You mean like a pimp?" he asks.

I nod. "Yeah. I mean like a pimp."

He's shaking his head. "Nah, man. She doesn't have nothin' like that, man. She just walks around downtown, you know? She just walks around and then does what she has to when dudes find her."

He sits down in the one chair in the room and puts his face in his hands. "We're never gonna find her are we, Sandman?" His voice is soft, filled with dread.

"Look at me, Allen," I tell him, waiting until he lifts his head from his hands and glances in my direction. "We're going to find her. I'll find a way."

He nods his head but his expression says he doesn't believe me. I suspect he's learned that people often don't tell the truth and tend to make promises lightly. And the reality is that I'm one of those people right in this moment since I have no idea how I'm going to find Lizzy.

Chapter 7

I'm in the shower at Lizzy's apartment, letting the warm water wash over my filthy body while Allen keeps watch at the window. I feel a little bad about using Lizzy's shower without permission, but I have the first inkling of a plan and I need to be somewhat presentable to implement it.

Before I got in the shower, I had pulled my laptop out of my backpack and fired it up, searching for an internet signal I could connect to. Allen gazed at me with wonder and shock, no doubt as surprised to see me pull a laptop out of the backpack as he would have been to see me pull a baby out of there. I didn't bother giving him an explanation, preferring to let him wonder than to give him a partial truth that might have to be expanded on later. I have a lot to hide, obviously, and he's the first person to ever see this sliver of my real life.

There was no internet signal that wasn't secured with a passcode, which means I need to go find one, which means taking my laptop in public, which means unless I want a bunch of other curious people ogling me the way Allen did when he saw the laptop, I need to change my appearance.

Thus, the shower.

I dress in my hipster clothes but skip the sandals, opting instead for my old tennis shoes. I don't want the granola look today, I just want a clean appearance, and my standard street clothes are too dirty and smell too bad for the image I need.

I leave my hair and beard looking scraggly and uneven, skipping the hair ties for the same reason I'm skipping the sandals.

Coming out of the bathroom, I see Allen still standing by the window, keeping watch as I'd asked him to do. He follows instructions well and I'm glad to have him helping me. I've been on my own for a long time and it feels good to have a partner again.

I fold up the clothes I've been wearing and place them in my backpack, putting the laptop in last, on top of everything else. The figurine that's so precious to me goes in its designated spot in the middle of my blankets, as protected as I can make it against accidental breakage.

"Let's go," I say to Allen, throwing the backpack over my shoulders and heading for the door.

We make our way back out to the street and turn right, headed for an area of East Fremont Street known as the Container Park. This is another project of Tony Hsieh and his fortune, basically a playground for both kids and adults made from old shipping containers. Full of bars, restaurants, shops and a metal treehouse and playground for the kids to enjoy, the Container Park covers one full city block. They usually search bags at the entrance to the park, and they wouldn't let Allen in even if we didn't have bags, but we don't need to actually go in. There's free Wi-Fi throughout the park, and benches along the sidewalk where I can sit on the edge of the fenced area, and that's what I'm searching for.

I position Allen across the street from the park, telling him to keep an eye out for anything unusual or suspicious. This is a bit borderline on my part as his paranoia causes him to consider a lot of things suspicious. Nevertheless, I need him to keep an eye out while I research things online. He pulls a sign out of his bag that says, *Homeless vet, anything helps,* and sits down on the sidewalk, his hat next to him, upside down.

Crossing the street, I sit on an empty bench in the shade of a large elm tree. I power up the laptop and connect to the Container Park Wi-Fi. The signal is good and I go immediately to the Clark County Jail website to do an inmate search. It takes only a second to get to the public inmate search page and I enter Panattiere's name in the box. Almost immediately, the record appears. The Inmate-In-Custody Status page comes up and I scan it to see that *Panattiere, Joseph* is currently in custody on a charge of MURDER, 1ST DEGREE with a bail amount of zero. This doesn't mean he can get out without posting bail, but rather that there is no bail available for him.

I gaze up from the computer screen, thinking. Panattiere is still in custody, and that means that he couldn't have left the note for me at Lizzy's apartment. Whoever left it for me knows I'm the one who captured Panattiere and called the police that night two weeks ago.

The only other person who saw me that night, as far as I know, was Panattiere's friend Reggie. Reggie didn't strike me as someone capable of pulling off a plan of this magnitude though. A plan to trap me by kidnapping someone I knew and luring me to Panattiere's house was complicated and tough to conceive and execute. Reggie seemed like more of a dim bulb who would prefer to roam the streets with a gun hoping to run into me.

The nature of the trap didn't fit with Reggie's type either. He wasn't the kind to lure me back to Panattiere's and then call the police to arrest me. He was the type who would take care of the

144

problem himself, never even considering calling the police to be a viable option. The same logic applies to any associates of Joseph's and Reggie's. They are just not likely to involve the police in their affairs in that way.

There is one other big question here, the main question actually, and that is, what's the connection (if there is one) between Joseph Panattiere and his gang, Jerry Bastain who he murdered, and the murder of my family two years prior? If someone kidnapped Lizzy to trap me and then called the police to arrest me when they thought I'd fallen into the trap, does that mean they know who I actually am? Do they want me arrested because they are the actual killers, or is there some other reason why my arrest would be desirable for them?

So many questions and no good answers. And none of this is getting me any closer to finding Lizzy, a sweet and kind girl, in danger now because of me.

I want to do an inmate search for Lizzy, just to cover all the bases and make sure she hasn't been arrested, but I don't know her last name. I consider running over and asking Allen, but it seems likely to be a waste of time. What else can I do here?

I pull up a Google search page and type in *Joseph Panattiere, Reggie* hoping to find some information about who Reggie is. It links me to an article from the Desert Sun Sentinel, and I click on it. Scanning the article, I see it's from ten months earlier and is about a jury tampering charge. Panattiere was on trial for extortion at the time and the jury was deliberating. The article says that Panattiere's associate, Reginald "Reggie" Sporado, had been arrested for jury tampering in that case. According to the article, he allegedly threatened the family of one of the jurors, causing a hung jury and a mistrial. The overall arc of the article is on how the mob is still an active part of the Las Vegas community. It goes on to mention several other arrests that had been made by the Las Vegas Metro Police's Organized Crime division in the previous year.

Armed now with Reggie's last name, I type it first into the Clark County Inmate search page. The only hits that come back are old ones, including the arrest for jury tampering mentioned in the article. I then type his name into the Google search page. It returns a bunch of hits and I scan them all. Most are links to the Desert Sun Sentinel article, and others are links to previous arrests. There's one link to a Facebook page and I click on that. It shows a picture of him but the account is private and I'm unable to view anything else on the page. It all seems to be a dead end.

Just out of curiosity, I do a Google search for my own name. Not David Sands, obviously, but my real name. There are lots of hits involving the murder of my family two years ago and I ignore those, not having any desire to relive that pain. I'd read them all in those first days and weeks after that horrible night. Almost all of them had made vague suggestions of my guilt, and the public comments were the worst. Everybody was sure of my guilt and, safe from fears of libel that bind the newspapers, they laid into me. That had been incredibly painful to read.

I do an advanced search for anything posted in the last month and I get several hits. Most of them are links to a newspaper article from the two-year anniversary of the slayings, and I avoid the temptation to click on those, knowing they'll be filled with details of the killings and I don't need to relive that. There is one link that mentions my house and I do click on that.

I read that article with dread. My house has been foreclosed on and there's going to be an auction for it this Friday, three days from now. The article mentions the case against me, of course, and that I disappeared two years ago and haven't been heard from since despite a massive manhunt that's still ongoing.

The thought of losing my house--the finality of it and the realization that some other family will soon be living there--leaves me in considerable pain. My wife and I bought that house five years before her murder, and we thought we'd raise our family there, that we would live there forever. We'd chosen it because of its proximity to great schools in easy walking distance. This foreclosure is the official end of everything that my life once was. It devastates me and leaves me shaking with fury and impotence.

I think about the piece of vacation property that we'd purchased a few years before we bought the house. The property is in the Sierra Nevada Mountains near Lake Tahoe, and we paid cash for it, using some money my wife inherited after her mother died the year before. That property, at least, nobody can take from me, nobody can foreclose on. I need to make sure I find a way to make the property tax payments on it at some point, but it's safe for now.

What about all of our belongings in the house? Family portraits, personal stuff? What will happen to all of that when the house goes to auction? Will the new owners just come in and throw everything away? The thought of that makes me feel physically ill and I want to throw up. It's Tuesday which means I have three days to figure that out before the house goes up on the block.

I shake myself out of my fugue and glance at Allen across the street. He's staring at me impatiently and I quickly shut down the computer. I haven't figured out anything useful other than confirming that it couldn't have been Panattiere who'd left that note for me. Stuffing the laptop into the backpack, I shoulder it and cross the street, leaving the nicely shaded bench I was on. It's hot out here, but not unbearable, the sun just beginning to dip toward the horizon and the shadows from the tall buildings lengthening on the streets.

"Let's go get something to eat," I say to Allen, waiting for him to gather his stuff and follow me.

I lead the way to the Las Vegas Rescue Mission, a walk that takes us about fifteen minutes. I don't often come here, mainly because I hesitate to take advantage of resources that should be used by those who deserve them, a category I don't feel includes myself. Today I need to make sure we get a good meal, though, as well as making sure we get out of the heat of the day for a short time.

The Rescue Mission has hundreds of beds that are first-come, first-served, though again, I rarely claim one of them. You probably think that's some kind of altruism on my part, but I have reasons that are more selfish. They search all bags for weapons for one thing, which doesn't work for me for obvious reasons. The few times I've rented a locker for my backpack and come here to get out of the cold during the winter, I've felt trapped and vulnerable, and that's the main reason I normally avoid the place.

Although the place is staffed by kind, generous, good-hearted people, it makes me nervous to be here. I've developed a fear of being in well-lit places full of people who don't ignore me—who try to help me actually. I suppose it's a result of my two-year desire for anonymity that causes this fear. Part of me wonders if I've joined Allen on the path toward irreversible paranoia when I feel this way.

Allen and I walk inside and I deposit my backpack by the front door. They don't search the bags of those stopping in for a meal, but they do make you leave your bag up front, a small security measure. The people here at the mission seem to appreciate the paranoia that's rampant out here on the streets, and they have a compassionate understanding that we're carrying everything we own, and those worldly possessions, meager as they might be, are important to us. I'll be able to sit at a table and keep an eye on my belongings.

The mission serves both breakfast and dinner and we're there just as the dinner service is beginning. Staffed by volunteers with smiling faces, the food is somewhat bland but nutritious and filling. And free.

Allen and I take our plates to a table near the door and I begin eating, ravenously stuffing the food into my mouth. I glance up to see Allen staring at me, his meal untouched.

"Allen, you need to eat."

"What are we doing about Lizzy, Sandman?"

"Eat and I'll tell you."

He reluctantly begins to eat, picking up a piece of fried chicken and taking a bite.

I scoop up some mashed potatoes and think about what to tell him. I honestly don't know what we're going to do.

"We need to find somebody who saw Lizzy last night, maybe one of her friends who was working with her. Do you know her friends?"

Allen nods, now attacking the food with some gusto. "Sure man. She's got lotsa friends."

"You know any of their names?"

"Yeah," he says, talking around a mouthful of chicken and mashed potatoes. "There's Annie; Lizzy and her are together all the time when they're working. And Star. And Becca, she's always around too."

"These girls are all working girls?" I ask.

"Yup. They all work Fremont."

I nod, chewing thoughtfully. If we can track down these girls tonight, maybe we can get an idea who picked up Lizzy last night, or where and when she was last seen. I still didn't rule out the slim possibility that she was arrested though. A lot of people think prostitution is legal in Las Vegas, but it's not. The cops don't usually do too much about it when they see it; it is legal in most parts of Nevada, just not in Clark County. Even so, they do occasionally crack down on it and make arrests.

"Do you know Lizzy's last name?" I ask Allen.

150

He rips a chunk off a roll and pops it into his mouth. "Bastain," he says.

My fork falls out of my hand. His mouth is full and I think I must have misheard him. "What?"

"Bastain. Her name is Elizabeth Bastain."

My mouth is hanging open and I'm staring at him. He continues to eat, oblivious to my shock. I pick my fork up and stare at my plate. Elizabeth Bastain. Jerry Bastain. Could it be that she's related to the man who had possession of my wife's figurine, the man murdered by Joseph Panattiere? I think about what I know of Lizzy. Jerry Bastain is Chinese but I know his wife is white. I always thought of Lizzy as a white girl, but now that I think about it, she does have a darker complexion. Her eyes also show some signs of a mixed race, the flatter appearance of some Asian influence. She has an exotic appearance to her that makes her beautiful, that men find attractive and appealing. She could be a Chinese-Anglo mix, now that I think about it.

"Do you know who her parents are?" I ask Allen.

He shrugs. "Her old man is some rich dude. She ran away a few years ago. She hates him."

I think Lizzy is probably in her early twenties. It can be tough to tell out here since this lifestyle tends to age a person faster than usual. But if she is that age, it would be possible that she's Jerry's daughter. That thought makes my head spin. Could it be that her kidnapping has nothing to do with me? That Jerry's murder and her disappearance are related to some family matter between them? But then what about the figurine in his glove box? And what about the note left for me in Lizzy's apartment? How do all those things tie together? None of this makes any sense.

I've lost my appetite, but they frown on wasting food here. I've seen enough hunger lately that I don't want to be the one who contributes to the rampant waste of food in this society, so I force myself to finish everything on my plate.

I have a feeling it's going to be a long night, and Allen and I have a lot of work to do.

Chapter 8

Allen and I are standing in front of Neonopolis, a large mall on Fremont Street just to the east of the famous canopy that marks downtown Las Vegas. Music blasts from speakers set overhead, and the buildings are lit up in a kaleidoscope of colors designed to draw the attention of the tourist like a peacock displaying its colored feathers.

The street is alive with pedestrians, most carrying some version of a large plastic cup filled with alcohol. This part of Fremont, east of the canopy, used to be a haven for the homeless, the mall behind us almost an unofficial apartment building for washed out drug abusers. Now, with the influx of new money into the area, businesses have returned, and this area is once again a tourist hot spot, the shops of the mall reborn with new and thriving businesses.

We aren't the only homeless people in the area. scanning around, I can see three others, two of whom I know by name. This area used to be packed with more transients than tourists or locals, but the police have been cracking down, harassing the vagrants and intentionally making the area less attractive for us. They've even been known to make arrests recently, which is why I normally avoid coming around here.

Tonight though, I have no choice. In order to find Lizzy, we need to find her friends and Allen assures me that this is the area they work most nights.

If we do run into any kind of trouble with the police, I can always step away from Allen and join the rest of the tourists. With my clean hair and clothes, I don't look much like a transient anymore.

After we ate at the Rescue Mission, Allen and I returned to Lizzy's apartment where we dropped off our backpacks. Although I hated leaving it behind, I can't be hampered by it tonight. I gave a lot of consideration to taking the gun with me, but eventually decided to leave it behind as well. Any contact with the police might be mitigated by my David Sands ID, but if they catch me with a firearm, it's going to be much more complicated. Not only that, I can always return to the apartment to get the gun if I feel that I'll need it later.

We were able to find a spare key at Lizzy's apartment which allowed us to lock the door behind us as we left. That made me feel better about leaving my worldly belongings behind, though still not completely secure about it. And of course, if Lizzy happens to return, she's going to wonder why two bags have suddenly appeared as if we've moved in.

Allen nudges me. "That's Star right there, man," he says, pointing to a young black woman wearing shiny gold short shorts and a pink halter top. She's showing a lot of skin and wearing a lot of makeup, along with heels that seem impossible to walk in. Even a fresh-faced mid-west kid straight off the cornhusker bus would have known she was a pro.

"Let's go talk to her," I say.

We cross the street to where Star is standing, leaning against the side of a souvenir store with her arms crossed, catcalling to passersby.

"Hey, Star," Allen calls to her as we approach. I'm walking slightly behind him, staying back just a bit so that she sees him first.

"Hey, Allen! How you doin' baby?" Star asks, a big smile on her face.

"Not good, Star. I'm trying to find Lizzy, you seen her?"

"Not tonight, baby. Not since last night."

I step up beside Allen and Star turns to me.

"Who's this?"

"This is my friend, Sandman. He's tryin' to help me find Lizzy, Star. I'm real worried 'bout her."

"What you say your name was?" Star asks me, staring at me with a frown on her face.

"I didn't, but it's David Sands."

"Uh huh. You the one they was lookin' for," she says, an expression of trepidation on her face.

I get a sick feeling in my stomach. "Who was looking for me?"

"Some guys last night. They was askin' all us who was workin' last night if we know who David is. They only knew your first name. They had a picture of you too. Your hair was in a pony in the picture though."

Oh crap. This is bad. Worse than I thought. Where in the world would they have found a picture of me?

"What was I doing in the picture?" I ask her.

She shrugs. "It was kinda fuzzy. You was standing by a slider door. You was lookin' in at it."

The security camera from Panattiere's house! The footage was recorded and they'd taken a screenshot of it; that had to be it.

"These guys, were they cops?" I ask her, dread building in my gut.

She laughs. "No way. They were mob, man."

"Mob?"

"Mafia. You know the type, Guido Italian dudes."

Allen is staring at me. "What's happening here, Sandman?"

I ignore him. "Did you know who any of them were?" I ask Star.

She shakes her head no.

"How many were there?"

"Just two. They was asking everybody who you were and showing your picture. You should ask Joni though. I think she knew them."

"Who's Joni?" I ask her.

"She's around somewhere. Allen knows her."

I turn to Allen. "You know this girl, Joni?"

He's frowning at me, I think finally beginning to realize that Lizzy's kidnapping has something to do with me. Eventually he nods.

"Where does she usually hang out?" I ask Star.

"I don't know man, she's just around; you'll have to find her. I need you guys to go now. I gotta make some cabbage, you know?" She motions with her hand, shooing us away.

I thank her for her help and Allen gives her a hug. We cross back to the other side of Fremont.

"What's goin' on here, Sandman?"

I ruminate over how to answer his question. I need to level with him to some extent. His paranoia is real and I can't have him deciding I'm one of the kidnappers or a secret agent or something. I can't have him run off, at least not until we find the guys who took Lizzy. The danger to her is becoming more and more real.

I'd completely forgotten that Panattiere had caught me that night on his security cameras. Or, more accurately, I hadn't thought about the fact that they might be recorded and that somebody might have been able to review them to see who I was. Joey and his associates would have wanted to know who I was of course, and he would have told somebody about the tape. I don't know how they decided to come downtown and ask prostitutes who I was, but they'd gotten lucky by finding Lizzy. She was the only one who would have been able to tell them my last name, the only way they would have been able to write it on the note they left in her apartment.

I pull Allen back off Fremont and into an alleyway, away from the throngs of tourists in their alcohol- induced fugues who would probably be mostly oblivious to what's happening with us anyway.

Allen stands there staring at me, his shoulders slumped, his Iverson jersey hanging by just one shoulder strap, the other having torn at some point without either of us knowing. He has a hangdog expression on his face, fear and worry mixed with confusion and distrust. I feel terrible that I'm the cause of those emotions in his already troubled mind.

"I don't know exactly what's happening, Allen. It appears that some people who were looking for me took Lizzy to make me come to them. That note we found in her apartment? It told me they had taken Lizzy to a house. I went to that house last night and she wasn't there; it was a trap. Now I don't know where to find her."

He's staring at me, silently, waiting.

"That's all I know, Allen. We need to find Joni and we need to ask her who the guys searching for me last night are. I don't have any other leads right now, no other clues or ways to find them."

"You think these guys asked Lizzy 'bout you and she told them she knew you so they took her?" He asks.

I nod. "I do. I think they thought I would come find her and they could grab me. But she wasn't there."

"That means she's prolly dead," he replies, a tear forming in his eye and rolling down into his black and silver beard, carving a track through the dirt on his face.

I shake my head, quickly. "I don't think so, Allen. They need her alive, to make sure they can capture me. They can't kill her because they might need her to set another trap. They're probably trying to set one up right now, actually."

He stares at me a long moment before speaking. "What we gonna do then, Sandman?"

"Can you find Joni?" I ask him.

He nods. "Yeah, prolly."

"Then we'll start there. We'll see if she can tell us where to find the guys looking for me last night, then we'll go see if we can find any clue to where Lizzy might be."

He takes a moment and then nods, turning and walking out of the alley without comment. I stare at his back for a second and then follow him back out into the bustling throngs of Fremont Street.

Chapter 9

It takes Allen less than ten minutes to find Joni standing near the entrance to the Golden Nugget, saying hi to men as they walk by and aggressively staring at them in an uncomfortable display of role reversal. Some of the men ignore her completely, others call out to her, whistle, or perform some vulgar gesture designed to elicit laughs and backslaps from their friends. Occasionally someone stops to talk to her, but they always move along within a few seconds.

Joni is an old hand at this, that much is obvious. She's a middle-aged white girl with big, fake boobs and a tight, trim body that she has on display in a short skirt and a flannel shirt, the shirt tied into a knot below her breasts and unbuttoned nearly to the knot to allow her cleavage to spill out. She's wearing high heels and has her hair in pigtails, obviously trying to convey a sense of innocence that's actually long gone given her age and occupation. She's appealing to me on a primal level, so she's getting something right, though on a physical level I've not been interested in anyone since my wife's murder.

"Let's go talk to her," I tell Allen.

"You gotta go on your own, man."

"Why?"

"She doesn't like me. And you see that guy standin' behind her?" He motions to a large, muscular man who's leaning casually against the side of the Golden Nugget, seemingly watching the crowd, his eyes shifting over to Joni every time someone approaches her.

"That's her boyfriend, man. He's called Gator. He don't like me neither and said he'll beat me up if I talk to Joni again."

I stare at Allen a minute. There's a story here but I decide I don't have time for it. "Okay, I'll go over there alone."

I cross the street and approach Joni. I see Gator's eyes track me briefly before dismissing me as a non-threat and going back to scanning the crowd.

"Hi," I say as I step up to Joni.

She puts a warm smile on her face. "Well hi yourself, stranger. Whatchu up to tonight?"

"I hoped we could have a talk."

She puts a hand on my arm and smiles. "I'm not that interested in talking, honey. But if you want to do a little more than talk, well then I'm all ears."

"It's about Lizzy," I say.

The smile disappears from her face and she glances back at Gator. He straightens up from the wall and stares at me. He couldn't hear what I said to her but he notices immediately the change in her posture.

I smile to put him at ease and then regard Joni.

"Not here," she says quietly. "Women's bathroom by the craps tables inside." She motions with her head back toward the Nugget. "Five minutes." She then laughs loudly and smacks my arm in a friendly way. "Get on your way, sugar. That's not gonna cut it!" She turns away and shrugs toward Gator who glares at me suspiciously.

I turn and walk into the Golden Nugget. I don't want to go back to Allen and tell him what I'm doing for fear that Gator will see him. Hopefully he'll just stay put and wait for me.

The Golden Nugget is jam packed tonight, the tables bustling with action despite it being a weeknight. Security is standing by the entrance as I walk in but they give me barely a glance. I keep my head down and move through the crowd. The cameras here use facial recognition software and I don't want to give that software an easy time. It's designed to help casinos spot known cheats and card counters but I don't doubt it could easily be manipulated to search for wanted felons as well. As long as I avoid the tables themselves where most of the cameras are focused, I should be safe. I don't think the police are able to tap into the casino security systems yet, but I've been away for too long and I can't be a hundred percent sure, hence my paranoia.

It takes me only a minute to find the bathrooms Joni mentioned and I walk inside the men's room first, relieving myself at the urinal and then taking the time to wash my hands, two luxuries I rarely get to enjoy.

Stepping back out into the vestibule between the men's and women's rooms, I lean against the wall and wait, trying to appear as non-threatening as possible.

I get a few frowns from women walking into the restroom, but I disarm them with my best smile. Joni finally appears a few minutes later, walking quickly toward me. I don't see Gator anywhere around and figure he must be waiting outside.

"Gator is coming inside any second, get in here!" She hisses as she passes me and steps into the women's room. I hesitate and her arm snakes back out, grabbing my shirt and pulling me into the women's restroom.

Uncomfortable. That's the best word to describe my feeling as Joni pushes by women attempting to leave the restroom, dragging me by the front of my shirt. I shrug and try to smile to the other women as they glare, first at me and then at Joni. I can only imagine the thoughts in their heads as they watch an obvious working girl dragging a man into the bathroom. I can also only imagine how long it will be before security shows up and detains us.

I seem to be struggling lately to keep a low profile.

"You're the guy Dominic was looking for last night, right? You're David?"

Dominic...It appears he was looking for me while I was looking for him. I nod my head at her.

"You got Lizzy involved in some bad shit, man," Joni says to me.

"I know, but I didn't mean to. Tell me about Dominic and tell me where I can find Lizzy."

"I gotta pee, stand by the stall," she says as she steps into an empty stall. I try to ignore the glowers I'm getting as girls come out of stalls and head either to the sink to wash or straight out the door. Luckily there seems to be a bit of a lull in the brisk pace of the bathroom and nobody is coming in. Or perhaps there's somebody outside warning people there's a man in the bathroom and casino security are on their way with the police right behind them.

"Look, Lizzy's a nice girl and I don't want to see anything bad happen to her," Joni continues from the stall. "But if Gator finds out I said something to you, he'll kill me for getting involved and for putting him at risk."

"Is Gator part of Dominic's crew?" I ask her.

She snorts. "No way. He's scared of them. They let him operate a few hos because he don't act up or step on anyone's toes. That's why he'd kill me if he knew I was talking to you."

"Does he know who I am? Did they show him my picture?" I ask, thinking about the way Gator stared at me and all of a sudden worried this might be a trap, worried that Gator might be calling Dominic right now. I glance nervously toward the entrance to the bathroom.

"Nah, he didn't see your picture. They just showed it to all of us girls, asking if we knew you or where to find you. Gator tends to disappear when those guys come around," she says, coming out of the stall, the toilet flushing behind her.

"How did they know my name? How did they know where to find me?"

"How do I know? I just know Lizzy told them she knew you and they told her to get in a car and they took her. Now listen up, I gotta get back out there before Gator gets suspicious. You gonna find Lizzy or what?"

"I want to but I don't know where to look."

"Dominic and his crew all hang out at Triple A Bail Bonds," she says, washing her hands at the sink. Two girls come into the bathroom just then, laughing loudly and carrying drinks. Hopefully that means nobody has reported me yet. They both glance at me and one of them turns to address the other.

"Oh look, another winner who wants to watch women pee because the gender-neutral bathroom policies allow him to be in here."

"I really don't, I uh…" I begin, not sure what to say. I have no idea what they're talking about or what these bathroom policies are.

"Ignore them," Joni says, glaring at them until they both disappear into stalls.

"Look," she continues, "at this bail bond place, they got a office above the place and a small warehouse back behind it. That's where I'd look if I was you. You know the place?"

I shake my head.

"It's behind the jail on Clark Avenue. Like maybe 3rd or 4th street. You get over there and you find Lizzy and you help her, you hear me?"

"Yeah, I hear you. Listen Joni, thank you for your help," I tell her, anxious to get moving, get out of this bathroom which is beginning to feel more and more like a trap.

She grabs a handful of paper towels and dries her hands then scrutinizes me.

"Don't thank me, just find her. These guys are dangerous and I'm afraid for her."

She tosses the towels in the trash and walks out.

I force myself to wait, telling myself to give her a full minute to get out of there before I follow her. I can only manage to wait fifteen seconds before my nerves begin to fray and I move to the exit. I peek my head out and don't see anything that alarms me. I hear behind me the sound of the girls exiting the stalls and I quickly step out of the doorway and work my way through the casino, suppressing the impulse to run. Will this feeling of being trapped whenever I'm indoors ever subside? I don't know the answer to that and I don't want to think about the long-term implications of my current situation. Lizzy needs my help and I need to focus on that and worry about myself later.

Chapter 10

It's nearly midnight and I'm sitting in the doorway of an attorney's office, huddled into the corner with my right shoulder against the door itself and my left against the wall. My backpack is between my legs and my jacket covers both it and me. This is causing me a bit of discomfort due to the still warm night, but I need the setup for camouflage. A breeze is blowing, relieving the warmth a bit as the dry air wicks the moisture from my skin.

I'm well supplied with water, a large plastic jug of it sitting at my feet. I don't know how long I'm going to be sitting here so I sip it sparingly, not wanting to have to get up to pee before I'm ready to move.

After leaving the Golden Nugget earlier, I met back up with Allen and filled him in on the basics of what I'd learned—that Lizzy had been taken by some bad guys and was being held a few blocks to the south. I didn't tell him she'd been taken because of me, though I know he's starting to put all the pieces together and realize that I'm responsible in some way.

And the truth is, I still don't know just how responsible I am for her kidnapping. Lizzy's estranged father, Jerry Bastain, was murdered by Joey under orders from Dominic. Dominic and his crew then kidnapped Lizzy while circulating a photo of me around the downtown area, specifically to the hookers down there. And Jerry Bastain had my murdered wife's figurine in his glove box. There's a connection there somewhere and I don't know what it is. Then of course, there's the police issue. When they tried to lure me into the trap at Joey's house, they called the cops to arrest me. I could understand a revenge motive...I had Joey arrested so they want to find me and hurt me or kill me. But I can't understand why they tried to lure me into a trap to have me arrested. And I don't know if that means my cover has been blown or not.

So, these are the problems I need to solve, hopefully tonight. I need to know if I can go back to the street, continue under my David Sands alias, or if I need to run, find a new cover, a new identity. I also need to know if Dominic and his crew murdered my wife and why. I need to know what it was that I did during my time as a police officer that got my family killed. And I need some revenge for their murders.

After I filled Allen in on the basics of what I knew, we walked back to Lizzy's apartment. The apartment was still locked up and appeared to be undisturbed. I grabbed my pack and the jug of water, told Allen that I needed him to wait there for me and that I was going to scout out an area where I thought Lizzy might be. Allen argued that he wanted to help, that he didn't want to be left behind again, but I convinced him to stay there. This was going to be tricky tonight and I didn't want to be worried about him while I was trying to find answers to all of my questions.

It was only seven or eight blocks from Lizzy's apartment to Triple A Bail Bonds, which I noted with some amusement was actually called *Triple A Bail Bonds* and not *AAA Bail Bonds* as you might expect. I thought the reason to call your company AAA anything would be to get your ad at the front of any alphabetical listing such as the yellow pages or an online directory. Calling it Triple A seemed counter-productive.

I'd found the lawyer's office with the recessed doorway just kitty-corner to Dominic's bail bond business, offering me a view of the front and side of the place, along with concealment from any prying eyes over there. The jail was just around the corner from my location, making this street a one-stop shopping center for the criminal. Go to jail, secure a bail bond, hire an attorney...all in one city block.

I've been sitting here for about twenty minutes and everything has been quiet across the street. Triple A Bail Bonds is still open for business which is surprising to me, though I don't know that much about how bail bonds work. Perhaps you can get bailed out of jail in the middle of the night?

There's a light on in the front window and a red *Open* sign glows brightly above the door. Nobody has come in or out since I've been here, though I did see a shadow move across the front window a few minutes ago. Above the storefront are three windows that could be the apartment Joni mentioned, though those are all dark. Behind the store, just visible from my location and attached to the back of the building, is another building that seems to have been added on after the original construction. Long and low-slung, it's a fairly large building, certainly big enough to be a warehouse with plenty of storage. I can just make out what appears to be a loading dock at the back of the building with two dumpsters against the wall beside it. There's a bunch of what appears to be construction debris stacked near the dumpsters, including pallets and boards and a few lengths of pipe that seem to have been set aside, possibly for later metal recycling.

There are two air conditioners mounted to the roof of the warehouse and they've been constantly humming since I've been here. Somebody is keeping that big building cool which leads me to believe there may be people inside. There are no windows that I can see from my place of concealment.

I see movement out of the corner of my eye and I turn my head slowly to the right, watching for it. Under my jacket, my hand grips the 9mm Glock I pulled out of the pack earlier. It's loaded and ready to go, the holster secured to the waistband of my pants. If Lizzy's in that building, I'm not taking any chances.

I don't see the movement again, but while I'm scanning, a car rounds the corner and pulls to a stop at the curb in front of Triple A Bail Bonds. It's a black four-door, newer model, possibly a Camry or one of those Kias that all look alike. Both front doors open and a man steps out of the driver's side, a woman out of the passenger side. She's holding some papers in her hand and she waits for the man to step around the front of the car. They both go to the front door and the man pushes a button.

Even from my position across the street, I can hear the tinny voice that comes from the speaker.

"Can I help you?"

The man replies, too softly for me to hear, and I hear the tinny voice telling them to come inside. A buzzer sounds and the man pulls open the door, motioning the woman to go in before him, the door closing behind him with a metallic *thunk*.

169

It seems to me these are nothing more than bail bond customers, two people here to secure a bond to get a loved one out of jail. The only thing of interest to me is the security of the front door. Locked and controlled from the inside, that's going to be a tough access point for me, especially if the employees inside have a description of me.

I think about the possibility of using Allen Iverson as a decoy, rushing the place when the employee buzzes open the door, but I can't even consider that without knowing the layout inside. If they keep cash inside, there may be even more security behind the door. I need a subtler approach plan than a mad bum's rush—no pun intended—through the front door.

After what seems to be about fifteen minutes, the front door opens again and the man and woman reemerge, his arm around her, the papers she had in her hand now gone. Titles and security against the bail bond perhaps, solidifying in my mind their status as customers. They get in the car and drive off in the opposite direction from the jail. Maybe that means you can't get released at night after all, which makes it somewhat curious why a bail bondsman would stay open all night. Of course, if Dominic's is the only place open at night when parents and girlfriends and boyfriends get the phone calls that their loved one has been arrested, he's more likely to get the business.

Cars zip by continuously on Main Street just one block over from my location, people going to and from the busy downtown area, even this late at night. Only rarely does a car turn down the street I'm on, though, the bail bond business being the only one open anywhere in the area. I peer to my right, trying to spot the movement I saw earlier, but I don't see it again. Could someone be watching me or watching the business like I am? Or perhaps it's just another transient settling into a dark corner for the night?

Another vehicle turns onto Clark, it's bright LED headlights splashing over me briefly as it makes the corner. I notice as it gets closer that it's a black Cadillac Escalade. It slows down as it passes my location and then turns right, down 4th street before turning left and pulling into the alleyway behind Triple A Bail Bonds. I glimpse it again as it reappears in my view backing up to the loading dock behind the warehouse building behind the bail bond business.

Two people get out of the Escalade and the back hatch lifts open with a beeping noise. The two walk out of my sight, headed toward what must be a door on the loading dock. I'm too far away to see what's happening and I suddenly regret my chosen hiding spot.

Making a snap decision, I throw off the jacket, shoulder the backpack, and cross the street, leaving the jacket in the doorway but not wanting to chance leaving the pack behind. The Glock is in my hand and I'm moving fast, surprising myself with this risky action I'm taking.

I run down 4th street and round the corner to the alleyway that runs behind Triple A Bail Bonds. Crouching behind a hedge, I can see the Escalade backed up to the loading dock. The two guys who were inside the car are now standing at a small door beside the large roll-up door that would be used for trucks to load and unload. The open hatch of the Escalade faces that door, and the interior light is on allowing me to see that the back seats have been laid flat for whatever it is they're picking up.

The two guys are both dressed in dark jeans and dark shirts, but the shadows are too deep for me to see their faces. They're waiting by the door and when it opens, the interior light shines out on them, allowing me to see them more clearly. They're both Asian, Chinese most likely, probably in their early to mid-twenties, black hair cut in similar styles, spiked up into waves on the top and short on the sides.

Why are two young Chinese guys doing business late at night with Dominic who by all appearances seems to be part of an organized crime racket involving mostly Italians?

The man who stands in the doorway is older than the other two, maybe late thirties, a white guy who's wearing a button-up shirt and dark slacks, the shirt untucked in a stylish, modern way. I don't know if this is Dominic himself or maybe one of the guys who was looking for me on the streets the other night. The three guys converse for a second and the man inside shouts over his shoulder, "Open it."

The big roll-up door begins to open, more light shining out into the alley and I burrow further into the hedges, trying to stay hidden. This is the part where, if this was a movie, I would jump out and run toward the warehouse, holding everybody at gunpoint while I found and rescued Lizzy. Am I a coward for remaining hidden behind a shrub?

I wrestle with my options here while my eyes probe the interior of the warehouse, scanning for any sign that Lizzy might be in there.

There are pallets of boxes shrink-wrapped and sitting in the middle of the warehouse floor. Against the walls are huge shelving units, also piled high with boxes. There are offices against the back wall, their windows dark, interiors hidden in shadow. The warehouse is not as large as I judged from the outside, but I think the amount of merchandise inside is what gives it the impression of being smaller.

Whoever opened the roll-up door is not in sight, so there's at least one person unaccounted for. The two Asians from the Escalade and the nicely dressed white guy walk up to a pile of boxes that are sitting on the concrete floor of the warehouse in front of the doors and ready to be loaded.

I'm dying to know what's in those boxes. Perhaps stolen goods being fenced through foreign contacts? What is the apparent connection between Dominic's crew and the Asian community? Is what I'm watching connected in any way to Jerry Bastain's murder?

All these questions are unanswered and racing through my head as I watch the two Asian guys begin loading the boxes into the Escalade. I'm afraid to move, afraid to act, though I do memorize the license plate number on the truck, something my mind tends to do naturally anyway. Perhaps I can run it later through my ex-partner at Henderson PD and get more information, if I can figure out how to do it without letting him know I'm in Vegas.

One of the two Asians yells back into the warehouse, snapping me out of my reverie.

"Hey, Dominic, I don't think these are all going to fit. We might need to make two trips."

The well-dressed man who opened the door reappears from behind a pallet of boxes that had been concealing him from view and yells back at the two.

"You idiots! I told Theo to send a truck and that fucking retard thinks this is a truck? Hurry the fuck up, I don't want to be here all night!" He steps back to whatever he was doing behind the pallet of shrink-wrapped boxes.

My heart is racing. I've found Dominic and he either has Lizzy or he at least knows where she is, where to find her. I need to figure out a way to get into that warehouse now.

It comes to my attention that the guys are just about finished loading and they're probably going to be leaving soon, driving right past my hiding spot. If I stay here, they'll certainly spot me as they drive past. I need to be somewhere else when they leave, and a basic plan is forming in my head to get into the warehouse.

Watching carefully, I wait until both of the guys are fixated on trying to stuff one more item into the Escalade, their heads buried in the back hatch as they shove boxes around. There's no sign of Dominic and I quickly stand and walk past the entrance to the loading dock driveway, moving out of sight behind a wall on the other side of the drive. I'm taking a big gamble here that they're going to leave the same way they entered. If they turn left instead of right as they come out of the loading dock drive and into the alleyway, I'll be right in their path and things will probably get bad for me.

The two Asians finally figure out the loading configuration and one of them pushes a button on the hatch, causing it to slowly lower and latch into place. Dominic is standing on the edge of the loading dock now, his arms crossed over his chest, glaring at the Escalade. There are six or seven boxes left at his feet that didn't fit inside.

"Hurry up. I want you back here in twenty minutes, no later."

One of the Asians nods his head and they get into the Escalade, the lights coming on as they start it. I duck my head back around the corner and wait. I can hear the Escalade coming toward me, its headlights beaming on the wall on the other side of the alley. My heart is thumping and my palm has gotten sweaty, the sweat loosening my grip on the Glock as I wait. If they turn left, there's going to be a confrontation most likely.

The Escalade noses out into the alleyway and I lean back against the wall, willing myself to melt into it. The driver doesn't even glance left as he makes the right turn, headed back to 4th street where he came from. I take a deep breath and will my body to relax. I force myself to loosen my grip on the Glock and wipe the sweat from my palm on my pants as the Escalade makes another right turn and accelerates out of sight.

Peeking my head back around the corner, I see Dominic's back as he walks to the rear wall of the warehouse. Both the smaller human door and the big roll-up door are still wide open and Dominic is headed to a control panel on the back wall. He reaches it and pushes a button which causes the roll-up door to start sliding down with a loud rattling noise. He starts back across the warehouse, headed toward the still open smaller door. This is the best chance I'm going to have and I take it.

Waiting until the last minute to make sure he won't see me under the descending warehouse door, I jump around the corner and take off at a run for the smaller door. My pack is bouncing on my back, something sharp hitting me in my spine with each lunging step. Something has moved around in there and isn't in its place, probably the case for my gun. I ignore it and lift the Glock, pointing it at the door as I get close. I remind myself that there's somebody else in the warehouse besides Dominic. I can't forget that, can't let my attention focus completely on him. I reach the four concrete steps that lead up to the door just as the door begins to swing shut. I still can't see Dominic, he's behind the door as it closes, but that means he can't see me either. I guess he hears me though, or otherwise senses that something is wrong, because the door stops closing and his face appears on the side of it.

It's too late for him to react though; I'm moving fast and I've taken the four steps in just two, keeping my speed up as I reach the door. Just as his face appears around the side, a bewildered mix of surprise and fear on his features, I hit the door with my shoulder at full speed. It slams open against its stop, ricocheting back to hit me in the head. It hurts but I shake it off. Dominic has been thrown back as well and he rolls over, coming to rest on his stomach, lifting his head to gape at me in shock.

"What the f-…," he begins.

I point the Glock at him. I'm breathing hard from both the exertion and the adrenaline that's coursing through my veins. It's been a while since I did this kind of thing and I feel alive even though my hands are shaking.

Trying to hide the shake and control my nerves, I loudly tell him, "Don't move, Dominic, or I'll shoot you right now."

He smiles, his face relaxing. He doesn't seem too concerned and that worries me.

"I'm not armed," he begins, showing me his hands. "I'm going to stand up. I'm not going to get shot on the floor like this, like a dog. I'm going to stand up and then we'll talk."

He doesn't wait for my reply but slowly puts his hands on the floor and pushes himself up, first to his knees and then to his feet. He lifts up his shirt to show me his empty waistband, spinning around to show me his back as well. I'm not convinced he doesn't have a gun, but at least he doesn't appear to have one within easy reach. He's controlling the situation, which I don't like, but unless I'm willing to follow through on my threat to shoot him, I can't do much about it. That's one of the problems with making threats you aren't prepared to carry out; sometimes your bluff gets called.

I won't have a problem shooting him if he rushes me, reaches for a gun, or I otherwise feel my life's in danger, but the code of conduct and the moral compass I lived my life under as a police officer is still strong in me.

Besides, I need to talk to him before I shoot him.

I haven't forgotten whoever else was in the building and I inspect the shadowy fringes carefully. Somebody rolled up the freight door earlier, but there's no sign of that person anywhere around. There are three doors on the far wall of the warehouse. Two of them seem to lead to offices, the windows of those offices dark. The third door presumably leads to the store front for Triple A Bail Bonds.

"Who else is here?" I ask Dominic.

He shrugs. "A couple of employees up front, that's all. They won't come back here though; you don't have to worry about them."

"Bullshit. Somebody opened the roll-up door earlier. Where's that person?"

Dominic smiles, an easy smile with a hint of malice and a disturbing lack of fear.

"Oh, you mean Reggie? I believe you've actually met him, no? You are David Sands, are you not?" he asks me, still smiling with that unhinged expression in his eyes.

I tighten my grip on the gun and my eyes search the warehouse again, scanning for any spots where Reggie could be hiding. The building is large enough that I'm not overly concerned about his ability to hit me with a pistol shot if he is concealed somewhere. If he happens to have a rifle, that might be a different story, but at least Dominic is between me and the majority of the warehouse.

The door behind me is still open and it worries me to have my back to an open door. On the other hand, I don't want to cut off my escape route by closing it. Instead I take a few steps to my right, toward the boxes the Asian guys hadn't been able to load, putting some space between me and the open door and positioning it in my peripheral vision.

"Where is Reggie?" I ask again.

Dominic shrugs again. "I'm sure he'll be around soon. But you're not here for Reggie, you're here to find Lizzy, am I right?"

I take a deep breath, keep the Glock pointed at Dominic and force my shoulders to hold still.

"Where is she?" I ask him.

"She's around here, don't you worry about that. In fact, we'll go see her in just a bit, and maybe you can even take her with you. But first, I think you and I should have a little chat. What do you say, *Harvey Conner?* Should we chat?"

I can't breathe. The warehouse begins to spin and my vision is blurred. Harvey Conner. My real name. The cover I've had for the last two years or more is blown. Dominic knows my real name. I can't make any sense of this, can't figure out how he would know.

He's smiling at me as I try to get myself under control. I want to sit down; my knees feel weak. I can't do that of course, and I consider running. Running right out the door and leaving everything, moving to a new town, getting a new identity. The desire to flee is strong, and I have to force myself to ignore it.

Thoughts of my family's murder and Lizzy's kidnapping are what snap me out of it. If Dominic knows my real name, he might have been the one who killed my family. My gaze refocuses and anger builds in me. I grip the Glock tighter and take three quick steps toward Dominic.

"Did you kill my family?" I ask, growling it out and moving toward him as I say it. For the first time, the smile on his face falters. His hands come up, palms toward me.

179

"Easy, easy. No, I didn't kill them. Relax."

I'm trying to relax, but my head is spinning, my muscles are tense and my heart is racing. *He knows my real name. He knows I'm Harvey Conner. How can he know that?*

"WHO KILLED THEM THEN, IF YOU DIDN'T?" I shout at him. My anger is raging and I tell myself to calm down, to take a deep breath.

Before he can answer the question, one of the doors on the back wall opens. I catch it out of the corner of my eye and I turn that direction, the gun following to point at the new threat. Dominic sees this and I notice his body tensing. I flick the barrel of the gun back toward his direction to stop him from any foolish moves and then yell across the room to the back offices.

"Whoever is back there, come out with your hands up or I shoot Dominic!"

There's a momentary pause and then a figure appears in the doorway. The room is dark and I can't make out the figure. It's an awkward shape, appearing not to be human. Until it steps out into the light. I finally realize it's not a single person, it's two people. The first is Lizzy. Her hands are behind her back and there's a piece of duct tape across her mouth. Behind her, his head appearing over her shoulder, is Reggie, an evil grin on his face, his missing teeth making the grin appear lopsided. He starts toward us, pushing her with one hand as they walk. His other hand holds a knife and the blade of the knife is against Lizzy's throat.

Out of the corner of my eye, I see Dominic smile, an evil grin that doesn't touch his eyes.

180

"Well, well, speak of the devil. You wanted to know who killed your family, Harvey? Let me officially introduce you to Reggie."

Chapter 11

Lizzy's eyes are wide, her features frozen in an expression of terror. I've got the gun pointed at the two of them, but there's no shot to take. They're too far away for one, and Reggie's head is much too small a target with Lizzy's body in front of him.

I turn back to Dominic who has taken a step closer to me with the distraction.

"Sit down on the ground right now, or I swear to God I'll shoot you right where you stand!" I'm yelling and I'm nearly out of control. Something in my voice or my posture conveys the veracity of my threat though, because he immediately sits down. It's a good decision on his part, because I was not bluffing that time.

I can hardly breathe and my vision is blurring. I spin back to Reggie and Lizzy who have come within twenty feet of me, Reggie's ugly face sneering at me. I can see now that he has Lizzy's hair clenched in his left hand and he's controlling her with that while his right hand wields the knife.

Can I make this shot? Reggie's head is above Lizzy's shoulder and is a good-sized target from this distance, but my hands are shaking and I haven't fired a gun in more than two years. At one time in my life I would have been able to make this shot easily, but now? I'm not sure and I can't take the shot without being one hundred percent sure of making it. If I miss, I hit Lizzy and maybe kill her. Or I miss the other way and Reggie just slits her throat. Either way, Lizzy dies. I can't take that chance. And, the way I'm shaking, I have no chance.

"Put down the gun!" Reggie screams at me.

I'm not going to do that, that's for sure. All that would do is assure both of our deaths. Lizzy is staring at me wide-eyed, her nostrils flaring. She's leaning back toward Reggie, I guess because of the pressure he's putting into his grip on her hair. I stare back at her, silently trying to convey to her that she needs to help. I need her to make a move, do anything to give me a chance to shoot Reggie. Slam her foot down onto his instep, make her body limp and fall to the ground, getting her head out of the danger zone, slam her body forward or backward, throwing him off balance. I'm wishing those thoughts across the room to her, trying desperately to telepathically send them to her, letting her know I need her to help.

My wife and son. Their killer is standing twenty feet away. I suddenly remember Reggie and Joey in their backyard, Reggie telling Joey that I looked familiar, that he thought he remembered me from somewhere. Dominic could certainly be lying, but deep inside, I know he's not.

The cold steel of the knife on her throat paralyzes Lizzy and she doesn't move.

"Put it down now or I slit her throat!" Reggie screams again, spittle flying from his mouth and landing on Lizzy's neck, his eyes bulging and his face a mask of manic fury.

"You killed my wife and son!" I yell at him, my voice cracking with anger and raw emotion.

The fury on his face disappears and he smiles. "Actually, I only killed your boy. Joey's the one killed that sweet piece of ass of yours."

I'm about to lose whatever little amount of control I'm still grasping. "Why?" I croak out.

Reggie shrugs, and nods toward Dominic. "Ask him."

Before I can respond, I catch movement from my left. My first fleeting thought is that Dominic is making a move, but it's only for a microsecond as I realize that's not it. The movement is accompanied by a scream and all four of us turn toward the open door, now filled with a dark shape moving fast.

It's Allen Iverson. In his hand is a length of heavy metal pipe and he's running, screeching a blood-curdling wail, his face contorted with rage, his gaze focused entirely on Reggie who's holding the woman he loves at knife point.

"Allen, NO!" I yell at him, but he's beyond hearing me. He charges toward Reggie and Lizzy.

Reggie pauses for only a second. I know that everything is moving extremely fast, but it all seems to slow down for me. I see Reggie's features change to surprise, his eyes wide. I see his hand tighten on the knife and his lips purse as he starts to form a word. He takes two steps back, away from the charging Allen Iverson and his metal pipe. He's a moving target now, and I can't take the shot. My finger tightens on the trigger anyway, but even in slow motion, everything is happening just too fast. I see Reggie's hand move, the knife blade sliding across Lizzy's throat. Her eyes widen in shock and pain, and blood gushes from her throat. Reggie lets her fall just as Allen reaches him, his rage giving him almost superhuman speed, strength, and agility. The pipe is raised over his shoulder like a baseball bat and he jumps through the air, over the inert form of Lizzy who has fallen at Reggie's feet. Reggie lifts the knife, trying desperately to defend himself against the monster now almost upon him. Allen swings the pipe downward, its steel barrel hitting the knife blade first, then Reggie's hand, then his head.

Reggie falls to the ground, the knife flung from his shattered hand, his eyes rolling back in his head. I scream at Allen again to stop but he doesn't. A strange noise is coming from his throat, almost a mewling or a whining noise but lower pitched. He raises the pipe and brings it down on Reggie's unprotected face, once, twice, three times, all in quick succession, hard, direct hits all of them. Reggie's face is a bloody mashed mess when he's done.

Allen then turns quickly and spots Dominic who immediately raises his hands.

"No, no, no, don't!" Dominic shouts at Allen.

I also yell, begging Allen to stop. I need one of them alive, I need to question them. I need to know why Tracy and Dillon were killed, and most of all, I need to know who ordered the killings, but Allen is beyond hearing and past stopping. Dominic tries to stand and fails, falling away and then crawling, screaming at the top of his lungs. Allen reaches him and swings the pipe against his skull. Dominic falls flat, and Allen slams the pipe into the back of Dominic's head again and again and again. He finally stops and glares at me. I'm fearful that he's going to attack me next, that in his rage he won't recognize me. If that happens, I'll have to shoot him. There's no reasoning with him in his demented state and I recognize that. I point the gun at him, my finger on the trigger, silently begging him not to come after me.

He doesn't. The pipe falls from his hand and clatters on the concrete floor of the warehouse. He runs over to Lizzy and grabs her head in his hands. Her eyes are wide; she's still alive but blood is flowing from her.

"Pressure! Put pressure on her wound!" I scream at him. I run over to Dominic and search his pants for a cell phone. His head is smashed in, blood pouring from it and pooling up beneath him. It's obvious that he's dead or about to be.

I glance back at Allen. He's sitting on the floor and he's cradling Lizzy's head in one hand while he desperately tries to put pressure on her throat with the other. Blood seeps out around his hand and tears are streaming down his face. He's pulled the tape off her mouth and she's gagging, blood coming out of her mouth now too.

"Noooooo. Lizzy, no. Stop bleeding Lizzy, stop bleeding, please. It's going to be okay, Lizzy, just stop bleeding, please," he mumbles over and over again. His body is shaking with sobs, his words choked with emotion.

I go to Reggie and search him for a phone. Lizzy needs help; I need to get her an ambulance. Reggie doesn't need help, that much is obvious. The rage Allen put into the four strikes to his head was more than enough to kill him. I would have killed Reggie myself, without remorse, but I get no satisfaction from his dead body. There are just too many unanswered questions, and my hopes of having them answered has died with him.

Reggie has no cell phone in his pockets either. No cell phone on either of them, right when I need one the most. I glance back at Lizzy and Allen, then to the offices on the back wall of the warehouse. There must be a phone in there, or for sure there will be one in the main office of Triple A Bail Bonds.

Before I can start back that way to find a landline, I hear a wail from Allen. I turn toward him again and see his head buried in Lizzy's chest. Her head lolls to one side, her eyes open wide, sightless, blood no longer spurting from the wound in her throat. She's dead and Allen realizes it.

I stop and my gaze flashes around the warehouse. There's blood everywhere, three dead bodies and one man sobbing uncontrollably, his body shaking with rage and grief. I holster my gun and, in a daze, I walk over to the boxes on the floor, the boxes the Chinese were loading into the Escalade. The boxes they're coming back for any minute now. Allen and I need to get out of here but I have no idea how I'm going to get him away from Lizzy, how I'm going to convince him to leave. His fingerprints will be on that pipe; I need to keep that in mind. I need to get things cleaned up, need to get him to a shower, get him some new clothes. He's covered with blood and I realize that I am too.

But despite all I need to do, I can't move my focus away from the boxes. What was Dominic giving to the two Chinese guys? I can't explain why it matters, for all I know they're just fencing some stolen goods or moving drugs, but in the back of my mind, I realize that there's a connection between the Chinese, Dominic, and me, the murder of my family. I don't know what the connection is, but I feel compelled beyond any logical reason to dive into the boxes, to see what they were moving, what they were taking to Theo, whoever that is.

I reach the first box and rip the tape securing it closed with my fingers. Pulling the flap hard enough to tear it free from the remaining tape, I open it and peer inside. Papers and picture frames. I'll never be able to explain how I know, but a feeling of dread builds in me as I reach slowly into the box and remove one of the picture frames. I turn it over and stare at the photo inside, unable to look away. Tears begin to form in my eyes, confusion and doubt pushed to the back of my mind as I'm overcome with emotion.

It's a picture of me, my wife, Tracy, and our son, Dillon. The picture was taken on Easter Sunday, just about a month prior to their murders. We're sitting on a picnic table, dressed in our nice clothes, smiling at the camera. A happy family with a bright future. A happy family, blissfully unaware that less than a month later that happiness will be ripped from us, Tracy and Dillon murdered and me on the run, evading charges for those murders.

I fall to my knees, holding the photo, my vision locked upon it. I know in the back of my mind that I need to flee this scene, that I need to get away and figure things out. I'm uncovering something huge here, I feel that, though I can't fathom what it is. I can't connect my family's murders, the Chinese, and the Italian mob guys. And at this moment, it doesn't matter. All that matters are my memories and all I want to do is jump into that picture, go back to that time, live in that moment forever or end my life right here and now and be with them again, wherever they are.

It's Allen who pulls me out of my fugue. I hear him calling my name.

"Sandman. Sandman!" His voice is racked with sobs. "She's dead, Sandman. Lizzy's dead. You said you would save her but she's dead!"

I shake my head, tear my gaze away from the picture and turn to him. Our eyes meet and we see the grief on each other's face, recognizing our shared losses, though he doesn't know the reason for mine. Allen looks back down at Lizzy and then slowly leans forward, kissing her softly on the lips before lowering her head gently to the floor and standing up.

"We can't leave her here, Sandman."

I nod to him and turn back to the boxes. I rip open two more of them and peer inside. It's my stuff, Tracy's and mine, all stuff taken

188

from my house: papers, photos, clothing…everything that I thought was still in my old house, now stored in these boxes and, presumably, the ones already on their way to Theo.

I take off my backpack and open it, gently placing the Easter photo inside next to the figurine I got from Panattiere's house. I want to take more stuff, all the photos, the papers with Tracy's handwriting on them. I want to search through everything for whatever I can find that will keep my memory of her alive, but logically I know that I can't carry all of this with me.

Part of me wants to burn it so that Theo doesn't get it either. I don't know who he is or why Dominic had my stuff and why he was giving it to Theo. I don't know why Dominic and his crew murdered Tracy and Dillon, or who ordered those murders, but I will find out. I have the license plate from the Escalade and I'll track Theo through that. Then I'll find him and when I do, I'll get answers and I'll get my belongings back from him. I'll make him pay for anything missing or damaged, make him pay physically. I don't know if he's the one responsible for my family's murder, but I do know that I'm getting closer to that discovery. I will discover the reason and I will get my revenge.

I close the boxes up and swing my pack onto my back. I turn back to Allen who's now carrying Lizzy, her body cradled gently in his large arms. I walk over to him and stroke Lizzy's cheek, closing her eyelids with my hand. They won't stay closed so I leave them open. I kiss the top of her head and then regard Allen who's staring at me, waiting.

"We can't take her, Allen. There's nowhere to take her. We have to leave her here."

189

He stares at me for a long while and then finally nods. Scouting around, he spots a table against the wall and walks over to it. Lowering her onto the table, he folds her arms over gently and kisses her one last time. He then turns to me, tears coursing down his cheeks. I walk over to Dominic's body and stare at him, the face of evil along with Reggie across the room. There are no answers to get from the dead bodies and nothing further for me here. I pick up the pipe, carefully keeping my hands out of the blood, and take a last look around. There's nothing else we've touched and I nod to Allen.

We walk out the door and I close it gently behind us, making sure it locks as it closes.

Chapter 12

It's Friday morning and I'm sitting on the steps of the courthouse waiting for the auction to kick off. This is the day my old house goes up for sale, and I'm curious to see who buys it.

A lot has happened since Lizzy's murder the other night. After Allen and I left the warehouse, we walked quickly, fleeing to the east to get out of the general search area. I didn't know if the two

Chinese guys would call the cops when they returned for the rest of the boxes of my stuff, but at some point, somebody would certainly call them. We needed to be long gone before the K9 tracks began.

I wasn't sure we were going to be able to move fast enough and I considered trying to hail a cab or hop on a bus, but Allen was covered in blood and I had a considerable amount on me as well. We would have left an impression we didn't want to leave.

I didn't want to return to Lizzy's knowing that the police would be showing up there eventually, once they'd identified her body and figured out where she lived. Unfortunately, I didn't have a choice. They'd be dusting her place for fingerprints at the very least and I needed to get all evidence of my presence removed.

I told Allen what we needed to do and we raced back for her place. I hoped the locked warehouse would stump the Chinese for a while and I'm hoping Dominic was telling the truth when he said the Bail Bond employees don't come into the warehouse. It seemed logical; after all, they were keeping a kidnapped girl in the offices back there.

We stopped to drop the pipe into a dumpster far from the warehouse, hiding it under all the trash. Even if it was somehow found, I made sure to wipe all prints off it. If dogs were able to get a track on us, the police might discover it but they wouldn't get Allen's or my prints if they did. We made it back to Lizzy's and I wiped down every surface I'd touched over the past few days while I got Allen into the shower. He hadn't wanted to do anything but hold Lizzy's things and cry, but I eventually conveyed the urgency of our situation. I'll admit to you that I once again used his irrational fear of the secret police to get him to move, something I'll always feel bad about.

He showered with his clothes on, washing the blood from them while I cleaned up at the sink, removing my shirt and running it under cold water to get the splashes of blood out. We were both dressed in wet clothes after that, but the night was warm enough that it didn't matter. I used a bottle of bleach I found under the sink and poured it down both drains, washing away any DNA and hopefully destroying any hairs that might be found in the traps, hairs that could be tested if the police decide to be that thorough. While wiping away all the fingerprints from every surface is necessary, it's also a red flag for the cops. I mean they expect to find at least Lizzy's prints everywhere, right? When they find precisely *no* prints, they know that somebody cleaned up and they tend to look a little closer.

We were out of there within thirty minutes of arriving, locking her door and closing it behind us, hopefully to buy us more time; the cops will need to secure a warrant before going in. We continued our flight, putting distance between us and the crime scene, staying on streets where lots of pedestrians walked, hoping to lose any dog that might be tracking us.

Luckily, it wasn't until the next morning that the crime scene was found by anybody at all, I later discovered from news reports. It was one of Dominic's associates showing up for work who found the bloody mess and three dead bodies in the warehouse, and by then our track was long gone. Apparently, the Chinese guys either didn't break into the warehouse to get the last of the boxes or they didn't call the police if they did. Either one of those possibilities seemed plausible.

We'd spent that entire night walking, making a long zigzag trail while our clothes dried on our bodies. The next morning, we found a thrift store and I used some of my dwindling cash to buy new clothes for both of us. We changed in an alley and tossed our old clothes into a dumpster back there, miles from the warehouse and well out of any search area. Allen tossed everything except the Iverson jersey, which he wouldn't discard despite all my pleas. He put it on over the new clothes, the broken strap still hanging down off his shoulder.

All day yesterday we rested and dozed out of the sun. I bought cheap food for us at a gas station deli and we both drank our fill several times from the faucet in the bathroom. We ignored the glare of the clerk who was not quite sure she should challenge us because our new clothes made us seem not quite like transients.

That night I sent Allen back to his normal haunts near Fremont Street and told him I would see him in a few days. He was disconsolate, not talking at all, robotic in his movements and actions. I still don't know how he found the warehouse that night, though I suspect he followed me, not wanting to be left behind yet again. I thought back to the movement I spotted while I was sitting and watching the warehouse, the movement I dismissed as a possible homeless person searching for a place to sleep. I was closer than I knew to being correct.

I knew Allen was grieving and I suspect he was blaming himself for Lizzy's murder. I tried to reassure him that Reggie was going to kill her anyway and that his actions were her best chance. I don't think either of us believed that though.

Now I'm waiting for the auction to begin, and I doubt you'd recognize me if you walked right past me. Gone are the long hair and the long, scraggly beard. I stopped at a barber shot yesterday and spent another precious bit of my money, directing the barber to give me a short, stylish haircut and trim my beard down to a normal beard length. I then stopped at a grocery and bought hair dye, gray dye which I wasn't even sure was available. I used the bathroom at the grocery store and locked the door, carefully applying the dye to both my hair and my beard. I now appear much older than my real age, which you might as well know is forty-six. With the sun-aged skin I've developed on my face over the last two years and my enhanced gray beard and hair, I now seem like I'm in my late fifties or maybe even older.

I still have the David Sands ID, though I now look nothing like his picture. I may need it again sometime, but for now it seems that alias is busted. I don't know how many people besides the recently deceased Dominic and Reggie are aware that my real name is Harvey Conner. The Chinese perhaps. The cops? I don't know. I'll find out the next time I contact my old partner at Henderson PD, but for now my disguise should work fine.

The auction has begun and the bidding, which uses sealed ballots, has closed. The auctioneer stands at a podium near a desk where several people are reviewing the bids. The bidders are sitting in chairs that are lined up facing the podium and the desk. I'm sitting on the steps behind them, inconspicuously leaning against a pillar and waiting for the announcements.

There are three houses up for auction today and my old house is the first one, though it's numbered as lot thirty-six. I stopped by the library yesterday and checked on the value of the place online. The taxes and mortgage owed comes to around $211,000 and that's the minimum bid. Online estimates put the value of the house at around $250,000, so I expect it will sell with that spread between value and cost.

I'm expecting to see the winning bid at somewhere in the $220,000 range, so I'm a little surprised when the auctioneer announces the final number.

From the podium, he speaks into the crowd. "The winning bid for lot number thirty-six is $300,000. The winning bidder is number twelve."

I stand up, trying to see who number twelve is. There are three men sitting together in the back row. They stand up and one of them reaches into a briefcase, handing some papers to the other. As he hands them over, he turns slightly toward me. He's dressed in a suit, his hair perfectly cut, his suit well-fitted and sharp, obviously expensive. He's wearing a gold watch that glitters in the sunlight.

Oh, and he's Chinese.

The man to his left has also turned toward the man on the right, the one who's now making his way up to the auction table, the papers clenched in his hand. This man is also dressed in a nice suit and he's also Chinese.

The third gent has made his way up to the tables and he hands the papers over to the clerk. She hands him other papers and he leans down to sign them. I'm guessing the papers he handed her were either bank guarantee notes or actual certified bank checks for the amount of the house which has to be paid for on the spot. The amount paid for my old house was exorbitant, but I can see both of the Chinese guys smiling. I still haven't seen the other guy's face but he doesn't appear to be Asian. He's dressed in jeans and a t-shirt with just a sport jacket over the t-shirt. Why is he the one who is signing the papers and why did the two Chinese guys give him the money?

I wait for him to finish signing and for the clerk to give him instructions. As he turns around to walk back, I get my first glimpse of his face. I freeze, shocked into immobility. I know this man. His name is Eric Townsend. He was once my best friend.

He was also my partner at the Henderson Police Department.

Part Three

Chapter 1

*T*he car's headlights splash across the front of the house, briefly

lighting up the yard as I turn in. I switch them off, but leave the car

running, leaning my head back against the rest and closing my

eyes. I'll go inside soon, but I need a minute to compose myself.

Some days are tough in this job, and this was one of the worst.

Responding to calls where there are dead kids is one of the great

tragedies of being a police officer.

Today I had to respond to a drowning. A four-year-old boy

drowned in the family pool. I'd been the first one on-scene, had run

around the house to the backyard, had shoved aside the parents

standing over the lifeless body of their son, doing nothing. They'd *been frozen in fear, grief, and disbelief. They'd not known basic CPR, or had been too paralyzed to attempt to use it, and that made me furious. I pushed them out of the way and leaned down over the child, his lips and eyelids blue, his face pale. He seemed like a doll lying there with his pale skin, not a real person. Part of me screamed that it was a practical joke, that any minute everybody would start laughing, and Ashton Kutcher would come running out telling me I'd been Punk'd.*

Another part of me, the rational part, sprang into action. I started CPR, prying open the small child's mouth, tilting his head back, pinching his nose, and locking my mouth over his, blowing gently as I watched his chest rise, making sure I didn't put too much air into his small lungs. Two breaths only, then down to his chest to start compressions. His parents stood there, the husband holding the wife, her face buried in his chest, sobs muffled by the husband's body but still loud. The husband watched me as I worked, not offering to help, his lips moving in silent prayer.

The medics came running around the house minutes later and I moved aside, staying on my knees, shaky and unable to stand, watching them work. A bag to do the breathing, an IV into a vein in the boy's leg, one of the medics counting out chest compressions. I glanced at the boy's face again, and through the plastic cup of the breathing bag, his face looks just like my own son's face. He looks

198

just like Dillon, and I feel tears in my eyes. I want to scream at his parents, who continue to stand there, helpless and impotent. How could they let this happen? Why weren't they watching their son? Why didn't they protect him? The medics bring a stretcher and lift the lifeless body onto it, the stretcher dwarfing the little boy, his arms and legs pointing limply toward the edges. The medics don't give up, continuing to work on the boy, but I see their expressions—grim realization tattooed onto their faces. It's too late for him and they know it.

Lifting my head from the steering wheel, I use my sleeve to dry my eyes. I push the button on the car's visor, and the garage door rumbles upwards, a noise I know Tracy will hear inside. "Daddy's home!" she'll be saying to Dillon, and he'll come running for the door leading from the garage to the house, waiting to jump into my arms. I'll hold him extra tight tonight, knowing that the nightmares will come, that the drowned boy will become Dillon in my dreams.

Tracy's car is parked inside the garage, and I skirt around it, taking one last moment to compose myself before I go inside. My backpack is slung over my shoulder and I'm in street clothes, having changed out of my uniform before coming home. My utility belt and gun are in the backpack, and I'll secure them in the safe in our bedroom right after I greet Dillon and Tracy. There will never be a loaded gun where Dillon can get to it in my house, not until he's old enough to know how dangerous guns are, and how to handle them safely.

I open the door and prepare for him to jump into my arms, but he's not there. I walk inside and let the door close behind me.

I call out, "Hello? Tracy?"

There's no answer, and I walk down the hallway. It seems longer than I know it actually is, and my vision begins to narrow, white fog blurring the walls as I walk. The hallway is a tunnel and I know in my heart it ends in death. I know when I reach the end, the drowned boy will be there, waiting for me, asking me why I didn't save him. I stop walking, trying to turn around, but it's too late. My feet lift off the ground and I'm carried in a rush to the end of the tunnel. I'm suddenly standing in my kitchen. This isn't right, *my brain tells me.* This isn't how it happened.

"It's close enough," *I hear myself say. The lights are blazing in the kitchen, but things are strangely quiet. I'm facing the stove and I hear a whimper behind me. The drowned boy. I turn around, dreading what I'll find, my heart racing and my palms sweaty. It's not the drowned boy. It's worse.*

I see Tracy. She's sitting in a chair, Dillon next to her. "Tracy?" I say, and she turns to me, her eyes wet with tears. I suddenly realize that

200

both she and Dillon have tape over their mouths and their hands are tied behind the backs of the chairs. My gun is in the backpack and I start to move, slipping it off my shoulder and taking a step back. Before I can fully react, someone grabs me, a big arm circles my throat and I feel a sharp poke on my neck. Things immediately begin to go fuzzy and I fall to the floor. I can see but can't move, and a pair of blue jean-clad legs steps in front of me. The backpack is ripped from around my arm and a moment later, I hear Tracy begin screaming through the tape over her mouth. My vision goes black as I hear two gunshots, then nothing.

I wake up with a start and lay there quietly, my heart beating wildly, my face damp with the tears I've been sobbing while I slept, my body drenched in sweat. This isn't the first time I've had this dream, nor the second, nor the third, nor the tenth. I've had some version of this dream dozens of times. I suspect I'll have it for the rest of my life. I always wake up at this point, the end of my sleeping nightmare which was only the beginning of my waking nightmare. When I'd actually awakened that night two years past, what I'd found was…I shake my head, deliberately suppressing the images that appear in my mind. I'm instantly craving a drink, a shot of whiskey, a warm beer, anything that will help me shake off the depression I'm feeling. I suppress those cravings as well. No more alcohol.

There's a light snoring sounding from next to me, and I glance over. Allen Iverson is sleeping five feet away, on the other side of the room. He could have his own bedroom, but since the first night, he's slept in the same room with me. He's never expressed a desire to take one of the other two bedrooms, and I haven't asked him to do so, understanding his need to not be alone during the night. It mirrors my own.

I get up, quietly, and roll up my blankets and sleeping pad. Taking the bundle out to the garage, I stow it in the corner, behind the hot water tank. Coming back inside, I take a seat on the floor near the window in the front room, sitting quietly, waiting and watching the street outside while I think.

It's been about two-and-a-half weeks since I sat on the courthouse steps and watched my old home get auctioned off to the highest bidder. Two-and-a-half weeks since I watched the winning bidder sign the paperwork. Two-and-a-half weeks since that bidder turned, and I saw it was my best friend and my old partner at the Henderson Police Department, Eric Townsend.

I'd been stunned into immobility when I'd seen him. I watched him walk back to the two people he'd been sitting with, two Chinese men, dressed in impeccable suits with serious demeanors. The three of them had left together, while I remained seated on the steps in stunned disbelief. I suppose it could have crossed my mind at some point that Eric was buying the house for me, that there wasn't anything nefarious about him purchasing it. But intellectually I knew that couldn't be true.

Foreclosed houses selling at auction have to be paid for at the time of purchase. Eric was a cop. He didn't have three hundred thousand laying around to buy a house. I watched the Chinese guy give him the bank checks to pay for it when he'd gone up to sign the papers. He'd partnered with them to purchase the place for some reason. I seem to keep running into Chinese connections with everything I find involving the murders of my family, and it seems that they've managed to turn even my partner against me.

I call Eric my partner, but in reality, there are no partners on the Henderson Police Department, at least not in patrol. When I'd first been hired, Eric had been my field training officer, or FTO as they were known. We'd ridden together for three months, patrolling the streets and responding to calls. I'd grown accustomed to calling him partner then, and the moniker had stuck through the remainder of my career. We'd become best friends, and our wives had also become best friends. Yet now I had to wonder just how good friends we'd actually been. I had to wonder just how much I'd been played by him, just how deeply he'd betrayed me.

I don't know if it sounds racist to assume that the Chinese connections I keep encountering are all related, but racist or not, it feels that they are. Jerry Bastain had been murdered and my wife's figurine was found in his car. He was the first of the Chinese connections. I'd then discovered the two Chinese guys loading boxes of my belongings into an SUV, driving off to deliver them to someone named Theo. Then the two Chinese guys who'd financed the purchase of my house. It was all too much to be coincidence.

I'd originally thought it was the Italian mob who were the primary suspects. I'd wracked my brain trying to think of what I could have done to piss them off, what I could have done to make them want to kill my wife and son. And while the mob guys seem to have been the ones to actually pull the triggers, I've begun to suspect the Chinese are behind it all, and I've been struggling to figure out what my connection to them could be.

I've done a small amount of research into known Chinese gangs in the last two weeks, focusing primarily on the 14K Triad, a large-scale gang operation based in Hong Kong. They seem to be the most active Chinese gang in America. They're heavily involved in drug trafficking and money laundering, but I don't recall any interaction with them whatsoever while I was a cop. In fact, they don't have a real presence in Las Vegas, according to the media. Nor do any other Chinese gangs. The Italian Mafia, sure, they've famously been here since the heyday of Vegas, but I can't figure out why I would have been a target for any of them. I'm at a dead end at the moment.

So now I'm sitting in a house in Las Vegas, and you're probably wondering how I managed to go from homeless to homeowner in the last two weeks. Well, I'm not a homeowner, but I have managed to find a home to live in, at least temporarily.

A few years ago, when the housing market crash occurred, Las Vegas became one of the hardest hit areas in the country. Housing prices tumbled dramatically, and many people lost their homes to foreclosures. There are still thousands of houses around Vegas just sitting empty, and many have become homes for squatters – homeless people who move into the empty houses and just make them their own. Many of them draw up fake leases, furnish the places, have the utilities turned on, and just simply pretend they belong there. Many others have completely destroyed the homes they've moved into.

I've been aware of this for years, and I'm also aware that the police occasionally crack down on these squatters. In fact, I read just recently that LVMPD has developed a unit of officers specifically to respond to the growing threat of the squatters, and that Las Vegas has created a law making squatting illegal, thereby empowering the police to take action on something that previously was nothing more than a civil matter.

Because of all this, I'd never considered trying to become a squatter and live in a vacant house. It is far too dangerous for me to put myself in a situation where the police may come to the door demanding identification and arresting the occupants for illegal occupation.

However, changing circumstances require changing risks.

For two years I've thought the murder of my family was nothing more than a home invasion robbery gone bad, or perhaps retaliation for some action of mine that I wasn't aware of. Now, though, it feels like a much more insidious conspiracy that reaches as close as my best friend.

So, I've adjusted my capacity for risk, despite what that might mean for my own safety or freedom.

The house I found, the house I'm currently sitting in, is located just down the street from my old house, the one sold at auction just two weeks ago. From where I sit in the front room of this house, I can see my house and can watch it for any activity. This seems to be my best bet for trying to figure out what has happened.

The problem is, I haven't yet seen anything that would give me any kind of a clue. When I first moved into this place, I saw a lot of activity at my old house. A dumpster was delivered to the driveway and I watched as construction workers, all young Chinese men, began bringing out wheelbarrow loads of debris, running the wheelbarrows up a ramp and dumping them in the big container. They tore up all the carpets in the house, took out the kitchen and bathroom cabinets, the showers, shelving, everything. By all appearances, they were simply doing a complete remodel of my old house.

It took them three days to complete the demo, filling two large dumpsters full of debris. Each day during that two weeks, twice per day, a black Cadillac Escalade pulled up. Each time, one of the workers would come out and speak to someone in the back seat, and then the car would pull away. After three days, the second dumpster was hauled away and all the workers left. They haven't been back.

Three nights ago, I took a chance and snuck over to the house sometime well after midnight. The neighborhood was quiet and I didn't see a soul as I boosted myself over the retaining wall fence and into my old backyard. The backyard was in rough shape, grass and bushes dead, debris from two years of storms accumulated along the back side of the house. The rear slider door was unlocked and I opened it quietly and went inside.

The entire house had been gutted. Walls were ripped apart so the studs were exposed, flooring was removed, leaving only the subfloor. The kitchen and bathroom cabinets were gone, along with all of the appliances. The house was completely destroyed, thoroughly emptied. The kitchen, where I was standing now, held only nightmares for me, the place where Tracy and Dillon were murdered, their blood staining the floor, their bodies limp, eyes open, staring, unseeing. I moved quickly through that room and into the living room.

I spent probably an hour inside the house, standing in the middle of each room, remembering how things had been. I spent most of the time in Dillon's old room, my eyes closed, picturing it how it had been when I'd last seen it, picturing Dillon lying peacefully in his small bed, the Buzz Lightyear blankets pulled up to his chest, the arms of his Thomas the Train pajamas on top of the covers. I could see the images clearly in my mind and I reveled in the memories.

I also spent time in the master bedroom, standing where the bed had once been, where Tracy and I had once slept and loved. The bed was gone, as well as the nightstands, pictures, keepsakes, and everything else, including the carpets and even the walls, but in my mind, they were still there, as vivid and fresh as if I'd traveled back two years in time.

I eventually left, tears fresh on my face, my mind clear and at ease. The trip inside the house, though it raised many more questions than provided answers, was therapeutic for me. I had a chance to say goodbye, to remember Tracy and Dillon, and to promise them again that I would find their murderers. That I would not rest and I would not forget.

I returned to this house where Allen and I were squatting, laying low, taking few chances and remaining as inconspicuous as possible. It had been a week since anybody appeared back at my old house, and what had seemed to be a thorough and complete remodel in progress was now looking like nothing more than a comprehensive and exhaustive dismantling of the entire interior of the house. It was eerily representative of the dismantling of my life over the last two years, and I wondered who was trying so hard to completely erase me from the world.

I have the license plate number of the Escalade that came by each day, twice a day, with the man in back to whom the construction worker spoke. That plate number is different from the one I have from the night at Dominic's warehouse. A different, though identical, black Escalade. The problem is, I don't have a friend in the police department to run the plates for me.

I can certainly no longer trust Eric, and I have nobody else I can turn to. Which means that my leads in this case are down to just one—Eric Townsend himself.

I leave the front window and walk quietly into the bathroom and undress, turning on the shower and stepping inside immediately. It's cold, but warmer than it will be in a few minutes when the water that's currently sitting in pipes inside the walls of the house flows through and is replaced by water that's in the pipes underground.

When I found this place, I contacted the water company and was able to give them a fake name (David Sands, of course) and get the water turned on. I'd simply had to tell them I had moved in and was leasing the place. I couldn't do the same with the power, or with the gas company, however. Water is a basic necessity, and the water company doesn't ask too many questions. They simply turn it on, and when you don't pay the bill, they send someone out months later to find out why. The power and gas companies are a little more stringent though. They want a social security number, and they want to run a credit check or get money up front. I wasn't able to provide that information, obviously, so we had running water, but no electricity or gas with which to heat it.

No heat isn't much of a problem, seeing how it's the beginning of June and the house falls below eighty degrees only late at night, staying in the upper eighties or low nineties during the day. That may seem hot, but it's not as hot as what Allen and I are both used to living with on the street during the summer. That heat also makes the water in the shower a bearable temperature, at least for the first few minutes, which is all I need to get clean anyway. I turn off the water just as it's starting to get uncomfortably cold, and I stand there, shivering but enjoying the coolness. The water will evaporate from my skin quickly in the dry heat of the house.

I do some stretching and some jumping jacks to wake myself up and to help the water evaporate and then get dressed in the same clothes. My clothes are just starting to smell bad again, but I'll wash them in the bathtub tonight, leaving them to dry while I sleep.

Once I'm dressed, I walk back to the bedroom to wake Allen. It's already late morning and it's time for us to leave. In order to minimize the danger that anybody will spot us homesteading here, and possibly call the police on us, we have a schedule that we adhere to. We leave the house after 9am, when most of the neighbors are gone to work, and we don't come back to it until midnight or later, when most of the neighbors are asleep. Other than the days I spent watching the demolition of my old house, this is our routine. Allen will spend the day panhandling and trying to stay out of the sun, avoiding the secret police he thinks are after him, and I will spend the day at Eric Townsend's house.

"Sandman," Allen says with a yawn as I wake him.

I've not told him my real name. I don't think he needs to know, nor do I think he'd even acknowledge it or understand. I grin at him, but he doesn't return the greeting. He's been in a deep depression since Lizzy's murder, and I haven't been able to shake him from it. You are probably thinking that I should have just left him to mourn on the street and live his life, while I do my own thing. You might be right. After all, I need to be able to move around unencumbered while I search for my family's killers, and Allen does add to my workload. But I couldn't do it to him. He's in need of a friend and I'm the only one he's got, now that Lizzy is dead. What kind of person would I be if I left a friend behind in the time of his greatest need? Not the kind of person I could live with, I'll tell you that.

So, I get Allen up, watch as he rolls up his bedroll and hides it next to mine behind the water heater that doesn't work. We clean the house of our presence each day before we leave. If any authority becomes suspicious that there is somebody squatting here, they will find no sign of us, at least not during the day when they're most likely to be checking for that. This is as safe as I can make us while taking the risk of illegally occupying an abandoned house.

I don't know how much longer we'll stay here. I've wanted to keep an eye on the goings on at my old house, now owned by Eric Townsend, though I suspect unofficially owned by some Chinese gentlemen. Right now, I have to travel from here to Henderson each day to watch Eric's house. If there's no further activity at my house within a week or so, it might be prudent to find another abandoned house in Henderson, somewhere near Eric's place. I'll have to talk to Allen about that later. I fear further change will only worsen his depression, taking him to an even darker place.

Allen blames himself for Lizzy's death, and I've been able to do nothing to convince him that it wasn't his fault. It will take time, and it will take patience, but I hope he'll someday be able to move on and to forgive himself.

We both fill large containers with water from the kitchen sink. I remove a package of granola bars from its hiding place on top of the cabinets, and we each take one. I hide my backpack in the attic, reaching it by standing on an old chair that was left behind when the previous owners moved out. Even if somebody comes into the house, they aren't likely to search up there, but I keep my gun and all my cash with me just in case. Necessary but limited risk, that's my new motto.

Allen keeps his pack with him and, glancing around one last time for any sign of our presence, we leave the house by the back slider, closing it quietly behind us. The house butts up against a dry wash, just like Joey Panattiere's house, and just like so many others in Las Vegas. This makes it convenient for us as we hop the wall and immediately become invisible to society. No longer trespassers on private property, but simply vagrants looking in the wash for cans or bottles to recycle in. Not worthy of anybody's attention, not even worth the time it would take to look upon us with disdain. Invisible, just the way we want it.

I need to remain inconspicuous because of my real problems with regard to being a wanted fugitive. Allen needs to remain unseen because of his imaginary issues with covert and secret police officers who are attempting to track him down. The invisibility of our presence in the dry wash works well for both of us.

Allen heads east along the wash, making for the Sahara onramp to I-15 where he'll spend the day with a sign asking for help, moving along with the shadow of the billboard as the sun traverses through the sky. He'll be lost in his own thoughts, his memories of Lizzy, along with whatever hell he lived through in a past life, but people will stop to give him money. Not many, but enough for him to buy lunch and dinner if he's careful. Possibly even enough for him to get a drink, a forty-ounce bottle of some cheap beer or a fifth of some rotgut whiskey. I don't think he'll buy the alcohol though. He hasn't had a drink since Lizzy's murder, and neither have I. His reason is unknown, but my own is simple: I was sinking into the trap of alcoholism, and it was affecting my drive to solve the murders of my family. I'm done with alcohol forever, a necessary decision that was easy to make. Easy to make but difficult to accomplish in fact, the cravings rearing their ugly head at various moments like this morning.

I head west, making my way up to a bus stop on Decatur where I know I can catch The Deuce, the double-decker bus that rolls all through the Las Vegas valley. I have a long ride, with two transfers to get to my destination around the area of Green Valley Parkway and Windmill in Henderson.

I spend the bus rides in silence, eating my granola bar and sipping my water, preparing for the day ahead. I made a decision while I sat at the front window this morning and, though I'm already mentally second-guessing that decision, I'm firm in my resolve. I'm out of options and further leads are currently non-existent. I have no option but to make the tough choice, the dangerous choice.

Today is the day I'm going to confront my old buddy, Eric Townsend.

Chapter 2

The bus drops me off and I start walking toward Green Valley Parkway. It's early yet, not quite 11 o'clock, and I know Eric's shift doesn't end until four o'clock, which gives me plenty of time. I've watched him carefully over the last two weeks, coming to this side of town nearly every day, and I've got his schedule figured out. Today should be a work day for him, and he seems to always come home right after his shift ends.

I no longer have the comfort of the homeless persona to hide myself from any close scrutiny, what with my fresh haircut, trimmed beard, and somewhat clean clothes. Having my hair and beard dyed gray does give me a new image that I can exploit though -- that of an old man.

What do old men do every day? I think they go to cafes, drink coffee, and read the newspaper. So that's what I do today.

I stop at a convenience store to buy coffee and the Desert Sun Sentinel and then sit at an outdoor table of a trendy coffee shop to read the paper and wait. I don't want to pay the exorbitant prices of the vogue coffee sold by the national chain, but I will take advantage of their table and chairs. They are unlikely to say anything to me about using their patio, if they even notice me. It would be far too confrontational and in direct conflict to their liberal ideals to insist I actually be a customer to enjoy the services of their business. Besides, it's going to be hot today and most patrons will be staying inside enjoying the air conditioning, so they shouldn't mind me taking up space.

I kill two hours reading the paper and sipping on my coffee. I go inside the store once during that time to use the restroom and, though the clerk gives me a suspicious glare as expected, she says nothing to me. It's close to one o'clock when I finally leave, stopping at the same convenience store where I bought the coffee, this time spending some more of my dwindling cash reserves to purchase two burritos and a banana, which I slowly eat while standing in the shade of the building.

That finished, I walk across the street to Walmart. I spend some time walking around the store, enjoying the air conditioning and using the restroom there as well, refilling my water bottle from the fountain before wandering over to the sporting goods section. I'm used to the curious glances I get; I don't want the attention, but I don't have a lot of choice at the moment.

In the sporting goods section, I find what I'm looking for—a can of tennis balls. I buy the cheapest ones they have that run me just over two dollars. Using the self-checkout, I put the balls in a bag and begin my leisurely walk to Eric's house.

By the time I arrive near his place, I figure it's after three o'clock, and I stop at a park just two blocks from his house. I take a seat on a bench in the shade of a large pine tree, sipping my water and holding the newspaper up like I'm reading it. I've already read the entire thing, so this time it's truly a prop, perfect for my image and as cover.

About an hour later, I see Eric's truck drive by. It's a silver Ford F-150, and I eyeball him over the top of the newspaper as he passes my location. He doesn't turn my way, staring straight ahead as he drives by. I stand up and amble over to the street watching him turn into his driveway two blocks away. His garage door, triggered by the opener in his truck, is going up but, as usual, he doesn't park in the garage. I know the reason for this — his wife, Alexa, parks her car in the garage. Eric leaves his truck in the driveway, off to the far-right side of the driveway itself, where Alexa can still get by him. I see his feet under the truck as he gets out, hear the door slam and see him walk into the garage. A few seconds later, the garage door starts smoothly down, the sound inaudible from my location.

I walk over to a garbage can and toss the newspaper away, then remove the container of tennis balls from the plastic bag. Opening the can, I throw the lid away and then stuff all three balls into the pockets of my light jacket. I consider the empty can for a minute. I may have use of it, though I dread the idea that's come into my head. After a minute, I decide to keep it, stuffing it into the inside pocket of my jacket where it hangs awkwardly. Not ideal, but it will have to do. That done, I walk back to my bench and set my water bottle in the shade. Nobody is likely to disturb it there, and it may be a while before I come back to it.

Now comes the tricky part. It's Wednesday and on each of the last two Wednesdays, Alexa has left shortly after Eric arrived home. She's been dressed in workout clothes each time, possibly going to the gym or to a yoga class, and she's returned home about ninety minutes later. If this is a pattern, she'll be leaving again this afternoon, anytime now. I do have a backup plan if she stays, but it's much riskier, both for me, and for Eric and Alexa.

I take my jacket off and, slinging it over my arm, stand on the sidewalk at the edge of the park, bouncing one of the tennis balls and trying to appear nonchalant. It's the hottest part of the day and there are only a few people outside which tends to make me stand out a bit. I'm slightly concerned about that, but it's a risk I need to take.

I wait fifteen minutes, the sun beating down on me, nerves and apprehension making me sweat although the dry air wicks it away as soon as it forms on my skin. I'm just getting worried Alexa isn't leaving today when I suddenly see the garage door start to go up.

Timing is everything now and I start toward the house, walking quickly but not so fast that I would draw any attention. Just an old man, out for a late afternoon stroll. I hear Alexa's car start up, the brake lights visible, the white back-up lights coming on as she begins to reverse out of the garage. I'm still a block away and I slow down just a bit, not wanting to get so close that she'll take notice of me. Her car, a white coupe, backs onto the street and I turn into the driveway nearest me, still four houses away from hers. She turns to the right, the rear of the car swinging in my direction, and I don't want to be visible in her rearview mirror as she backs onto the street. I stop at the top of the driveway, hoping the occupants of the house aren't looking outside, and wait for her reverse lights to go off. As soon as they go dark, I walk quickly back onto the sidewalk and start at a fast walk toward Alexa's car which has now started moving forward away from me.

Their house is on a corner lot, and Alexa is heading toward that corner. She's hit the button in her car and the garage door is starting to slide down. I'm still two houses away and I pick up my speed, breaking into a jog, hoping she doesn't glance back and see me. I've got one of the tennis balls in my hand and just as Alexa makes the turn, when I know her focus will be on the street in front of her, watching as she rounds the corner, I launch that tennis ball toward the garage, over the top of Eric's truck, aiming for the corner of the garage door. It bounces into the garage and hits a shelf with a clang that I hope isn't audible inside the house. The garage door continues its downward track and I quickly grab another tennis ball from the jacket pocket. I'm close now. Alexa's car is out of sight and I throw the second ball. This time it bounces on the driveway and hits the garage door, careening back into the street. One ball left. I pull it from the pocket of the jacket slung over my arm. The garage door is only two feet from closing and I'm at the rear of Eric's truck, just at the corner of their driveway. I stop and take aim, launching the last tennis ball toward the sensor, the garage door nearly closed. The ball skips on the driveway and for just a heart-wrenching second, I think it's going to bounce up and hit the door like the last one. But it doesn't. It slips under the door with maybe an inch to spare, triggering the invisible safety beam as it bounces into the garage. The big door reverses its downward slide and starts back up, and I step behind Eric's truck, hidden from the house, watching for any sign that I've been seen or that Eric has heard noise from the garage.

The door reaches the top of the tracks and comes to a stop, the light flashing three times inside. I glance around quickly. There's nobody watching, nobody seems to have noticed anything. Casually, my heart racing, I step into the garage and walk to the front wall where the door to the house is located. I hit the button on the wall and then step to the side, into a shadow behind a rack of shelves which holds boxes containing sporting and camping equipment. The door slides down quietly and comes to rest, the garage now still and quiet.

The garage door opener is a new model, quiet and smooth, but I still wait a full minute to make sure that Eric didn't hear the sound of the tennis balls. After a minute, I slip my gun from its holster and walk quietly to the door of the house.

Taking a deep breath, I turn the knob and quickly push open the door, avoiding the classic movie mistake of the slow opening door that squeals out. It makes no sound and I step inside, closing it over softly behind me, gun held out in front of me. There's a washer and dryer on my left and an open doorway that leads to a hall with several rooms opening off it. From around the corner, toward where the living room is, I can hear a TV, some type of sitcom playing with an accompanying laugh track that has always annoyed me.

My training comes back to me, and I don't head straight for the living room. Quietly I clear the two guest bedrooms and the office first, leaving no room for anybody to sneak in behind me. The master bedroom is next and I have to cross the adjoining hallway which leads to the rest of the house to get to it. My vision shifts rapidly between the master bedroom and the hallway as I slide quickly but carefully across, my heart racing, my palms beginning to sweat. I've still not seen anybody, but I know Eric is somewhere in the house.

The master bedroom is messy, clothes on the floor at the foot of the unmade bed, makeup and hair products scattered on the counter of the twin-sink master bath. I probe into the walk-in closet, my gun still held out in front of me, trying to move quietly. It's clear.

223

I step back to the hallway and move down toward the living room, stopping to quickly clear the small guest bathroom that opens to my left. There's a closet on the left at the end of the hallway, the door closed, and I decide to ignore that. If anybody's hiding in there, they know I'm here and things are going to get ugly anyway. As the living room area comes into my view, I see the large television and a white, sectional couch that I recognize immediately. Despite Eric's recent ability to come up with three hundred large to pay cash for a new house, he hasn't bothered to upgrade his furniture.

On the couch sits a man, his back to me, his head sticking up above the back of the couch. I recognize my old partner from just the back of his head. He's watching an old episode of *Friends*, Ross is on the screen whining about some injustice while Rachel prattles on about how awful the current guy she's dating is. These are definitely not things I miss from my old life.

The kitchen and dining room open up to my right, and though I want to clear those, if I move any further forward I'll be in Eric's peripheral vision. I need to get his attention before I do that. I stand there a moment, calming my nerves, poised for action, my gun pointed at the back of his head. I know that Eric is no longer my friend but I don't know why. I don't know if he'll try to kill me, if he'll comply with my orders, or if only one of us will walk away from this encounter, but it's high time for this confrontation to happen. Long overdue questions are going to be answered, even if I have to hurt Eric and wait for Alexa to get home to get those answers.

Readying myself, I say, "Hello, Eric," while I take a step forward. This allows me to see his hands which I immediately see are holding only a cell phone; at the same time, the movement brings me into his peripheral vision. He jumps off the couch, his breath coming as a gasp, his eyes wide and focused on the gun, his phone flying from his hands.

"Don't move!" I shout at him, and for just a second he almost does. I see him glance at the end table where I notice for the first time his gun in a holster. I never would have missed that in my glory days.

"If you move toward the gun, you die, and so does Alexa." I hope my voice conveys more assurance and confidence than I'm feeling at the moment.

He freezes at the mention of Alexa and stares at me, his hands raised in the air, his body tense. A frown comes over his face as he stares. I figure he recognizes my voice but can't reconcile it with my current appearance.

I wait, giving him a moment, and the recognition comes suddenly. His eyes widen even further.

"Harvey?" he says in disbelief, his hands lowering toward his side.

I motion with the gun. "Uh-uh. Keep them up high."

"Harvey, what are you doing? What's going on?" His voice is higher than usual with nerves and adrenaline.

"That's what we're going to find out in just a minute, Eric. But first, I want you to move slowly over to the corner there and kneel down." I motion to an empty corner of the living room but Eric doesn't move, he just stares at me.

"Whatever's going on here, Harvey, let's talk about it. Whatever you think I've done, I promise you I haven't."

I smile as I recognize this for what it is, a complete lie. If he truly hadn't done anything wrong, the first thought for why I was holding him at gunpoint would not have been that I was there because he'd done something. It was the classic understanding of the correct reason for the confrontation and an immediate attempt to deflect it, something I've seen criminals and suspects do a hundred times. Sort of like when the SWAT team kicks down your door and you immediately scream out, "I didn't murder that girl!" How did you know we weren't here on a search warrant for drugs?

226

"Move to the corner and kneel down facing the wall, Eric. I really don't want to have to shoot you, but I will if you don't comply."

He must have recognized the truth in my statement because he shrugs and walks to the corner, kneeling down away from me.

"Hands on your head, fingers interlaced, ankles crossed," I tell him. "You know the drill."

He does what I say and I take the opportunity to peer into the kitchen and dining room just to make sure there's nobody there. I then walk over and carefully pat him down, making sure he isn't armed. When I'm finished, I step over to the end table where his gun is and I slip it into my pocket.

"Step into the kitchen," I tell him, walking backwards ahead of him, my gun held tightly, trained on his chest.

"Grab one of the chairs and take it to the wall, then straddle it backwards, your back against the wall, facing me."

He does as I ask. This will keep him from making any sudden movements and will allow me to relax just slightly.

When he's settled in, I stare at him, waiting. He stares back at me for a moment and then contemplates his lap.

I wait, not saying anything. I know he'll speak eventually and he finally does.

227

"I'm sorry, Harvey."

My stomach clenches. Even now, I hope I've been wrong, that I misconstrued what I saw. His apology is like a knife in my guts.

"Why am I here, Eric?"

"You're here because I betrayed you." He continues to focus on his knees as he says this.

"Look me in the eye," I tell him. He does, slowly.

"Did you help murder Tracy and Dillon?" I ask, anger, dread and gorge bubbling up, my hands shaking. If he averts his eyes I don't know if I'll be able to stop myself from pulling the trigger right now.

His eyes widen. "Oh my God, no! Jesus, Harvey, you have to believe me, never. I would never, oh my God." His eyes fill with tears and relief spreads over me. I'm still shaking and I will myself to calm down.

"Who did?"

He shakes his head. "Honestly, Harvey, I don't know. Do you think I would have been involved in anything if I knew that? Do you think I wouldn't have moved mountains to try to find the answer to that? I loved those two like they were my own family."

Now both of our eyes are tearing up.

"Then what's going on here, Eric? What have you done?"

He takes a deep breath and shakes his head.

"I don't even know where to start."

"Why don't you try the beginning? That's where most stories start."

I grab one of the chairs and sit in it, my gun resting in my lap but still pointed at Eric. I'm across the kitchen from him, my back to the sink where I can see him as well as the rest of the house just in case anybody slips in without my knowledge.

Eric wipes his eyes and starts talking.

Chapter 3

"It started about a year before Tracy and Dillon were killed."

"Before Tracy and Dillon were *murdered*," I correct him.

He stares at me a moment and nods.

"Before they were murdered. I got in some trouble betting sports. I was losing and I owed my bookie a big number."

"You mean to tell me this is about a gambling debt?" I ask in disbelief. "Who's the bookie?"

"A guy named Dean Scofield. I lost about thirty grand to him. I paid him ten of it but I couldn't pay the last twenty."

I'm confused. "What does this have to do with Tracy and Dillon?"

"Nothing at first. Scofield was putting pressure on me to pay him and I just didn't have the money. I didn't want Alexa to know and I told him I needed some time. Then Tracy and Dillon were murdered. I ignored Scofield for a while because I was helping you, spending all my time making sure you were okay. Then word came down you were going to be arrested."

That memory was vivid. It had been two weeks since the murders and I'd been frustrated with LVMPD. They hadn't made any progress on identifying the killers and I'd been dragged in for several interrogations with the homicide detectives. I was on leave from Henderson PD, of course, and staying at a hotel, my house a crime scene; even if it wasn't, I had no desire to go back there.

Early one morning, Eric called me. He'd heard from a friend of his at LVMPD that I was going to be arrested later that day. I'd been pissed off, angry beyond belief, but not surprised. There were no other suspects. Tracy and Dillon had been murdered with my own gun and I had a story about being knocked unconscious with a needle to the neck. They'd taken my blood and found no evidence of any drug present. They'd confronted me already about that and I'd had no answer. If I'd been in their shoes, I would never have believed my story either.

So Eric had warned me and I'd fled. It became painfully obvious that LVMPD was looking at nobody but me for the murders, and I had no desire to prove my innocence in a court of law which would have meant directing energies away from finding the real killers. You know what happened after that. An overwhelming desire to find the killers had slowly melted away after two years of living as a transient.

Eric was still talking. "I called you and warned you and you disappeared. I told the Metro homicide guys that you were innocent and that they needed to be searching for the real killers, but they just barely gave me the time of day, and even that only because of some sense of professional courtesy. They stopped looking for anybody else, focusing only on you as a suspect. But I never believed it. That's why I kept helping you every time you called me."

"Except you were actually working against me," I say to him angrily.

Eric shakes his head. "No. I was never working against you. But one day, about three months after you fled, Scofield came to see me here at my house. Alexa was gone and he showed up at my front door. He told me I needed to settle my debt right then and there and I told him I didn't have it. That's when he told me he had another option."

He pauses and I prod him. "And that was?"

"He didn't say at first. He left and a couple of days later he shows up again, with another guy this time. This was his boss, the actual money behind the betting operation..."

Before he says the name, I know who it is.

"...a guy named Dominic Carvelo."

It would be too much of a coincidence for this to be a different Dominic. This must be the same Dominic from the warehouse.

"Tell me about Dominic. What does he look like, what do you know about him?"

He describes the man from the warehouse and then shrugs. "I did a criminal history check on him when I went back to work, of course. He was relatively clean, no arrests, suspect in a couple of burglaries from way back, but never charged. Clearly tied to mob activities, but it doesn't matter now anyway."

"Why's that?" I ask, already knowing the answer.

"Because he's dead. He was murdered two or three weeks ago in a downtown warehouse along with another guy and a girl."

I nod but don't say anything further. I see no need to give Eric any inkling of what I know or don't know.

"Continue."

"Dominic begins threatening me, telling me I owe him a lot of money and he wants it now. I tell him I'm a cop and he says that's the only reason he hasn't already taken further steps. He then tells me he's going to be having a chat with Alexa next." Eric shrugs. "I was between a rock and a hard place and I told him that wasn't acceptable. He smiled and told me there may be another option. Then he said he'd let Dean explain it to me, and he left."

Holding the gun level is beginning to get uncomfortable and I spin the chair around, straddling it and propping my arm up on the backrest, continuing to point the gun in Eric's direction.

"What did Dean say?"

"He told me they knew I'd been the one to tip you off before you fled."

"How did they know that?"

Eric shrugs. "I don't know. They didn't say and I didn't ask. I was more worried about why your name was being brought up in the first place. Then Dean told me they had a vested interest in your whereabouts and that if you were ever in contact with me, they wanted to know about it."

"And you told them every time I contacted you. Told them where I was and everything," I say, my anger bubbling up again.

"Not really," he shrugs, "what could I tell them? One of the reasons I agreed to cooperate was that I honestly didn't know anything useful. You always told me you were in Florida; even when they made me track you by installing a program on my computer that could backtrack your IP address, it became instantly obvious that you were using an IP hiding program. There was nothing I could tell them that was useful."

"Until about a month ago when I asked you to run a plate that came back to Joseph Panattiere," I say to him.

His gaze drops. "Yeah, until then. I reported that you'd contacted me and that you'd asked me to run a plate for you. I didn't think it was too meaningful, but apparently it was."

"How long after I asked you for the plate information did you pass it on to Dean?"

"The next day. I sent him a message the same day, telling him you'd been in contact. He called me the next morning and I told him about the plate and name I'd run for you."

"What happened when you mentioned the name Joseph Panattiere?" I ask.

"He got excited and told me he'd call me back. That's when I took a peek at the call logs from LV Metro from the night before and saw Panattiere on the arrest report. That was the first time I connected the dots and knew you were still here in town and the first time I actually began to get worried that my reports to Dean were going to have consequences."

They had consequences all right. Dean passed the information on to Dominic and together they figured out I must have had something to do with Panattiere's arrest. They would have contacted him in jail and found out he had video of me at his house. Joey would have certainly confessed at that point to taking Tracy's figurine from the car after he killed Jerry Bastain. He would have wanted to let Dominic know about my reaction to finding the figurine, about how I'd gone off the deep end and stabbed him with the scissors. Assuming Dominic knew the significance of the figurine, it would have instantly told him who I was. If he didn't understand the significance, he would have figured it out when he saw me on the video, even though I don't look quite the same as in any other photos they might have of me.

"Did Dominic or Dean show you a photograph of me at any time? Or a photo of anybody that they wanted you to identify?" I ask Eric.

"No." He frowns at that question.

They must have pulled the screenshot of me from the video and then started asking around, starting with downtown where Panattiere had killed Bastain. They would have guessed that I'd witnessed the murder. What other conclusion could they have drawn? Panattiere had murdered Bastain, and a few hours later an ex-cop on the run from the law contacted his old partner and had him run the plate number of the vehicle Panattiere used for the murder. Later that night, Panattiere had been captured in his home by someone who asked him about that murder, tied him up for the police, then freaked out about a figurine stolen from the scene of the murder that just happened to have previously been owned by that ex-cop's murdered wife. Too many coincidences to come to any conclusion other than that the person who'd captured Panattiere must be the missing Harvey Conner.

By the time they got around to showing the photo to Star, they'd already had my moniker, David Sands, which meant somebody had identified me before they got to her. Possibly the same person who told them of my friendship with Lizzy eventually putting her in danger. Or perhaps she was going to be in danger anyway as the daughter of the man they'd just murdered. All of which raises so many possibilities that my head is beginning to spin trying to sort it all out.

"You said Dominic was murdered a few weeks ago. What do you know about that?"

Eric shakes his head. "Not much. He was found beaten to death in a warehouse downtown, along with another guy and a woman who'd had her throat slit. From what I heard, it appears to be mob-related in some way, but I don't know any more than that."

"What about Dean Scofield? Have you spoken with him since Dominic was killed?"

"Just once. He told me nothing had changed and that with Dominic's death, he was now in charge." Eric pauses for a minute.

"He also told me some other guys would be in contact with me shortly and I was to do whatever they asked."

"Is there any point at which you were ever going to say no to this guy?" I ask him. "Any point at which you would have reminded yourself that you're a cop, maybe got your dignity back and considered doing the right thing?"

His expression is one of misery, though it has no effect on me. I have no compassion for him.

"They hadn't yet asked me to do anything that would have made me say no. Reporting your contacts with me seemed harmless; every police officer in the state and surrounding states had been searching for you for two years. I didn't think my telling them you'd contacted me was going to do any harm and it was keeping me from having to do something worse to pay them the money I owed."

All the while apparently never upsetting your morals, I don't say out loud. Life circumstances can make all of us stretch the boundaries of our morals at times, something I'm instantly reminded of when I recall that I'd asked Eric to commit a felony by helping me out and not reporting our contacts to the police.

"Why do these guys want me so badly, Eric? What do they want with me?"

"I don't know, Harvey."

"If they wanted to kill me, they could have done it the night they murdered Tracy and Dillon. Why now?"

"I don't know the why, but I do know they don't want you dead. They want you arrested."

I glower at him. "How do you know that, Eric?"

He stares at the floor and massages his forehead. "A couple of weeks after Panattiere was arrested, we got word from Metro that they'd acted on a tip the night before and thought they had you at a residence on the west side of town. I pulled up the call and saw it was Panattiere's house. I spoke to one of the officers involved in the call.

I remember the night, of course, the man in the sedan who'd made the call when Nick, my decoy, had appeared. How quickly the cops had arrived...

"What did he say?"

"He told me they'd been tipped off that you were going to appear that night. The caller told them to stage a few cars at the Vons at Charleston and Decatur. The cop involved told me it'd been a false alarm. They got the call, stormed over there, and it wasn't you."

Who would have the kind of influence to make a phone call and get Metro to assign two patrol cars and four officers to stage that way? I pose this question to Eric.

"I don't know, Harvey, but it's something you should think about. Whoever it is wants you arrested and they have pull. That's better than wanting you dead I suppose."

I consider this, but I don't have an easy answer. There aren't a lot of people who could get that kind of response from the police without giving away information and control, but I don't have a grasp on enough facts to narrow the possibilities. It could be a dirty cop at Metro, possibly someone in command, or it could be another situation like Eric's here, an otherwise good cop who's being blackmailed and manipulated. Whatever it is, it will have to wait until I know more. It's time to get to the heart of the matter and make sure Eric's being honest with me.

"Who were the guys Dean put you in contact with after Dominic was killed?"

"A couple of Chinese guys. They didn't give me their real names. They introduced themselves as Mr. Smith and Mr. Jones, and they told me I was about to become the owner of a house that I was going to buy at auction with their money."

He won't look at me while he tells me this, though of course I know the reason why.

"They took me to a public auction and had me bid on a lot there. I did what they asked and we won the auction. They then handed me cashier's checks and I paid for it, signing the paperwork."

"When did you realize it was my house?" I ask, and his eyes flash up at me sharply.

"That's why you're here," he says.

"That's why I'm here," I acknowledge.

"Look, Harvey, I didn't know it was your house until after I'd made the purchase. I was riding back with the two guys and they told me I wasn't to sell the house, or do anything at all with it until they were done, at which point they would be gone and I could do with it whatever I wanted." He stops and shrugs. "It didn't make any sense, but who was I to argue? It sounded like I was going to get a free house out of the deal, which I could then use to pay off my debt to Dean and get out of my mess."

You and I both know there are no free lunches, I think but don't say. I'm pretty disgusted with my former best friend and the decisions he's made. Of course, you're probably saying that I've made some pretty poor ones myself and I shouldn't judge others.

And you'd be right. It still doesn't make me any less angry with him though.

"You haven't answered the question. When did you realize it was my house?"

"After they dropped me off back here. I pulled up the auction records online and saw that it was yours."

"Why? What the hell is going on here, Eric?"

"I don't know, Harvey. If I did, I'd tell you. I promise."

"Who ordered Tracy and Dillon's murders?"

"My God, Harvey, I don't know. You have to at least believe that much. If I knew that, I would have done something about it a long time ago!"

He has tears in his eyes and I think I believe him. His past deceptions leave me with some lingering doubts, of course.

"Have you heard the name Theo from any of these guys?"

Eric thinks for a minute and then shakes his head no. "Who's Theo?"

I don't know, and I don't answer him.

"I've been wracking my brain, Eric, trying to figure out what I did to incur the wrath of the mob guys or the Chinese. And I can't think of anything. I don't remember any incidents with either group. I don't remember any arrests I made on them. Why did they come after me? It was serious enough for them to have killed my wife and son, why can't I figure out what I did?"

"I don't think it was you, Harvey."

"What are you talking about? Who else would it have been?" I ask.

"I think it was something Tracy did."

Chapter 4

My stomach sinks. Something Tracy did? That seems impossible.

She was a geologist; what could she have possibly done to have earned a death sentence from some gangsters?

"Why do you say that?" I ask him.

"It was something one of the Chinese guys said on the way back from the auction. He made a call and when the other person answered, he said, "We got it. If she hid it in there, we'll find it." Remember, at the time I didn't know it was your house I'd just bought. I didn't make the connection until later."

What did these guys think Tracy had hidden in the house? I wouldn't believe Eric if I hadn't seen just a few days ago how they'd completely dismantled my house, all the way down to the bare walls and subfloor. This would also explain why they'd emptied my house of all belongings before they purchased it at the auction. They must have broken in and stolen everything in the house and then realized that in order to do a more thorough search, they were going to have to buy it.

But what could Tracy have possessed that would have possibly been worth completely wasting three hundred thousand bucks just on the off chance she'd hidden it in the house? To take on that expense, whatever it was, would have to be worth millions. What could she possibly have that was worth millions? It seemed impossible. How could she hide something like that from me? Why would she hide something like that from me?

"I need more, Eric. There's got to be more."

"That's all I know, Harvey. Honest, that's all I know. I have no idea what these guys are up to or what this is about."

Should I believe him? I want to, but I also don't want to be a chump. I stare at him and he stares back at me, his pitiful expression filled with sorrow. Or am I just seeing what I want and hope to see? Do you blame me for not wanting my former best friend to be a deceitful traitor?

I glance at the clock on the stove and realize it's time to go. Alexa will be returning soon and it seems Eric has no more to tell me.

I step over to where Eric's phone landed when he jumped off the couch and I grab it and slip it into my pocket. Holding the gun on him, I walk backwards through the kitchen to the sliding glass door. Reaching behind me, I unlock it and then slide it open.

"Eric?"

He frowns at me. "Yeah, Harvey?"

"Do me a favor. Don't move for a while. I seriously considered shooting you when I came here tonight, but I've changed my mind. Don't make me change it again by doing something stupid."

I don't wait for his reply. I step through the door, then close it, watching him through the glass. He doesn't move, staring back at me, an expression on his face that seems full of sadness and regret. I turn and take five quick steps to the masonry wall that separates his yard from the street. Holstering the gun, I plant my hands on the top of the wall and boost myself over it, landing softly on the sidewalk on the other side. I immediately turn and begin jogging, putting distance between myself and Eric's house. As I round the corner, I recognize Alexa's car coming toward me. She doesn't so much as glance at me as she passes, oblivious to my presence as she turns down their street. I pick up the pace.

I don't know if Eric will call the police to report me or not. I want to believe what he's told me, but I'm not foolish enough to risk my freedom and my safety on that desire. By taking his cell phone, I've delayed his ability to call the police, but with Alexa arriving home, he might be making the call right now. If he does call, he's going to get a full and immediate response from all available units. They'll come in force and they'll bring a police dog, possibly a helicopter. There are only a few ways to avoid a tracking dog, and one of the only surefire ways is to create distance.

I pause just long enough to dump Eric's phone into a sewer. I then take the plastic water bottle out of my pocket and walk over to a recycle bin that's on the curb. The water bottle would have made a nice little silencer for the pistol, but I'm relieved I didn't need it.

Now I continue running, crossing Green Valley Parkway, wanting to get a major thoroughfare between myself and Eric's house. If the police are coming, they'll be setting up containment: parking patrol cars in a circle around Eric's place, lights flashing, blocking the major intersections, the goal being to get me to go to ground, to hide somewhere. Hiding is what most criminals do, and it's pretty damn tough to hide from a tracking dog. That's a great way to not only get arrested, but to also get some flesh torn from your arm or leg when the dog finds you. If I can move faster than they expect me to move, I can be outside the containment area. The police will move the containment wider as time goes on, and they'll also start a roving containment if they have enough units, and a helicopter with a search light and forward looking infrared, known as FLIR, will also make things more difficult, but distance will be my friend. Run now, hide later.

I continue to move, now in a straight line, trying to get as far away as possible, listening for sirens and watching for flashing lights. I hear nothing and I see no police cars, and eventually I slow down to a jog, then to a walk. I'm breathing hard, sweating in the still, hot air of the summer evening despite the arid conditions. It's still early and traffic is busy, and now's the time for me to blend in with the other pedestrians, hiding my scent among the many others who are out tonight.

After fifteen minutes, I begin to relax. If Eric had called the police, I would have heard sirens by now, would have seen and heard police cars rushing to the call. Just as I'm feeling confident that I'm safe, I hear a siren approaching and I see flashing lights in the distance coming toward me. My heart starts pounding, and I step off the sidewalk, walking into a parking lot, preparing to duck behind a parked car. The siren and lights get closer and I relax again as an ambulance flies by, running through the red light at the intersection and turning left, the noise from its siren fading as it speeds away.

I wander around for the next thirty minutes, making random turns but moving in a direction away from the vicinity of Eric's house. I'm probably being more cautious than I need to, but prudence is why I've lasted as long as I have.

Eventually, I find a bus stop and hop on the next arriving bus, paying a buck fifty and watching the driver carefully. If Eric did call the police, they've had enough time to get my description out to every bus driver. He gives me barely a glance, his expression unchanging, and I settle in to a seat near the back, not caring about the direction the bus is traveling, just wanting to relax for a minute and think.

For more than two years now, I've assumed Tracy and Dillon's murders had something to do with me – something to do with my job as a police officer. For the last month, I've been focused on the Italian mafia and the Chinese *14k Triad*. Now, thanks to Eric, I have a new line of thinking. Could this have been something Tracy was involved in?

On the surface, it seems ridiculous. Tracy was a geologist who worked for the United States Geological Survey. She mostly worked out of an office, supervising the work of other geologists and mineral surveyors on her team, occasionally traveling herself to areas around the western part of the United States to conduct her own surveys. I know that much of her work involved identifying and monitoring fault lines and ground shift as part of an effort towards building an earthquake early warning system.

Of course, she was also tasked with locating and identifying sources of mineral deposits for the government, and that leads me to thinking something else: Could this be about gold? Could Tracy have discovered some previously undiscovered gold deposit and kept the information to herself? This seems absurd, though, after I think about it a bit more. I don't know a lot about gold mining, but I do know that most, if not all of the easily and readily available sources of gold in the western United States have already been located and exploited. Sure, mining companies may discover new

249

veins, but they find those in established mines deep underground. A novice gold miner may find a new, small, source high in the Rockies or the Sierra Nevadas, but it's not going to be something so significant that it would draw the attention of the Chinese and organized crime.

As unlikely as this seems, I think I need to set aside the doubt and make a few assumptions: the first is that Eric is telling me the truth, the second is that the "she" he overheard the Chinese guy talking about in the car was actually referring to Tracy, and the third is that Tracy discovered something in the course of her work as a government geologist, and that she held something relating to that discovery. If these are true, then the Chinese must think that whatever it is she possessed was hidden in our house. They didn't find it in the belongings that they carted away, or had the mob guys cart away, so they decided she must have hidden it somewhere in the house itself.

So, what could she have hidden in the house itself?

It would have to be small. The Chinese work crew had completely gutted the house searching for it. They'd dismantled the walls and the floors which tells me they hadn't found whatever it was they were looking for. If Tracy had hidden it under the carpets or behind the kitchen cabinets or anywhere else that was easy to locate, the crew wouldn't have needed to continue ripping up the walls and floors. They would have stopped when they found it, which means they hadn't found it.

If they didn't find it in the house, then where could it be?

The "what" I may not know, but the "where" I should be able to figure out. After all, I knew Tracy better than anyone. If I make the assumption she did indeed hide something of value, then who better than me to be able to figure out where she might have hidden it?

I stare out the window of the bus and realize the sun has gone down and darkness has settled in over the valley. The bus is approaching downtown Las Vegas and I decide to get off. I won't be meeting Allen for a few hours still, and the five-mile walk back to the house we're staying in will give me some time to think. I exit the bus at the next stop, the driver completely ignoring me again.

As I walk, I think about where Tracy might have chosen to hide something. I try to ignore what the object might be, and instead focus on where it might be, but that proves to be tough. Without knowing what it is or how big it is, how can I know where it is? It has to be small and not easily identifiable. If it was a twenty-pound gold nugget or something ridiculous like that, the murderers wouldn't have bothered removing everything from my house.

I wrack my brain as I walk, conceiving of and discarding ideas. Could she have had a safety deposit box that I wasn't aware of? Could she have left it with a friend, left it at her work, her gym locker? These things would have been thought of by the people searching for it. They wouldn't have gone to the extreme measure of buying and ransacking my house if the answer was this simple.

By the time I've reached Sahara and the ramp to I-15 where I meet up with Allen every night, I've still not been able to figure out anything useful. Allen isn't on the ramp and I walk around peering into the shadows for him. Sometimes, when he has a good day panhandling, he'll wander into the Denny's restaurant and order a few things off the 99-cent menu. I check the restaurant and don't see him. I check the AM-PM gas station in case he stopped there to get water or use the restroom. He isn't there either.

I'm beginning to get worried. In the few weeks that we've had this routine, Iverson has always met me, always been waiting anxiously for me. It's not like him to be gone. I walk under I-15 and check the other onramp, as well as the offramp. Nothing. I check the nook between the overpass and the earthen berm, in case he's decided to crawl up there and take a nap. No sign of him.

I walk rapidly back to where he was supposed to have sat out the day. Despite the late hour, cars whiz by me, ignoring me, unaware of my unease that's slowly turning to panic. I stand on the shoulder of the onramp, spinning around, trying to figure out where he might have gone. Suddenly I notice a piece of cardboard. It's flattened up against the wooden post of the guardrail, possibly blown there by a car as it accelerated up the onramp, held there by the post until another gust of wind from a slightly different direction might send it tumbling down the slope toward the back of the AM-PM. I walk quickly to the cardboard and grab it. Scrawled across it in shaky handwriting are the words:

Homeless Veteran – anything helps. God bless you.

This is Allen Iverson's sign, and I know he wouldn't abandon it willingly. Without any real way to easily recreate it, he's careful with it, always keeping it under his shirt, careful not to bend it too much or to lose it.

My gut sinks with near panic. If Allen fled for some reason, leaving behind this sign, I might never find him. There's a small part of me that feels relief at the thought of him being gone, the burden of caring for him lifted from my shoulders. I'm just being honest with you, but I instantly feel awful about it and I quickly bury those selfish feelings. I need to find him.

I step over the guardrail and hop down the slope, dirt and rocks tumbling away below me as my feet dig in to the soft dirt. I feel a rock slip inside my shoe, poking irritably into my sole. I ignore it and cut through a shallow drainage ditch, stepping onto the asphalt behind the AM-PM store. There's a dumpster back here, as well as a stack of pallets, several tall stacks of milk crates, and a bin nearly full of cardboard. It's dark back here, the store blocking most of the light from the street, and I don't feel up to stumbling around in the dark, so I call out to him.

"Allen? Allen, are you back here?"

There's no answer at first, and then, just barely audible, I hear: "Sandman?"

Relief floods through me and I step forward peering into the darkness for him.

"Where you at, Allen?"

"Here. Behind the dumpster. Get back here, quick. They're out there, man," he answers, just loud enough for me to hear.

I step behind the dumpster and see him. He's sitting, knees bent up, just barely visible in the gloom as my eyes adjust. I crouch down next to him.

"What happened, Allen?"

"They found me, Sandman. They found me."

In the dim light, I can see streaks on his face where he's been crying. His body shakes, his eyes are wide, and he's hugging his knees, rocking slightly back and forth.

"Relax, buddy. I was just out there. There's nobody around. Tell me what happened."

He stares at me. "You sure? You sure there's no one out there?"

I nod and touch his shoulder. "I'm sure. It's clear. You got away and they've moved on."

He nods and seems to relax just slightly.

"They found me though, Sandman. I saw them. They was watching me, then they started toward me. I ran."

I nod at him. "You got away though, Allen. They're gone. What do you say we head home?"

He glowers at me a moment, then nods. "If you're sure, Sandman. Only if you're sure."

I tell him that I'm sure, and we walk around to the side of the store, Allen shadowing me. I glance back and see him scanning the darkness, tense and alert. I ask him if he's eaten tonight and he tells me he hasn't. A customer pumping gas stares at us and I stare back at him until he looks away. We walk into the AM-PM and ignore the dirty stares from the clerk. I take Allen to the cold case and grab two large Gatorades. I then order burritos and corndogs from the clerk, and pay for it all with a twenty, bemoaning the expenditure but needing to get Allen calmed down and fed. We take the food outside and start walking to our house, Allen looking around carefully between bites, calmer but still watchful.

His paranoia has worsened and I'm worried. He's going to need some medication, and if he was truly a veteran, I could take him to the VA to get checked out. He claims to be a Vietnam vet though, and I know that can't be true, which makes me doubt that he's a veteran at all. That means no free healthcare and no medication for his paranoia and his delusions. Which means caring for him is only going to become more difficult at a time when my own life has become more complicated.

There are some tough choices coming up, and I'm worried about the decisions I'm soon going to be forced to make.

Chapter 5

I'm dreaming again, but this time I know I'm dreaming. It's the

same dream as before, though it starts in the hallway of my house

this time. The walls are blurred, shifting, almost ghostly. The light

at the end of the hallway is beckoning, yellow but tinged with red,

and I know why it's tinged with red. It's a warning, and in this

version of the dream, I know what the warning is. I know what I'm

going to find if I walk to the end of the hallway. My understanding

is almost a conscious understanding, even though I know I'm

asleep and dreaming. I even know what this is called, a lucid

dream, and I laugh to myself as I realize that.

I have a choice this time, apparently. I know what happens if I walk

down the hallway toward the kitchen. I know that means death for

Tracy and Dillon. So instead, I turn right and walk into the

bedroom.

Our bed is there, made up neatly, decorative pillows stacked in a

way that only a woman could possibly appreciate. The dresser sits

in front of the bed, a large mirror attached to the back of it, and I

see myself in the mirror. It's the younger version of myself of

course. The version that doesn't have two years of living on the

street etched into every line on his face. The version that was

happy. Of course, I understand that the happiness for this Harvey

Conner is about to come to a screeching halt. I understand that what has been done cannot be undone, and it saddens me.

I start to turn and something catches my eye. It's a piece of paper, sticking out from behind the mirror. Only the corner of the page is visible, and I walk over to it and start to pull on it. As I pull, words begin to appear. Bold, black letters in a large font. The words read, "**Chinese 14k Triad in Las Vegas.**" *Below that is a list of names. Theo is written at the top of the list, and his last name is listed as well, but the letters are indecipherable and I can't read them. I scan down the list and realize that I can't read any of the other names either. I wonder if this is what the Chinese were searching for, but that doesn't quite add up. Before I can puzzle it out any further, I hear a moan behind me.*

I turn around and see Allen lying beside the bed. He's in his sleeping bag, his Iverson jersey just barely visible, peeking out of the bag. He's asleep and he moans again, tossing back and forth. I frown, wondering why he would be intruding into this private and personal dream. As I stare at him, I hear a loud bang, followed by shouting voices.

I whip around, dread pulsing through me, thinking the shots that killed Tracy and Dillon have been fired despite my attempts to delay them by refusing to follow the hallway.

"Hey, idiot." It's my reflection in the mirror, now my older self, my current self.

"It's not part of the dream. It's real life," the other me states.

"WAKE UP!"

I bolt awake, the dream fading rapidly as I hear another large *Bang*, the house shaking. I realize it's the front door and I see flashlight beams from the hallway at the same time I hear voices shouting:

"FBI, come out with your hands up! FBI!"

My stomach lurches and panic floods over me. I consider reaching for the gun under my sleeping bag, and just as quickly eliminate that option. They're coming down the hallway, and there's nothing I can do.

Allen wakes up and gapes at me, eyes wide, panic-stricken.

"Sandman…," he starts, suddenly cut off by the appearance of a flashlight and a submachine gun barrel, followed by a man, then several others, large letters that read **HRT** just visible on their chests, and under that, **POLICE**, all of them shouting loudly for us to get our hands up. I see a red dot appear on Allen's chest, followed by another, and then several more on my own chest. I'm still in the sleeping bag, but I slowly and carefully raise my empty hands.

259

"Okay, don't shoot!" I yell, terrified for both Allen and for myself.

The men swarm us, roughly shoving me to the ground, one of them planting his knee on my back as he wrenches my arms behind me. I feel a set of plastic cuffs zip closed firmly around my wrists, cutting off my blood supply and making my hands go numb. Beside me, Allen is screaming and fighting, and I turn toward him.

I'm now panicked for him. I've only wanted to protect him and now I've led him to his worst fears. He's being arrested, caught up in my crimes by doing nothing more than associating with me. His greatest fear has come true and I'm despondent over the impact this is going to have on his fragile psyche.

"Leave him alone!" I shout to the officers. "He hasn't done anything! Get off him!"

"Shut up," one of them yells at me. They get Allen's arms behind his back and fasten another set of plasticuffs to his wrists. He's screaming, sobbing, and attempting to pull his legs up into the fetal position. My heart breaks for him. I'm sorry for the pain and the damage this will cause him, the wretched expression on his face causing me to tear up.

"I'm so sorry, Allen," I yell to him.

"I told you to shut up!" the officer shouts to me. I glare up at him, marking him, angry at his lack of empathy.

"Search 'em," one of the officers growls to the others, and they pull us both from our sleeping bags, dumping us on the ground beside them and searching our pockets. We're both wearing clothes, our backpacks against the wall to the side of the room. One of the officers finds my David Sands ID in my back pocket and hands it to the officer who appears to be in charge.

"David Sands, huh?" he asks with a sneer. I know the reason for the sneer, but I say nothing. They know who I really am of course, but there's nothing I can say that will help me out. The officer also finds my envelope of money, opening it up and showing it to the officer with my ID. He stares at me for a minute and then orders it returned to my pocket. I'm surprised by this but don't say anything.

"No ID on this one," says one of the officers searching Allen.

"That's okay, we don't need ID for him," the officer who's clearly in charge answers. "Search the backpacks."

They tear open our bags and rifle through them, the officer searching mine finding the wrapped figurine and tossing it aside.

"Be careful with that!" I scream at him, and the pressure on my back increases as the officer on top of me digs his knee in deeper. The officer at my backpack tosses my clothes on top of the figurine, then finds my laptop. He tosses that aside too, seemingly uninterested in it which surprises me. In Allen's bag there's almost nothing beyond some dirty clothes and a few trinkets that the officers examine closely before returning to the bag. I'm sure they'll search the sleeping bags next and that they'll find my gun, but surprisingly they don't. The officer in charge glances at his watch and then turns back to the other men.

"We'll take them both with us until we can sort out why they're together. Leave their belongings here; let's move out."

This entire thing feels rushed but I'm too dazed to figure out why they're moving so fast. They roughly stand us both up and force our shoes onto our feet. Allen's head hangs and he doesn't gaze at me, even when I call out his name.

The officers line us up and march us to the front door where I see that the sky to the east is just starting to lighten with the rising sun. The pre-dawn raid. The modus operandi of raiders since the time of the Vikings, or maybe earlier. I'd participated in several of those myself in the past. The time when suspects are most likely to be sound asleep, and it worked perfectly in this case, as it always has throughout history.

There are two black vans parked in the driveway and the officers shove us roughly to the sliding door of one of the vans. I suddenly realize that these are not Las Vegas Metro officers. I was too overwhelmed, having been woken with such a start, but I realize now that they were yelling out FBI when they stormed the house, and the letters on their chest read *HRT* which I happen to know stands for the FBI's elite Hostage Rescue Team. I've been completely unaware that my fugitive status has reached the attention of the FBI.

As they shove Allen and me into the van, I realize that it must have been my implied flight over state lines that had brought my case to the FBI's attention. Still, there should have been an LVMPD presence at the scene of my arrest, and their absence is both surprising and a bit disturbing.

Allen and I are forced to lie on the floor of the van, unable to see where we're going. The men guarding us sit on benches against the wall of the van and say nothing.

"Where are we going?" I ask one of them who stares at me but doesn't reply.

"He's not part of this, let him go," I say, motioning with my head toward Allen who lies motionless, his eyes closed.

"Shut up," the agent replies, and I do.

My focus has been on Allen and his reaction to this arrest, but I suddenly realize what this means for me. The end of everything. I'd begun to feel that I was making the smallest amount of progress

263

toward finding my wife and son's murderers and now it's at an end. My arrest means the end of my investigation, and nobody out there is going to believe my story that some shadowy figures in the Chinese and organized crime underworlds were the actual culprits. My proof is missing and nobody is there to step up to take my place. My heart aches at this realization. Not so much for myself, but for justice that's now been denied for Tracy and Dillon.

They still have to convict me of course, but the evidence against me is pretty significant. Not only that, but even if they don't convict me, I'll be held without bail through the trial which could be a year or more down the road. Judges don't tend to look too favorably on defendants who've been fugitives for two years when it comes time for the bail hearing.

Not only that, I have no money and no assets to leverage in order to hire an attorney, which means, barring some miracle where a pro-bono attorney steps up, it's a public defender for me.

Yup, my future appears bleak indeed, and as that realization sets in, depression comes with it. I close my eyes, and mourn silently, my thoughts on Tracy and Dillon.

The van comes to a stop, and the door slides open. I open my eyes at my captors' prodding and step out of the van into a sally port, its tall walls topped with coils of razor wire. They push Allen out beside me and then march us to a door with letters that read *Las Vegas Metro Police – Spring Valley Area Command.* I frown at the realization that they've not brought me to the Clark County detention facility for booking, but I quickly realize that doesn't matter. That will be my final destination regardless of where I'm going to start this journey.

One of the agents pushes a button near the door and speaks into the intercom. The door buzzes and they escort us through. I glance at Allen, trying to catch his eye, but he seems to be in a trance. His eyes are glazed and unfocused, his expression set. He's checked out, his mind somewhere else, and my own seems to be trying to go the same place. I can barely focus as we're brought inside. Someone frisks me thoroughly, removing everything from my pockets, including my David Sands ID card and all of my remaining money. They also take my shoes and my belt. My handcuffs are removed and I'm pushed into a holding cell, the door slamming behind me.

The holding cell contains a cot with a thin, green, plastic-coated mattress and a stainless-steel toilet with no lid or seat. There's nothing else. The walls are made of cinderblock, painted white, and the floor is concrete, sloping from all sides toward the middle where there's a drain. There are stains on the floor, vomit, blood, shit...who knows what. Years of bodily fluid accumulation that nobody cares to expend more than a token effort cleaning.

These cells are designed to temporarily hold suspects for interrogations before they're booked into the actual jail located downtown. The cell is about six feet by six feet and the cot takes up almost half of it, running from front to back with the toilet next to it against the back wall. I walk shakily over to the cot and sit on the lumpy mattress. There's no pillow, so I lean against the wall and close my eyes.

The cell is bright, a fluorescent light inset into the ceiling casting its sharp glare down onto me, the light piercing even my closed eyelids.

I wonder how long I'm doomed to sit in this hellhole. I'd take a cell at the Clark County jail over this place. I've booked suspects into the jail a hundred times. It's not as bad as this.

I hear the cell door next to me slam shut and hear footsteps walking away. Standing up, I walk to the door which has a thick, plexiglass pane about one-foot square inset near the top. Just enough for a jailer to peer through before opening the door, a safety feature against violent and desperate criminals.

"Allen!" I call out.

Nothing.

266

"Allen! You there?"

Still no answer.

I sit back down on the cot and wait. Right now, officers will be calling the LV Metro detectives who worked the case of Tracy and Dillon's murders. They'll be coming to interrogate me, which will be a complete change from my interactions with them two years ago. Those were called interviews. There's a very subtle, yet critical difference between an interview and an interrogation.

The press will be notified, I'm sure. They'll send reporters outside the police department to talk live on the air about how the man who murdered his family (Allegedly. They'll use the word *allegedly*, or the word *accused*, but the viewers will only hear *the man who murdered his family*) and has been on the run from police for these last two years has finally been captured.

I'm amped up and I can't sit still, so I stand up to pace. Two steps up the cell and two steps back down. I quickly get dizzy from the turns that are too close together and I sit back down.

I'm going to need an attorney, but I won't be able to afford one. Maybe the money I have remaining will be enough to get me started with one? You're probably laughing right now and you're right. I have only around $1500 left. That won't even be enough to get a good criminal attorney out of bed.

I walk over to the door again and try to get Allen's attention. He doesn't answer and I'm miserable for him. His severe mental problems have led him to be deathly afraid of any interaction with the police and now I've managed to get him arrested, his only crime his proximity to me. Unknowingly associating with a wanted felon. When the detectives arrive, I'll refuse to talk to them until Allen is released and delivered somewhere safe. Maybe to the shelter downtown. They'll want badly enough to hear what I have to say that they should be willing to accommodate me, especially with such a simple request to release an innocent man who's done nothing wrong.

I sit back down on the cot and close my eyes, a futile attempt at rest. A few minutes later, I hear footsteps coming back toward my cell. I open my eyes and see a man peer through the glass. The door bolt slams open with a loud *thunk* and the cell door opens.

"Sands," the man says, gruffly. "Come on out."

I wonder why they're still calling me Sands, but I step out. The jailer directs me down the hall toward the booking area. He doesn't put handcuffs on me and that also seems strange. As we pass Iverson's cell, I try to get a peek inside, just an attempt to see his face, to make sure he's okay. I catch just a glimpse of him through the small, barred window. He's crouched in the corner, his knees pulled up to his chest, arms around them in a fetal squat, his face buried. The jailer pushes me before I can see more or call out to him, and we continue on.

We reach the booking area where the booking officer sits behind a desk. The lead FBI guy from the arrest is sitting there also and he glances over at me.

"Put him in the interrogation room please, officer," he says, nodding his head toward one of the two interrogation rooms that leads off the booking area.

The officer directs me to the first one and opens the door, motioning me inside. The interview room is nicer than the jail cell, but only marginally. A desk with a chair on each side awaits. The walls are padded with some sort of acoustic tile, designed to make conversations less likely to be overheard. Can't be having anybody overhear the snitches snitching. The only thing missing from making it appear like a low-budget TV set is a two-way mirror, but I do notice a camera hanging from the ceiling, pointed at me as I take the suspect's seat against the wall.

Two minutes later, an FBI agent comes in. He hasn't identified himself yet as such, but I can instantly tell the type. Smug and arrogant. I have no doubt he'll also be condescending as soon as he opens his mouth. He's in his late thirties, dressed in a brown suit with a blue tie that's littered with wrinkles, as if he's just pulled it out of a suitcase. Which doesn't make a lot of sense because the FBI has a large office here in Las Vegas, so any agent assigned to my case should be a local.

He sits in the chair across from me. "I'm Special Agent Nick Trahillo with the FBI. I have a few questions for you and I need you to answer them honestly. Do you think that's something you can do?"

See? Condescending. What a surprise.

I consider asking for a lawyer right then, but decide to simply stare at him instead. If I ask for a lawyer, they'll probably throw me back in the cell, so I might as well milk it a little here in the interview room. I can also probably get some coffee and food if I play it right. Might as well make the best of it I suppose.

I don't say anything and he takes a deep, impatient breath.

"Look, Mr. Sands, you do speak and understand English, right?"

I'm wondering why he's continuing to call me Mr. Sands, maintaining this farce. There must be some end-game behind this, some interrogation technique or psychological warfare aspect behind allowing the continued use my moniker and not acknowledging my real name.

I smirk at him and decide to answer. "I speak English, yes."

"Good. So, how long have you known Irvin Wallace?"

I've never heard the name Irvin Wallace. I think for a bit, trying to figure out who that might be, but I draw a blank.

I shrug. "Never heard of him."

Trahillo shakes his head in annoyance. "You were just arrested with him. You were sleeping next to him. Now you're going to claim you never heard of him?"

I frown. He's talking about Allen Iverson? Suddenly everything starts to click, to fall into place, the fog of my early morning, abrupt wake-up call beginning to recede. The agent's continued use of the name David Sands, the agent on the scene of the raid saying they didn't need ID from Allen, the disregard of my laptop and other belongings when they grabbed us from the house. Could it be possible this isn't even about me? The agent at the house had said to take both of us in and I'd thought he'd been considering leaving Allen behind. Could it be that they had considered leaving me behind?

I'm thinking quickly and Trahillo is staring at me impatiently. They haven't fingerprinted me which means they ran my David Sands ID and nothing unusual returned. It's expired, yes, but apparently the real David Sands renewed the ID without reporting it missing. I
271

don't look like the picture at all, but apparently the FBI hasn't cared enough about me to notice the discrepancy. Or is this all just a sham, a big con to give me false hope, some kind of interrogation technique that I've not yet considered?

"I never knew his real name," I eventually tell him. "I knew him only as Allen."

The agents certainly heard me call him by that name at some point, so it seems logical to admit to that much. I'm feeling cautiously optimistic here, but careful not to show too much, not to tip off the agent and make him dig a little deeper into me. I'm also careful not to get my hopes up too much, lest they be dashed by this being a con.

"Okay. How long have you known him?" he asks.

I shake my head. "Not long. I met him just a few weeks ago. I was squatting in the house where you arrested us and he was homeless. He asked if he could stay there with me. I said yes. That's it."

Irvin Wallace. Allen Iverson's real name. I'm stunned, mostly by the fact that it's beginning to appear that there actually were agents out to get him, that he really was being hunted by people. I seem to keep getting fooled, to keep jumping to conclusions without questioning things further, and I have no doubt you're wondering how bad a cop I must have been with this kind of naïve stupidity. I'm starting to wonder the same thing.

"Did Mr. Wallace ever say anything to you about his previous life? Anything about where he came from or what he did before you met him?"

I shake my head. "No. We never talked about any of that." This part is actually true, though I do know that Allen claimed to have been a Vietnam vet and to have seen things that the government couldn't allow him to see and continue living free. At the time, I just thought he had severe mental issues. Now I'm beginning to wonder.

"He never said anything to you about why he was homeless, why he was on the run?"

I shake my head again. "He never talked about it. None of us ever does. Have you ever been homeless, Agent Trahillo?"

The condescending smirk is back. "Of course not."

"Well, those of us who do live on the streets don't ask too many questions. We mainly want to be left alone, to live our lives. And some of us, like Allen or Irvin or whatever his name is, need help. He has pretty severe mental health issues. I hope you're going to get him some help."

"Unfortunately for Mr. Wallace, things are going to get worse for him before they get better," he replies.

"What did he do, anyway?" I ask, still trying to come to terms with the idea that this arrest has nothing to do with me. I realize that the longer I'm here, the more likely they'll be to question my identification.

"I'm not here to answer questions Mr. Sands, I'm here to ask them," he says.

"Well, I don't have any answers for you, Agent Trahillo. I barely knew the guy, but I do know that he needs help, and if he did something wrong before I met him, it was not the same guy. This man I know as Allen wouldn't hurt a fly."

I say this tongue in cheek of course, as I watched Allen beat two men to death with an iron pipe just a few weeks ago.

Trahillo studies me for a minute and then exhales sharply in annoyance. "Thank you, Mr. Sands." He walks to the door and opens it. As it closes, I hear him say, to someone out of my sight, "He doesn't know anything. Let's kick him loose."

I'm in shock. I can't believe it, and the cynical part of me is sure they must still be making some play here. I don't want to get my hopes up, but another agent comes in and tells me to follow him. I step back out to the booking area where the Metro officer hands me my shoes and my belt. I put those on and he hands me a plastic bag that contains my David Sands ID card along with my envelope of cash. I shove them both into my pocket.

I'm still waiting for the hammer to drop—still waiting for the FBI agents to say, *"Haha, just kidding. Harvey Conner, get back in here, you old murderer you!"* But it doesn't happen. The booking officer asks me if I need a ride anywhere and I mumble an answer about being fine without one, and they send me out the main door and into the scorching heat.

I stand there for a minute, blinking in the sun like an owl who's just been shaken awake in the middle of the day. My senses are reeling from the temperature difference between the heavily air-conditioned building and the midday desert heat. After a few seconds, I start walking, resisting the urge to run, maintaining a calm expression though I'm actually shaking. I clear the parking lot and turn left on Durango, checking behind me every few steps, expecting pursuit which never comes. I find a bus stop at the corner of Durango and Desert Inn, and get on the first bus that appears, not caring about its direction of travel or destination, only caring to put distance between myself and the bear trap I've somehow managed to escape. I settle into a seat and try to calm my nerves as the bus driver releases the brake with a hiss and the bus rumbles away.

Chapter 6

An hour later, a different bus drops me off in Henderson near

Eric Townsend's house. I walk directly to his house, not bothering

with any of my old furtive moves. His truck isn't in the driveway,

but I don't expect it to be. I know he's at work today and that he

rotates days off starting tomorrow, which factors in nicely with the

plan I've started to piece together on the bus ride.

I walk right up to the door and ring the doorbell. From inside the

house, I hear a voice yell, "Coming!" It's Alexa's voice, and she

opens the door, a half smile on her face. I wait. It takes her about

three seconds before the smile disappears.

"Harvey?" Her mouth gapes open, her eyes wide.

"Hi, Alexa."

"Oh my God, Harvey. Are you okay?"

She's not acting. Nobody is this good at a spontaneous, ad hoc

performance like she would have to be putting on if she had any

idea I was in the area, or that I'd visited Eric the previous evening.

That meant that he hadn't told her anything.

"I'm sorry to drop in out of the blue, Alexa. I need to talk to Eric and I know he's working. Would you mind if I come in and we could call him together?"

She nods and steps back quickly. "Yes, get in here, Harvey, get out of this heat. How are you? Are you okay?"

I step into the cool house, relieved to be out of the sun. Alexa's face shows genuine concern, and it's apparent that she hasn't yet considered the fact that she's currently committing a felony by aiding and abetting a known fugitive. At one time, before the murders, Tracy and I had been good friends with Eric and Alexa, and she apparently still remembers that. She also apparently still believes in my innocence, and that's a good thing for me because I'm going to be needing her help.

"I'm okay, but I'm kind of in trouble and I need your help, Alexa."

"Okay, Harvey. What can I do?"

"First, can I get some water?"

"Oh my gosh, of course." She runs into the kitchen and fills a large glass of water, bringing it back to me. I'm parched from the sun and from my walk and I drink it down at once. Alexa fills it back up for me and then offers me a seat at the kitchen table. I sit in the same chair I'd used the night before.

Can you call Eric, please?" I ask.

She nods.

"Make sure he's somewhere private, where nobody can overhear your conversation."

She walks over to her cell phone on the kitchen counter and picks it up, hitting a few buttons and holding it up to her ear. I consider asking her to put it on speaker, but I want to trust her and I want her to see that I trust her. I need to establish two-way trust between us for what I have in mind. I also need Eric to know that I trust them both, even though I certainly don't trust him yet. If he follows through for me today, then I will, but not until then.

Eric answers and Alexa tells him she needs to talk to him and asks him if he's somewhere private. Now I motion for her to put the phone on speaker and she does.

"Okay, nobody's around, what's up, babe?" Eric says through the speaker.

"Eric, it's me, don't say anything, don't say my name," I say to him.

"What are you doing? If you hur..." He's about to threaten me, worried about Alexa's safety, and I understand why. I did hold a gun on him for an hour just the other night, but I can't have him saying anything that would put Alexa on the defensive or make her suspicious.

"Eric," I cut him off, "I know you're surprised to hear from me and I'm sorry to drop in on you guys unannounced like this, but I need your help. Will you help me, Eric?"

There's no immediate answer and a frown appears on Alexa's face until Eric finally replies, "Of course. What do you need?"

"Two men were arrested this morning. They were arrested by the FBI, but they were taken to Metro's Spring Valley precinct. Their names were David Sands and Irvin Wallace. I need you to find out everything you can about Irvin Wallace. Why he was arrested, what his crime was, what's happening to him next, where he's going to be booked, everything."

"Okay, that should be easy enough," he replies.

"Good. I'm also going to need a car. Do you guys mind if I borrow Alexa's car for the day?"

I study Alexa while I say this and she nods immediately. I smile at her, grateful. I actually feel my eyes start to water as I realize the risk she's willing to take to help me. It feels good after so much time alone to be able to ask for help at last.

Eric answers that it's okay as well, and I motion to Alexa to stay still while I take the phone and walk into the other room, taking it off speaker. When I'm out of earshot of Alexa, I tell Eric the three other things I need from him. It takes me a little while to explain exactly what I need, but when I'm finished, he's agreed to help. I hope that Eric isn't going to backstab me, that he truly feels remorse for his previous actions, and that he's going to follow through for me today. Am I being a fool to put my trust in him? It's possible, and I'm risking everything right now, but I no longer have a choice. The time for discretion has come to an end and it's time to start taking risks.

I hand the phone back to Alexa and she says goodbye to Eric then gets her car keys for me. She takes two bottles of water from the fridge and asks me if I want anything to eat. I spy a banana on the counter and ask if she minds if I take that. She jumps over to it and hands it to me. I eat it quickly, and we then go out to the garage and she takes a few things out of the car. She gives me a hug and tells me she's missed me and she prays for me every day. I appreciate that and I feel my eyes welling up again. I need to leave before I break down. I'm feeling immense pressure right now but I can't take the time to share anything with her, nor can I afford the risk that telling her everything would take. I'm putting a lot of eggs into one basket right now, but I'm not going to put them all in.

Alexa opens the garage door and I start the car. It takes me a moment to get used to the feeling of being back behind the wheel of a car. It's been more than two years since the last time I drove, but it all comes back to me quickly as I back out of the driveway and head toward I-215.

It's already after 11am, and I'm in a bit of a hurry, but I drive carefully, following the traffic laws, slowing down for the construction zone on I-215 even though all the other motorists are zipping by me. My Sands ID held up earlier today, but that was probably only because the FBI agents were almost entirely engrossed in Allen Iverson and their interest in me ended with what I might know about him or what he might have told me.

I take the exit for I-15 and follow it past the famous Las Vegas Strip, north to Charleston Avenue where I exit, taking the side roads to the house where Allen and I had been staying. We're clearly done with this place, its usefulness having come to an end with the FBI raid, and I go inside for just long enough to grab all of our belongings including our backpacks and sleeping bags and my gun, of course, which I slip back into my waistband. Throwing everything into the car, I lock up the house, leaving things just as we found them when we first began squatting there.

I head back south on the 15, exit at Flamingo and head east, crossing Las Vegas Boulevard and turning into the large office complexes off Howard Hughes Parkway. A cul-de-sac of high-rise buildings and lush green grass surrounded by towering palm trees, this area is an oasis of wealth in the middle of the poverty of east Las Vegas.

Alexa's white Lexus coupe fits in nicely here among the cars of the upper middle class, and I navigate to a tall glass and steel tower at the back of the complex finding a parking spot where I can see the front entrance. I glance at the clock on the radio and see that it's almost noon, which is perfect timing.

As I rode the bus from the police station to Henderson this morning, my thoughts were divided between Allen/Irvin's problems and how I could help him, and my own problems and how I could solve the mysteries of what happened to Tracy and what she'd been involved in. Allen was going to have to wait until later, unfortunately. I needed to work on my own issues.

And that work was going to start with Tracy's former best friend, Vanessa Marquette.

If Tracy had been involved in something that got her killed, and she'd told anybody at all about it, that person would have been Vanessa. Inseparable best friends for the last decade, Tracy would have almost certainly confided in her. There are two big problems, however. The first is that I would have thought she would have also confided in me, which could well mean she chose to keep everything to herself. The second is that Vanessa almost certainly thinks I'm the one who murdered Tracy and Dillon.

Confronting a woman who thinks I murdered her best friend definitely has risks but, as I mentioned, I'm at the point where it's time to take those risks.

The office building in front of me houses numerous businesses, the largest of which is a casino risk management company called Gemini Risk Management, and this is where Vanessa works. Or at least where she worked two years ago. Employee turnover in Vegas is high in general, but Vanessa was in upper management here at Gemini and I'm hoping she's still here.

I sit in Alexa's car with the air conditioning going full blast, waiting and enjoying this rare commodity and the barely-remembered feeling of being cool in the middle of summer.

Just after the dashboard clock registers noon, people begin coming out of the front entrance to the building, some heading to their cars, others heading out on foot, on their way to the numerous restaurants that ring the plaza and service all of the employees who work here. I spot Vanessa almost immediately. She exits the building and starts walking at a fast pace down the sidewalk away from me.

I jump out of the car and hustle up behind her. I want to get close to her, but not so close that I'll cause her to bolt or to scream out in alarm. When I'm about ten feet from her with nobody between us, I call out.

"Vanessa!" I say, not too loudly, not wanting to scare her or draw attention to us. She turns and glances back, a half-smile on her face, searching for the person who called out to her. She's not on guard in any way, nor should she be, considering it's a beautiful sunny day and she's walking within view of many of her co-workers.

I take a few steps closer to her as her eyes settle on me, and then stop. I don't want to seem threatening by getting too close. She doesn't immediately recognize me.

"Vanessa, it's me. Harvey. Please don't run, I need to talk to you, I need your help. Please." I hold my arms out, palms facing her in a non-threatening gesture that lets her see I'm hiding nothing. Nevertheless, she immediately takes a step back, holding her purse to her chest, her eyes wide.

"Please Vanessa. You must know I didn't do it. You must know I could never do that. Please tell me you know that."

I'm pleading with her and my expression is earnest. My eyes are tearing up as well, and it's not an act. I need her to believe me.

I needn't have worried. She steps toward me and then grabs me in a bearhug.

"Oh my God, Harvey, it's really you."

She steps back and holds my face in her hands, peering up at me. Vanessa is about 5'6" tall and she's wearing heels which make her slightly taller. She's also wearing tight black jeans, a dark green top, and a black, fitted, lightweight sport coat. She has dark brown hair that falls down past her shoulders in soft curls. If I remember correctly, she must be thirty-five years old or so. I also notice a large diamond ring on her left hand that wasn't there when I last saw her more than two years ago.

"God, Harvey, you look so different. I wouldn't have recognized you. What's happened to you? You've changed so much and you're so thin!"

Her eyes are filled with concern, and that makes my own tear up even more.

"It's been a rough couple of years, Vanessa," I say, trying not to cry. Her concern and the love in her face is overwhelming. "But the gray hair is mostly artificial and the beard is just so I'm not recognizable."

285

"Oh my God, where have you been? What's happening?"

"Can we go someplace and talk?"

"I'm on my way to lunch, are you hungry?" She steps back and studies me again. "What am I saying? Of course you are. Look at you, you're so skinny. Come on."

She grabs my hand and leads me down the sidewalk and toward the Panera Bread restaurant that's just around the corner. We go inside and I excuse myself to the restroom to wash up. When I come out, Vanessa has just finished paying. She directs me to a table in the corner and then goes back up to the counter where she grabs two sandwiches and two large lemonades.

"Eat this," she says, setting the sandwich in front of me.

The sandwich is chicken salad and I take it gratefully, digging into it with gusto. When I've finished the first half, I glance up at her.

"You don't know how much it means to me that you're willing to talk to me, Vanessa."

She swallows a bite of her own sandwich and takes a sip of her lemonade. "Tracy was my best friend and she loved you. I love you too, and I was devastated when, after everything happened, you had to run."

"I didn't do it, Vanessa. You know that, right? I didn't kill them?"

"Of course I know that, Harvey," she says, staring into my eyes. "I never believed it for a second. After you fled, the police came to interview me. I screamed at them for a good thirty minutes telling them they were wasting their time pursuing you when the real murderers were still out there. They wouldn't listen to me, didn't believe me."

I nod. I'm incredibly grateful to Vanessa and it feels unbelievable to just have one solid person I can rely on after so much time on my own. I think humans are meant to be able to rely on one another, to not have to go through this life on their own, and for the last two years I've had nobody. I saw a quote once that read, *"Without a family, man, alone in the world, trembles with the cold."* That's been me, and the love I'm feeling from Vanessa is finally beginning to thaw me out.

That being said, I still don't blame the detectives for turning their attention to me. They'd done a blood draw on me the day after the murders, and there'd been no trace of any kind of drug in my system. I still had the tiny pinprick on my neck where I'd been stuck with the needle, but it was deemed inconclusive and easily faked anyway. I had a small knot on my head where I'd hit the floor, but other than that, there was no physical evidence to corroborate my story. No fingerprints were found in my house other than ones that should have been there, no hairs or DNA was found that would incriminate anybody else. And, a trace amount of gunpowder residue was found on my hands and clothes. I'd had no explanation for that. I'd not fired a gun in weeks, so that discovery weighed heavily against me.

But, in spite of all this, Vanessa believes me. And that gives me immense feelings of gratitude and relief.

"Why did you run, Harvey? We could have fought this together, so many of us would have stood with you."

I let out a short, bitter exhale of breath and shake my head slowly. I'd considered staying but at the time, the thought of going to jail and preparing a defense while the murderers remained free with nobody after them had seemed unbearable. I would have gone crazy being locked in a cell, unable to pursue leads. Unbeknownst to me at the time, living as a transient and hiding from the police was almost the same thing, or possibly even worse than being incarcerated. I leave the last part out and try to explain the rest to her, and she seems to get it.

"But still, it was terrible for many of us when you fled. It felt like we'd lost all of you, although there were some who looked on your flight as evidence that you were guilty."

She says this last part with anger in her voice and I tell her I don't want to know any names. I don't want to judge my old friends for those beliefs in a time of great sorrow for so many people. I also don't want to know what Tracy's family or my own thought of me, for that matter. I hadn't been close to them anyway and only rarely saw or spoke to them even before the murders. Disappearing for two years didn't change much in that area.

"So, what's changed, Harvey? Why are you back? Why now?"

I take another big bite and chew it before answering. "I found the guys who pulled the trigger, Vanessa."

Her eyes widen and I tell her about witnessing the murder of Jerry Bastain, tracking down Joey Panattiere, and finding the figurine. She remembers the little statue well, and she's astonished by my story. I skip most of the details but tell her I was able to track Reggie to a downtown warehouse where I confronted him and he confessed to Panattiere and him being the triggermen. I tell her he died—not by my hand—before I could find out more. She seems as if she's about to ask more information about that but then changes her mind.

"The problem is, I don't yet know who ordered the killings. I know who hired Joey and Reggie to do the killings, but not who hired the guy who hired them. And I don't know why, but I do know this goes way up somewhere and that it was some kind of big conspiracy."

Vanessa and I both take another bite of our sandwiches and then she says to me, "Harvey, Tracy told me, shortly before her murder, that if anything ever happened to her, I should tell you it was the Chinese government." She gets a sad expression on her face. "She laughed after she said it, and I thought it was a joke. We were at a happy hour and she'd had a few drinks. I asked her about it afterwards and she told me she'd just been kidding around."

"Why didn't you tell me this?" I ask.

"I was in too much shock after her murder. Then you disappeared so quickly. I did tell the police when they questioned me, but what did I know? The detective wrote it down but I didn't have anything more to go on."

The Chinese connection has been obvious to me recently, but Tracy had used the words, "Chinese government." I ask Vanessa if she's sure Tracy had said, "government," and she confirms that's what she remembers her saying.

"How could Tracy have been involved in anything that has ties that high? All the way to the government?" I ask her in disbelief.

"I don't know, Harvey, I only know that's what she said. Like I said, I didn't think much of it at the time because she told me she was joking, though I did think it was an odd joke to tell, and it was said out of the blue."

We bat this around for a while, but come up with nothing else. I tell her about my house going up for auction and about the two Chinese guys who bought it, leaving Eric's name out of the story. I then finish by telling her how I watched my old house get completely demolished inside and my theory that they were searching for something. I then tell her that the Chinese think Tracy may have hidden something inside the house.

Vanessa frowns as she chews a bite of her sandwich before replying. "Hidden what?"

I shrug. "That's what I don't know. I can't figure out what she could possibly have hidden, but I think it may have had something to do with her job."

"She was a geologist, Harvey. She filed reports on fault lines and tested rocks to see how old they were. What could she have possibly known that would have gotten her killed?"

I tell her I don't know and then mention the idea that Tracy might have found a gold source or other precious metal supply.

Vanessa seems doubtful. "Maybe, but is it likely she found a vein of gold large enough to have somebody kill her for it? And wouldn't it have belonged to the government anyway, if Tracy had found it while she was working?"

"I think so. I'm not sure," I reply, plaintively. This conversation with Vanessa is bringing back a flood of memories, times we all shared together. I shake my head to clear it of the distracting memories.

"Vanessa, if these guys think she hid something, and they didn't find it in my house, they might start checking with her friends. Has anybody approached you, or anything suspicious happened lately?"

She frowns again while she thinks. "Not that I can think of."

"You haven't noticed anybody following you, watching you, any suspicious cars in your neighborhood, anything like that?"

She shakes her head. I finish the last bite of my sandwich and then motion toward the ring she's wearing.

"Did you get married?"

She grins and holds up her left hand. "Yes! Just a month ago, Harvey! He's a great guy, his name's Brian, I can't wait for you to meet him! I had just started dating him when Tracy...," she trails off, the smile fading from her face. "But of course, you can't meet him, can you?"

I shake my head. "I can't take the risk, Vanessa. I'm a fugitive wanted for a double murder. I hate to ask you this, but I need you to not say anything to your new husband about seeing me."

She nods, slowly and sadly, then stares down at her plate for a bit, pushing the crust of her sandwich around without saying anything. I'm quiet too, lost in my own feelings of sorrow and loss. Tracy had been trying to fix Vanessa up for years, wanting nothing more than for her to settle down and to start a family, have kids that could grow up with Dillon and the future children we'd have together. All things that would never happen now.

"I'm so happy for you, Vanessa. He must be an amazing guy and I hope to be able to meet him someday."

She smiles and then directs the conversation back to Tracy and her work. We bat around a few more ideas while we finish our meals. Eventually, Vanessa checks her watch and says she needs to get back to work. We leave the restaurant and I walk back with her, both of us lost in our own thoughts as we move quickly along the tree-lined path, the sun beating down mercilessly from directly above us.

"Have you checked with her attorney? If she did hide something, maybe she hid it with him."

I stop suddenly and stare at her. "Her attorney?"

"Yes. Don't tell me you didn't know she had an attorney?"

I'm quiet, shaken by this. The secrets I've been recently discovering about the woman I thought I knew so well. She had an attorney? It seems so underhanded, so deceitful, so unlike her.

"What kind of attorney? Who is it?" I ask her.

She thinks for a second. "His name is Rosenthal or something like that. He works right here in my building. I think he's a contract attorney or something like that."

Vanessa goes on to tell me about the day a year or so before Tracy's murder when she ran into her in the lobby of her office building. Tracy had at first been somewhat coy and secretive, but had eventually told Vanessa she was there for a meeting with her attorney regarding some contracts she'd needed reviewed.

My mind is spinning and I'm having difficulty reconciling the woman I'd known with the woman who'd been meeting in secret with an attorney. I resist the urge to ask the questions I truly want to ask Vanessa. The questions that would come to your mind too, if you found out that your wife was secretly meeting with an attorney, as well as hiding other things from you. I won't give voice to the doubt, won't dishonor her memory with the pall of suspicion that's rearing itself in my head. I won't spout out the words, but I can't help the expression that must be on my face, the expression that causes Vanessa to stare at me with care and compassion.

"Harvey, Tracy was not cheating on you and she was not leaving you. I know that's what you're thinking. I don't know why she was keeping secrets from you, but I can tell you, with one hundred percent certainty, it's not what you're thinking. I would have known, I promise you that."

Her words make me feel better but at the same time, make me feel guilty for even thinking such things. I push aside the shame and guilt and nod to her. "I think I need to see this attorney. Can you show me his office?"

She nods and we continue toward her office building. When we reach it, we go into the welcome air-conditioning, and Vanessa leads me over to a board in the lobby where there's a list of tenants listed in a plexiglass shadow box. Vanessa's company, Gemini Risk Management, is the largest of the companies, taking up three entire floors of the eight-story building. There are two lists, one an alphabetical list, the other by floor. Vanessa points to a name on the alphabetical list.

"Here he is, Rosenberg, not Rosenthal."

I see the name, *G. Andrew Rosenberg*, followed by a placard that reads, *Attorney at Law*, and then his suite number, *210*.

295

I nod and then thank her again for meeting with me and for lunch.

"Hang on a sec," she says, running in her high heels over to a podium where she grabs a piece of paper and a pen and writes something down. She then digs into her purse with her back turned to me before coming back to where I'm standing.

"Here," she says, handing me a piece of paper and some cash. "This is all the money I have at the moment, but I can get more for you. I've also written down my cell phone number and my office number; please call me if you need anything." She sees me start to shake my head, start to push the cash back to her. Her hands come up. "No way, Harvey. I won't take it back. It's not much anyway, less than two hundred bucks. You need it and you can't even tell me you don't. I want to get you more too, I have plenty of money to spare, so please call me, any time. I'm here for you, whatever you need."

My eyes are tearing up again and I quickly hug her and thank her, stuffing the money and the paper with her numbers on it into my pocket. I then turn quickly to the elevator and get on one with a group of people that has just arrived, probably returning to work from the lunch hour. Vanessa gets on with us, and I hit the button for the second floor. We don't say a word as the door opens and I step off, turning back to make eye contact with her as the door closes on the crowded car. We don't say anything, but we don't need to. I can see the love on her face, her eyes glistening with tears as the doors close, and that means more to me than any words she might have said.

Chapter 7

I'm standing at the reception desk in the offices of G. Andrew Rosenberg, Attorney at Law while the receptionist speaks quietly on the phone, her back turned toward me so that I can't hear what she's saying. When I arrived, I'd asked to see Mr. Rosenberg, and of course she asked if I had an appointment. When I told her I didn't, she told me that I needed an appointment and that she would be happy to make one for me for the next week. This wasn't going to work for me, so I told her I was there regarding a client of Mr. Rosenberg's who'd been murdered, and that it was quite urgent I speak with him immediately.

She'd asked for my name, but I refused to give it to her, telling her I would speak only with Mr. Rosenberg. Everybody loves a good murder mystery, and I had a hard time believing that I would be turned away without an audience. I'm proven correct when the receptionist hangs up the phone and gave me a pleasant, though clearly annoyed, half smile.

"Please have a seat, Mr. Rosenberg will be available shortly."

I thank her and sit in one of the comfortable leather armchairs in the waiting area, basking in the luxury of the soft padding, thinking to myself that one of these chairs, which you would consider a terrible alternative for a night's sleep, would make for a more comfortable bed than I've had in years.

There's a coffee table in front of me with a neat stack of law journals and periodicals, as well as the requisite collection of top ten magazines. The receptionist is eyeing me suspiciously, so I intentionally scatter the pristine display while pretending I was only trying to get to the latest National Geographic.

There's a sticker on the magazine that reads, *G. Andrew Rosenberg* along with the address of this office building. I thumb through the magazine, not actually reading the articles, just making a clumsy attempt to mask my nervousness. I keep waiting for the outer door to spring open and a police officer to walk in, called by the receptionist while I'd thought she was talking to Rosenberg. After what seems like a long time, the receptionist's phone buzzes and she answers it, then hangs up without saying anything.

"Mr. Rosenberg will see you now," she says stiffly. "Please follow me."

She stands and walks down the hallway without glancing back. I follow her to a door with a frosted glass pane stenciled with Rosenberg's name. She knocks once and then, without waiting for a reply, opens the door and motions me inside. I step into a spacious office and the receptionist closes the door behind me.

A man, G. Andrew Rosenberg presumably, stands to my right, his back turned to me as he pours a thick, viscous concoction of some sort from a blender into a tall glass. When he turns around, I see there are chunks of green and red blobs floating in the creamy liquid. Rosenberg is wearing dark blue warm-up pants and a white, long-sleeved t-shirt with the name of a charter fishing company from Costa Rica. He's in his late fifties but appears fitter than I did in my prime. Clean shaven with short, gray hair, he seems every bit the professional, despite the workout attire.

To my left is a large wooden glass-topped desk, clear of papers or debris, a black leather blotter and dual computer monitors the only objects on the desktop. There's a large brown leather chair behind the desk, and two slightly less comfortable leather armchairs in front of it. I stare at the two chairs, thinking to myself that Tracy probably sat in one of those chairs at one time, wondering what it was that could have possibly brought her to this office. With that thought, I turn back to Rosenberg who is standing with his back to the bar, studying me carefully while he sips his drink from a large plastic cup.

"Can I get you anything? A smoothie perhaps?" he asks, a quizzical expression on his face.

"No, thank you."

"You sure? They're amazing." He holds up the cup so I can see the smoothie better. "All the superfoods blended together with a ton of protein powder and a scoop of peanut butter. Delicious." With that, he takes another large sip.

"I'm sure, thanks anyway."

He nods and stares at me a moment longer before motioning to his desk. "Won't you have a seat?"

I sit, relishing the feel of the soft leather. Rosenberg sits in his large chair, the smoothie in his left hand.

"Well, you managed to get past Angie without an appointment, which I think is a first. Mind telling me which of my clients has been murdered?"

"My wife. Tracy Conner." I watch him closely for any sign of recognition, but I see nothing. He takes a sip of the smoothie and then studies the ceiling for a moment.

"You're Mr. Conner, I presume?"

I nod. "Harvey."

"Well, Harvey, I'm sorry for your loss. Maybe you can tell me what your wife was seeing me about and what exactly I can do for you."

"I'm hoping you can tell me why she was seeing you," I reply. "Maybe you can look up her file?"

He smiles. "That's not how it works, Harvey. Client confidentiality extends even beyond death."

"Look, Mr. Rosenberg..."

"Call me Rosie, please," he interrupts.

"Okay, Rosie. Look, two years ago my wife and toddler son were murdered. The murderers have never been found. I'm trying to find them and I just recently discovered my wife was a client of yours shortly before her murder. I'd appreciate if you could help me in any way at all."

His eyebrows go up and he stares at me a moment.

"Let's say I do remember this." He stares at me sharply. "If I remember correctly, the police think you're the one who killed them."

"Yes, they do," I answer simply.

"Yet I can't help but notice you seem to be conspicuously un-incarcerated."

"I'm a fugitive," I reply. I've decided to be honest with him in an attempt to earn his trust and hopefully get him to tell me why Tracy hired him. As I reply, though, I start to wonder if maybe he'll feel the compulsion to turn me in. "Speaking of client confidentiality, is our conversation privileged?"

He nods. "Yes. But you should know that I'm not a criminal defense attorney. And if you're a fugitive, I do have some legal obligations that might override privilege. Let me ask you something, why do you think you're a fugitive?"

I shrug. "Well, the police are searching for me and I'm on the run."

"How do you know the police are looking for you?"

"A friend," I answer, vaguely.

"If you haven't officially been notified by law enforcement or the courts that there's a warrant for your arrest, then you're not a fugitive. You didn't flee across state lines, did you?"

"No, I've been here in Las Vegas the entire time."

"Then you're definitely not a fugitive. You've simply been taking some alone time to deal with your grief."

That seems like a lawyerly way to put it. And it doesn't change my status—I'm still wanted and I'll still be arrested by the first officer who realizes my actual identity. But it does help with one thing.

"So, if people I know have helped me, they can't be charged with anything?"

He shakes his head. "No, not with aiding and abetting a fugitive. You're not a fugitive. They could potentially be charged as an accessory after the fact, but that's almost impossible to prove in a situation like this. Any reasonably competent attorney could get a charge of that nature dismissed."

I smile slightly in spite of myself. I'm relieved to know that Vanessa can't get in trouble for helping me, and that I might actually be able to rely on her help again. And, to a lesser extent, Eric and Alexa.

Rosenberg is staring at me without speaking, and I stare back at him. Eventually, he takes another drink of his smoothie and then leans forward and pushes a button on his phone.

"Yes, Mr. Rosenberg?" the voice of the receptionist comes through the speaker.

"Angie, please pull the file for Tracy Conner and bring it to me. It's going to be from two or three years ago."

"Yes, sir," she replies.

He glances back at me. "Do you have any identification with you?"

I shake my head. "I'm on the run from the police. Carrying identification seems like a bad idea."

"How do I know you are who you say you are then?"

I shrug. "Perhaps you can pull up my picture online. I was in the news pretty extensively two years ago and my picture was all over the internet. My appearance is a little different today, but I think you'll be able to tell."

He slides a keyboard out from under the desktop and types a few things on it, staring at the monitor that I can't see from where I'm sitting. He glances back at me, then back to the monitor again before sliding the keyboard back from where it came.

"Okay, I'm convinced you are who you say you are. I have to tell you, I only vaguely remember your wife, and I can't say anything further until I review the file. Even then I may not be able to say anything to you about her case, is that clear?"

I nod. "It is. But you should know that anything you can share with me will be helping to potentially bring her murderers to justice."

"Unless, of course, the murderer is you," he replies, softly.

His words raise my ire, but I push it down and remain calm. "If you believed that, you wouldn't be helping at all," I reply.

He shrugs. "I have no reason not to believe it. And, I've found that the police are usually correct when they think someone has committed a crime. But, I can't say whether or not I'll help you until I review the file and refresh my memory I need you to wait in the conference room while I do that. When I'm done, I'll let you know what I can share...if anything."

I nod, and Rosenberg escorts me to the conference room where he closes the door. I see Angie walk by a few minutes later with a manila folder in her hand. I stare at it wistfully as she passes by the windows of the conference room. Whatever secrets Tracy had are contained in that folder, and I desperately need to know what they are. I lower my head and take a deep breath, willing my heartbeat to calm, preparing myself for a long wait while Rosenberg reviews the file.

The minutes tick by slowly, and I feel myself nodding off. I stand up and walk around the room to stay alert. I'm nervous, as I'm sure you understand. After about fifteen minutes, Angie opens the conference room door.

"You can come back now, Mr. Conner."

She's holding the file folder in her arm and I can see the edges of several sheets of paper. She sees me staring at it and she curls it up to her chest protectively.

"Mr. Rosenberg's waiting for you in his office, sir," she says, glaring at me suspiciously.

I nod to her and walk back down to Rosenberg's office where he's waiting behind his desk. A few sheets of paper are stacked in front of him, face down on the desk. He motions for me to have a seat in the armchair.

He doesn't make me wait. "I've reviewed your wife's file, Mr. Conner. I'm inclined to share a few things with you. Mostly because Mrs. Conner left specific instructions that I could share this information with you if you should ever show up asking."

I smile. The relief I feel is tremendous. The idea that Tracy had thought of me despite hiding things from me is uplifting. Yet, it seems to me Rosenberg should have made some effort to find me after Tracy's murder. I mention this to him.

Rosenberg leans back in his chair and stares at me a moment before replying.

"You know, Mr. Conner, I'm a contract attorney. I have thousands of clients. Your wife hired me for one specific task, and it was more than a year before her murder. I met with her one time for about an hour. When I heard about her murder on the news, I recalled that the name was familiar, but nothing more. I can't be expected to check my files with every murder in this town to see if the victim was ever a client."

He's defensive, and I don't want him that way. I nod. "I didn't intend that, nor would I expect it, Rosie. Please continue."

He nods. "One of the things I specialize in is mineral rights. And that's what Mrs. Conner hired me for."

My eyes widen. *Mineral rights?*

"She told me that she wished to retain me for potential future representation on a mineral rights claim that she owned. She said she had no intention of doing anything with the mineral rights at that time but that she anticipated she'd need me at a future date.
307

We signed a contract, and she left the original assay report on the land with me."

He leans forward and picks up the papers lying face down on his desk. He glances at the top one and then holds them toward me. "This is a copy of that report. The original will remain with her file."

I anxiously grab the papers and begin scrutinizing the first one. Rosenberg sees my face and remains quiet while I read.

I've seen mineralogical surveys on numerous occasions when Tracy would bring her work home, but I'd never bothered to learn how to read one. This one is full of numbers and bar graphs that mean little to me. I flip through the pages, scanning for words I recognize, simple words like *gold* or *silver* or *uranium*. I see none of these. Instead I see words such as *Bastnäsite, Cerium, Lanthanum, Neodymium, and Gadolinium*. I've never heard of these minerals, yet they appear numerous times throughout the report, along with other, similarly unfamiliar names, with percentages and concentrations listed next to them. The entire report is written in a scientific vernacular that is way over my head. I eventually glance up from reading the report to see Rosenberg staring at me.

"Does it mean anything to you?" he asks.

"Nothing. Have you read it?"

"I glanced at it. I'm a mineral rights attorney, but I've never heard of most of the minerals listed there. Most everything I do in this field has to do with precious metals, gemstones, or oil. Around here, it's mostly gold or silver, a little platinum. I'm not an expert on the minerals themselves, just in the law around claims and property owner rights."

I can see that I'm not going to be able to interpret this document myself, and I have a thought. I flip back to the front page of the document and read the heading. Directly under the USGS logo and the contact information for the Las Vegas regional office is Tracy's name, email address, and office phone number. Under that is a subheading that lists the name of the agent who conducted the survey and authored the report. It reads, *"Erin Fogler, Lead Mineralogist."*

I smile as I realize I know this name. I've met Erin on several occasions, most recently at the company holiday party just a few months before Tracy and Dillon's murders. Erin will remember me and hopefully, she'll help me interpret the report.

"Did Tracy tell you where this survey was done? What area it was for?"

Rosenberg shakes his head. "Not exactly. In my notes, I'd written down that she owned the property though, and that it was located up north in Washoe County."

I sit back in the armchair and smile slightly. Washoe County is where Lake Tahoe is located. It's also where Tracy and I bought a piece of land a few years before her murder. She'd picked out the property, had in fact told me she'd discovered it while she was doing survey work. It hadn't even been for sale, but Tracy and I had flown up there one weekend and contacted the owner, asking if he'd consider selling. He'd been reluctant but had finally offered a price. Tracy had convinced me that we should buy it, and I'd gone along, mostly because we were using funds she'd inherited following her mother's death the year before, and I felt she should be able to spend that money however she wanted. We'd paid cash for the property, with plans to build a cabin and possibly a retirement home at some time in the future. That future had been abruptly interrupted when she'd been gunned down, along with my little boy, but the pieces were finally beginning to fall into place. The picture was still fuzzy, but it was becoming clearer with each new lead.

Even though I don't know what the minerals listed on this report are, I feel that I have the *why* of Tracy's murder at last. I need to work a bit more on clearing that up, then discover the *who*, but at last I have a good lead and a good place to start. I also know exactly where to go from here. Erin Fogler was a top mineralogist for the USGS, and even if she's no longer employed there, she shouldn't be too hard to find.

Before I can do any of that though, I have one more important thing to do. Irvin Wallace, AKA Allen Iverson, needs my help. Even though I'm not the one who got him arrested, I'm not about to leave him stranded. I know him as well as anyone, and he's not going to survive his captivity. I don't yet know what crime he's committed, but that is one of the things I asked Eric to look into. Assuming he has some answers for me, I'll make a plan for how to help Allen.

With the report in hand, I thank Rosenberg for his time and his help, and he shows me out of his office.

Part Four

Chapter 1

"Irvin Wallace was wanted by the FBI for treason and violations of the espionage act. He's been on the run for more than eight years."

I'm sitting in the living room at Eric and Alexa's house. After I left Rosenberg's office, I drove to Henderson where I stopped at the library to use a computer. I pulled up the USGS website and searched for Erin Fogler only to discover she wasn't listed as an employee in their Western Division office. They don't list all the employees of course, but Fogler had been a director when I'd known her before, and she should have been listed. I'd used the phone at the library (something much easier to do since I've cleaned myself up) to call the office, and a nice receptionist had been kind enough to inform me that Fogler had transferred two years prior to the Southwest Division office in Dallas.

I have about as much chance of getting to Dallas to see her as I would of getting to Paris to see her.

Nonetheless, I called her office in Dallas and talked to her assistant who told me Erin is currently on a field assignment in Flagstaff, Arizona, and won't be back until Monday. She wouldn't give me a phone number for her but did offer to take a message and pass it on. I declined and hung up.

After that, I returned to the Townsends' house where Alexa was waiting for me. She made some snacks for us and we sat in the kitchen making small talk while we waited for Eric, all of which seemed abnormally normal. By that I mean I remember a time when this sort of thing would have been normal for me, but it feels almost dreamlike and wrong in this moment.

At one point, Alexa offered me a beer, and while the idea of a cold beer sounded amazing to me, I turned her down and asked for water instead. I felt proud of myself for that decision.

When Eric arrived home, he'd done the things I'd asked of him earlier, which restored a bit of my faith in him. Not to mention, he didn't arrive with a S.W.A.T. team, which of course, was also a big plus.

So, here we are, sitting around the living room as if I haven't been on the run for the last two years, living in grief on the streets of Las Vegas. Like I said, abnormally normal. Eric is telling me what he discovered about Irvin Wallace who I know as Allen Iverson.

"I tried to find out exactly what his crime was, but nobody I talked to seemed to know, or at least they didn't want to tell me. It all seemed quite hush-hush. I actually spoke to the FBI Special Agent in Charge here in Vegas but he wouldn't tell me much, just that there were federal warrants for him. Then he started asking me why I wanted to know, what was the reason for my interest and such, so I decided I better get off the phone."

That wasn't very helpful, and I'm wrestling a little here with my conscience.

I want to help Allen but, at the same time, if he's truly a felon and possibly a dangerous one, it might be best if I don't try to help him. Quite a little dilemma wouldn't you say?

"One other thing," Eric continues. "I was able to find out from a Metro buddy that they're moving him first thing tomorrow morning. He's scheduled to be checked out of the holding cells at the Metro substation and transported by the FBI, with Metro's help, to Henderson Executive Airport where they're flying him somewhere. I wasn't able to find out where."

Well, that explains why they took us to the nearest holding cell as opposed to booking us into the Clark County Detention Center. They'd had no intention of holding me and hadn't wanted to book Allen into the Clark County jail since they were arranging transport elsewhere.

Eric and Alexa both seem relaxed and at ease with me. It's obvious that Eric hasn't yet had a conversation with Alexa about his activities, but I'm not inclined to be the one to fill her in. As of right now, he's making up for it by helping me, and I need a few more things from him.

"Any return on those plates I gave you?" I ask Eric. I'd given him the license plate numbers from the Escalade that night at Dominic's warehouse and the one that came by my house for a few minutes every day during the demolition.

"Yes. Both of them return to 2013 Cadillac Escalades. Looks like they were both leased at the same time. They're registered to a company called QTZ West Holdings, LLP. The address on the reg is a mail forwarding company here in Henderson. I tried to dig a little further into QTZ West, but I didn't have any luck."

That was fine, it was probably a dummy corporation anyway. These guys were just too slick to not have several layers between them and the public face they presented. I'd have to do some serious digging, maybe even hire a private detective, to follow the paper trail and find the owners. Before I went to that trouble, I had other leads to follow and more important things to do.

"Did you get the phone for me?" I ask.

He nods and pulls a cell phone from his pocket.

"Here you go. It's activated from a prepaid credit card and will be good for a month. The number's on a sticker on the back. It's a Vegas number."

"Thank you." The cell phone is going to be necessary for the things I need to do in the next couple of days.

"Harvey," Alexa asks, a glimmer of concern in her eyes, "what's going on? Have you figured out who killed Tracy and Dillon?"

"Not yet. But I'm working on it and I'm getting close. I just need a few more days, I think. Which brings me to the last thing I asked you to do, Eric. Are you guys all set to leave?"

Alexa shoots a sharp look in his direction but Eric ignores her.

"We're all set. I have a three-day weekend, but to be honest, I don't want to leave, I want to stay and help you."

"Where are we going, Eric? What's going on here?" Alexa asks.

"Honey, I'll explain everything to you, I promise. We're just going away for the weekend. Can you go pack a bag, please? I promise I'll explain everything soon."

It's a lame deflection, but I do understand that their conversation is one that needs to happen in private, between the two of them. Regardless, Alexa gives him an angry glare over his dismissive tone and appears about ready to blow up at him. I interject before she can.

"I'd love for you to stay and help, Eric, but you know as well as I do that you can't do that. It would be too dangerous for you guys, and you'll be helping me a lot by leaving. Alexa, will you do this for me? Please?"

She pauses a moment and then gives me a sharp, abrupt nod, walking out of the room without saying anything.

When I told them that being out of town will help me, what I actually mean is that Eric and Alexa being out of town will give them plausible deniability. My plan has the potential to have serious consequences for Eric, and I want to give him the best possible chance to get out of this trap he's in without ruining their life. I do feel a little bad about what I'm about to do and the fallout that's going to land right on his head but, again, he put himself into this position and he owes me. It's time for me to collect a little on that debt.

When Alexa is out of the room, Eric leans in closer.

"Harvey, Dean Scofield called me today. He said he wants to chat. He's coming by tonight around nine o'clock."

I nod, slowly. This complicates things, but it might also fit in well with what I have planned. In fact, I realize, if I do things right, Scofield showing up tonight might actually help me.

"You're done with him, Eric," I tell him. "It's time to step up and be a man. You know that, right?"

He stares at me a moment and I see his features harden. "You're right. I'll call him right now and tell him I'll get him the money when I can, but I'm done with him. I'm not going to help him with anything, anymore."

"Good, Eric. But don't call him. I need him, and his coming over here just makes things easier. You can call him Monday when you guys get back."

He agrees and doesn't ask me any more questions. I've told him about all I want to anyway. We sit there quietly until Alexa walks back into the room with a small roller suitcase. She's still clearly annoyed, but she tells Eric she's ready to go. He walks down the hall and I hear him quickly packing a bag.

"Can you at least tell me where we're going?" Alexa asks me.

"You're taking a long weekend down to Laughlin. You're going to have a great time. You guys will stay at a hotel, eat at nice restaurants, rent jet skis on the river, maybe see a show or two. You'll have a nice time and, when you get back, hopefully everything here will be resolved, knock on wood."

And, hopefully, there won't be an arrest warrant waiting for Eric, I don't add. I'm determined to keep him out of any trouble, but there is a small amount of risk.

Eric and Alexa gather their things and say goodbye to me. I don't walk them out, on the off chance a neighbor is watching, but I do watch them through the window as they get in Eric's truck and take off down the street and around the corner. Nobody follows them.

Chapter 2

It's almost nine o'clock, and I'm watching out one of the upstairs windows, waiting for Dean Scofield to arrive. In the five hours since the Townsends left, I've been busy, though I did find time to take a nice nap in their guest bedroom. I have to say, I enjoyed the luxury of a bed and a pillow, and I slept better than I have in a long time despite the stress of the last few weeks. I was exhausted though—it's been a long day, what with the early and abrupt wakeup call courtesy of the FBI this morning.

Not only that, but for the first time in my life I'm about to knowingly commit a slew of felonies—serious ones at that, and upcoming criminal activities apparently tend to make a person sleepy.

After my nap, I made a pot of coffee and some food from items in the refrigerator. It took longer than it might have otherwise, as I kept staring at the extravagant appliances, marveling in how long it had been since I was comfortable around them. Who knew a toaster could be such a wonder?

After the meal and coffee, I took a long, hot shower, shaving off my beard using a razor and fresh blade I found in one of the bathroom drawers. I also found a hair trimmer, and I used the number four setting to shave my head down to a crew-cut. It felt strange to see myself with no hair and no beard for the first time in more than two years. I spent a good amount of it staring at my face in the mirror, seeing how much I'd actually aged. Two years of spending nearly twenty-four hours a day exposed to the wind and the sun have taken their toll. I look a little strange, what with the tanned skin around my eyes and the white under the rest of my freshly-exposed face, but luckily the sun has had a chance to reach my skin for the last few weeks through my short-trimmed and dyed gray beard, so the contrast isn't too shocking.

After I was cleaned up, I raided Eric's closet, finding a Henderson Police Department polo shirt and a pair of Dockers that were both slightly too big, but fit well enough. I added a belt and then attached my own gun in its holster. I then raided Eric's patrol bag, attaching his badge to my belt, followed by a set of twin handcuff cases. A pair of socks and dress shoes, as well as a ball cap that says *Henderson Police*, and my outfit is complete.

I look every bit like a plainclothes police officer. Hopefully I can pass for Detective Townsend of the Henderson Police Department.

I'd like to use a different name, to deflect and separate responsibility from Eric a little bit, but I don't have a choice. The badge has his name on it and if anyone studies it closely—though I don't truly expect that—I need it to match up with the name I give.

I also gathered a few more things from Eric's including some clothes and some toiletries, and I tossed them all in a duffel bag which I placed in the back seat of the car. Allen's backpack and my backpack I put into the trunk, jamming them into the small space, hopefully without crushing my laptop.

Dean Scofield is late, and it's ten minutes after nine before a late model Chevy Camaro pulls up to the curb in front of the house. A white male gets out and scans carefully around the neighborhood. He's wearing blue jeanshorts and a white, V-neck t-shirt. I'm surprised to see he's young, somewhere in his mid-twenties. For some reason, I'd expected someone older. He's talking on a cell phone but disconnects the call shortly after getting out of the car. He appears to be around five feet ten inches tall and weigh somewhere in the neighborhood of 170 pounds. I've lost a lot of the muscle mass I once had over the last two years, but Dean Scofield doesn't look like he'll be too much of a problem.

As he walks up the sidewalk, I make my way down the stairs, arriving in the living room just as he knocks on the front door.

Arriving at the door, I call out, "Who is it?"

There's a pause, probably as he tries to figure out the voice, then, "It's Dean."

I draw my pistol and hold it in my right hand, hiding it behind my right leg so he can't see it. Then I open the door, pulling it quickly and startling him. I reach out with my left hand and grab a handful of his V-neck shirt, then jerk him into the house, sticking my foot out to trip him as he passes me. He falls to the ground, and I kick the door closed and jump on his back, sticking the pistol into the back of his head.

"Police!" I yell. "Don't move! You're under arrest!"

"What the fuck?" he shouts.

"You're under arrest. Get your hands out."

I grab his left arm and wrench it behind his back, holstering the pistol and pulling one of the sets of handcuffs from my belt. I snap it on his left wrist and then pull his right arm behind him, fastening the other side of the cuff.

"What's going on, man?" Dean asks, a whine coming into his voice.

"I just told you. You're under arrest." I pat down his lower back and then his jean shorts, pulling a pocket knife from his right pocket and slipping it in mine. I roll him over and finish the pat-down, then sit him up, his back resting against the back of the couch.

"Under arrest for what?" he cries.

"I haven't decided yet. We'll start with bookmaking and extortion. Maybe we'll end up with being an accessory to murder. I'll figure it out shortly."

Dean drops his head immediately and mumbles *oh fuck* under his breath. I have to admit, I'm disappointed. This is the guy who was able to extort a police officer? This whiny little bitch who didn't even put up a fight was able to get my best friend to turn on me? Disappointed isn't actually strong enough. I'm pretty disgusted.

I empty his pockets which contain his cell phone, a stack of cash that amounts to $740, some coins, a wallet, a lighter, and a piece of chewing gum. Keeping my eye on him, I step into the kitchen and grab a Ziploc bag, dumping all of his belongings into it. I'm tempted to take the cash. After all, what's a little theft once you've decided to impersonate a police officer and kidnap someone? Not to mention what I'm about to do. My moral compass isn't quite pointing due south yet, though, and I zip the bag closed with the cash still inside it.

I crouch down next to Scofield who's contemplating me warily, a mournful expression on his face.

324

"So, let's begin by talking about how you've been extorting a police officer over a gambling debt, and how you're involved with organized crime."

Now he frowns at me. "Aren't you supposed to read me my rights or something?"

I take a deep breath and contemplate the ceiling for a moment. I guess I might as well add assault to my charges. Lowering my gaze back down to his face, I punch him in the throat. Not hard enough to do any real damage, but it doesn't take much when the contact point is the soft, vulnerable flesh of the throat.

Scofield starts gagging, leaning forward and retching, struggling to breathe. I sit there on my haunches, watching him, waiting. It takes him about five minutes to catch his breath and stop choking, then he leans back, a fearful expression in his eyes, watching me and not saying a word.

"Let's get something straight. Have you heard of the Patriot Act? Nod if you have."

He pauses a moment and then nods quickly. I'm not surprised. Nearly every American is familiar with that contentious piece of legislation.

"Good. I'm with Homeland Security. You're under arrest under the Patriot Act. I'm trying to decide right now if you're going to jail

325

here in Las Vegas, or if you're going to be flown to Guantanamo Bay, Cuba, where you'll never see another friendly face again. You don't have any rights, you don't get to be silent, you don't get an attorney, and you don't get a phone call. Are we clear?"

This is all bullshit, of course, and I can hardly believe what's spewing out of my mouth. I mean, who would actually fall for this stuff? Dean Scofield, apparently. He nods again, terror on his face, and I'm disappointed once more in Eric.

"Now, Mr. Scofield, here are your choices. You don't have any rights, but you do have choices. The first option is that you can be honest with me. Absolutely and completely honest. If that happens, you'll go to jail for the night. You'll be released in the morning, and you'll end up going to court at some point in the future. A real court, with a real judge and your own lawyer, and all your rights intact. It's not you we're after, it's somebody else. Somebody you know. Cooperation goes a long way here at Homeland Security."

He's not a complete ignoramus, and I see him glance at my badge. "I know it says Henderson P.D. I'm a Henderson detective assigned to Homeland Security," I reply to his unasked question, cutting off that line of thought before he can get too suspicious. "Interagency cooperation and all that. If you don't believe me, I'll get some of the actual Homeland special agents here to convince you, but that won't work out very well for you, believe me."

He does. "Okay," he says. "I believe you." His voice is slightly hoarse from the punch to the throat.

"Good. Now option B, and I don't think you're going to like this option, but it is a choice. You decide not to talk to me, or you decide not to be honest with me, or you decide you're going to try to exercise some kind of right that you don't have, anything like that, and you still go to jail tonight. The only thing is, in the morning, instead of being released, you get transferred to Henderson Executive Airport where there's a nice private jet waiting for you. This jet is owned by the military, and it's scheduled to fly with one passenger tomorrow, nonstop to the beautiful Caribbean island of Cuba. Except you won't see anything beautiful because the window shades will be closed the entire flight and you'll be landing on a U.S. Navy base where you'll be instantly transported to a small cell." As I say this, I suddenly wonder if this is actually where Allen Iverson is headed tomorrow. I mean, I'm completely making this up on the fly here, but what if Allen was involved in something serious? What if that flight he's scheduled on tomorrow is actually headed to Guantanamo?

I continue. "I'd rather not describe what's going to happen to you in that cell because, quite frankly, those things are extremely distasteful, but I think you get the point. Do you get the point?"

He simply nods, a miserable expression on his face.

"Good!" I smile broadly at him. "So, which option would you like."

"The first one," he says, with no hesitation. I'm beaming with pride for him.

"Excellent. Question number one, and remember, the first time I think you're not being completely honest, we move immediately to option two. It's not a problem because everybody is completely honest once they've experienced option two for a little while." I don't know this firsthand of course, but I have to think it's probably true. "Question number one is... Who are Smith and Jones?"

By the time I've finished questioning Dean Scofield, it's an hour later, and full darkness has descended on Las Vegas. I've learned quite a few answers to questions that had been bothering me, connections that I hadn't had the information to be able to make. Dean was a bookie and a loan shark who'd been financially backed by Dominic Carvelo. When Eric had been unable to pay his sports betting debt, Dean had informed Dominic just as a matter of course. Dean had then put what he called "a normal amount of pressure" on Eric, which simply meant your basic bookie harassment: phone calls, text messages, lightweight threats, etc.

Then, one day about two years earlier, Dominic had called Dean in and told him that Eric was going to be allowed to work off the debt. Dean told me he'd been surprised, but that Dominic was guaranteeing the debt in exchange for Eric reporting in anytime he'd been contacted by one Harvey Conner. All of this was completely in line with what Eric had told me the night I confronted him at his house.

Dean filled in a few more blanks by telling me that after Dominic had been found dead in the warehouse, he'd been contacted by another of Dominic's associates and told he was wanted at a meeting in an office building downtown. When he'd arrived, he met with Mr. Smith and Mr. Jones, who were introduced to Dean as Mr. Nguyen and Mr. Ang. They'd told him he could continue to make money by occasionally working for them and that they wanted him to introduce them to Eric.

Dean had been present at the auction where Eric and the two Chinese *gentlemen* had purchased my house, though I hadn't seen him at the time. He told me he didn't know their first names or the name of whomever they worked for. With his honesty elsewhere, I tended to believe him.

He'd been sent to Eric's tonight to find out if he'd heard any more from Harvey Conner recently. He didn't seem to have any information about who I was or what I look like, and I was positive he had no idea that I was actually Harvey Conner.

He told me a lot of other information, mostly nonsense that was irrelevant to me, and keeping him on track was difficult. He was apparently incredibly anxious to avoid a prisoner transport flight in the morning and was a fount of information that would have been incredibly interesting had I actually been a law enforcement officer, but was nothing but background noise to me now. I eventually realized I had nothing more of value to learn from him, and I told him he was done.

Now, I stand him up and walk him outside, turning off the lights in the house and locking the door as we leave. I take him to Alexa's car and seat him in the passenger seat, then pull the seatbelt around him, locking it into place, his hands still cuffed behind him. I get in the driver's side; he shifts uncomfortably and then studies me suspiciously.

"Why are we driving the wife's car?"

I'd anticipated this question. "It's not the wife's car, Scofield. It's an undercover car. "The wife," as you call her, is an undercover officer." I'm really stretching things now, and my story has more holes in it than a horse trader's mule, as Slim Pickens might have said. Any more questions from him and it's likely to all fall apart, so I tell him to be quiet for the remainder of the drive.

You're probably wondering just what my plan is here. I'll just tell you that my plan is to rescue Allen. If you want to know exactly how I'm going to do that, well, I can't tell you. Mostly because I'm not quite sure myself. I have some semblance of a plan, but as far as the details? No friggin' clue. So many things can go wrong, and planning can take care of very few of them. I need to stay light and fluid, so I haven't developed a comprehensive plan.

No doubt your next question would be, why am I taking this risk? Why am I diverting from my true purpose when I'm so close to finally discovering the answers to the questions I've had for years? The answer is, I don't know why. I've come to care for Allen, to consider him a friend. I know what captivity will do to him. The one glimpse I got of him, curled into a ball inside his cell, his face buried…it broke my heart and I just can't stand by and do nothing. I don't know what his crime is, but I do know that he wants nothing more than to be left alone, to live his life in peace. If right now you're saying to yourself that I should let the criminal justice system work, or that if he's a criminal I shouldn't help him, I don't disagree. I just can't bring myself to ignore him and do nothing to help, not when he's been my best—and one of my only-- friends for the last two years. His mental state is also a factor to me. In other circumstances, I could perhaps find him a lawyer, one who could have him submitted for a psychiatric evaluation, but not in this scenario. The fact that they're flying him away in the morning to an unknown location means I have to act now, before they leave, or I'll have no chance whatsoever.

I do understand, intellectually, that saving Allen is more important to me than it should be just because of my inability to save Lizzy and my complete failure to save Tracy and Dillon. You probably figured that out already, but I'm just understanding that at a deep level. I sort of get it, and I know that affects my judgement here, but I push that knowledge aside because it doesn't change anything. I have to do this regardless of the potential consequences.

And, if I discover later that Allen's crimes were heinous enough that he deserves to be in jail despite the cost to his psyche? Well, I can always change my mind and drop him back off with the cops, right?

Chapter 3

I pull in to Las Vegas Metro's Spring Valley Command substation

and park on the side of the building, well away from the booking area. This morning—was it really just this morning?—the FBI had pulled their van directly into the sally port, which is what most cops do when they bring prisoners here. To the best of my recollection, though, it isn't unusual for some cops, particularly when driving unmarked cars, to park outside the sally port and walk their prisoners in. I'm hoping that hasn't changed because the last thing I want is to be completely committed by driving into the sally port or for the booking officer to see the white Lexus and start to get suspicious.

I help Dean from the car and grab the Ziploc with his cash and belongings, then walk him up the sidewalk and around the corner to the sally port entrance. There's the large, roll-up car door entrance and the smaller door for walk-ins, and we step right up to the walk-up door where I hit the intercom button. Since we rounded the corner we've been on camera, and I keep my head down, obscuring my face as much as possible. I don't know the quality of the cameras back here, nor do I know if they're recorded or have night vision capabilities, but I'm going to assume the worst and try to show my face as little as possible.

333

"Can I help you?"

The disjointed voice coming from the speaker box is tinny and of low quality, and that gives me hope the cameras might be the same.

"Hey there. Detective Townsend, Henderson PD with one for a temp cell."

I try to keep my voice light and airy. No stress here, just a neighboring city detective who needs a temporary cell for a prisoner.

A moment goes by, just a moment, but my heart is thumping madly. Suddenly a loud buzzer sounds, making me jump. The door unlocks with a loud *click*, and I reach out and pull it open, my right hand on Dean's forearm as I march him through and pull the door closed behind me. The closing door has a foreboding feeling to it as I've just voluntarily put myself into a cell, but I remember that it can be opened from the inside by pressing two separate, hidden buttons, the location of which I thankfully remember from a couple of previous trips here.

Because Henderson and Las Vegas are neighboring cities, it's somewhat, but not completely, unusual for a Henderson detective to use the cells here. Also the FBI, as I saw this morning, Nevada Highway Patrol, the Nevada Division of State Parks, Fish and

Wildlife, and Gaming Control Board officers to name just a few. So, the booking officer here will be used to seeing outside agencies although a Henderson detective will be a little unusual, so I have a story prepared.

There's another door to enter the building itself, and I hit the buzzer for that door as well, again keeping my head down. This time it unlocks without the voice, and I pull it open and march Dean inside. Cool and confident, at least on the outside, though my heart is hammering.

The cells here, as I mentioned before, are simply temporary holding cells, designed to house prisoners for short time periods while they're being interrogated about crimes prior to their transport to the actual county jail which is in downtown Las Vegas. With that, things here are much more relaxed than they would be if it were a bona fide booking.

The officer in charge of the holding cells is sitting at a podium, and he glances up as I walk in. There's nobody else in the room, and I say a silent thanks for that small favor. I tell myself that he sees only a cop, nothing more. The mind sees what it wants to see— and even more importantly, what it *expects* to see. This officer expects to see a police officer with his prisoner.

"Hey man, what's going on?" the booking officer asks.

"Hello. Detective Townsend with Henderson. I have one for a holding cell for just a few hours, and I should be on the schedule to interview a guy you currently have in here, Irvin Wallace?"

He frowns and glances down at his desk, then frowns at me.

"I don't have any kind of note on that. Who'd you speak with?"

I shake my head in mock disgust. "Of course you don't. Fucking FBI. I talked to Agent Trahillo earlier today. I got this guy Wallace as a suspect in a string of residential burgs out there and Trahillo tells me they're flying him out tomorrow morning early. Said I could interview him but it had to be tonight or it wouldn't be happening, maybe ever."

The officer snorts. "Fucking FBI. I'm surprised they even answered your call. Especially that asshole, Trahillo. Elitist fuck." He gives an exaggerated sigh, as if the effort is too much to contemplate, and then stands up. "Okay, no worries, I'll grab your guy; he's in cell three. You need an interview room?"

"If you got one available, that'd be great, otherwise I can just sit him down over there and chat with him," I say, pointing to a bench in the corner of the room.

"It's a slow night," he replies. "We got plenty of room, you can use room one, through that door right there." He points to the door that leads into the main area of the police department where all of the patrol bays and offices are located. "You know where it is?"

"Sure do, thanks. I appreciate it."

"Yeah, no worries. I gotta tell you though, I don't think you're going to get anything. Wallace hasn't said a word since I've been on shift, probably nothing since they brought him in. FBI guys seemed a little frustrated when they were trying to interrogate him. He's just sitting there saying nothing. I'm not even sure he knows what's going on, to be honest. Sign your guy in here, would you?"

He spins the booking log around to me and I fill it in with Dean's name. Next is the arresting officer, and I write, *Townsend, E*, and just as I'm about to write the rest of Eric's name, the booking officer, whose name I still haven't seen and who is standing behind me, speaks up.

"Did you say your name is Townsend?"

I nod, my heart jumping into my throat.

"I know a Townsend over there. Patrol guy, Eric."

I can hardly speak. Four hundred officers in Henderson, thousands here in Metro, and I get the booking officer who happens to know the officer I'm impersonating. *Get it together!* I turn around and force a smile and nod. "Yeah, good guy, good cop. I'm Edward Townsend, no relation." I turn back and finish writing Edward on the report. As I fill out the rest of the form, I study Dean out of the corner of my eye. He's frowning and staring at me, awakened probably by the realization that I have the same last name as Eric Townsend. Another hole in the mule, and I need to end this before things fall apart.

"Are you going to take him from here?" I ask, and the booking officer nods.

"Yeah, let me go get Wallace for you and then I'll bring your guy back to a cell. I need to search him and we just got the one guy back there, so I'm by myself tonight. I'll need you to listen for the sally port buzzer while I'm doing that. You good with that?"

"Sure, no problem," I smile at him. "I'll leave his belongings on the desk here for now."

"Cool. Be right back." He pulls open the metal door leading to the cells and it closes behind him.

I glance at Dean whose expression tells me he's about to start asking questions. I need to head that off.

"You did good tonight, Dean. You're going to spend the night in the cell back there and then in the morning, you'll be released, probably no later than 10 o'clock, as soon as the courts can get

338

you an arraignment date. Don't rock the boat tonight, and I guarantee you'll miss that flight in the morning." He's actually going to be released as soon as they realize he wasn't booked by a real cop. I can only hope that's hours from now.

He stares at me without saying anything, and I don't like the expression on his face, but I turn away as if nothing's wrong. A few minutes later, the booking officer opens the door and comes in pushing Allen in front of him.

Allen is wearing the same clothes that he's worn since that night after the warehouse killings, the clothes I bought him after we fled, including the Allen Iverson jersey that he refused to part with. His hair is dirty and tangled, and his head is hanging down so that I can't see his face. The booking officer gazes at me and wrinkles up his face, waving his hand up and down in front of his nose in a gesture designed to let me know that Allen smells bad. I nod and smile at him, though I feel anything but humor at the moment.

"Here you go," he says, "Irvin Wallace. I'll take your guy back there and I'll bring you back your cuffs when I'm done with him." He points at Allen, "you can uncuff him yourself when you get to the interview room, or not, it's your choice. He seems pretty docile."

"Sounds good, thanks," I reply, staring at Allen, waiting for him to react to my voice. Nothing.

I take his arm and the booking officer takes Dean and prods him to the door. He pushes him through and down the hallway, and before the door can close, I hear Dean say, "Hey man, something's wrong here."

I tense up, but the booking officer pushes him again and says, "Shut up. Get down to cell five, now."

I need to get moving, and I focus on Allen. He's handcuffed behind his back and still hasn't raised his head.

"Allen?"

Nothing.

I realize that I don't need him to be cognizant of what's happening as long as he'll walk. With one last glance at the doorway to the cells, I grab his arm and push him gently but quickly to the door leading out to the sally port. Leaving him there, I run back to the booking desk and flip the switch that unlocks it. It buzzes and clicks open, and I run back to Allen, pushing open the door and nudging him through it, slamming it behind us. I realize that cameras are rolling, both in that room and out here in the sally port, but I still don't know if they're recorded, and I can only hope they aren't.

Turning left, I prod Allen the twenty feet down the sidewalk to the exterior sally port door. Just as we reach it, I hear a buzz from the other side. Someone has pushed the button to request entry into the sally port.

Chapter 4

I have no choice at this point. Even if I wanted to turn around, I have no way of getting back into the jail area. I'm the one who's supposed to be manning the desk, and I'd have a lot of explaining to do if I'm found out here in the sally port with the prisoner who I was just supposed to be interviewing. Taking a deep breath, I push the two hidden buttons which unlock the door and I push it open.

Standing there is a Nevada Highway Patrol officer. He has a prisoner with him, a man in his sixties who's clearly intoxicated, swaying on his feet and yelling.

"I tol' you, man, I only had a coupl'a beers! I'm not fuckin drunk, man."

I force a smile again. "Hey. Good timing, come on in. Looks like you got a fun one," I add, nodding toward the drunk.

The trooper nods. "Yeah. Not drunk supposedly but managed to sideswipe a guardrail then ram a parked car on 215."

I laugh. "Well, the booking guy in there is tied up with a prisoner who's giving him some problems, so it might take him a minute at the next door."

"Alright, no problem. Have a good one," he says, pushing the drunk guy by me.

"You too."

I kept my head down and the hat pulled low, but this is another witness, and I have no doubt they'll have a good description of me when they start searching for me. Which could be any minute. I push Allen through the door and it bangs closed behind me. Practically running now, I push him down the sidewalk and across the lot to Alexa's car. I'm holding him up by the cuffs, which can't feel good, but he still hasn't said a word. He's also offering no resistance, moving his feet at the speed that I'm pushing him, and I'm grateful for that. Opening the passenger door, I push him inside, none too gently, then slam the door closed and run to the

342

driver's side glancing around wildly for any witnesses or pursuers. There are none. I don't bother with seatbelts, starting the car and slamming it into reverse, squealing the tires slightly as I hit the accelerator too hard. My legs are shaking with adrenaline and I hit the brake too hard as well before throwing it into drive. Forcing myself to drive at a speed that won't attract attention, I pull out of the parking lot and onto the street, heading toward I-215, determined to get distance between us and the pursuit that's sure to soon become an all-out manhunt.

I get onto I-215 eastbound and follow it all the way through Henderson, forcing myself to keep my speed right at the limit. Taking deep breaths, I calm my nerves, and by the time we reach the I-515 /US 93 interchange, my heart rate has slowed to something normal. I turn east on 93 and cross Railroad Pass, entering the town of Boulder. While I drive, I try to imagine what might be happening back at the Metro substation.

When the booking officer comes out, he'll first think that I simply failed to man the desk and brought Allen directly into the interview room. That notion will change quickly enough once he realizes the state trooper is standing outside the door waiting to be let in. That was a piece of exceptionally bad luck. If the trooper hadn't arrived exactly at that moment, the booking officer might have waited hours before coming to check for us in the interview

343

room. As it is, though, he'll wonder how the trooper got through the first sally port door. When he tells him that the Henderson officer let him in, there might be a few minutes where everybody is confused and unsure of what's happened, but it won't take too long for them to realize that I've left with their federal prisoner, Irvin Wallace. That part has almost certainly happened already.

The next thing that will happen will be a call to a supervisor, who'll tell the booking officer to give a call to Henderson PD and find out just what in the hell this asshole Detective Townsend thinks he's doing. That will result in more confusion as they discover there is no Detective Townsend, but there is an Officer Townsend, and more time will be wasted while they sort that out. The one benefit to me having used the Townsend name.

It's possible they'll then try to reach Eric. I gave him instructions to not answer his phone until tomorrow. Assuming he follows through, this will result in even further delays while they sort all of that out and check the camera footage, if it exists, to try to figure out just who I am.

I figure the first call to the FBI will take just about one hour. Had that trooper not shown up when he did, it might have taken three hours. Just bad luck.

Eventually, they'll reach Agent Trahillo who will probably be sleeping when they call, getting ready for his early morning private jet to its undisclosed location. He'll react quickly and order an APB, an All-Points Bulletin, but I don't think they'll have a description of the car I'm driving. I'm confident there were no cameras facing the parking lot outside of the precinct, another reason why I parked out there instead of driving into the sally port. All they'll have for the APB will be whatever description they have of me and, of course, a good description and name for Allen.

Speaking of Allen, he's begun to moan in the passenger seat, but is still staring down at his lap. I want to remove his handcuffs, but need to stop the car to do that, and I want to get out of Nevada first. The APB will start with the Las Vegas Metro area and Henderson. When they don't find us after a couple of hours, they'll expand it to all surrounding states. I figure the APB will go out in southern Nevada about seventy-five minutes from the time I left with Allen. Call it sixty minutes exactly just to be safe, and that's how long I have to get into Arizona. The good news is I'm only about fifteen minutes from the border now.

The surrounding states APB should go out about two hours after that, which now won't quite give me enough time to reach my destination, which you might as well know is Flagstaff, Arizona.

It's an hour and thirty minutes to Kingman, Arizona where I'll get off the lonely Highway 93 and join the busy Interstate 40 for the remaining two-hour drive to Flagstaff. If I reach I-40 prior to the APB going out to the Arizona Highway Patrol, and if they don't have a description of the car I'm driving, I should be able to safely reach Flagstaff. Too many "ifs," but I don't have any way of eliminating them.

Briefly, I consider stopping somewhere to steal a license plate just in case they have mine, but I decide that's too risky. If they don't have mine, then having the wrong plates on the car will only put me in more danger. Leaving Boulder City behind, I descend down the long hill toward Lake Mead, then wind back up to the Pat Tillman Memorial Bridge which bypasses the old route that used to cross the top of Hoover Dam. The clock on the dashboard reads five minutes to midnight as we cross the bridge and enter Arizona. I breathe a small sigh of relief. The first step is complete and, in spite of the fact that for the first time in my life I've knowingly committed several major felonies, I feel good. I feel like I've done something good, something right and just.

Reaching out, I gently massage Allen's shoulder and talk to him softly as we drive on into the dark Arizona night.

Chapter 5

Traffic is light, mostly big trucks hauling cargo, climbing the hills

slowly and barreling down the other side. The moon is bright,

illuminating the barren, isolated countryside as we drive. The

emptiness encourages speeding, but I avoid that temptation by

setting the cruise control for exactly the speed limit. I'm sure I

don't need to say it, but getting pulled over would be a disaster.

I managed to get Allen's handcuffs off him while we drove,

swerving across the lane several times while I struggled with one

hand to unlock them, Allen not helping at all, remaining docile as a

lamb, moaning softly. Once I got them off, I tossed them out the

window, then began tossing out the other items that I'd taken

347

from Eric's, including the polo shirt with the sewn-on badge, replacing it with a t-shirt from the duffel bag I'd thrown in the car earlier.

I tossed the items out the car window, scattering them over a good twenty miles of roadway. It's so dark and barren out here that I doubt anybody should ever find more than one of them. The two sets of handcuffs I made sure to throw into ravines as we drove over them. Eventually, flash floods coming down the hills will wash them into the Colorado River. I debate what to do with Eric's badge, but eventually decide having possession of it is just too dangerous. I wait for us to cross a deep ravine and toss that as well.

The only thing I keep is my gun which I stuff under the seat. After I've gotten rid of everything, I work on Allen again, calling out to him. He stares at me but I see no flicker of recognition in his eyes. I have time, but I'm worried about him.

I realize that one of the most distinct things about him, the thing that's going to mark us for sure when the APB goes out, is the Iverson jersey he's wearing. That thing needs to go, and this might be the time to do it. Grabbing it, I begin pulling, figuring it should rip off him pretty easily. As soon as it starts to tear, Allen reaches up and grasps my wrist tightly.

"Allen?"

He's staring at me with a different expression now. "Sandman?"

"Yeah, buddy. It's me. You're safe now."

He leans back against the car door and then his gaze flashes around, his grip still firm on my arm.

"Where are we? What are we doing?"

"We're in a car, in Arizona. We're heading to Flagstaff."

"Why?"

"Can I have my arm back, buddy?" He stares at his hand gripping my wrist and then lets go.

"Thanks. Do you remember getting arrested?"

He stares at me a moment and then nods. "Yeah."

"It was the FBI, Allen. I managed to get you away from them, but Las Vegas isn't safe for you anymore. They know you're there now, and they'll find you again if you stay."

He nods slowly then peers out the front window, contemplating the desolate landscape before replying. "Thanks, Sandman."

"How did they find you this time, Allen?"

"They been searching for me a long time, Sandman. I tol' you that, lots of times. One of them seen me the other day. I done tol' you that already too."

I have to give him that. He had told me…many times. I'd always figured it was paranoid delusions from a failing mind.

"How did they find us at the house though? You remember the raid this morning where we got arrested?"

He glances at me again. "I'm sorry you got tied up in that, Sandman. Wasn't right they arrested you too. You didn't do nothin' wrong."

It's kind of ironic that I'd felt the same way about him while the arrest was happening, thinking they were there for me. I suppose how they found us isn't important, and I can guess anyway. Allen had been sitting on a busy onramp, panhandling. The FBI has an office here in Las Vegas, and an observant agent must have noticed him and somehow recognized him. He saw the agent and hid, but when I found him hiding behind that convenience store, they must have already seen us and followed us back to the house where we were staying. In order for them to put together a raid like they executed instead of just grabbing us as we walked down the street, Allen must be pretty damn dangerous, and I'm a bit nervous as I come to this realization.

"Allen, I need to know why you were arrested. What did you do?"

He doesn't answer at first, staring out the window into the darkness. I'm about to ask again when he finally starts to speak.

"I can't tell you too much, Sandman, but I owe you somethin'. I used to work for the government. I was assigned to the U.S. Embassy in Ho Chi Minh City. Saigon, we all called it. From there I traveled all over Asia. I can't say what I did, but basically, I was s'pose to gather intelligence on certain people. Follow them, watch them, sometimes more." He pauses a minute again, then turns and regards me. "You get what I'm sayin'?"

I nod but don't say anything. He was a spy. He worked for CIA or DIA, or some other three-letter agency performing covert operations. That's what he's telling me, though I'm not 100% certain I believe him. It's just hard for me to reconcile the image I've had of this man for the last two years, with an image of him as a covert operative for the government.

"Good. Anyway, one day I jus' had enough. I had a way out an' I used it. Got back to the States and just went into hidin'. But my out wasn't secure and I knew it. They knew I didn't git killed or captured or whatever. The way my out worked, they knew I'd fled and they couldn't have that. I knew too much and I'd seen too much, so they had to look for me. Had to capture me."

He's told me all of this before, of course; I just never listened. He'd told me before that government agents were searching for him because they could never let anybody go who'd seen the things he'd seen. He'd told me he was a Vietnam vet, and I'd just made the assumption he meant from the Vietnam War, in which he was too young to have served. I'd made a false and erroneous leap to him having mental problems. Of course, he obviously does have mental issues of some type, though I now think they're not the kind that need medication, but rather the kind that a psychiatrist could help with. I'm not a doctor and I'm not an expert on mind issues, but I've seen a lot of people with mental problems during my time on the street, and I'm quite sure most of them can be helped only with medication, if at all. Allen doesn't seem to have a condition that severe, though my faulty observation and analysis of him led me to believe he did. Allen has always had moments of clarity since I've known him, and he's having an acute one now.

"Did you commit a crime, Allen?"

He stares down at his lap and takes a minute to answer. "I committed lots of crimes, Sandman. I committed crimes against people and crimes against God. I did them all 'cause I was ordered to. They don't want me 'cause I did those crimes though. They want me 'cause I stopped doing them. They call it treason. But that's just 'cause I ran and they can't have me out here. They

352

afraid I gonna talk eventually, or they think maybe I already did. But I ain't never tol' nobody nothin'. I think you know that. If I ever tol' anybody anything it would'a been you or Lizzy. And she dead now, so even if I tol' her somethin', she can't tell nobody else."

I wait for a minute to see if he'll say more, but he's quiet, gazing out the front window again, still in enormous pain over Lizzy's death.

"Allen, we gotta gid rid of the Iverson jersey. I know you love it, but it marks you, identifies you, and we've gotta toss it."

He doesn't say a word, just nods and pulls the jersey over his head. Lowering the window, he regards the jersey for just a second, and then tosses it out. I laugh softly. All of his attachment to that thing, his refusal to get rid of it after the massacre at the warehouse, and just like that, he tosses it without a second thought. A moment of clarity in a mind that has seen too much and just wants to forget.

"Why Flagstaff, Sandman?" he asks, turning to study me again.

"I need to go there anyway. There's somebody there who can help me find my wife and son's killers. Once we're there, I can give you money for a bus, though, if you don't want to stay. You can go anywhere you like, but if you travel, you're going to have to change your appearance. There will be posters out on you with your picture exactly as you look right now."

He nods. "I've been doing this a long time, Sandman. Haircut and shave will change my appearance completely. Flagstaff is as good a place as any I suppose."

We arrive in Kingman at around 1:30 in the morning, and I stop for gas at a busy truck stop right at the Interstate 40 junction. I tell Allen to wait in the car. He's way too identifiable, even without the Iverson jersey, and his long hair and beard will make him memorable to the clerk or to any other customers. He tells me he has to use the restroom and I tell him we'll stop at a rest area somewhere down I-40.

I go into the store to pay for the gas, keeping my head down, avoiding the lenses of whatever cameras may be there. I buy two cups of coffee, a couple of bottles of water, and a bunch of snacks, including the last two corndogs in the case, which are of questionable quality, but will almost certainly not be the worst food Allen and I have ever eaten. Taking a guess, I prepay for $40 worth of gas. I want to get enough in the tank to get to Flagstaff, but not so much that I need to come back to the store for change. The clerk, busy with all the truckers getting fuel, gives me hardly a glance as he rings me up.

I hand Allen the supplies from the store and begin pumping gas, keeping a close eye on the rest of the customers, watching for anybody who might be eyeballing at us too closely. I have no idea if the APB has gone out to neighboring states yet, and I don't know if the police have a line on this car. This is arguably the most dangerous part of the trip, sitting still under the lights of a busy gas station.

Just as I'm finishing up the fueling, a Kingman police car rolls through the lot, moving slowly, the officer inside eyeing the cars at the pump. He shoots a glance directly at me and I nod, forcing myself to stay calm. Nodding back, he keeps driving, then suddenly pulls into a parking spot and sits in his idling car.

I'm nervous, of course, but there's nothing to do but continue on. If he has our info then he has us, and there's nothing I can do about it. If I act even more suspicious and he wasn't there watching us, then I'll have drawn his attention for no reason. I get back in the car and start it up.

"We okay, Sandman?" Allen asks, his eyes focused on the police car as well.

"We'll know in a minute. Just stay calm," I reply.

I pull out of the gas station and turn toward the Interstate 40 interchange. The patrol car doesn't move, but I have no idea if the officer is watching us, so I get on the onramp for westbound I-40. I travel a few miles west on I-40 before taking the exit for historic

Route 66 and getting back on I-40 eastbound. There are quite a few cars and trucks on this major interstate even this late at night, but nobody follows us. If the police officer is ever asked later, or remembers us for some reason, he'll tell whoever asked that we went east on I-40, headed toward Lake Havasu and, eventually, the Los Angeles area. The more I can throw off the inevitable search, the better.

We stop just once at a rest area just outside of Kingman, and I park well away from the building, out of the lights, in the area where people walk their dogs. Allen and I take turns peeing in the bushes, avoiding the building itself and all the people. I'm tired and want to stop to sleep, but it's too dangerous. Far too many highway patrol officers check out the rest areas during the late hours of the night. Allen naps while I drive, the coffee giving me some much-needed energy.

We make it into Flagstaff right as the clock on the dashboard reads 4:00am. We're in the Mountain Time Zone, but with no daylight savings time in Arizona, it's the same time as it is in Vegas. This far east, however, the sky is just beginning to lighten when I pull to the side of the road in the middle of town.

Neither Allen nor I know this town, but he's going to have to learn it. I'm giving him a head start by dropping him off near the

Sunshine Rescue Mission which I found using the map on the prepaid phone Eric got me. There are several people sleeping on the sidewalk around the mission, and the air is cool but not cold. I open the trunk and remove both of our backpacks. After locking the car, Allen and I move over to an open doorway, spread out our jackets and sit next to each other, leaning back against the wall.

I'm exhausted and need a nap, and this seems like as good a place as any. The car is parked in an area where the meter doesn't need to be fed until 9:00am, and I've removed my gun and all other belongings from it. From where I sit, I can see if any police officer notices it and, even though I no longer look like most of the transients around me, I'll still be able to blend in somewhat with my olive-green jacket, huddled next to Allen who definitely matches the part. His societal invisibility shield will extend to cover me as well.

Chapter 6

I wake up several hours later to the noise of cars and pedestrians passing by. It's Sunday morning, and the business we're huddled in front of hasn't opened yet, but it's time for us to get moving. I glance over to Alexa's car and see that it appears to be undisturbed. Shaking Allen awake, we eat the remainder of the snacks I bought at the truck stop last night. We then move out into the sunshine and sit down on a bench on the sidewalk.

Reaching into my backpack, I pull out the envelope of cash and peel off $500, which is almost half of my remaining money. I hand it to Allen who tries to not take it at first, eventually accepting with tears in his eyes when I insist. I tell him to spend it wisely and carefully, and he assures me he will.

We say our goodbyes; Allen looks me in the eye for a minute and then nods and walks away. I have to admit, it's hard to leave, knowing that I'm unlikely to ever see him again. Eventually, he rounds a corner and I throw my stuff in the car and drive away. What else can I do?

Despite my sadness, I feel some relief at separating from him. Being together doubled the danger for both of us, especially while in this car. I can't get rid of the car just yet, but I can find out if there's any immediate danger driving it. Using the cell phone, I dial Eric's number.

He answers on the first ring and tells me he has two missed calls and messages from his department. Not answering is making him anxious, but I tell him to please hold off a little longer.

"Eric, you're on a nice weekend getaway with your wife. You've been ignoring your phone completely and haven't seen the calls. It's that simple."

He's reluctant but agrees to wait a while longer. It's possible— even likely—that Henderson PD has already sent officers to his house, but I locked up when I left, and with no cars in the driveway and an empty look to the house, they'll be reluctant to break in.

I hang up with Eric and immediately dial Erin Fogler's Dallas office number. A receptionist answers and I tell her my name is David Sands and I need to reach Erin regarding an old friend of hers named Tracy Conner. I leave my number and tell her I'm in Flagstaff and it's imperative I reach Erin as soon as possible. I figure that will pique her interest and get me a quick call back if she gets the message. I could tell by Eric's voice on the phone that he was feeling a lot of pressure, and I need to get the car back to Las Vegas as soon as possible.

An hour later, I'm sitting in a Starbucks, facing the door, drinking an overpriced coffee and reading a local newspaper when my phone rings displaying a Dallas number. I answer and Erin identifies herself. When I explain that I have information regarding Tracy Conner and her murder, Erin agrees to meet with me. She tells me she's five minutes away and she'll meet me here.

Five minutes later, she walks in the door, glances around, and before I can wave to her, she spots me and walks up to my table, sitting down in the seat across from me.

"Hello, Harvey. I thought that was your voice," she says.

I'm astounded and I laugh. "And you still came? Without the police?"

She waves a hand. "Please. I worked with Tracy for years. I met you before and I'm a good judge of character. Plus, Tracy talked about you often, how amazing you were. If you were a bad guy, I'd have known. I know you didn't have anything to do with her murder. And your son? Come on. Even if you were the type to kill your wife--your son? No way. I never bought it for a second."

"I'm surprised you recognized me."

"Tracy had a picture of you on her desk, Harvey. I saw your face every day. Plus, we met a couple of times. You've aged a bit, obviously, but there aren't that many people in here."

I smile at her. I'm amazed at how everybody I've run into lately never believed in my guilt. Maybe I shouldn't have run after all. I can't second guess that decision though; it certainly seemed like the right one at the time.

Erin excuses herself and goes to the counter to order a drink. She's wearing a denim long-sleeve shirt and dark blue cargo pants with hiking boots. There's dirt on her pants, and I suspect she's been in the field doing survey work. It's exactly how Tracy used to dress when she would go into the field, though that happened much less frequently in later years after she was promoted and spent most days in the office.

Erin is about 35 years old and has green eyes, pale skin with a scattering of freckles around her nose, and long, dark red hair that is tied back in a ponytail behind her head. Her hair is slightly messy and I guess she was wearing a hat before she came in to meet me.

She comes back to the table with an iced drink and sits down. She hasn't asked me where I've been or what I've been up to the last two years, and, though she must be curious, she doesn't ask now either.

"So, what can I do for you, Harvey?"

I reach into my back pocket where earlier I stuffed the survey report I got from Tracy's lawyer. I hand it to Erin who starts to read it.

"This report was prepared by you. I just wanted to find out more information about it."

She's frowning as she reads it. She flips through it, studying each page until she reaches the last one. She sets it down and regards me.

"I didn't write this report."

I jerk back and frown at her. "Okay. Why's your name on it?"

She shrugs and picks up her coffee, taking a sip before she replies. "I guess someone put my name on it for some reason. Where did you get this?"

"Before I answer that, I need to know how sure are you that you didn't write it. I mean, you must write these types of reports all the time, so how can you be so sure you didn't write this one?"

She laughs. "Because I'd remember this one, Harvey. You see those elements listed there?" She points to the names of elements I'd seen on the report but been unable to identify. Bastnäsite, yttrium, cerium, neodymium, and the like. I nod to her.

"Well, I've filed plenty of mineralogical assay reports like this one, but never in my life have I filed one that had concentration numbers like this. Believe me, I'd remember."

"What are these elements?" I ask.

"Uh-uh. Your turn. Where'd you get this?"

I'm not anxious to tell her that, but she's staring at me fixedly and I don't think she'll respond without some reciprocity.

"Tracy hired a lawyer before she was murdered. I recently found him and he gave this to me. I think this report is the reason Tracy was killed, but I don't know what it means."

She leans back in the chair, sipping on her drink and studying me for a bit before she replies.

"Well, then I think the author of the report must have been Tracy. And, for some reason, she felt the need to put my name on it."

"What is this? What does it mean?" I ask.

"That depends. Do you know where this survey was conducted?" She flips the paper around and points to the map coordinates on the front page. "Where these coordinates are?"

"Supposedly, they're located on a piece of land that Tracy and I bought about eight years ago. A piece of property in the mountains of northern Nevada, near the California border."

363

"Well then, if that's the case, this means you're the owner of a very valuable piece of property."

Stunned would be an understatement. I'm completely floored.

"How valuable?" I manage to croak out.

She shrugs. "That depends. And actually, the value fluctuates a lot, but it's possible that soon, if the assessment is correct, the land could be worth an awful lot of money."

"I'm lost, Erin. Can you help me understand this?"

"I can try. Have you ever heard of *rare earth elements*?"

"I don't think so."

"Okay, so I need to start there then. Rare earth elements, sometimes called rare earth metals, are a set of seventeen different chemical elements. They're all found on the periodic table ranging from an atomic weight of twenty-one up to seventy-one. Are you familiar with the periodic table?"

"About as familiar as any high school C grade-in-chemistry student can be."

She frowns at me.

"No, not really," I clarify.

"Okay, well then I'll skip over the technical parts. What you need to know about this survey is that this shows a very high
364

concentration of bastnäsite. The highest I've ever seen, actually, as I mentioned."

"Okay, and what does that mean? I've never heard of it; is it worth a lot of money?"

"Well, yes, technically it is, but not on its own. Bastnäsite is a mineral, a rock to be accurate, that binds together many of the rare earth elements. Most of the bastnäsite we find is bastnäsite-(Ce), which means it's mostly composed of cerium, and cerium is one of the most abundant rare earths out there. Cerium is listed here, and these are very high quantities, but nothing I haven't seen before. However, if you look down here," she points further down the page on the survey, "you'll see that this bastnäsite is also very heavy with lanthanum, neodymium, yttrium and gadolinium."

She lost me way back at "technically," and I tell her that. "At the risk of sounding dumb, I don't really get it. You're telling me that the piece of property that Tracy and I bought has a high concentration of these rare elements, this lantha-whatever and neo-whatever, and that makes it worth a lot of money?"

She nods. "It appears so, from this report. Additional surveys would need to be done in other test areas around this just to make sure, but yes, this appears to be a very high concentration of these elements. You should also understand that rare earth elements, at least these ones on this report, are not actually all that rare. In fact, cerium is something like the 25th most common element in the Earth's crust, at about the same concentration as copper."

I frown, more confused than ever. "So then, why are they valuable if they're common and abundant?"

"Because they're rarely found in concentrated amounts that can be easily extracted. They're found scattered all over in small quantities where the cost to mine them would be significantly higher than the value of the ore itself. There are actually only a few places where these rare earths are found in concentrations like this. One of those places is the Mountain Pass Rare Earth mine in California. Most of the rest are in North Korea and China."

"China?" Something clicks in my mind. Another piece of the puzzle is falling into place.

Erin nods. "Yup. China controls the vast majority of the rare earth market. About 95% of it, actually, maybe a little more."

"Okay, so what exactly are rare earths used for?"

She laughs. "Just about everything that has anything to do with current technology. From LED televisions, to lasers, to electric car motors, to cancer treatments, to the display screen on your iPhone. They all require rare earth elements to work. Rare-earth magnets are the lightest and most powerful magnets we can

366

make, and they're used in all kinds of applications like computer disc drives, gyroscopes, and windmills. And that's just a small sample; many of the things we use on a regular basis require REEs to work. Then of course, there are the military applications. They're used in rocket technology, GPS devices, sonar systems, fuel cells, you name it. Almost everything technology-based that we use today, wouldn't work without rare earth elements."

"And China controls 95% of the world's supply of these things?" I'm getting a very bad feeling.

"They do."

"Isn't the government concerned about that? Aren't they doing something about that?"

She nods. "They're trying. At least some of the people in charge are concerned about it. They became a lot more concerned in late 2010."

"Why? What happened in 2010?"

"A territorial dispute between Japan and China. They both claim ownership of some islands in the East China Sea. I don't remember the name of them, and it's not important. A Chinese trawler was wandering around in those disputed seas and it collided with a Japanese Coast Guard vessel. The Japanese arrested the captain and crew and caused a major diplomatic incident. Even though

367

they were eventually released, in retaliation, the Chinese quietly enacted a ban on the sale of all rare earth elements to Japan."

"So the U.S. became concerned they could do the same here?"

"Sort of. I mean, think about it. Enacting a ban on the sale of rare earths because of a diplomatic incident involving the collision of two boats doesn't make any sense. Most of us at the USGS, when we heard about that, realized exactly what it meant."

I don't quite get it, and I tell her so.

"It's not an appropriate retaliation or punishment. It doesn't correlate. They didn't block other trade, just REEs. Plus, they denied that they'd enacted the ban. They claimed Japan was lying about it, and that was even more of a red flag. At the time, Japan was buying a surplus of REEs, enough to sell a relatively small amount to the U.S. We got 100% of our REEs from China and Japan then, but when China enacted the ban on selling to Japan, Japan decided to stop selling any of their own surplus abroad. They understood that they needed to hold it for their own future needs."

"And that made the United States 100% reliable on China," I say, connecting the pieces.

She nods again. "Yup. Now, China has the world's largest mineable deposits of rare earths, and the second largest source is in North Korea. Are you familiar with our relationship with that country?"

"I've been off the grid for most of the last two years, but yeah, I did manage to read the newspaper some days."

"So then you know that we have trade sanctions with them, and our relationship just keeps getting worse, thanks to Kim Jong-un who's an absolute maniac and is unstable and dangerous. Not to mention the fact that China is North Korea's biggest ally and their biggest trading partner despite all of the U.N. sanctions against trade with them. China just does what it wants. Basically, what it comes down to is, if China ever decides to cut off sales of rare earths to the U.S., it will bring our entire economy to its knees. We'll crash and go from superpower to third-world country in a matter of months. Imagine what it'll be like if you break your cell phone and can't get a new one because there are no rare earth elements from which to make one."

This sounds a bit alarmist, to be honest, and the cell phone analogy isn't pertinent to me as I just acquired my first cell phone in more than two years. I get the point though. With the United States 100% reliant on China, the Chinese could set their own prices and their own supply quotas for nearly all of our everyday technology. And, if they cut us off completely, what little amount we are able to produce ourselves would go straight to the military. The United States is certainly not going to let our nuclear submarine force be unable to replace a sonar system or our strategic rocket forces be grounded due to faulty guidance systems just because the rare earth elements needed to build new ones are being used to make LED televisions for Jim Bob to purchase at Walmart.

"What about the rest of our trading partners?" I ask. "Great Britain, France, Russia?"

"Great Britain and France, as well as most of Europe are in the same boat with us. They have the ability to mine their own supplies; there are abundant deposits in Canada, Greenland, Australia, and a few other places. But to get those mines operational and processing ore would take years. In the early 2000s, China undercut the prices of all the REEs and the world stopped mining their own supplies. Everybody gets them from China. Russia has its own sources, mostly in Siberia, but do you think they'd help us? For starters, they'd begin hoarding whatever supplies they have in anticipation of China cutting them off too. Then of course, there's the fact that Russia would love to see us fail. China has the ability right now to become the world's dominant superpower, and I believe it's only a matter of time until we start seeing signs that they're taking first steps toward that goal."

And they may already be taking those steps. If it's true that they're trying to control the world's supply of REEs, then the logical first step would be to lock up all known and unknown supplies, as far as possible. And my wife had apparently located a large, previously unknown deposit. The question is, how did the Chinese discover this?

"Have you seen any sign that the Chinese are searching for rare earth elements in the United States?" I ask.

"Yes, and not just in the United States, all over the world. It's been well known at the USGS that China is quietly searching for supplies outside of Asia, but the rest of the world has been too cocooned to see it happening. We've only just begun to recognize the danger, despite the fact that your wife, me, and a few others have been telling everybody who'll listen just how much danger there is."

I'm stunned. I can't believe the short-sightedness of those that allowed us to be put in this situation. On the other hand, the *why* of Tracy and Dillon's murders is coming together, and I'm beginning to understand the importance of Tracy's find. What I don't understand, though, is why she hid it. Why didn't she notify the government of her find?

The reason for my visit suddenly occurs to Erin. "Wait, you think the Chinese killed Tracy and Dillon over this report?"

"I do now," I tell her. I take a moment to tell her about two Chinese agents buying our house at the county tax auction and me watching them tear it apart. "They were looking for something, and I think it was this report."

She nods, slowly. "If Tracy had filed this report, I'd have heard of it. She must have kept it hidden."

I want to ask why she'd do that, but I skip that question for now and ask, "So the U.S. must be doing something. Somebody must understand the importance of this, right?"

Erin laughs. "You'd think so, but it's surprising how little we're doing about it. Back around the end of 2014, I helped publish a fact sheet about REEs and what they were used for including the dangers of the Chinese dominance of the market. It was published online and distributed through the government, but it got only minor attention. We are actively searching for new supplies, not just the U.S., but also our allies, but it's slow and there's no sense of urgency from anybody in charge. Recycling technologies have improved a lot, and we can process used REEs from batteries, magnets, and fluorescent lights now. The Mountain Pass Mine in California still has a large mineable quantity of Rare Earths. In fact, it was the U.S.'s largest territorial supplier of rare earths, but it shut down, I think around 2002, just because it was cheaper to buy the rare earths from China and Japan than it was to mine and process them here. You have to understand, mining REEs is an open-pit job, which means it has a huge environmental impact. Also, there are a lot of radioactive isotopes generally found with the REEs which makes clean-up a real bitch. China doesn't have the same environmental standards that we have. In fact, their mines are true environmental disaster areas, but they don't care. They cover it all up and mine away. We can't do that here."

"So, the Mountain Pass Mine is still closed?"

"Well, it reopened in 2010 when China banned imports to Japan but, like I said, the mining company is in a constant struggle with environmentalists and they've had a ton of problems getting production back up. Last I heard, the owners were in bankruptcy, and mining operations had ground to a halt. In fact, in the calendar year of 2016, and so far all of this year, the United States has produced exactly zero REEs at Mountain Pass or anywhere else."

Which makes Tracy's discovery even more valuable. It also explains why she hadn't pushed me to get a cabin built on the property, even though I'd suggested on numerous occasions that we move forward with building our retirement place. She'd always gently nudged me away from that, putting it off to something we'd do in the future, and I'm beginning to see why. She never planned to use it as a vacation or retirement property.

I take the assay report from Erin and spot the date on it. The report had been completed in August of 2009, and we'd bought the property just a month later, in September. I point this out to Erin.

"Yeah; so at that time, we were happily getting all of our supply of rare earths from China and Japan, with no territorial issues about environmental impacts or anything like that."

"So at that point, Tracy couldn't have known what was going to happen in the future. From what you've told me, at the time it wasn't economically or environmentally feasible for the U.S. to mine the rare earths for ourselves anyway."

"That's true," she replies, "but even back then, some of us could see the handwriting on the wall. We knew that rare earth elements were going to be a problem for us in the near future. In the years before the China-Japan incident, we never even searched for rare earths when we did our mineral surveys. I mean, we'd note them when we found them, but we didn't actively search for them. Keep in mind, back in the early 2000s, there were no iPhones, no Teslas with electric motors, rare-earth magnets were needed for hardly anything, flat panel TVs were just becoming popular, and they were plasma screens, not LEDs. We didn't use rare earths for all that much, and the Mountain Pass Mine was providing most of the world's supply. In fact, back in 2000, we were the ones who controlled the supply; no other country even bothered with them because they were so difficult and messy to mine. The environmentalists destroyed that for us and put us in the bind we're in now. They made it easy for the Chinese to step in and take over with their disregard for any environmental considerations. And that happened right at the time when rare earth elements were becoming more and more critical to technological innovation, either through coincidence or some great foresight on their part."

I know it's true, but it's still hard for me to fathom that just ten years ago, nobody had ever heard of an iPhone. Fifteen years ago, few people owned flat-screen TVs. Technological advances are occurring exponentially, and the rate at which we adapt is incredible. When I graduated college in 1993, I'd never been on the internet and nobody I knew owned a cell phone. That's hard to fathom as I sit here just twenty-some years later.

I gaze at Erin again. "When exactly was the USGS ordered to start actively searching for rare earths?"

She glances upward, thinking. "It wasn't until after the Japanese were cut off by China in 2010 but, like I said, many of us could see the potential problem years before that. When Tracy did this survey, she couldn't have known what was coming, but she would have known it was a possibility." She pauses for a moment. "Let me ask you this: is the property good for anything else besides the rich supply of rare earths?"

I nod and tell her that it's a beautiful area of mountainous terrain with great views.

"So, at worst, you guys were going to have a nice piece of vacation property. And at best, you guys were going to be able to sell the mineral rights to the U.S. Government for a pretty penny. Not a bad deal."

I don't want to know the answer to my next question, but I have to ask.

"Is what she did even legal or moral? She used government resources to locate a mineral supply and then purchased the land herself."

Erin shrugs. "Illegal? No. Unethical? Maybe. She was surveying the land for some reason, which we don't know, and she found a vast supply of rare earth elements. At the time, the U.S. would have done nothing with the information anyway. The land was privately owned, right?"

I nod. We'd purchased it from a guy who'd owned it for almost twenty years.

"So, the report would have been filed away and nothing would have been done with it anyway until the China-Japan incident the next year when a few key people recognized the growing Chinese threat. Then the U.S. Government would have made the owner of the land an offer and probably would have started mining. All Tracy did was fail to file the report. If she'd filed it and then purchased the land, that would have created some problems for her and she could have been brought up on some ethics charges probably. It would have also created some problems for you. You were a police officer; I doubt that as a public employee you would have kept your job. You guys bought the land as a married couple, your superiors wouldn't have believed you had no knowledge of the mineral value that Tracy had discovered."

I nod, slowly, my head hanging. This isn't the Tracy I knew. The girl I fell in love with and married was honest and ethical to a fault. At least that's what I'd thought. Could money corrupt anybody, even someone as genuine and virtuous as Tracy?

"That's what some people will think. Now, let me tell you what I think actually happened," Erin says, seeing the pain on my face and giving me some hope. "The Tracy Conner that I knew wouldn't have stolen a paperclip. And I don't believe she intended to steal anything here either. When Tracy conducted this survey and found such a high concentration of rare earths, I think she knew exactly what would happen. This survey would have been filed with the USGS and become a part of the public record. At the time, nobody really cared about REEs. They were being sold cheaply by China, and it wasn't profitable to mine them. If these had been found on public land, it would have been fine; the government would have owned them and nothing would have needed to be done. But the minerals, and the access to them, were located on private land. If Tracy had filed this report, anybody could have contacted the owner and purchased the land or the mineral rights. But because there was no urgency, the government might not have acted before someone else could have. And I think she knew at the time that the Chinese were beginning their searches for worldwide supplies of REEs. I think she knew that the USGS was doing all the work here in America for the Chinese, filing surveys that the public could access so the Chinese didn't even have to do their own work. You think the Chinese file publicly accessible surveys when they find high value mineral deposits? No chance. I think Tracy just wanted to even the playing field a little."

"What do you mean?"

"Tracy didn't file the report because that would have left it open for the Chinese to find it, contact the landowner, and purchase the mineral rights. By keeping the report to herself, she could lock up those rights and keep them out of the hands of the Chinese. For all we know she was going to simply sign them over to the United States government at some point in the future, when she knew the government was aware of the Chinese threat and would protect the rights. Or, maybe she'd sell the rights for what you guys paid for them. We don't have any information that she was even considering trying to make a profit."

I ponder this a little. If Erin's theory is correct, Tracy had decided to bury the report and keep me in the dark to protect me, to protect herself, and to protect the country. And that decision cost us her life and the life of our son. I hang my head and stare at my lap, overcome with sadness and emotion. I recognize that Tracy has some small amount of blame in this, but I feel nothing but pain for her. I believe Erin, not just because I want to believe her, but because Tracy was a good woman, a smart woman and a thoughtful woman. Erin is correct; Tracy wouldn't have ever considered stealing from the government or anybody else for that matter. Her intentions had been pure, but she had underestimated the threat and made a mistake in judgement. Mistakes in judgement are not supposed to cost you so much. To cost all of us so damn much.

Erin sees my pain and my emotion. "I'm so sorry, Harvey."

I nod and wipe my eyes, taking a deep breath. "The Chinese are actively searching for this report, Erin. They've spent a lot of time and money trying to find it. Why would they do that? Why's the report itself so important?"

She thinks about it for a minute before replying. "Well, it was never filed. And, if Tracy had the only copy and the Chinese were able to get their hands on it, then nobody would ever know this large deposit ever existed. Unless we did another survey in that area, which might be decades down the road."

She pauses again, chewing on her lip while she thinks. "It's helpful to them if the survey never sees the light of day…extremely helpful actually. If nobody knows of the existence of a deposit of REEs, then the Chinese still own the monopoly and still have the leverage. But it's even better for them if they own the land or they own the mineral rights. But they don't, you do. I wonder if they ever tried to purchase them from Tracy."

I don't know the answer to that, but the answer to a huge question suddenly hits me like a lightning bolt. For the last two plus years, I haven't been able to figure out why the Chinese didn't kill me that terrible night. And, why they tried to have me arrested that night at Panattiere's when they set the trap after kidnapping Lizzy. It hadn't made any sense, but it suddenly does.

"What is it?" Erin asks, seeing me sitting up suddenly, eyes wide.

I don't answer her right away, thinking it through. If the Chinese had tried to get Tracy to sell them the land or the mineral rights and she'd refused, they may have decided to kill her. But, better than killing her would have been framing me for the murder. If I'd been arrested, I would have needed to hire an attorney. A long, drawn-out legal battle would cost me hundreds of thousands of dollars…money I didn't have. If I'd been in the middle of a court battle for my freedom, and I'd been approached by someone offering to buy the vacation property we owned, offering cash at a great price, I'd have accepted in a second. I would have needed the money for my defense, and I'd have thought it was a great decision. I would have probably even been grateful and thankful to the purchasers for stepping forward at that time, like angels from heaven. I'd have never known that selling to them was trampling on everything Tracy had fought to prevent. I might have never discovered what I'd done.

381

The plan was evil, heinous, repulsive...and brilliant. And it almost worked.

Instead of allowing myself to be arrested, I'd run. When they got a lead on my location after a long two years during which nobody discovered the lode, they thought they had another opportunity to have me arrested. They set the trap at Joey Panattiere's house, had police officers staged and ready to go, and I'd narrowly avoided that, mostly through luck and the paranoia I'd cultivated after two years on the streets.

I need to discover who is the mastermind behind this—Theo, or maybe someone to whom he reports. And who is well enough connected to have been able to generate that level of police response? I suddenly realize that I've forgotten one person who might be able to help, one person who was very much connected to Theo and the rest of the Chinese, but who is as much a victim of their savagery as I am. I can hardly believe that I've overlooked this potential source, and I'm a bit angry with myself for the oversight.

Jackie Bastain, wife of the Asian Businessman of the Year, Jerry Bastain. Jerry had been murdered by one of the same people who murdered my family, likely on orders from Theo. And then Lizzy Bastain had been murdered by Reggie. Joey and Reggie murdered my wife and son, and then they murdered Jackie's husband and daughter. Like the negative of a developed photograph, her husband and daughter, my wife and son, killed by the same people on orders from the same man. Jackie is a victim and, though she'd been gone that night long ago when I climbed over the wall of the community where her house was located and snuck into her backyard, there is a good chance she's home by now.

Chapter 7

I spent another half hour talking with Erin, learning more than I ever thought I'd need to know about rare earth elements and the Chinese monopoly on their production. I finally told her I needed to head back to Las Vegas. Before we parted, I left her with the copy of the assay report. If I need another one, I can probably get it from the attorney, Rosenberg, but the most important thing to me now is to make sure, at any cost, that the Chinese plot doesn't work, regardless of what happens to me. I told Erin if she doesn't hear from me in a few days, to start disseminating the report around the USGS and the rest of the government.

I'm now driving and am almost to Kingman where I'll need to fuel up again. I just got off the phone with Eric who had bad news for me. Henderson PD put too much pressure on him and, when first his lieutenant and then his deputy police chief had begun calling Alexa's cell phone, he decided he had to answer. They ordered him to report back to Henderson immediately, and he was on his way.

It's only a bit more than an hour's drive from Laughlin to Henderson which means Eric is going to reach it ahead of me. When he gets there, he'll claim his house was broken into and Alexa's car was stolen and a few minutes after that, this car will go out on the net as a stolen vehicle, greatly elevating my risk.

I pull into Kingman and stop at the same gas station. This time when I go in and prepay for the gas, I purchase a bottle of bleach-based cleaner and a pair of leather driving gloves designed for winter driving but thankfully uninsulated.

While the gasoline pumps, I take time to clean every bit of the interior of the car, wiping down all the surfaces that Allen and I might have touched. I then drive around to the back of the truck stop where there's a vacuum cleaner system. I take twenty precious minutes to thoroughly vacuum and then liberally spray the cleaner all around the interior, hopefully getting every bit of hair and DNA, my main concern being those belonging to Allen. If this car is ever forensically examined, finding my DNA has far fewer consequences for me than finding Allen's DNA would. It's bad if the police tie me to the car, but not terrible. All I would need is for Eric to not press charges for motor vehicle theft and I'll walk away. It's a guaranteed twenty years in prison for me, though, if they manage to tie Allen and me both to the car.

With some trepidation, I take my old backpack out of the trunk and carry it over to the dumpster behind the truck stop. Digging through it, I take out the remaining cash and stuff that in my pocket, then pull out the gun case and the laptop in its neoprene sleeve. I carefully unwrap the white, porcelain figurine of the mother holding the child, etched with the inscription *H.C. + T.C. = Forever*, the figurine that started this whole journey. I place that gently with the laptop. I then take one last gander at the clothes in the backpack, the winter gloves and jackets, the blankets that kept me warm on cold nights, the only things I've owned for the last two years. I'm done with them. No matter what happens in the next couple of days, I'm finished with being a transient, finished hiding and finished running. I leave the pack leaning against the dumpster. Maybe another transient will wander along and claim it for his own, or perhaps a store clerk will toss it away. Either way, I don't care. It's part of my history now.

Back in the Lexus, I head north on highway 93, wearing the driving gloves, the air conditioning blasting to make sure I don't sweat, the back windows of the car rolled down slightly to blow out the sickly smell of the bleach cleaner. I use the internet on the phone to find a number for the guard gate at Jackie Bastain's place, and when I call and identify myself as a police detective with LV Metro, the security guard forwards the call to Jackie's residence. I'm thrilled when she answers the phone, and when I tell her I have information about her daughter's murder, she agrees to meet with me.

I arrive in Boulder City just after six o'clock and roll through slowly, crossing Railroad Pass and then going down the long hill into the Las Vegas Valley, merging onto I-215 westbound. As it seems to happen every time you hope to not see any police officers, you seem to see them all, and I pass three highway patrol vehicles parked in the shade under overpasses, monitoring traffic as it crawls by, the evening rush hour in full effect. Thankfully, none of them pulls out after me, though I'm a nervous wreck while passing each one.

I hadn't counted on the heavy rush hour traffic, and I pull up to the guard gate a little after seven o'clock, more than thirty minutes after I told her I would be there. For the homeless, rush hour is simply a time when panhandling the freeway onramps is most profitable, not something to factor in to a commute.

"Detective Conner to see Mrs. Bastain," I say to the security guard at the gate. She checks her list and then nods and presses a button. The large, heavy, iron gates begin to slowly open and I nudge Alexa's car forward, pulling through as soon as there's room. It continues to amaze me that nearly everybody remains oblivious to the discrepancies in the character I'm impersonating. Nobody questions the ridiculous notion that a police detective would have a Lexus coupe as his on-duty vehicle. Present an image to someone and they accept it, despite what would seem to a careful observer to be glaringly obvious incongruities.

When I helped Allen escape, I'd been Detective Edward Townsend, Henderson PD. When I'd called Jackie Bastain earlier, it seemed better to retire that name. Plus, I didn't even have a badge with a last name engraved on it to show anymore, which made using a real name unnecessary. So, today when I called Jackie, I introduced myself as Detective Allen Conner, Las Vegas Metro Homicide, helping with the investigation into her daughter's murder. Not real original by any means, but the name was easy for me to remember.

I arrive at the Bastain house and drive past slowly, turning around at the end of the block and parking three houses away. When there's an all-points bulletin out on the stolen car you're driving, it's rarely a good idea to park it in front of the house where you're actually going to be located. In the driveway of the Bastain residence is a black Lincoln SUV. Walking past that, I glance through the garage door window and see the Tesla still parked inside, plugged into the supercharger. I'm reminded again of the Olds Cutlass that Jerry Bastain was murdered in. His driving that old car is a mystery that's bugging me, though I'm sure it has no relevance to the goal of my investigation. Still, I'm hoping to tie up that loose end today.

I approach the large, glass and iron double doors at the front of the house and ring the doorbell. The chime is a deep, sonorous bell that echoes through the house for a full ten seconds. Through the smoky glass, I see a woman approach the doors. I immediately recognize Jackie Bastain from the newspaper pictures I'd seen from when Jerry won the Asian Businessperson of the Year award. She's blonde, tall, and slender, dressed in blue, cut-off denim shorts and a white tank top. Her feet are bare and she wears no makeup, though that does nothing to detract from her good looks.

In her right hand, she's holding a glass containing ice cubes and an amber liquid.

I hold out my hand. "Mrs. Bastain, we spoke earlier on the phone. I'm Detective Conner with Las Vegas Metro. I'd like to speak to you about your daughter's murder."

She studies me blankly for a moment and then finally reaches out and shakes my hand, her grip loose and unenthusiastic.

"Come in," she says, turning and walking toward the kitchen. "You're late."

"Sorry about that." I close the door behind me and follow her through the grand entryway and into an enormous kitchen. The kitchen and living room are combined as one expansive room separated by an island and a bar made from a beautiful, enormous slab of granite. On the bar is a bottle of Scotch, only about a quarter of the amber liquid remaining in the bottle. Five large, tall chairs line the bar, but Jackie walks past them and into the living room. The living room contains a large LED television (made with rare earth elements, as I've just learned) inset into a richly-colored, built-in, wooden cabinet that stretches from the floor to the high ceiling. In front of the television are several dark brown, leather sofas arranged into three quarters of a rectangle. Jackie plops onto one of the couches, her long legs curled under her, a dour expression on her face. She motions for me to have a seat across from her and I do.

"Can I get you anything to drink?" she says, half-heartedly, making no effort to get up.

"No, thank you, I'm fine."

"Well then, what can I do for you? Quite honestly, I've had about enough of the interviews and I'd like to be left alone, so let's make this quick."

Her words are slightly slurred, and I can tell this isn't her first glass of Scotch today. I hardly blame her for the alcohol, nor for the sullen and unfriendly attitude. In the span of less than a month, she lost both her husband and her daughter to murders. Either one of those would be a devastating blow, and both of them coming so close together makes life tough to deal with. I should know.

"Mrs. Bastain…"

"Jackie," she interrupts, taking a sip of what I presume to be the Scotch in her glass.

"Jackie. I have to be honest with you. I'm not actually a cop."

She looks at me, really scrutinizes me for the first time. I see her eyes widen slightly with interest, though there's no apprehension.

I would expect to see some fear given that her husband and daughter were both recently murdered.

Before the fear she should have can work its way through the alcohol and pain-induced dullness, I continue. "I have reason to believe that the same men who killed your husband also killed your daughter. And I have further reason to believe that those same men murdered my wife and my son."

She frowns at that and glances at her drink before leaning forward and setting it on the coffee table between us. She then motions for me to go on.

"Through what was partly coincidence and partly design, I happen to have been present for both your husband's and your daughter's murders. I'm so sorry for your losses. As I mentioned, I lost my wife and son, so I know what you're going through."

"Who are you? What do you want from me?" she asks, inflection in her voice for the first time, though still no fear.

"My name really is Conner, Harvey Conner, and a little more than two years ago, my wife and my son were murdered. I never saw the murderers, and I was left alive so that I could be framed for their murders. I ran and, with nowhere to go, I took to living on the street. Last month, I happened to be there when your husband was murdered during a meeting with a guy downtown. I saw the murderer and I tracked him down."

"If that's true, then you can tell me his name," she replies.

"His name is Joseph Panattiere. He pulled the trigger, but he's not the one who's actually responsible for your husband's murder. He was simply hired to do a job. He was a hired hitman."

She nods, slowly. "I know."

I raise my eyebrows. "You know? How do you know that? What do you know?"

"Not yet," she replies. "First, tell me about my daughter."

"I first met your daughter a little over a year ago. I knew her only as Lizzy, and she was a sweet girl who had nothing but kind words for everybody she met."

Jackie grimaces and tears well up in her eyes. "Elizabeth was always a compassionate child. She never saw a stray dog she didn't want to bring home. When she ran away, I was devastated. I searched for her, even hired a private investigator to find her. He found her living downtown in a filthy apartment, doing God knows what with whoever for money. I begged her to come home but she wouldn't. I went to the police, but by then she had turned eighteen; she was an adult and they wouldn't do anything."

She leans forward and grabs her drink again, draining the Scotch and setting it back down. "It was Jerry's fault. They fought constantly all during her teens. They were just different people." She looks me in the eye and then glances down again. "Elizabeth had a boyfriend. Just a kid, a nice Chinese boy from a nice family. They were poor however, and Jerry was having none of that." She laughs, bitterly. "I guess he forgot that he was poor once, before he met the right people and got a huge hand up."

She stops talking and I prod her. "What did he do?"

"You have to understand something about my husband, Mr. Conner. He was a pillar of the community. The Asian community. Did you know he was named the Asian Businessperson of the Year a few years back?"

"Yes, I did actually."

She seems surprised by this, but continues. "It was all a sham. He's never done anything but follow orders. He was a puppet, Mr. Conner. A puppet on a string, incapable of denying his masters anything they wished for."

I'm not quite following, and I desperately want to know who the puppet masters are. I don't interrupt though, letting her continue at her own pace. She stands up and carries her glass over to the fridge, filling it with ice cubes and then pouring most of the remaining Scotch into it. She takes a paper towel and dabs her eyes with it, then walks back over to the couch where she sits down again.

"Jerry caught Elizabeth one night with the Chinese boy. They were having sex in the car, just down the street from our house. It was the boy's car. The same one Jerry was later murdered in." She laughs again and takes a large swallow. "Oh, the irony."

"What happened?"

"Jerry ripped open the door and grabbed the boy. He beat him senseless and then dragged him into the house, Elizabeth following, screaming and crying. Somebody, one of the neighbors, called the security guard over the commotion and he came up. Jerry met him outside and talked to him. Probably paid him off. That's what he was trained to do. Then he called his men. They showed up and took the poor boy away. Elizabeth never saw him again."

"What happened to him?" I ask, mortified by this story, and by my new understanding of the type of person Jerry Bastain was.

Jackie shrugs. "No idea. Maybe he was sent away, maybe back to China. Maybe they murdered him and buried his body. I don't know. I live in a bit of a bubble up here in this gated community, if you haven't noticed. Jerry never allowed us to associate with what he considered lower types. It wasn't good for our image. I like to hope his family was just bought off and they moved, but I dread that I'm wrong."

"How did Jerry end up with the Olds?"

She laughs, humorlessly. "He bought it from the boy's family. Or maybe he stole it from them. I don't know, but he showed up driving it the next day. He parked it in the driveway as a reminder to Elizabeth. She was seventeen years old, almost eighteen, and her father not only made her boyfriend disappear, he also parked the boy's car in the driveway as a reminder." Her next words are bitter and full of resentment. "Elizabeth hated him after that. She ran away a few weeks later and never came back. I'm convinced she became a prostitute just to punish her father. And it worked. He was never the same when the private investigator came and told us what he'd found, where she was living and what she was doing for money. Everything changed after that."

I'm saddened by this story and by the tragedy of poor Lizzy's life and death, but as much as I don't want to, I need to hear the rest of it.

"Everything changed how?"

She motions toward me with her hand. "No. It's your turn. I want to know how you knew my daughter and how she died."

Fair enough. I tell her about meeting Lizzy and about Allen (I don't tell her his real name, just refer to him as Allen; nor do I mention his age, thinking the fact that he's more than twice her daughter's age wouldn't set well) and his love for her. I tell her stories about Lizzy's kindness and her generosity. I explain the day Lizzy disappeared and about Allen's search for her. With trepidation, I tell her that I'm partially responsible for Lizzy's murder. I tell her about the note in the apartment, and how Lizzy's kidnapping was an attempt to lure me out. I skip over the details about Nick and the police who responded to Panattiere's house, and instead tell her that I followed clues that led me to the warehouse. I tell her about Dominic and Reggie and that Allen tried to save her but Reggie murdered her before he could. I don't go into the graphic details of her throat being slit and blood pouring out everywhere, though I do tell her that Allen beat Reggie to death with an iron pipe. I think it would help a mother to know that her daughter's murderer died a violent death. Although I try not to think about it, I know deep down that I felt a small amount of satisfaction when I saw Reggie's caved-in face and his sightless eyes.

When I've finished the story, Jackie nods. She sat motionless for the entire thing, never glancing away from me, holding her drink while the ice cubes melted. Now she takes another sip.

"I'll never forgive myself for letting her go. I'll never forgive Jerry for chasing her away. I'm glad he's dead."

She's eerily still, and I feel terrible for her. She's in such pain right now and I want to be able to tell her it will be all right, that the pain will fade. I'm surprised at that thought, but I realize that the pain of my own tragedy has dissipated slightly, in such small increments that I haven't realized it. The memories will never disappear altogether, but the worst ones are mostly gone, and the good ones are still sharp and bright. The happy times Tracy, Dillon and I had are still vivid in my mind. The images of their lifeless bodies are blurred and unclear. The human mind is capable of incredible levels of recovery from tragedy, but it takes time, and I know any words to say to her that will come across as more than empty platitudes, so I say nothing. Instead, I commiserate with her in silence.

After a minute or two, I focus on her.

"Jackie, I'd like to know who ordered the murders of my wife and son, and I think you know who it is."

She takes a deep breath. "Do you know why they were killed?"

"I know they were killed on orders from some representative of the Chinese government. I have reason to believe the man at the top is named Theo. My wife held something that the Chinese desperately wanted. To get it, they needed her dead and me charged with the crime. I need to find out who that man is."

"What will you do if you find out?" she asks.

"I'll kill him," I answer, without preamble and without emotion.

She takes a moment and then nods. "Good. The man you're looking for is Theo Zhao. He's the west coast representative for the Chinese government here in the U.S. He's also the one who gave orders to my husband."

Theo Zhao. I finally have the name, and my heart soars.

"What kind of orders did he give your husband?"

"The Chinese have a master plan, Mr. Conner. They want to take over the world, and they know it's going to take generations to do it, but they don't care. They think long term and they plan long term, and Americans will never understand that level of commitment, that depth of thinking and intricacy of plotting. That's why it will work, because the Chinese will labor in the shadows until they own everything and it's too late to stop them."

I nod. A few months ago, I'd have thought this nothing more than a racist rant by a white nationalist. Now I know better. While I don't necessarily believe the Chinese are trying to take over the world, the information Erin Fogler gave me about the Chinese monopoly on rare earth elements was frightening and eye opening.

She continues. "I first met Jerry a little more than twenty years ago. He was young and ambitious, good looking and funny. He'd been born in America, though his parents came here illegally. Being born here made him a citizen automatically and made it easier for his parents to eventually gain citizenship as well. Anyway, he was raised in L.A. but came to Vegas shortly after his eighteenth birthday. He owned a single coffee shop when I met him, and it was incredibly successful. So successful that he was able to open several more."

She pauses to take another sip of the Scotch, and it's obvious that she's becoming impaired. Her words are slurring regularly now, and she's laughing spontaneously during her story. I'm hoping she can get through it before she gets too drunk.

"I fell in love and we married. I was already pregnant with Elizabeth when we got married, which is one of the reasons I was willing to marry him so quickly. If only I'd known then..." she trails off.

"Known what?" I prod.

She snorts. "That Jerry was a shill. A fraud. He was successful only because the Chinese were all forced to support other Chinese businesses. None of them would have been caught dead with a cup of Starbucks in their hand. Nope, nothing but SHANGHAI ESPRESSO for the Chinese!" She shouts this last part, lifts her glass and then laughs again.

"Even back then, the plans were well underway." She focuses intently on me. "You knew he was the Asian Businessperson of the Year. Do you know how he won that *honor*" She emphasizes the word *honor* sarcastically.

"No."

"The commendation that accompanied the title said it was for all of his support of Asian-owned businesses and the Asian community."

I nod. I remember reading that.

"What it should have said was *Chinese*-owned businesses and the *Chinese* community." But of course, they couldn't say that; it would sound too distinctly nationalist. And, it would provide a hint of the takeover plan! So they said, *Asian-owned businesses*, which is a joke. All of those guys are complete racists when it comes to other Asian races. You think any of those businesses he supported were Japanese? Please. Any Korean businesses, any Vietnamese businesses? No fucking chance. Every business he supported, every student he sent to college, every charity he wrote a check to—they were all Chinese. Every last one."

She pauses, holds up her glass and shouts, "Here's to Chairman Mao and the future Communist States of America!" She downs the remainder of the Scotch. I watch her, the pieces slowly falling into place. Most of them anyway.

"So then why was he killed?"

She looks at me, soberly but not sober. "He wanted out. He'd had enough. Nobody gets out, and he knew that, but he wanted out anyway."

It seemed to me, surveying their expansive and decadent house, that he had a pretty good thing going, so I ask, "Why?"

She's quiet a minute before answering. "Freedom. He had no freedom. In the land of the free, he had less freedom than a normal person even in Communist China would have. He was subject to the wills and whims of his overlords, and God forbid he ever said no or ever questioned an order. I'd had enough of it years ago, and he finally decided he'd had enough too."

I think back to Tracy's figurine that was in his car. "Was your husband involved in my wife and son's murders?" I ask, dreading the answer.

"I wish I could say he wasn't, but who knows?" She gives an exaggerated shrug of her shoulders, stands up and starts pacing. "If Theo was involved, then Jerry probably was too. He was Theo's right-hand man; he did everything Theo asked of him."

I describe the figurine I found, explaining it had belonged to my wife and that it had been in Jerry's car when he was murdered. "Did you ever see anything like that?" I ask her.

She nods. "Yup. I saw it in the Olds. He kept it in there all the time. I asked him about it once but he wouldn't tell me what it was or where it came from. Just another secret in a long list of them, that bastard."

She's angry and pacing faster, but I persist. "How do you know he wanted out? How did you find out he was going to quit?" I ask.

She stops pacing and the anger disappears, replaced by a sadness. It's clear that she's miserable, and the range of emotion she's displaying is disquieting. "He told me the night before his murder. It was almost a confession. He said he had done things he wasn't proud of, things that haunted him to this day, and that he was getting out of it all. I thought at the time he was talking about Elizabeth and her poor boyfriend, but who knows? If he was involved in your wife and son's murder, maybe that was it. Maybe he kept that figurine as a reminder of what he'd done. I'd like to believe he felt some remorse for his actions."

I don't care if he felt remorse or not. It's starting to appear as if Jerry Bastain was involved in my wife and son's murders. If Theo ordered the murders through Jerry, then Jerry was the one who hired Dominic, who gave the job to his two henchmen, Joey and Reggie. Jerry, Dominic, and Reggie are all dead, and Joey is in jail, untouchable at the moment, which just leaves Theo. I feel a little like Arya Stark from *Game of Thrones* as I make a mental list of people I need to kill and, for the first time, I truly understand her character.

"Jackie, what I don't understand is why did the Chinese use the Italian mob guys as the trigger pullers? Why not use their own people, 14K Triad or something like that?"

Jackie starts pacing again and laughs. "There is no 14K Triad, at least not out here in Vegas. Not yet anyway. Once they show up, this city is really fucked. Everybody thinks they're just another gang, like the Bloods or the Crips, but they're not. They're much worse. But even if they did have a presence here, Theo would have never used them. The 14K is anti-China and anti-communist. They're based out of Hong Kong which isn't even really a part of China." She tries to take another sip of her drink but it's empty, and she sets the glass back down. "Theo has his own group, but they're small. They have a presence all over the country, but there's only a few of them in Vegas right now. But they'll grow, believe me. They're known as *JiaFeng Zhu*, which means *The Liberators*, and they're the international enforcement arm for the Chinese army, the People's Liberation Army. Do you understand how serious that is?" She stops pacing and stares at me with wide eyes. "The Chinese already have an army on American soil. The *JiaFeng Zhu* are nothing more than an extension of the Chinese military, taking orders from the government. Someday they'll be ensconced throughout the country, and then wait and see how bad things get. But they aren't big enough here in Vegas yet, so Theo uses other groups to do his wet work."

"Groups like the Mafia. Organized crime syndicates," I state.

"Exactly," she replies. "And mostly the crew that was headed up by Dominic Carvelo."

I nod. It makes sense. Theo decides Tracy needs to die, and maybe Dillon as well, so he hires Dominic who turns the job over to Joey and Reggie. Or, perhaps Theo orders Jerry to facilitate it all, and Jerry hires Dominic. Then, a couple years later, Theo decides Jerry Bastain needs to die, and he again hires Dominic who sends the work to Joey once again. And I happen to be in the right place to witness it, which is absolutely astonishing when you think about it, though I'd had no idea at the time that what I'd witnessed was going to have such an impact on my life. I consider asking Jackie to help me find and trap Theo, but I realize she's become very drunk and loud, and it's time for me to make my exit.

"How do I find this Theo Zhao?" I ask her.

She snorts. "It shouldn't be too tough. Just go downtown to city hall any weekday and you'll find him. He's a Las Vegas City Councilman."

Chapter 8

My shock at hearing that the man who ordered the murder of my wife and son is a Las Vegas Councilman dissipates pretty quickly. I mean, it makes sense that such a man, executing such an agenda as the Chinese allegedly have, would have inserted himself into a position of power. This was why he was able to get such a heavy response from the police that night during the ambush at Panattiere's house. A councilman calling someone high up in the police department and saying he has information regarding the whereabouts of a wanted fugitive is going to get any response he asks for. Power combined with a willingness to abuse it is a dangerous thing.

I could go downtown and try to confront Councilman Zhao, but that seems complicated and dangerous. How would I do it? Just walk up to him on the street and put a gun in his side? How would I even facilitate running into him like that? If this was a movie, I'd simply go down there and happen to catch him walking to lunch, or parking his car, or something similar. But real life is rarely that easy.

Also, I'm pretty familiar with City Hall. It's located just a few blocks from Fremont Street, an area I've roamed nearly every day of the last two years. I've maintained enough of my observational skills that I can recall lots of security cameras around that area, both on the streets and on the City Hall building itself. The jail is across the street from City Hall, and police patrols are almost constant all through that area. There's a good reason I avoided the block of streets immediately surrounding City Hall while I lived in that area.

Perhaps I can confront him at his house. A man of his social stature will almost certainly live in a gated community. Gated communities in Las Vegas are a dime a dozen, and anybody who's anybody lives in one. The most exclusive, such as the one I'm in right now, have guards at the gate 24/7, as well as roving patrols, intruder alarms tied right to the gate house, resident panic buttons, and such. It won't be like it was at Joey's where I simply hopped the wall behind the house. Nor will it be as easy as the first time I came here to Jerry and Jackie's house and snuck into their backyard while nobody was home.

I need a solid plan. I need to be able to question him. I'm not going to take Jackie's word for it that he's the one who ordered my family's murders, even though there's no part of me that doubts that, not for a second. The evidence all points to him, including the independent evidence I've gathered over the last month. But I know that in order for me to be able to ever move on, to ever have any semblance of a normal life, I'll need to talk to him. To ask Theo Zhao why. Why, with one order, was he able to alter the course of so many lives with so little thought? And, if I'm truly going to kill him, I need to be one-hundred percent sure he's responsible.

Jackie has been talking while I've been thinking, and I tune back in to hear her saying, "...Theo recruited Jerry before I ever knew him; he brought him into the fold quickly and completely. And, that worked out real well for Jerry and for me." She motions around the expansive and beautifully decorated house and laughs. "I guess I have nothing to complain about, do I?"

"Jackie, no offense, but you deserved better. I've learned in recent years that belongings are not the key to happiness. You have a beautiful home, but I doubt it was worth the pain you're going through right now and the pain you're going to feel in the future."

She nods slowly and sits down next to me.

"I need some water, please," she says, her head in her hands.

I grab her empty Scotch glass and dump it in the sink on my way to the cabinet. Pouring some water from the fridge, I bring it back to her and stand beside her while she drinks it. She's drunk, she's depressed and sad, and while I feel bad for her, I just don't have time for it. It's time for me to go. I tell her as much and thank her for her help.

"Wait," she replies, standing up and grabbing my hand. "I want to help you."

"You already have, Jackie."

"No. I want to help you kill him."

I shake my head with exasperation. "Jackie, I don't know what I'm going to do yet. I don't know how to confront him or how to question him. I need more information and I need time to come up with a plan. And, I work alone. I can't have you there."

"Harvey, I can help you. I *know* Theo. I can set up a meeting, I can make something up and get invited to his house, his office, whatever. Let me help you!"

She's slurring her words slightly, but her offer appears genuine and sincere. And, I could use some help with the planning, even though I don't intend to use her in the operation itself. I sit back down on the couch with her and we spend the next hour discussing different options. At one point, I get up and make a pot of coffee which I make her drink, trying to sober her up. I tell her the most important thing is for me to have time alone with Theo. I need to get answers from him, to make sure there wasn't anybody else involved in Tracy and Dillon's murders, and to tie up some disturbing loose ends.

We have the beginnings of a decent plan when the doorbell rings.

"Are you expecting company?" I ask Jackie.

"No. Hold on a sec."

She grabs the remote control from the coffee table and turns on the TV. A security camera view of the front door appears and I see two Metro police officers in uniform, peering through the window panes of the front door.

"Oh, crap," I say.

"I'll get rid of them," Jackie says, standing up.

I grab her arm. "Jackie, this is important. I'm not here, there's nobody here, you're alone. You have no idea who I am, haven't left the house, haven't seen anybody, is that clear?"

She shakes her arm free from my grasp. "Relax. I said I'll get rid of them."

She marches around the corner and into the entryway and I turn back to the TV, seeing the door open just a crack, Jackie's face appearing on the screen.

"Can I help you?" she asks, her voice coming from down the hallway, slightly out of synch with the video.

I have a moment of panic. If the police officers checked in with the gate guard, they know someone's here, and I just told Jackie to say she hadn't seen anybody. It's too late to warn her now.

"Hi ma'am, Las Vegas Metro," I hear one of the officers say. "We're here because there's a white Lexus parked down the road from you and we're looking for the driver. Have you seen anybody?"

"No, I sure haven't." I see her on the television smile tightly at them and then start to close the door.

One of the officers places his hand on the door, holding it open. "Excuse me, ma'am, but we checked with the gate guard and they tell us that car entered the property bound for this address. The driver identified himself as Detective Conner with Metro PD. Are you telling me you don't know who this is? Because according to the guard at the gate, Jackie Bastain phoned down to them about an hour prior to him showing up, authorizing entry for a Detective Conner."

There's a slight pause from Jackie and I move to the back door, a sliding glass door that leads to the backyard. I can see a large yard with an enormous swimming pool, as well as a cabana and an outdoor bar area. There's a high block wall at the back of the yard, and I know from my last trip here there's a large drop-off on the other side.

"Well, officers," I hear Jackie saying, "a Detective Conner was supposed to meet me here over an hour ago now and he never showed up. Perhaps you can call him and find out where he is. I have to tell you, I'm a little bit pissed off. What's wrong with you guys that you can't keep your appointments? And if he drove up here, he sure didn't come to the door, so where did he go? And what kind of detective drives a Lexus anyway?"

I glance back at the television and see the two officers give each other a confused glance. Jackie is scowling angrily and has opened the door further. She has her hands on her hips and is staring at the nearest officer, waiting for a reply.

"So, you did have an appointment with Detective Conner? Do you know his first name?"

"No, I don't know his first name. He called and said he was Detective Conner and he needed to speak to me."

"Do you know what it was regarding, ma'am?" I hear the other officer ask.

"I assume it had something to do with my daughter's murder a few weeks ago, which you guys haven't managed to solve, or perhaps my husband's murder from over a month ago, which you also haven't managed to solve."

Jackie's voice is full-on angry now, and I can't help but smile a little at the marks of contrition on the officers' faces.

"Ma'am, are you telling me both your husband and your daughter were murdered in two separate incidents?"

"I believe that's exactly what I'm telling you, officer. Jerry and Elizabeth Bastain if you want to check. Now, are you telling me that not only do you not have information for me on who murdered my family, but you've also now got a rogue detective who drives a Lexus and seems to be missing? Is the entire force as incompetent as you three?"

The first officer is quiet a moment and then replies, "Ma'am, is it okay if we come inside and check your house just for your safety?"

Please say no. Please say no. Please say no.

"Check my house for what? Your rogue detective? I already told you, he's not here."

"Ma'am," I hear the first officer say slowly, "we checked with dispatch after we stopped at the guard gate. We don't have a Detective Conner on the force." The officer lowers his voice and I can hear him talking but can't understand the words. I see on the television that both officers now have their hands on their guns, though, and I can guess what they're saying and what's about to happen.

I see Jackie glance up at the camera, and I know the officers are asking her if she's under duress. I also know what her glance means. She's going to have to let them in. If she doesn't, they're not going to be satisfied she's safe.

Fuck.

I stride quickly over to the sliding glass door and open it quietly, stepping out and sliding it shut behind me. Just before it closes, I hear Jackie say,

"If it will make you feel better, come on in. I'm alone here, though, I promise you that."

I walk quickly over to the patio bar, poring over the yard for a place to hide. I've done house searches before. Even when you're sure it's nothing but a false alarm, when the ninety-year old woman tells you she heard a noise upstairs and wants you to check, you still take the time to check every spot where a person could hide. I'm in big trouble.

It's going to take them at least twenty minutes to check the house, as big as it is, so I have time before they get to the yard. Unless they happen to gaze out a window. I can possibly jump into a neighbor's yard, or over the back wall. I check the back wall first, grabbing the top and pulling myself up, poking my head over slowly. As I suspected, there's a steep, rock-covered slope that falls away sharply down to the road about fifty feet below. I might be able to navigate the hill, but it's quite likely I'll break an ankle if I try and, even if I don't, I'll make all kinds of noise sliding down that rock-covered slope. I suddenly notice something that makes even that last-ditch option completely out of the question...a patrol car is parked on the lower road, watching the back side of the houses for anybody attempting to flee in that direction.

The neighboring yards seem to be my only option. I'm headed for the southern border when a noise suddenly registers. I've been hearing it for the last fifteen seconds or so, but just now realized the significance of it. Scanning the skies, I spot the helicopter headed right for me, it's searchlight, the midnight sun as it's known, already turned on, tracking its path as it flies toward me at 200 feet. It's not quite dark just yet, but the searchlight will pierce whatever shadows I might have tried to use.

They've called in an airship for support, and I'm screwed.

Chapter 9

In addition to the searchlight, the helicopter will also have a

thermal imager, the FLIR system, able to pick up body heat from a person hiding where the searchlight won't penetrate. The air is probably too hot for it to work well, but if the search goes on into the night, they'll be able to make good use of that feature.

There's only one option left, and with a quick glance back at the house, I slip quietly into the pool.

The pool is a large one with a rock formation against the back wall of it, water pouring down over the rocks in a beautiful shower that's supposed to be pleasing to the senses. I'm hoping it's more than just for looks though.

I swim underwater to the rocks and surface behind the waterfall. It's not a large waterfall, and there's nowhere near enough volume to hide me from a searcher on the ground, but the overhanging rocks shield me from the helicopter which I can now hear circling the neighborhood, the whine of its powerful turbine engine audible even over the sound of the water. My hopes for the rock pile the water spills over are realized when I rub my eyes to clear them of the water and spot the grotto.

A cave, recessed in the rock, with ledges just below the water level for swimmers to relax. I swim forward and lift myself onto the ledge, pulling myself up and back behind the wall. There's no walking path that allows access to the craftily hidden grotto, and the cops will have to get wet if they want to find me here.

I sit still, not moving, not wanting to risk a splash that might be heard, unable to see the yard or to know if the search is still ongoing. The air inside the grotto is humid and warm, so getting chilled isn't a factor, though my wet pants and shoes quickly grow uncomfortable. I have no way of knowing how long it's been, and when I check my phone, I realize it doesn't work, destroyed by the plunge into the pool.

Everything in my pockets is soaked, including my gun which I don't worry about. It's a Glock, and it's designed to fire while totally submerged in water, so I know it'll be fine. I don't need it now anyway; if the police find me, I'll give up; I'm not shooting a cop.

After what I guess to be almost an hour, I realize I don't hear the helicopter anymore. Night has fallen while I've been in here, and it's completely dark in the grotto, so I take a chance and slip back into the water, taking care to not make a splash. I swim slowly under the waterfall and then surface my head, blinking my eyes to clear them, prepared to duck back under if I see anyone. There's nobody in the yard. Just as I'm about to swim to the edge of the pool, I see Jackie approach the glass door and slide it open. She peers into the yard.

"Are you out here, Harvey? It's all clear."

She could be tricking me I suppose, but if she wanted to turn me in, she had ample opportunity to do it, and she certainly knew about the grotto and must have guessed that was the only place I could hide.

"I'm here," I reply, and swim to the edge. I climb out on the underwater steps and stand dripping on the pool deck.

"I'm sorry," she says, grinning slightly and looking anything but sorry. "I didn't think I had much of a choice but to let them in. I thought you would just jump the wall to the neighbor's or something."

"They had a helicopter," I say, walking to a basket of towels and grabbing one to dry off.

"Yeah, I noticed that afterwards, when the cops finished searching the house and came back here to look. I figured you'd discovered the grotto when I saw the helicopter and they didn't find you."

I know she didn't have a choice but to let them in, and I'm grateful she didn't make matters worse by refusing. That would have likely worked out poorly.

"How did they find the car so quickly?" I ask her.

"Mrs. Nancy Nosy down the road called it in," she replies. "She calls in a complaint every time someone parks on the street in front of her house."

It figures that I'd park in front of the neighborhood busybody's house. "Did they tow it?" I ask. My laptop and gun case are still inside, along with the figurine. I don't have any need for them right now, but the laptop will certainly have information that will identify it as mine if they do a forensic examination of it, and my prints are going to be on all the items.

"No. They told me they're going to sit on it, whatever that means. They're still searching for the driver."

That gives me some time to contact Eric and make sure he tells them the stuff belongs to him.

"Come on in and get dried off. I made dinner too. The police went to search the neighbors' houses, and the helicopter stayed around for that, so I had time before I could come get you."

She leads me into the house and directs me upstairs where she points out her husband's closet.

"Find something in there that fits you and we'll throw your clothes into the dryer; then we'll eat and plan out how we're going to take down Theo."

"What's with this *we* stuff? I already told you I don't need your help; I'm going after him alone."

Jackie smiles at me sweetly and walks out of the room without replying. I shake my head with a grimace and then walk into the huge closet, searching through the clothing for anything that will fit. Most of it is too small, but I manage to find a dress shirt that works, and a pair of swim trunks that I could have made better use of a couple of hours ago. It feels strange to be putting on a dead man's clothing, but I've certainly worn worse clothes the last few years.

I bundle my soaked clothes together and carry them to the bathtub where I wring them out. Finding the washer and dryer in the hallway, I throw them all into the dryer and start it. I then head downstairs to eat some dinner and, for the first time, plan the capture and possibly the death of the man responsible for the murder of Tracy and Dillon.

Chapter 10

It's almost 11pm, and I'm lying on the floor of Jackie's SUV as she

pulls out through the gates of her subdivision, waving to the security guard as she drives past the booth. To sneak me out of the house, she'd opened the garage door and backed the SUV in, pretending to load a few things in the back while I climbed in, just in case anybody was watching, though I suspected the watchers, wherever they were, were focused on the Lexus three houses down from hers.

Nobody stops us or challenges us as we head out of the neighborhood and turn onto Durango, headed south to I-215. I wait until we've merged onto 215 going east before I climb up into the front passenger seat and buckle myself in.

We came up with the plan over dinner and, even though I didn't want Jackie's help, I came to realize that I need it. With the cops watching Alexa's car, I no longer have transportation, and at the very least I needed her help on that front, something she wasn't willing to offer without full involvement leaving me handcuffed, so to speak.

Step A of the plan had been Jackie making a phone call to Theo, telling him that she'd found something while cleaning up Jerry's study. The one thing Theo seems to want more than anything is

Tracy's assay report on the rare earths, so I had Jackie tell Theo what she had for him was a sealed manila envelope with his name on it. If he asked her to open it, I gave her enough information from the real report for her to convincingly pretend that's what was inside the envelope, but he doesn't ask. Instead, he arranges to meet her downtown at midnight. According to Jackie, it was not unusual for Jerry to have late-night meetings with Theo downtown, often even in his City Hall office.

We're plenty early when we arrive, and I jump out at a stoplight a couple of blocks from the meeting location while Jackie drives another block away and parks to wait. I'm wearing the light-colored khakis and white t-shirt I borrowed from Eric's house yesterday, freshly washed and dried courtesy of Jackie's pool and dryer. I would have preferred something dark so I could blend in to the night, but nothing in Jerry's closet fit me, so I'm going to have to make do.

The meeting is set for the southern end of the parking lot of the Plaza Hotel, which means we'll be directly across the street from Theo's office, also known as City Hall. He chose the location, not the best option for us, but it is the option that should raise the fewest alarm bells in his mind if he's at all suspicious.

As I mentioned before, ever since they built the new City Hall here several years ago, there are a lot of street cameras in the area, and I keep an eye out for them as I stroll down Main street. Just north of the MTO café, there's an alley that runs between the café and a warehouse, and I turn down that alley, making my way behind the city parking garage, walking quietly through the darkness of the alleyway. There are two dumpsters from the MTO café back here, and I spot the familiar sight of a pair of legs sticking out from the space between them. A transient lies on a double piece of cardboard, a blanket over him as he sleeps.

I walk cautiously past him and reach a chest-high wire mesh fence that separates the alley and the city building from the vacant lot that serves as overflow parking for the Plaza Hotel. This is where, in about twenty minutes' time, Jackie is supposed to meet with Theo, and I'm scouting for a spot I can hide and observe the meeting take place.

The fence has been pulled away where it once touched the warehouse building, curled back to allow transit through it, likely done by a transient, possibly by the same one sleeping just a few feet away. As I'm well aware, transients aren't often dissuaded by property boundaries, fences, or *No Trespassing* signs. Getting arrested just means a temporary cot and three squares for most of them.

I push through the gap in the fence and move slowly up to the corner of the warehouse. There's a stack of pallets in front of me which makes for good cover and allows me to peer through the gaps while still remaining hidden. The problem is that the parking lot area is huge, and I don't know exactly where the meeting will take place. I curse at myself for not thinking to bring binoculars and for not having darker clothing.

Leaning against the wall and adjusting my gun, which is in a holster at the small of my back, I settle in to wait, taking deep breaths of the hot air which, even this late at night, is still in the mid-nineties. Not uncomfortably hot like it is when the sun is pounding down on you, but certainly not a desirable temperature at almost midnight.

I glance around the parking lot, checking for any movement. I see two men walking about two hundred or so yards away. They're Plaza Casino employees, and they stand at a car talking for a couple of minutes and then separate, each getting into his own car and driving off. There are other cars scattered throughout the parking lot, including a few within fifty yards of my location, though the vast concentration of cars is on the north end of the lot much closer to the Plaza.

After the two Plaza employees leave, I see no further movement at this end of the lot until about twenty minutes after I arrived. I see

Jackie's Lincoln pull into the lot and turn towards me, driving slowly. She circles the northwestern end of the lot and then comes to a stop under a light pole just thirty yards away, turning off her headlights but leaving the engine running, parking lights on.

I have Jerry's phone in my pocket, returned to Jackie by the police after his murder and loaned by her to me for this operation; it vibrates. I don't check it, knowing it's just a text from Jackie telling me she's in place. The protocol we set up requires me to respond only if I need her to park in a different location and, even though I'd love her to be closer, it might seem suspicious to Theo if she's too close to the buildings and fence. The place she is will have to work, and I've already confirmed that none of the cameras on Main Street should have coverage of this part of the lot.

We maintain our positions for another ten minutes, and I'm itching to check the phone for the time, but I don't want the light from the screen to give away my position if anybody is watching. Just as I decide to risk it and check, I see a black Cadillac Escalade drive into the parking lot. It comes from across Main Street, from Lewis Avenue, which runs directly behind City Hall and also happens to be where key members of City Hall have a private parking lot. I stand up straighter, moving closer to the pallets to get a better view, adjusting the gun to a more easily accessible position.

The Escalade pulls up and parks directly in front of Jackie's vehicle, nose to nose. The engine shuts off and the driver's door opens. In the glow from the streetlight, I can see a man dressed in a dark suit and he's Asian. He peers through the window of Jackie's Navigator and makes a motion for her to get out. She opens the door and steps out, the interior light from the Navigator illuminating the inside of the vehicle. The Asian steps forward and peers through the windows of her vehicle checking the back seat and the cargo compartment, and I'm relieved we decided against having me hide there.

The man in the suit then walks back to the Escalade and opens the rear door, and I get my first glimpse of the man who ordered the murders of my family and changed my life forever.

He's Chinese, obviously, dressed in a dark suit as well, though he's not wearing a tie. I place him in his late fifties, possibly early sixties, with a slight middle-age paunch above his belt. His black hair is streaked with gray, thin and slicked back. He's wearing round frame, silver glasses, and he stares a moment at Jackie, then gestures to her to walk over to him while pulling a pack of cigarettes from his pocket, putting one in his mouth, and lighting it.

Jackie steps between the vehicles and approaches Theo Zhao, the manila envelope in her hand. She appears stiff and nervous to me, and I don't blame her. Everything about Zhao, from the driver/bodyguard who checks things out before opening his door, to the dark vehicle, expensive suit, posture, bearing, and flippant expression, screams of power.

I'm too far away to hear their full conversation, although I catch snatches of it on the gentle breeze that's blowing from the north. The plan is for Jackie to ask him about Jerry's death, to confront him about his involvement in it. When he's distracted by her question, I'll approach from my hiding spot with my gun. We'll subdue the driver that Jackie knew was always with him, and then we'll take Theo to a place Jackie knows, a house belonging to a friend of hers who's on vacation. From there we'll have all the time we need to question him and decide what to do with him.

I can't hear their conversation, but we anticipated that possibility. Jackie is going to ask Theo the question just after she hands him the envelope, before he can open it and see that it's nothing but blank papers. She reaches out with the envelope, and Theo takes it from her. I draw my gun and prepare to step out, approaching them from the bodyguard's blind side. Just as I'm taking the first step, I hear the sound of two car doors opening, and spot a flash of light. It's coming from one of the parked cars, one of the cars that I thought was empty, about fifty yards back from where Jackie's and Theo's vehicles are parked. The doors close and two men approach the three of them. They're too far away for me to see them clearly, and I freeze, waiting to see what happens. Theo, Jackie, and the bodyguard all turn to watch the two men approaching. Their backs are turned toward me, and I can't see their faces, but I do see Theo take a drag from his cigarette, a relaxed gesture that makes me think the two new guys are not friends of ours. As they arrive in the pool of light from the streetlight, I notice first that they're Asian, and second that they're the same guys from the auction, Mr. Smith and Mr. Jones, AKA, Mr. Nguyen and Mr. Ang. The third thing I notice is that they're both holding drawn guns pointed directly at Jackie.

Chapter 11

I melt quietly and slowly back into the shadows behind the stack

of pallets, cursing again my light-colored clothing that's surely making me stand out in the darkness if anybody looks closely. Jackie is turning her head rapidly back and forth, scanning for me I'm sure, and I silently beg her to stop. It's four against two now, with at least two guns on their side, and I have no chance whatsoever.

I hear Jackie shout, "No. Don't!" and the bodyguard grabs her arm and squeezes, hitting a pressure point and causing her legs to buckle.

"Get in the vehicle, please, Mrs. Bastain," carries across the lot to me, Theo's voice as he motions with the cigarette.

Jackie looks as if she wants to fight, but must realize that the odds are impossible, because she scans the area again and then meekly walks to her Navigator. The bodyguard who was driving Theo's car gets behind the wheel of Jackie's, while one of the others, Nguyen or Ang, gets in the backseat with her, gun drawn and pointed at her.

I'm helpless to assist at the moment and decide to stay hidden and wait for an opportunity if one presents itself.

It doesn't.

Theo has a quick word with the other guy who then walks back across the lot to the car they'd been waiting in. He gets in and starts it up, and the Navigator drives slowly off, the other car pulling in behind it, following it out of the parking lot and onto Main Street where both vehicles turn left.

Theo watches them go, his back to me, puffing on the cigarette as he leans his elbows on the hood of his Escalade. I reach into my pocket for the cell phone Jackie gave me, pulling up an app and hitting a button before putting it back into my pocket and then stepping out from the shadow of the pallets. I walk quietly up to Theo, who's still standing there, manila envelope in one hand, cigarette dangling from his mouth. He rips open the envelope as I approach and pulls the sheaf of papers out, staring at them. Despite the danger and uncertainty, I can't help but smile at his expression as he sees the blank pages.

He drops the envelope and starts hastily shuffling through the papers, glancing at the front, then the back, before dropping each one beside the envelope. His distraction allows me to get close, the gun pointed at him, and I step up to within five feet of his back.

"Not what you expected I'm guessing?" I say quietly.

He whips around, papers in both hands, cigarette still hanging from his lips, and stares at me.

"Who are you?" he asks, concerned but not fearful.

"Someone who's been searching for you for a long time. And someone who you've wanted to find as well."

He stares at me a moment and then drops the rest of the papers, pulling the cigarette from his mouth and blowing smoke up into the air.

"Ah, yes. Hello, Mr. Conner," he says, rather coolly for someone who has a gun aimed at his head.

"Theo Zhao. Las Vegas City Councilman. Head of *JiaFeng Zhu.* Head of Chinese interests for the west coast of the United States. Murderer, thief, and apparently as of tonight if not before, kidnapper. Also, I might add, all-around scumbag."

He smiles at the last part and takes another drag from the cigarette, blowing the smoke upwards and then dropping the butt, grinding it under his heel.

"That last one is a bit hurtful. And you certainly can't prove the others, though I will say it appears you've done some homework."

"It's long past time you and I had a little chat," I tell him.

He nods at the gun in my hand. "We don't need a gun to have a chat, Mr. Conner. I've been wanting to meet you for a long time now, but you've been notoriously hard to find."

"Well, now's your chance. But first, take off your jacket."

He pauses a minute, and then shrugs and slips his jacket off, holding it in his hand.

"Lift your shirt and spin around."

"I assure you, Mr. Conner, I'm not armed. I have people for that." He smiles at me.

"Do it anyway. No offense, but I'm not that inclined to take your word for it."

He shrugs again and lifts his shirt, spinning around slowly so that I can see his waistband.

"Lift your pant legs, please. One at a time so I can see."

He does that, showing me that he has no ankle holster. I have him toss me his jacket and I feel the pockets for any weapons, and then toss it back to him. I'm fairly certain he's clean, and he certainly doesn't scare me physically, so I put the gun back into the holster. There's no reason to cause a stir if someone happens to come by while we're standing here.

"Can I make a suggestion?" he says to me, his eyebrows raised.

"Go ahead."

"I suggest we go to my office and have our chat."

"I think we're just fine chatting right here," I answer. I'm not inclined to go to his turf, where he certainly might have a gun hidden.

"Mr. Conner, it's hot out here and my office is air-conditioned. Plus, I have something to show you. Something you're going to want, I'm quite sure."

I think about that for a minute. "There are too many cameras around that building. I'm not going there."

"There's a back entrance and private elevator for the exclusive use of the city council and the mayor. There are cameras, but they're disabled. I made sure of that a long time ago, with the mayor's blessing, I might add." He shrugs, "None of us wanted everybody knowing every detail of our comings and goings, not to mention some of my co-councilmen are, shall we say, prone to certain indiscretions when it comes to their sex lives. City Hall is apparently a bit of an aphrodisiac."

If this is a lie, it's a good one, and I'm inclined to believe him for the simple reason that it makes a twisted kind of sense. Exactly the kind of sense that could only exist in the political arena. I decide to take a chance.

"You drive," I tell him, drawing my Glock again and walking around to the passenger side, sliding in and keeping it pointed at him. I haven't checked the vehicle for weapons and I don't want him pulling some kind of Ray Donovan shit by crashing the car into a wall, so I also buckle my seatbelt.

Theo gets in the driver's side and adjusts the seat before starting the Escalade and driving to the parking lot entrance.

"What did you do with Jackie?" I ask him.

He glances at me and then shrugs again. "She's becoming a bit of a problem, so she's taking a vacation."

"A vacation to where?"

"She's being driven to Los Angeles where she'll be put on a boat that's leaving tomorrow for China. She'll be fine, I promise you. I just need her out of the way for a little while."

I don't believe him for a second and suspect that Jackie will never reach China. Thinking about the kid, the boyfriend of Lizzy's who disappeared, I wonder if this is the same thing that happened to him, and how many others it's happened to as well. The good news is there's only one main route to Los Angeles, and they'll be on the road for the next few hours, giving me plenty of time to notify the highway patrol.

We cross Main Street and turn into the small parking lot at the rear of City Hall; signs announce that parking is for permit holders only and that unauthorized vehicles will be towed. The parking lot is well-lit and empty, and Theo parks in the spot nearest the door.

Theo sees me surveying the area, no doubt a nervous expression on my face. "I assure you, Mr. Conner, everything will be fine. I only want to show you something, and it's not in my best interest for anything bad to happen to you."

"Except for me to be arrested," I tell him.

He shrugs. "Based on the fact that you found me, and found Jackie, I can only assume you know what this is about, which makes having you incarcerated of zero value to me at this point."

That's quite true. The point of having me arrested was to get me to sell the land to be able to hire an attorney. Now that I know that, my arrest is pointless for him.

Nonetheless, I'm cautious as I get out, gun holstered in case there are any witnesses. I stay close to Theo as he climbs the short flight of stairs to a metal door. There's a smoked glass globe above the door, clearly designed to house a camera. I watch Theo closely, making sure he doesn't give any kind of sign, my paranoia in full effect. He takes no notice of the camera, though, pulling a key card from his pocket and swiping it at the reader on the side of the door, then entering a six-digit pin code on the keypad.

The door unlocks with a click and Theo pulls it open. It opens into a small lobby, vacant save a bench, two plants, an elevator, and a door with a sign that says it's a stairway.

"Pull the door closed behind you, please," Theo says, striding over to the elevator and pushing the call button.

I close the door and then join him as the elevator doors open. Once inside, Theo uses the keycard again, swiping it on the sensor and then hitting the button for the seventh floor.

"All of us councilmen have offices on seven," he says. "I just came from here before my meeting with Jackie and I was the only one here, so no one will see us."

The elevator door opens onto an expansive hallway, floors and walls of white marble and intricate glass design work, backlit by blue lights giving a comfortable, warm glow. The regular lights are turned off, causing deep shadows along the hallway. Theo turns left and I follow him through the gloom to a large door. There's a plaque on the door that reads, *Councilman Qiang "Theo" Zhao,* the first time I've realized his full name. It strikes me for some reason, and I stare at it as Theo unlocks the door and pushes it open. I suddenly realize the significance. When Eric ran the plates to the Escalades, they both came back to QTZ West Holdings, LLP. QTZ – Qiang Theo Zhao. A clue hidden in plain sight. An unnecessary and dangerous arrogance from a man striving for anonymity while at the same time seeking recognition. An arrogance of a sort that should be exploitable in some way.

Chapter 12

Theo's office is large and beautifully decorated, no doubt at the expense of the taxpayers of Las Vegas. The walls are covered with artwork that appears to be of high quality, framed elaborately and lit from below by soft lights, the room's only illumination. We cross a reception area and enter another door in the back wall that leads to his inner domain. He hits a switch, washing the office in bright light and starts toward his desk against the wall of windows at the back of the room.

"Hold on," I tell him. "You can have a seat right there." I point to a couch against the wall on the right side, a glass and wood coffee table in front of it, a decorative rug underneath. He pauses a

437

minute and then shrugs, tossing his jacket over the back of one of the chairs that faces the couch. He sits and leans back crossing his legs, his arm on the back of the couch in a relaxed posture.

As I stare at him, I realize this is the face of evil, the face of a man who ordered the death of my wife and my son, as well as Jerry Bastain, and probably Jackie just a few minutes ago, the man who was directly responsible for the death of Lizzy and who knows how many others. And yet, the evil doesn't show. His features are grandfatherly, warm and friendly, trusting and kind. It's easy to see how he got elected to this position. The charisma and charm ooze from him and I find myself wanting to like him, questioning whether I actually have the right person thinking this man can't possibly have done these heinous things. I suddenly imagine what it will be like convincing a jury that this individual was the one that ordered the murders of Tracy and Dillon Conner. I picture him sitting in the courtroom, smiling at those jurors, they returning his smile, unable to imagine the monster beneath the surface.

I draw my gun and point it at him again, not wanting to be lulled into a false sense of security. He glances at the gun and smiles at me.

"I told you, that's really not necessary. This isn't the old west and we aren't gunfighters. Why don't we be civilized and have a conversation like gentlemen?"

"You ordered the deaths of my wife, Tracy, and my son, Dillon," I say. "A four-year-old boy, and you ordered someone to shoot him in the face." My voice cracks as I say this, and I force myself to maintain control.

"I didn't, actually," he says, calmly. "It was a judgement call by the man on the scene. We didn't know your son was going to be there that day, and in reality, I told them to kill your wife only as a last resort."

It's an admittance of a sort, and I suddenly find myself wanting to pull the trigger. Wanting to blow that calm smugness off his face, but I have more unanswered questions.

"As a last resort?" I say.

"The objective was to get her to sign over the mineral rights to your vacation property. You know about that, I presume?"

"Rare earth elements," I reply.

He nods. "Rare earth elements. I take orders myself you know. Our geologists had located the large concentration that your wife discovered a few years earlier. We didn't know at the time that she

439

was a geologist, of course. We simply pulled the ownership info on that land and then we called her. She refused to sell, so we sent agents to meet with her one day. We offered twice, then three times what you two had paid for the land. She refused again. Then we threatened her." He shrugs and shakes his head. "She didn't believe us, I guess. We told her we weren't going away. By then, of course, we knew she worked for the USGS. We knew she must have done a survey herself and found the REEs, but we also knew she hadn't filed the report with the USGS. We knew you worked for Henderson Police Department. And we knew about your son. We told her we knew all of that, and she still wouldn't sell. It was really unfortunate that things had to go as far as they did."

I'm barely able to control my anger at his calm demeanor, his utter lack of concern as he speaks of blackmail and threats to my wife and son.

"So, you broke into my house and kidnapped them," I tell him through gritted teeth.

He shrugs. "We figured it would get her to finally cave. Of course, at that time I'd come up with the backup plan to kill her and frame you. My superiors thought we could just kill both of you and search the house for the report. They knew it hadn't been filed with the USGS and that she must have been holding it, trying to profit from it. But I knew that if we killed a cop, the entire police department would come down on us. The scrutiny would be tight and they wouldn't give up until they found your killer. But if they thought you were the killer, well then...things would be quite different."

"You just said the plan wasn't to kill her," I tell him, taking deep breaths to keep my emotions under control.

"That was only the back-up plan. We thought she'd most likely capitulate once we showed her the kind of force we were willing to use. She didn't though." He shakes his head as if he's disappointed in her. I'm struggling to not just pull the trigger right now, and my hand is shaking. *Control, Harvey.* "So, my guys went forward with plan B, which they were prepared for. Of course, your son being there was tough, but we really didn't have a choice; I'm sure you must be able to see that."

I realize he's lying. If they'd done their homework as he said they had, they'd have realized Dillon was home every night. Theo knew he'd be there when he sent his hired guns to pressure Tracy. They'd also come prepared for the set-up, including the drugs to knock me out and the gunpowder residue to put on my hands, to make it seem that I'd fired the shots. Tracy and Dillon's murders were always the plan that night, only Tracy hadn't understood just what she was up against. She hadn't realized how dangerous these guys actually were.

I also know that Tracy, faced with the danger to Dillon, would have given up. She would have told them they could have the land, have the minerals, anything they wanted. She would never have allowed mineral rights, no matter how important to the country, to endanger our boy. Which meant it had been too late. Theo had already moved to part two of the plan, and his hired guns ignored her, there at my house with instructions only to kill her and frame me. Theo is a liar, and he's smooth. Nothing in his face or voice betrays his lies, or any discomfort even, despite the gun pointed at him.

"They jumped the gun anyway," Theo continues. "They used too much force too quickly. I was very disappointed."

Lies. "But not too disappointed, apparently. You used the same guys to kill Jerry later, even though he was your partner," I tell him.

"Partner? No. Jerry was someone we used to accomplish an objective. He profited enormously from our relationship, and then he turned on me." He smiles at me. "Do you know why Jerry was downtown the morning he was killed?"

I shake my head, no.

442

"He was searching for you."

I'm sure he's lying again. I was completely off the grid at that time, they didn't know where I was hiding.

"What do you mean?" I ask.

He smiles. "Jerry had already figured out at that time that you were living as a bum on the streets. His daughter was a prostitute, as I'm sure you know. He had a P.I. follow her and take pictures of her. One of the pictures was Elizabeth talking to a homeless guy with long hair and a beard. Jerry flipped past it at first, but something about that homeless guy looked familiar. By then, we'd been looking for you for quite some time. Eventually Jerry went back to the picture and recognized you. He didn't tell me about it though."

I'm in shock, but I manage to ask, "Why not?"

"Because that idiot decided he was sorry for what we'd done. He thought it crossed a line. He decided he wanted to confess to you. He apparently didn't understand the magnitude of what we were doing. He didn't see the end-game." Theo shrugs and adjusts his glasses. "He had some little statue that his guys had stolen from your house that night, and he was going to show that to you to convince you."

Tracy's figurine. That was why Jerry had it in the car that morning. That was why he was down there in the first place. He was looking for me to confess to being responsible for Tracy and Dillon's murders. So much would have changed if only he had found me.

"How long was he looking for me?" I ask Theo, who seems to be enjoying the shock on my face.

"Not long. I don't put full trust in any of my key people, ever, Mr. Conner. I have them all watched, have them all checked on occasion. Word got back to me pretty quickly that Jerry was acting strangely. Then he called me and told me he wanted to quit. That's not really an option in my organization, if you know what I mean."

"So you had him killed."

He shrugs. "He knew the consequences going in. He knew what it meant to join. It's a lifelong commitment. The only way out is death, and Jerry knew that. By asking to get out, he was asking for his death."

It takes a sick mind to think this way, to justify murder like this, and I realize that Theo is mentally unstable in his own way.

While I'm quietly considering everything he's telling me, Theo leans forward and stares at me earnestly.

"I'm very sorry about your wife and son, Mr. Conner. If I could go back and change that I would. We made a lot of mistakes, and not all of them were my choice. Like I said, I answer to people in China, I take orders from them. They expect results and they aren't known to be patient. I'd have liked to have done it a different way, please believe me."

I smile, though I want to throw a piece of lead through his teeth and into his brain.

"What about Lizzy?" I ask. "Jerry and Jackie's daughter. She was kidnapped by Dominic and his crew. Was that because of me or because of Jerry?"

"Both actually!" he says, leaning back again. "Before Dominic's guy Joseph killed Jerry that morning, Jerry confessed to him that he was downtown scouting for you. He told him about seeing you in the picture with his daughter. Jerry knew what was coming, of course, as soon as he saw Joseph there to meet him. He was trying whatever he could to save himself. It took us a while to find her, but we were looking for you as well. When we did finally track her down, I realized we could use her to lure you into a trap and to keep Jackie under control if she decided to talk to the authorities. We were going to send her pictures of Elizabeth held captive, maybe an ear or a finger or whatever. But, somehow those idiots messed it all up and killed her." He frowns at me. "Were you there in the warehouse? Do you know what happened that night?"

I don't answer him and instead ask, "Who was watching Panattiere's house from the car the night you guys set the trap for me?"

"That was my associate, Le Ang. He was one of the guys you saw tonight. He had your picture, and I was able to get the police to understand they had a good chance to catch a wanted fugitive that night. Nice job, by the way with the decoy, that other transient. Very clever. You're a resourceful man, Mr. Conner. All that you were able to accomplish, just the fact you were able to get here, to me, shows your resourcefulness." He smiles at me and nods and again I see a hint of his charm and his charisma.

"Do me a favor," he continues, "can I go to my desk? Please, keep the gun on me if you need to, I just want to show you something."

I pause and then nod. I'm out of questions and I have everything I need so I might as well see what he has to show me. I also haven't figured out yet just what to do with him. I mean, I'd love to kill him, I have a desire to kill him, but I can't just shoot him here in his office, can I? I know he's a liar and I can't trust that the cameras haven't recorded me. Would Tracy have wanted me to murder this man for revenge? I don't think she would have. I don't think she would have wanted me to risk going to prison to avenge her murder.

Theo stands and moves to the desk with exaggerated slowness, keeping his hands in sight. I move with him and stand behind him, peering over his shoulder as he opens the desk drawer.

"Do you mind?" he asks, pointing to his chair, a leather behemoth that looks big enough and comfortable enough to sleep in.

I nod and he sits down, then removes a leather folder from the desk. He opens it and points to the inside. It's a checkbook, a fancy one like the type business owners used to use exclusively decades ago.

"This is a just an ordinary checkbook, but it draws on a special account. A very special account. I know things have been difficult for you, and I know you hold me responsible. I hold myself responsible as well, I assure you. I'd like to make it up to you. I know I can't change the past, but I can change your future. I can make you a wealthy man. You own something that my country desires, and we're willing to pay for it.

He takes a pen and fills out the check with my name, then signs his name at the bottom. He rips the check out and lays it on the desk, then contemplates me, quizzically.

"Name your price, Mr. Conner. Change your future and move on from this. A successful man allows himself to adapt to what life throws at him. This is the best way I have to make it right to you. Sell me the land and create a new life for yourself, anywhere in the world you want to go. The check is good, I assure you."

I stare at the check, lost in thought. Theo takes that as a sign that I'm considering his offer.

"While you think about it, what do you say we have a smoke? I can't smoke in here, but I could really use one. I usually go to the roof to light up, do you mind?"

I nod to him and motion for him to get up. He goes to his jacket and pulls out his pack of cigarettes and a lighter.

"Follow me; we'll take the stairs up."

He opens the door to the office and turns left back to the elevators. I follow him and he opens the stairwell door next to the elevator. We climb two flights and he uses his keycard to open the rooftop access door which is secured from this side. As we pass through, I take note that a keycard isn't required to get back into the stairwell.

The roof is dark, the lights that illuminate the great glass building not penetrating through the waist high parapet that encircles it. Large satellite dishes and antennas dot the surface, no doubt local radio and television stations taking advantage of the elevated public building to broadcast their signals. A large array of solar panels takes up an entire wing of the building, facing the sky to the south, providing free and clean energy for the high-tech building.

Theo walks to the edge of the parapet and leans against it, lighting his cigarette and inhaling deeply, blowing smoke into the night sky where it's illuminated briefly by the lights that shine upwards along the sides of the low wall.

"Why don't you put the gun away, Mr. Conner. We both know you're not capable of murder, and I'd hate to see an accident happen, one we'd both regret."

There won't be any accidents tonight, that's for sure. I nod to him to placate him and holster the gun. I don't need it anymore. I then reach into my pocket and pull out the cell phone. I call up the app, the one I opened just before I came out from behind the pallets earlier in the parking lot.

"What are you doing?" he asks, a frown on his face.

"Turning off the voice recorder," I tell him, turning the phone so he can see that it's been recording our entire conversation.

He smiles and takes another drag from the cigarette. "Surely you realize that it's not going to be admissible in court, don't you? You've held a gun on me all night. It's what's known as a coerced

449

confession. I felt in fear for my life and I would say anything to keep you from shooting me, blah, blah, blah. Come on, Harvey. You're better than this. This just isn't necessary."

"I don't need it to hold up in court, Mr. Zhao. I just need it to clear my name. Doubt is all I need, not proof that you murdered them."

He shakes his head. "I'm disappointed in you. I have all the contacts I need to clear your name. I even have the perfect person to take the fall in your place." He smiles at me and takes another drag. "We'll set up someone else for your wife and son's murders and you'll walk away free and rich. What could be better? Name your price, Mr. Conner. Let's get this over with and move on."

"You were right about two things tonight, Mr. Zhao," I say, slipping the phone back in my pocket.

"What are those?" he asks, an impatient scowl crossing his face.

"I definitely used to be incapable of murder. And a successful man allows himself to adapt to what life throws at him."

I quickly grab Theo by the back of his belt, shoving him forward into the parapet and lifting at the same time. His breath comes out with a gasp as he drops the cigarette and grabs for the edge. Just briefly, his fingers grasp a hold and our eyes lock together. My face is blank as I shove again. He slips from the edge and tumbles through the air. There's no scream like you always hear in the
450

movies, no sound at all, just a body, falling silently toward the concrete below. He falls for seven floors and then hits the edge of one of the twenty-foot-high pillars that dot the courtyard below, solar panels elevated above the park-like setting of the patio, providing both energy for the building and shade below. His body pinwheels off the edge of the pillar and I hear glass breaking on one of the solar panels, followed by a sickening thud as he lands on the concrete of the courtyard.

There's nobody down there, no scream from a passing pedestrian, no shout of alarm. I watch a pool of blood spread rapidly from his head. I feel nothing, no remorse, no joy, no satisfaction, just an emptiness as I stare at his dead body. I don't know if Tracy would have wanted this, but I suspect she would not have. I came to a realization up here on the roof, though. It doesn't matter what Tracy would have wanted. I'm the one who has to continue in this life without her. I'm the one who has to live with whatever decisions I make tonight. I needed the finality of this, the finality that never would have come with years of trials, years of appeals, hours, days, and weeks spent in courtrooms, reliving every detail of Tracy and Dillon's murders. So much time, watching this man work the jury with that charm, that charisma, the grandfatherly face accused of a heinous crime he may not have committed.

I couldn't put myself through all that and, despite what Tracy would have wanted, she no longer has to deal with those issues. It's now about what I want.

Turning from the edge, I grind out his cigarette with my heel and make my way back to the stairwell.

Chapter 13

"Hello, Agent Trahillo," I say, sitting down at the table where the FBI special agent is playing with a plastic cup containing an iced drink of some type. He's dressed casually today in a polo shirt and slacks, the shirt tucked in, his badge and gun visible, attracting the occasional glance from the other customers.

He nods to me. "Hello, Mr. Conner. Or is it Mr. Sands?" He has a wry, half-grin on his face.

"A lot of that depends on what you have to say to me right now," I reply.

"Maybe there's a SWAT team outside about to storm in and arrest you right now," he replies, his eyebrows raised.

"Maybe," I reply, shrugging. "But I doubt it. I don't like to overestimate the intelligence and savvy of the FBI, but I think you guys are a little smarter than that. You know I didn't do anything."

"We know you didn't murder your wife and son, but we wouldn't care if you did anyway. Murder is a state crime. However, there is the small matter of the escape of a federal fugitive that still hasn't quite been cleared up."

Now it's my turn to smile. "While I certainly can't say I have any information about that, Agent Trahillo, I will say that I'm not sorry he escaped. He didn't do anything and I think you know that."

"I don't actually know anything of the sort, and he has the kind of information that can't be floating around out there. Especially if he's mentally unstable. You must know that."

"I'm not here to argue with you. What I know is that I knew that man better than most for the last two years, and he never once breathed a word to me anything of any significance to national security." Other than the vague, *"I've seen things that they can't let nobody see,"* which I don't feel the need to pass on to Trahillo.

He shrugs. "Okay, well that's neither here nor there. We can't prove you were involved in his escape and I doubt very much that you're going to admit that you were. I'm just here to give you this."

He hands me a sealed envelope that has *Mr. Harvey J. Conner* typed on the front.

"What is this?" I ask, though I think I know.

"It's a letter from the District Attorney. It states that you are no longer wanted in connection with the murder of your wife and son, or any other crimes at this time, and that all wants and warrants concerning these crimes have been quashed and are no longer valid."

I hold the envelope tightly. I won't let Trahillo see any emotion, but the relief I feel from having this letter is overwhelming. Of course, there is one more thing.

"Anything else?" I ask.

"There's also a certified check for five million dollars from the United States Treasury. Of course, I'm supposed to take that back from you unless you have something for me."

I smile again and reach into my back pocket, removing a thick sheaf of paperwork.

"Are you a notary public, Agent Trahillo?"

"No, but I brought one with me." He motions to another table, and a man dressed in a suit and carrying a briefcase, stands up and walks over, setting his briefcase on the table and pulling over a chair from another table.

I unfold the paperwork and turn it to the last page, the signature page. The notary doesn't say a word, but opens the briefcase and hands me a pen. I sign my name at the bottom, and the notary then takes the paper and affixes a stamp, also taken from the briefcase, before filling in his information and then signing above my signature.

"Aren't you supposed to check my I.D.?" I ask him.

"That won't be necessary," he says, speaking for the first time. "I've been told that might be an issue for you."

Well, that's certainly true.

"We won't tell if you don't tell," Trahillo adds.

He studies the paperwork for a couple of minutes and then nods, folding it up and handing it to the other man who simply places it into the briefcase, closes the lid, stands up and leaves without a word.

Trahillo takes a sip of his drink and then stares at me. "So, the United States government now owns the mineral rights to your land, and you're five million dollars richer. I have to admit, I was a little disappointed that you asked for that much money. It seemed to me you might have transferred those rights just out of a sense of patriotic duty."

I stare at him. "Want to trade places with me, Agent Trahillo?"

He locks eyes with me a moment and then nods in understanding. "No, I suppose not."

"It seems to me that the government should have recognized the threat sooner and acquired those rights a long time ago. In which case, my wife and son would still be alive."

He doesn't answer, lifting his drink and sipping through the straw.

"I'm sure you heard that we located Jackie Bastain alive and well?" he asks.

I nod. As soon as I left City Hall that night, I called the police and gave them a description of Jackie's vehicle and the vehicle following it, as well as a probable location and destination. The California Highway Patrol had found them.

"It became a kidnapping that crossed state lines, so it's an FBI investigation now," he adds. "It seems they were taking her to a ship. From what Jackie says, the guys in the car made sure she overheard them saying she was to be thrown overboard once they were well out to sea."

The depravity of these people seemingly knows no bounds. The good news is that with Theo's death and the arrest of the three people directly under him, the Chinese will have to rebuild their network out here, and that will take some time. Time that hopefully the FBI will use to its advantage to level the playing field a bit.

"Did you get your belongings back from Alexa Townsend's car?" he asks.

I smile at him. When the Metro officers got tired of waiting at Alexa's car that night in Jackie's neighborhood, they called Eric and Alexa to come pick it up. Eric told them the laptop, gun case, and figurine in the car belonged to him, and he was able to remove them before the techs went over the car for prints. They hadn't found anything inside to tie me to it. Trahillo's question is a trap, but I can tell his heart isn't in it.

"Is there anything else, Agent Trahillo?"

"Do you want to tell me anything about Theo Zhao? Maybe anything about his death?" he asks pointedly.

"As far as I'm aware, it was a suicide. Poor guy."

"There are some who aren't convinced. Some who think it may have been a homicide."

I shrug. "Suicide is much cleaner. Better for everybody involved, wouldn't you agree?"

He frowns but says, "I would, actually. And I told the LVMPD homicide guys that a finding of suicide would be just fine with the government. Hard to say if they'll play ball though. Last I heard they still wanted to interview you as you were the last one to see him alive."

They'll have to find me first, but now that I'm no longer wanted for the murder of my family I won't be trying so hard to hide.

"It's too bad there wasn't anybody from the government watching him who might have saved him."

He nods, thoughtfully. "Only a few people know this, but we actually were watching him. Loosely. We aren't completely blind, Mr. Conner. We've been aware of Chinese activities here in the U.S. for some time and we knew Zhao was involved."

This doesn't call for a response, and I don't give one.

"One other thing. We analyzed the digital recording you gave us, of course. All those things go straight to the lab. They say it was edited for length. The meat of the recording itself was unaltered, obviously, or you wouldn't have been cleared, but the lab tells us there was more to the recording that was edited out. More at the end."

I couldn't leave the part on the recording where Theo asked me to go to the roof, of course. After I left the roof that night, I went back to his office and took the check he'd written to me tearing it up and scattering the pieces on the street. Then I edited the recording so it ended just before Theo asked me if we could go to his desk. They knew I'd been in his office the night he flew off the roof, but I told them I'd left after getting his confession. Nobody believes that, of course, but believing and proving are two different things.

"Is there a question in there somewhere?" I ask.

"I'm just wondering what else was on that tape," he answers.

That's not a question either, and I stand up. "It was a pleasure doing business with you, Agent Trahillo. No offense, but I hope this is the last time we have any sort of business together."

He nods and stands as well. "You know, Conner, we could use someone like you. Not at the FBI, of course, but I do have contacts in some other agencies that would be very interested in speaking with you."

I stare at him a moment before answering.

"I think I actually prefer Sands. It reminds me of the desert: shifting sands, blowing sands, wandering sands, subject to the forces of wind and earth. Traveling grains nearly unnoticeable...irrelevant and anonymous. That's me in a nutshell." I grin at him, stuff the envelope in my back pocket, turn and walk out.

THE END

Enjoyed this novel? Would you mind leaving a short review on Amazon? The success of Indie writers like myself is dependent on great reviews and it would mean a lot to me.

Be sure to check out my other novels:

Drawing Dead

Chesaw

Reasonable Doubt

Also, be sure to check out my blog at AuthorRickFuller.com, and email me anytime at:

DetectiveRyanTyler@gmail.com.

I love to hear from my readers!

Thanks for reading!

Rick Fuller – 10/24/2017

Printed in Great Britain
by Amazon